Jayfeather shivered against the dread hollowing his belly. Clan cats, cats who lived beside the lake during their waking moments, surrounded him. He could feel their warm hearts beating, quickened by the lies of the dead. There was no hiding now from what was happening: Cats from *every* Clan were being trained by Dark Forest warriors to rise against their Clan-mates, trained to break every part of the code the Clans had long fought to protect.

WARRIORS

THE NEW PROPHECY

POWER OF THREE

OMEN OF THE STARS

EXPLORE THE WARRIORS WORLD

OMEN OF THE STARS

WARRIORS

NIGHT WHISPERS

ERIN HUNTER

HARPER

An Imprint of HarperCollinsPublishers

Night Whispers

Library of Congress Cataloging-in-Publication Data

Hunter, Erin.
  Night whispers / by Erin Hunter. — 1st ed.
    p. cm. — (Warriors, omen of the stars ; bk. 3)
  Summary: As Jayfeather, Lionblaze, and Dovepaw continue to seek answers to the mysterious
prophecy that binds them, they learn that another cat may play an essential role in defeating the
Dark Forest.
  ISBN 978-0-06-155517-6
  [1. Cats—Fiction. 2. Prophecies—Fiction. 3. Adventure and adventurers—Fiction. 4. Fantasy.]
I. Title.
PZ7.H916625Ni 2012   2010015313
[Fic]—dc22   CIP
                                                                                              AC

Typography by Hilary Zarycky
14 15 C G / O P M   10 9 8
❖
First paperback edition, 2012

Special thanks to Kate Cary

ALLEGIANGES

THUNDERCLAN

__LEADER__ **FIRESTAR**—ginger tom with a flame-colored pelt

__DEPUTY__ **BRAMBLECLAW**—dark brown tabby tom with amber eyes

__MEDIGINE GAT__ **JAYFEATHER**—gray tabby tom with blind blue eyes

__WARRIORS__ (toms, and she-cats without kits)

GRAYSTRIPE—long-haired gray tom

DUSTPELT—dark brown tabby tom

SANDSTORM—pale ginger she-cat with green eyes

BRACKENFUR—golden brown tabby tom

SORRELTAIL—tortoiseshell-and-white she-cat with amber eyes

CLOUDTAIL—long-haired white tom with blue eyes

BRIGHTHEART—white she-cat with ginger patches

MILLIE—striped gray tabby she-cat

THORNCLAW—golden brown tabby tom

SQUIRRELFLIGHT—dark ginger she-cat with green eyes

LEAFPOOL—light brown tabby she-cat with amber eyes, former medicine cat

SPIDERLEG—long-limbed black tom with brown underbelly and amber eyes

BIRCHFALL—light brown tabby tom

WHITEWING—white she-cat with green eyes

BERRYNOSE—cream-colored tom

HAZELTAIL—small gray-and-white she-cat

MOUSEWHISKER—gray-and-white tom

CINDERHEART—gray tabby she-cat
APPRENTICE, IVYPAW

LIONBLAZE—golden tabby tom with amber eyes
APPRENTICE, DOVEPAW

FOXLEAP—reddish tabby tom

ICECLOUD—white she-cat

TOADSTEP—black-and-white tom

ROSEPETAL—dark cream she-cat

BRIARLIGHT—dark brown she-cat

BLOSSOMFALL—tortoiseshell-and-white she-cat

BUMBLESTRIPE—very pale gray tom with black stripes

APPRENTICES (more than six moons old, in training to become warriors)

DOVEPAW—pale gray she-cat with blue eyes

IVYPAW—silver-and-white tabby she-cat with dark blue eyes

QUEENS (she-cats expecting or nursing kits)

FERNCLOUD—pale gray (with darker flecks) she-cat with green eyes

DAISY—cream long-furred cat from the horseplace

POPPYFROST—tortoiseshell she-cat (mother to Cherrykit, a ginger she-cat, and Molekit, a brown-and-cream tom)

ELDERS (former warriors and queens, now retired)

MOUSEFUR—small dusky brown she-cat

PURDY—plump tabby former loner with a gray muzzle

SHADOWCLAN

LEADER **BLACKSTAR**—large white tom with huge jet-black paws

DEPUTY **ROWANCLAW**—ginger tom

MEDICINE CAT **LITTLECLOUD**—very small tabby tom
APPRENTICE, FLAMETAIL (ginger tom)

WARRIORS **OAKFUR**—small brown tom
APPRENTICE, FERRETPAW (cream-and-gray tom)

SMOKEFOOT—black tom

TOADFOOT—dark brown tom

APPLEFUR—mottled brown she-cat

CROWFROST—black-and-white tom

RATSCAR—brown tom with long scar across his back
APPRENTICE, PINEPAW (black she-cat)

SNOWBIRD—pure-white she-cat

TAWNYPELT—tortoiseshell she-cat with green eyes
APPRENTICE, STARLINGPAW (ginger tom)

OLIVENOSE—tortoiseshell she-cat

OWLCLAW—light brown tabby tom

SHREWFOOT—gray she-cat with black feet

SCORCHFUR—dark gray tom

REDWILLOW—mottled brown-and-ginger tom

TIGERHEART—dark brown tabby tom

DAWNPELT—cream-furred she-cat

QUEENS

KINKFUR—tabby she-cat, with long fur that sticks out at all angles

IVYTAIL—black, white, and tortoiseshell she-cat

ELDERS

CEDARHEART—dark gray tom

TALLPOPPY—long-legged light brown tabby she-cat

SNAKETAIL—dark brown tom with tabby-striped tail

WHITEWATER—white she-cat with long fur, blind in one eye

WINDCLAN

LEADER

ONESTAR—brown tabby tom

DEPUTY

ASHFOOT—gray she-cat

MEDICINE CAT

KESTRELFLIGHT—mottled gray tom

WARRIORS

CROWFEATHER—dark gray tom

OWLWHISKER—light brown tabby tom
APPRENTICE, WHISKERPAW (light brown tom)

WHITETAIL—small white she-cat

NIGHTCLOUD—black she-cat

GORSETAIL—very pale gray-and-white she-cat with blue eyes

WEASELFUR—ginger tom with white paws

HARESPRING—brown-and-white tom

LEAFTAIL—dark tabby tom with amber eyes

ANTPELT—brown tom with one black ear

EMBERFOOT—gray tom with two dark paws

HEATHERTAIL—light brown tabby she-cat with blue eyes

APPRENTICE, FURZEPAW (gray-and-white she-cat)

BREEZEPELT—black tom with amber eyes
APPRENTICE, BOULDERPAW (large pale gray tom)

SEDGEWHISKER—light brown tabby she-cat

SWALLOWTAIL—dark gray she-cat

SUNSTRIKE—tortoiseshell she-cat with large white mark on her forehead

ELDERS	**WEBFOOT**—dark gray tabby tom
	TORNEAR—tabby tom

RIVERCLAN

LEADER	**MISTYSTAR**—gray she-cat with blue eyes
DEPUTY	**REEDWHISKER**—black tom
	APPRENTICE, HOLLOWPAW (dark brown tabby tom)
MEDICINE CAT	**MOTHWING**—dappled golden she-cat
	APPRENTICE, WILLOWSHINE (gray tabby she-cat)
WARRIORS	**GRAYMIST**—pale gray tabby she-cat
	APPRENTICE, TROUTPAW (pale gray tabby she-cat)

MINTFUR—light gray tabby tom

ICEWING—white she-cat with blue eyes

MINNOWTAIL—dark gray she-cat
APPRENTICE, MOSSYPAW (brown-and-white she-cat)

PEBBLEFOOT—mottled gray tom
APPRENTICE, RUSHPAW (light brown tabby tom)

MALLOWNOSE—light brown tabby tom

ROBINWING—tortoiseshell-and-white tom

BEETLEWHISKER—brown-and-white tabby tom

PETALFUR—gray-and-white she-cat

GRASSPELT—light brown tom

QUEENS   **DUSKFUR**—brown tabby she-cat

MOSSPELT—tortoiseshell she-cat with blue eyes

ELDERS   **DAPPLENOSE**—mottled gray she-cat

POUNCETAIL—ginger-and-white tom

CATS OUTSIDE CLANS

SMOKY—muscular gray-and-white tom who lives in a barn at the horseplace

FLOSS—small gray-and-white she-cat who lives at the horseplace

OTHER ANIMALS

MIDNIGHT—a star-gazing badger who lives by the sea

Hareview Campsite

Sanctuary Cottage

Sadler Woods

Littlepine Road

Littlepine Sailing Center

Littlepine Island

River Alba

Whitchurch Road

Abandoned Workman's House

Quarry Road [disused]

Quarry

Hare Hill Woods

Crystal Pool

Sanctuary Lake

Hare Hill

Hare Hill Riding Stables

Hare Hill Road

Knight's Copse

Deciduous Woodland

Pine Forest

Marsh

Lake

Footpaths

NORTH

PROLOGUE
❧

Torn clouds streaked the stars. Branches whisked the night-black sky and showered leaves over the shadowed glade. Wind hollowed the shallow clearing while, around its rim, bushes stirred and rustled as though wolves paced through them.

At the center of the glade, an old she-cat hunched her shoulders against the growling air. Starlight sparkled on her matted gray pelt. She flattened her ears as two feline shapes padded down the slope to join her.

"Yellowfang." A white-pelted she-cat spoke first. "We've been looking for you."

"Lionheart told me." Yellowfang lifted her chin. Rain specked her muzzle as the medicine cat blinked at her former mentor. "What is it, Sagewhisker?"

Sagewhisker answered sharply: "We've been talking."

"The whole of StarClan has been talking," her tortoise-shell companion cut in. "Every cat thinks you should have stopped it."

"The battle between ThunderClan and ShadowClan?" Yellowfang flicked her tail. "Do you think I have that much power, Fernshade?"

1

Sagewhisker leaned forward. "You could have sent a message to ThunderClan."

"If you had, Russetfur might not have died." Fernshade stepped closer. There was a hint of claws in her words. "I trained her, you know."

"I hadn't forgotten," Yellowfang rasped.

Fernshade narrowed her eyes. "I'm the one who's going to have to fetch her."

Yellowfang's shoulders sagged. "She was old," she murmured. "Maybe she'll be glad to join us."

Sagewhisker lashed her white tail. "No warrior wants to die. Especially in a battle that should not have happened."

Fernshade curled her lip. "You knew what the cats from the Dark Forest were doing. There was no need for Firestar to challenge Blackstar over that worthless stretch of grass. Did you *want* cats to die?"

Wind swirled through the hollow, tugging ears and tails, as Bluestar's mew sounded from the top of the slope.

"Enough!"

The ThunderClan leader stalked down to greet the others. She nodded to Sagewhisker and Fernshade in turn. "The battle was unfortunate, but it was a lesson we needed to learn."

Sagewhisker met her gaze. "A lesson in what?"

Bluestar stood with her paws rooted in the streaming grass. "We know what we're up against now. The Dark Forest cats can change the destinies of the Clans. This battle would not have been fought if not for them."

Yellowfang shuddered. "I should have known the Clans

would suffer the moment I saw Brokenstar in the Dark Forest."

Sagewhisker jerked her head toward her former apprentice. "And whose fault is it that he is there? Or that he was ever born at all?" Her eyes glittered. "You broke the warrior code and kitted him. What did you expect?"

Yellowfang flinched.

"Blaming each other won't help." Bluestar brushed past Yellowfang, drawing her tail over the old cat's knotted pelt. "We've all made mistakes in our time."

Fernshade's whiskers twitched angrily. "Not *every* cat breaks the warrior code!"

Bluestar didn't blink. "Mistakes are where we learn the most," she meowed evenly. "And we can learn from this battle. We must set aside old grievances. The Clans must join forces."

"Brokenstar has already punished me more than I ever deserved," Yellowfang muttered. "And now he's trying to punish me again by destroying the Clans I once called my own."

"This isn't about you!" Sagewhisker snapped. "Whatever's going on in the Dark Forest affects us all. We need to deal with it before it does any more harm to ShadowClan!"

A growl rose in Bluestar's throat. "Not just ShadowClan! Firestar lost a life, too!"

Lightning flared. The cats crouched and blinked upward, pelts bristling. As thunder rolled in the distance, more cats began to slink into the glade.

"Lionheart!" Bluestar called. There was relief in her voice as she saw her old friend lead Mudfur and Oakheart down the slope.

"What's going on?" Lionheart stopped beside Bluestar.

"We know the Dark Forest was behind the battle between ShadowClan and ThunderClan," Bluestar told him.

"ThunderClan started it!" Fernshade growled.

"The cats from the Dark Forest started it!" Bluestar reminded them. She glanced at Yellowfang. "Not just Brokenstar. Tigerstar and Hawkfrost, too."

Oakheart narrowed his eyes. "Do we know who they're training?" His slick RiverClan pelt was starred with beads of rain.

Yellowfang showed her cracked and stained teeth. "Brokenstar will claim any soul he can reach."

"What if they recruit a Clan leader?" Fernshade growled.

Mudfur, the old WindClan medicine cat, shook his head. "We can no longer trust any cat."

"Or Clan," Sagewhisker muttered darkly.

Mudfur stiffened and tasted the air, ears pricking. "Who's there? Mudclaw? We weren't expecting to see you here."

The cats turned to watch the WindClan warrior hurry down the slope. "I came as soon as I heard. What's the plan? How are we going to deal with the Dark Forest cats?"

Grass ripped beneath Bluestar's paws as she unsheathed her claws. "We must persuade the Clans to join forces and fight this threat together."

Sagewhisker flattened her ears. "How will they know who to fight?"

"Why don't the Dark Forest warriors just come and fight us, if they're so hungry for a battle?" Fernshade snarled.

Lionheart stared over the rippling grass. "Because that would be too easy. They know they'll hurt us much worse if they attack the Clans we left behind."

"Is there no other way to defeat them?" Oakheart fixed his questioning gaze on Bluestar.

She froze for a moment as though she were scanning his thoughts. Then she blinked. "Tigerstar has only ever understood violence."

Oakheart looked away.

"That's all *any* Dark Forest cat understands," Bluestar pressed. "If we try to reason with them, they will see it as weakness."

Sagewhisker snorted. "Just as long as no one's blaming ShadowClan for Brokenstar." She glanced at Yellowfang.

"As far as I can see, it's ShadowClan who's suffered most this time," Fernshade added.

Thunder cracked overhead.

Sagewhisker nudged Fernshade. "You'd better fetch Russetfur."

As she spoke, the skies opened. Rain pelted the glade, and the cats scattered, racing for the shelter of the trees.

"Fernshade!" Yellowfang called after the tortoiseshell warrior.

Fernshade skidded to a stop and glanced back. "What?"

Rain blurred Yellowfang's gaze. "Have a safe journey." Her voice cracked. "And tell Russetfur that I'm sorry."

CHAPTER 1

A yowl sliced through the shriek of battle, sharp with grief more than rage.

Dovepaw ducked out of Toadfoot's way and spun around.

Firestar!

The ThunderClan leader was being dragged away across the battle-crowded clearing. The grass glistened crimson behind him. Birchfall sank his teeth farther into Firestar's scruff and heaved him over Spiderleg's shoulders, then helped to carry him away into the trees.

Horror pulsed through Dovepaw. Around her, the fighting was shuddering to a stop as cats sheathed their claws and stared in bewilderment. Firestar's deputy, Brambleclaw, his broad shoulders wet with blood, padded toward Blackstar. The ShadowClan leader didn't look up. His head was bent over a dark ginger pelt.

Brambleclaw dipped his head. "The battle is won," he growled. "The clearing is ours. Do you concede or shall we fight for it again?"

Blackstar flashed a look of burning hatred over his shoulder. "Take it," he hissed. "It was never worth the blood that has been spilled here today."

As Brambleclaw backed away, Dovepaw recognized the ginger pelt.

Russetfur! Is she dead?

The ShadowClan deputy lay unmoving, apart from the blood that trickled from her lips. Her Clanmates began to step carefully past the ThunderClan warriors and head for the pines. Scorchfur, Tigerheart, and Rowanclaw stopped beside their leader. While Scorchfur nudged Blackstar to his paws and guided him gently into the trees, Tigerheart grabbed Russetfur's pelt and slowly, gently, heaved her onto Rowanclaw's shoulders. Then in silence they followed their battered Clanmates into the mist-wrapped trees.

Dovepaw stared after them, the energy draining from her as she saw Tigerheart's tail snake into the shadows. She looked around for Ivypaw. Her sister was helping Blossomfall limp toward the forest.

"Come on, Blossomfall," Ivypaw was murmuring to her Clanmate. "Jayfeather'll fix you up." There was no hint of their past quarrels in her mew.

Squirrelflight was checking Leafpool's wounds, while Leafpool scanned the battlefield, her eyes round with worry. "Lionblaze is okay," Squirrelflight reassured her sister.

Brightheart lay panting on the grass, her one good eye so wide that a circle of white showed around the blue.

Cloudtail nudged her with his muzzle. "Come on, you'll feel better once you start moving," he urged.

Brightheart let out a low moan as she hauled herself to her paws.

Bumblestripe, one ear torn, surveyed the flattened grass. "I think we showed them," he declared.

Hazeltail glanced at him with scorn in her eyes and pressed closer to Mousewhisker, lapping at her sister's bleeding, ruffled fur. "Showed them what?" she muttered between licks. "How much blood can be spilled in a pointless battle?"

Only Lionblaze looked uninjured. A smear of blood stained his flank, but Dovepaw knew it wasn't his. She frowned, doubts flocking into her mind like starlings. Lionblaze was part of the prophecy, like she was. His power was the ability to fight any cat, any creature at all, without being hurt.

Why couldn't Lionblaze have saved Firestar? What's the point of having all that power if he couldn't help his leader?

In front of her, Brambleclaw crossed the stained grass where Russetfur had lain, and touched the tip of his tail to Lionblaze's shoulder. "Russetfur was too old for this battle," he murmured. "It wasn't your fault she died."

Lionblaze hung his head.

Oh, StarClan! Dovepaw's belly tightened. *Lionblaze killed Russetfur?* Her mentor looked shattered, his eyes dull. She hurried to his side and pressed against his flank. She felt utterly helpless. Her power was the ability to hear and see things that were happening far away, much farther than other cats could sense; she should have known what ShadowClan had been up to. Instead it had been her sister, Ivypaw, who had told Firestar that Blackstar was planning to invade ThunderClan's territory and steal more land for hunting. Had StarClan sent a dream to Ivypaw because Dovepaw had refused to use her powers to spy on the other Clans? Maybe if Dovepaw had been listening and watching, as Lionblaze had asked, she'd have known what ShadowClan was going to do. She could have warned Firestar about it before there was no choice left but to fight.

Could I have prevented this?

She felt Lionblaze's warm breath as he touched his muzzle to the top of her head. "Come on," he whispered wearily. "Let's go home."

Dovepaw pressed close to Lionblaze as they trudged on heavy paws through the whispering trees.

CHAPTER 2

❧

Jayfeather reached a paw into the far corner of his medicine store. He could smell stale marigold tucked beneath the rock; it was the last of his supply and so old that he wasn't sure it'd be strong enough to keep infection from Sorreltail's wound. But he clawed it out anyway and pawed it together with the last of his dried oak.

"This might sting," he warned Sorreltail.

The tortoiseshell-and-white she-cat had been sitting patiently beside Briarlight's nest. "That's okay." From the echo of her voice, Jayfeather could tell she was watching the dozing young warrior. "Her breathing sounds rough."

Briarlight had fallen asleep before sunset despite the steady flow of injured warriors and apprentices through the den. Sorreltail was the last, having insisted on waiting until the others had been treated, though the gash in her shoulder was deep and still oozing blood.

Jayfeather pressed on the poultice and reached for cobwebs to cover it. "She has a chest infection," he explained, draping sticky white strands across the wound. "I'm not sure whether to make her exercise harder to clear her chest or to let her rest and fight it from inside."

Sorreltail brushed his shoulder with her muzzle. "Have you asked Leafpool?"

Jayfeather flicked his tail crossly toward the wads of blood-stained moss and herb fragments that littered the den floor. "Does it look like I've had time?"

"I just wondered," Sorreltail replied mildly.

"Besides," Jayfeather muttered, "Leafpool's busy checking injuries."

"I suppose." Sorreltail got to her paws. "Thanks for the herbs."

Regretting his sharpness, Jayfeather touched her flank with his tail. "Do you want poppy seeds to help you sleep?"

"No, thanks." Sorreltail padded away. "Brackenfur's snoring lulls me better than any medicine."

Jayfeather had treated the golden warrior earlier, snapping his wrenched shoulder back into place before sending him to his nest with strict instructions not to move until sunrise. The rest of the Clan had been spared serious injury. Only Firestar's wound had required careful attention. The tear in his neck had been closed with cobwebs and firmly bound. It would heal, but the life that had seeped away could never be replaced. Jayfeather pictured the faint warrior in StarClan, a little less transparent now, his flame-colored pelt one shade more vivid against the greenness of StarClan's hunting grounds.

As Sorreltail limped from the den, Briarlight stirred. "What a mess," she rasped over the edge of her nest.

"How are you?" Jayfeather sniffed her, relieved to find

that her ears were cooler.

"Sleepy. How's Firestar?" Briarlight blinked.

"Asleep in his den," Jayfeather told her. "Sandstorm's watching over him. He'll be fine in a few days."

"If only Russetfur hadn't attacked him." Briarlight had heard all the gossip from the other warriors. "Then Firestar would be fine, and Lionblaze wouldn't have killed Russetfur."

Jayfeather tensed. "Russetfur was *too old* to be fighting!"

The brambles swished, and Jayfeather breathed the familiar scent of Lionblaze. The warrior padded heavily into the den. "I should have realized that before I attacked her."

"What else could you do? She was killing Firestar." Jayfeather shook out his fur and crossed the den to greet his brother. "Is Dovepaw okay?"

"She's fine," Lionblaze reassured him. "Still quiet. But fine."

Dovepaw had returned from the battle shivering and speechless with shock. Jayfeather had offered her thyme, but she'd refused, saying she was just tired. Unlike her Clanmates, who were keen to share every battle move, Dovepaw had sat silently while Jayfeather checked her over, only mentioning when prompted that Lionblaze had saved her from Dawnpelt.

Is it fair to make apprentices fight alongside warriors? Worry for Dovepaw tightened Jayfeather's belly. Sometimes she seemed so young. At least Ivypaw was okay. She seemed rather pleased with herself, actually. And with only a bruised tail to show for her run-in with ShadowClan's fiercest warriors.

But she hadn't mentioned her dream again. The dream she'd blurted out to Firestar where ShadowClan had invaded

ThunderClan territory and set the forest streams running with blood. In fact, when Jayfeather had slipped into Ivypaw's thoughts, it had vanished from her mind. How could she forget a nightmare so vivid that it had sparked the battle between ThunderClan and ShadowClan?

Jayfeather turned his blind blue gaze on Lionblaze. "Was it worth it?"

"The battle?" Lionblaze stiffened. "Of course!"

"But to lose two lives over a worthless piece of grass!"

"We've sent ShadowClan a message they won't forget."

"At what cost?" Jayfeather sighed.

"We must not turn soft now." Lionblaze's voice dropped to a whisper as Briarlight's attention pricked across the den. "Who knows where the next blow might fall?"

Jayfeather's shoulders sagged as Briarlight began coughing again.

Lionblaze nosed him toward his patient. "We can't afford to ignore any signs now," he hissed. "Go on, see to Briarlight. We'll talk later."

As his brother swished out of the cave, Jayfeather began massaging Briarlight's flank with his paws. Her coughing subsided, and she laid her chin on the side of her nest, her breath quickly easing into sleep.

"Is she okay?" Leafpool's hushed mew sounded at the den entrance. She padded over to Briarlight's nest.

"A little cooler." Jayfeather could hear Leafpool scraping cobwebs from her paws. He could tell by the scent that she'd been repatching Cloudtail's gashes. "How's Brackenfur's shoulder?" He was worried that wrenching it back into place might have damaged more than it fixed. "Did you get a chance to look at it?"

"Y-yes." She hesitated. "What do *you* think?"

Jayfeather's belly knotted. In the past, her question would have been a test. Now Leafpool sounded like she *really* wasn't sure. Why mumble like a nervous apprentice? It was as though she was frightened of putting a paw wrong. His mind drifted back to when she used to boss him around in this very den. He'd answer back, and she'd snap in return. The air would fizz and crackle as he rebelled against her overcautious fussing.

The memory hurt. He'd *known* Leafpool in those days; he'd been able to predict her every objection. Since he had found out that she was his mother, he felt as if he didn't know her at all.

Ignoring her question, he dismissed her. "Will you check on Firestar, please?" He lifted a paw to wash.

Leafpool's whiskers brushed his toes as she dipped her head. "Of course."

Stop acting like a mouse! Jayfeather thought indignantly, while he tugged a sprig of thyme from between his claws. The brambles swished, and Leafpool's pads scuffed away across the clearing.

Jayfeather paused from washing and listened to his Clanmates settling down for the night. Poppyfrost was washing Molekit and Cherrykit inside the nursery. Purdy's rumbling mew droned in the elders' nest. Brackenfur was snoring just as Sorreltail had predicted. Blossomfall was fixing her nest in the warriors' den underneath the fallen beech; perhaps she was trying to make it the way it was before the tree had crashed into the hollow.

Jayfeather shuddered as he remembered the day it had fallen. Its roots had been loosened by rainfall, and the great tree had slid from the top of the cliff and smashed down into the camp, crushing the elders' den and demolishing the thornbush where the warriors used to sleep. Longtail had died. Briarlight had been crippled, her back broken so that she could no longer feel her hind legs. It was only Dovepaw's powerful hearing that had prevented more cats from being killed or maimed.

For half a moon the Clan had worked to rebuild their home, clearing twigs, leaves, and branches as much as they could. They had rebuilt the elders' den by weaving the old honeysuckle tendrils around a frame of splintered wood. The beech still spanned the camp, its trunk like a spine, its boughs a rib cage jabbing into the clearing, its roots gripping the bramble nursery like claws. Every night was filled with the sound of leaves and twigs being tugged and adjusted as the warriors worked on their nests in their new den beneath the strongest bough of the fallen tree.

Jayfeather was still finding it hard to navigate the camp, tripping on unexpected branches or piles of twigs that had been brushed to one side but not yet cleared. Longtail, the blind elder, would have struggled even more to adjust. Perhaps he was lucky to be with StarClan, luckier than Briarlight. She had a chest infection now because she couldn't run and hunt like her Clanmates. She could only drag herself to and from the clearing, her hindquarters dead as fresh-kill.

Jayfeather shook himself. Fretting wouldn't help. He rinsed his paws in the pool, shuddering at the chilliness of the water, then padded to the bracken pile beside Briarlight's nest.

As Jayfeather curled into the smooth stems and closed his eyes, Ivypaw's dream pricked his thoughts. Why had StarClan set this battle in motion? He couldn't shake the nagging suspicion that StarClan would never share dreams with Ivypaw. Why choose *her* and not one of the Three?

I'll talk to Lionblaze about it in the morning. Tired to the tip of his tail, he let his mind drift into sleep.

The stench of decay made him shudder. Blinking open his eyes, he found himself in the Dark Forest. Shadows pressed like dark pelts around him. He glanced nervously over his shoulder. What was he doing here? Was Tigerstar planning to recruit him?

No. Tigerstar was no fool.

He tasted the air. A familiar scent bathed his tongue. Stiffening, Jayfeather peered through the gloom.

"Hello!" A cheerful mew sounded in a clearing ahead.

Ivypaw?

A gruff mew answered her. "Sorry if I scared you today."

Who is she talking to?

"You didn't scare me at all." Ivypaw didn't sound frightened or even surprised to be in the Dark Forest. "I knew you wouldn't hurt me. You're one of the Clanmates, aren't you?"

The Clanmates?

Crouching low, Jayfeather ducked into the mist and crept

forward. Ivypaw stood a fox-length away, ears pricked, tail high. Beside her, Jayfeather recognized the broad shoulders of a dark brown tabby.

Tigerheart!

The ShadowClan warrior leaned close to the Thunder-Clan apprentice. "I saw you with Hawkfrost the other night while I was training with Brokenstar. I never guessed you'd be one of us."

One of us? Jayfeather crept closer.

Tigerheart circled Ivypaw. "You're good." Ivypaw fluffed out her chest as Tigerheart went on. "It was a shame our Clans had to fight, though. How did that happen?"

Tell him about your dream!

Paw steps scuffed in the shadows, and cold fear traced Jayfeather's spine as a rumbling mew interrupted the two young Clan cats.

"Come on, Ivypaw! You're wasting time!"

Jayfeather's breath caught in his throat as he recognized the speaker. *Hawkfrost.* Tigerstar's son, endlessly furious that he had been killed by his half brother, Brambleclaw, when he was trying to take Firestar's remaining lives and leave Thunder-Clan leaderless and vulnerable for his and Tigerstar's own cruel ambition.

"You fought well today," the former RiverClan warrior growled. "But you got the move wrong when you attacked Scorchfur. Never turn on two legs when you can manage on one!" He beckoned Ivypaw away with his tail. She followed without question, disappearing after him into the mist.

Hawkfrost's growl shot back from the shadows. "Wait there, Tigerheart. Brokenstar's coming for you soon."

Jayfeather stared in horror, his paws frozen to the chilly earth.

As the mist swirled around him, mews and growls began to rise from the shadows; young voices chirped with questions and called for approval while older mews snarled in reply, urging them on, pushing them ever harder. It was the noise of training sessions from any Clan by the lake—except this wasn't the lake, it was the Place of No Stars. Jayfeather glimpsed sleek, oily pelts wrestling in the shadows and smelled RiverClan. Beyond a line of gray ferns, lither shapes reared and swiped at each other.

WindClan, too?

"Unsheathe your claws!"

"Fight like a warrior, not a kit!"

The scents of decay swamped Jayfeather's tongue.

Then Breezepelt's mew rose from the shadows. "I wish I'd fought in the battle today." The WindClan warrior sounded tense with frustration. "I'd have fought on your side if I'd been given the chance."

Who is he talking to?

Jayfeather tasted the air, reaching through the foul tastes of the Dark Forest and shuddering as he recognized a ShadowClan scent. Breezepelt was swearing allegiance to a ShadowClan cat!

Another shape moved between the trees. Jayfeather spotted the long dark spine moving through the mist like a snake.

Yellowfang had given this cat a name on his last visit to the Dark Forest—a name she had spat from her tongue like poison.

Brokenstar.

"Don't worry, Breezepelt," the black-furred warrior growled. "There'll be many more chances to fight. We'll destroy the warrior code. Once it's gone, there'll be no limit to what we can achieve."

Breezepelt growled excitedly as Brokenstar went on. "With no mouse-hearted rules telling us what to do, we can rebuild the Clans stronger than ever."

Jayfeather shivered against the dread hollowing his belly. Clan cats, cats who lived beside the lake during their waking moments, surrounded him. He could feel their warm hearts beating, quickened by the lies of the dead. There was no hiding now from what was happening: Cats from *every* Clan were being trained by Dark Forest warriors to rise against their Clanmates, trained to break every part of the code the Clans had long fought to protect.

CHAPTER 3

"Mouse dung!" Lionblaze grumbled under his breath as Birchfall, snoring, flopped his legs onto Lionblaze's belly for the third time.

I wish I could sleep! Lionblaze heaved Birchfall away roughly. He got to his paws.

"Ouch!" A sharp twig jabbed Lionblaze between the ears. The roof was low and as prickly as a hedgehog, bristling with twigs that still needed to be trimmed. The *whole den* needed trimming.

Lionblaze wrinkled his nose. The air was rank with the stench of combat-weary warriors. Unease tightened his belly as he thought about the battle. Russetfur shouldn't have died. The skirmish over the Twoleg clearing should have played out till the strongest Clan had claimed the territory. Death had no part in a fight over boundaries.

Lionblaze brushed past Millie, tucked into a ball beside the entrance, and pushed his way out of the den, cold air nipping his nose. He blinked, relishing the chill, pulling free of the trailing branches that dragged at his pelt. The clearing glittered in bright moonlight. Frost silvered the cliffs that circled the camp, and the ground felt like stone. Lionblaze's warm pads stung for a few paw steps, then grew numb with the cold.

He paused and listened. In the medicine den, Jayfeather soothed Briarlight as she coughed. Molekit was purring in the nursery, probably warming himself with Poppyfrost's milk. The battle seemed like another world away.

A faint crack sounded from the top of the hollow. Lionblaze jerked his gaze upward and saw a piece of grit catch the moonlight as it fell. It landed with a tiny snick on the frozen clearing.

Something's up there.

Lionblaze headed for the barrier. Jayfeather had warned that the Dark Forest was rising against them; no sign could be ignored.

"Lionblaze?" Cinderheart squeezed from the den entrance behind him. "Are you okay?"

Lionblaze glanced over his shoulder. Cinderheart's gray tabby pelt was still ruffled from her nest. "Did you hear something out there?"

The thorns rustled, and Hazeltail slid into the hollow. "What's up?" Firestar had assigned her to guard the entrance with Graystripe. The ThunderClan leader always doubled the guard after battles.

"Have you seen or heard anything tonight?" Lionblaze glanced back up to the top of the hollow.

Hazeltail followed his gaze. "No."

"Has Graystripe?"

"Did someone say my name?" The gray warrior peered in through the barrier. His fur was fluffed up against the cold.

"Has anything happened while you've been on watch?" Lionblaze pressed.

"Nothing."

Hazeltail stretched, stifling a yawn. "It's been silent as the stars all evening," she agreed. "Why? Are you expecting something?"

The fallen speck of grit glinted on the frosty ground.

"It's probably just prey," Lionblaze muttered.

"Mmm, prey." Graystripe licked his lips and ducked back out of sight. Hazeltail shook out her fur and padded through the thorns to join him outside.

Cinderheart eyed Lionblaze. "Shall we go and check?"

Lionblaze hesitated. "It'll be freezing in the forest."

Cinderheart shrugged. "A run will warm us up."

"But it's the middle of the night." He didn't want to share his unease with her. And what if there was something there? He felt a protective surge rise in his chest. "You stay here. I'll check."

Cinderheart's eyes flashed in the moonlight. "I'm not a kit!"

Flustered, Lionblaze flicked his tail. "I didn't mean—"

Cinderheart marched past him. "And I'm not going to stand here till my paws freeze to the ground!"

Lionblaze sighed as she stalked toward the camp entrance. If Cinderheart was going to be stubborn, there was nothing he could do about it.

He followed her to the barrier. "We'd better be on the lookout for ShadowClan," he warned. "They might still have a taste for ThunderClan blood."

Cinderheart glanced back at him sharply. "You think?" She

pushed her way through the tunnel.

Lionblaze snorted, annoyed with himself. She was right; he was treating her like a kit.

"Where are you two going?" Graystripe challenged as they emerged from the wall of thorns.

"Can't sleep," Cinderheart explained.

"Be careful," Hazeltail cautioned.

"We won't stay out long." Lionblaze's breath billowed in front of him. "It's too cold." He followed a narrow path through the frosty bracken and up through the trees.

At the top of the hollow, they emerged from the forest into moonlight. Lionblaze sniffed at the grass edging the cliff top. It was limp with frost, and he could smell nothing but frozen leaves and ice.

"Are you okay?" Cinderheart's mew was hushed with concern.

"What do you mean?"

"About Russetfur." Cinderheart tipped her head to one side. "About her dying."

Lionblaze stiffened. "About me killing her, you mean?"

"You had to save Firestar."

"I don't want to talk about it." Lionblaze turned back to the grass, following the glittering stalks around the hollow's edge toward a fallen branch. He could only smell ThunderClan scents. No sign of intruders, or prey.

"You have to talk about it," Cinderheart persisted. "Every other cat will be talking about it. You can't just pretend it didn't happen."

"It shouldn't have happened!" The words burst from Lion-blaze, anger flooding quickly after. He sprang onto the fallen branch and turned on his Clanmate. "I never meant to kill her!" He tore at the bark, ripping chunks out with his claws. "I was just trying to save Firestar! But I didn't even manage to do that. He still lost a life!"

Cinderheart flinched from the spray of splinters. "You *did* save Firestar." Her voice was firm. "Who knows what Russetfur would've done next? She might have taken all his lives."

Why was she making him remember? He was suddenly back in the battle, Russetfur struggling in his grip as he tried to rip her from Firestar. He shuddered as he felt her grow limp beneath his claws. Why had StarClan let him *kill* her?

Cinderheart kept pushing. "Every warrior knows they might die in battle. Why are you so upset? Are you afraid ShadowClan will retaliate?" Her dark blue eyes reflected the stars. "Why should they? Death happens. Clans have more to worry about than losing a warrior."

"She was their *deputy*!" Lionblaze snapped.

Cinderheart met his gaze. "She was old."

Lionblaze's anger weakened its grip. He was suddenly sorry he had let his temper get the better of him. "A true warrior doesn't kill to win," he murmured. "Remember the code?"

Cinderheart blinked, her pelt smoothing, then turned and stared into the trees as though watching a thought drift into the forest. "Maybe times are changing," she breathed.

Lionblaze stiffened. "No!"

Cinderheart shifted her paws.

"What do you mean?" Lionblaze pressed. "The warrior code is the same as it always was. How can something *that* important to all the Clans change?"

Cinderheart shrugged. "Can't you feel it?"

"Feel what?" Lionblaze felt his pelt start to prickle. Had Dovepaw given something away about the prophecy?

"Something . . ." Cinderheart seemed to be searching for the right words. "Something feels different. The battle was so vicious—too vicious for a fight over boundaries—almost as if it was just the beginning of something much worse." Her eyes were round, dark pools.

Lionblaze stared at her. Was she the only cat to feel this way? He was used to the prophecy: *There will be three who will hold the power of the stars in their paws.* He'd known for moons that ancient enemies were stirring. The Clans were on the edge of darkness. The knowledge colored every moment for him now; it shaped every thought. But the rest of the Clan must be protected from knowing. It was more than they could comprehend, more than they could cope with, however hard they trained, however much they believed in the warrior code.

"Have you had a dream? Some warning?" he demanded. "If you have, you should tell Firestar."

Cinderheart shook her head. "No. It just feels wrong that Russetfur tried to kill Firestar. She was a fine warrior. Why try and kill him? She must've known StarClan would disapprove."

Lionblaze leaned forward as she went on.

"It was like something darker was driving ShadowClan."

A shriek from the trees made them both spin, fur on end, claws unsheathed. A white owl wheeled from between the trunks. It dived toward them, the air from the downbeat of its wide, snowy wings lifting their fur as it swooped past.

"What in the name of StarClan?" Lionblaze gasped.

A wing tip whipped against his muzzle, and he fought to keep his balance on the branch as, with another shriek, the owl whirled away over the hollow. With a startled yowl, Cinderheart pelted into the trees, her tail bristled like gorse. Lionblaze hared after her.

He started to call to his denmate, to reassure her, but he stopped himself. Running would wear out her fear soon enough. Besides, the cold night wind felt good in his fur. He felt powerful. Trees blurred around him; branches trembled as he passed. Cinderheart's tail, a fox-length ahead, was already beginning to smooth, snaking behind her as she plunged through a stand of bracken. He followed, the frozen stalks scraping his pelt.

Cinderheart swerved as they burst from the bracken. The forest floor dropped away in a short steep slope that Cinderheart leaped in an easy stride, landing lightly and racing onward. She veered to skirt a knot of bare brambles. The trees grew thicker around them as they headed deeper into the forest. Lionblaze let Cinderheart lead, enjoying the warmth of her wake, matching her pace, concentrating only on the ground beneath his paws.

When Cinderheart began to slow, he slowed too, flanks heaving, breath coming in hard gasps, as together they pulled to a halt. Lionblaze was surprised to see the abandoned Two-leg nest, dark against the darker trees. He hadn't realized they had run so far. They trotted past in silence and headed up the oak-lined slope behind the stones. Brambles sprang in front of them, but Cinderheart kept pushing her way through until she stumbled into a tiny clearing.

Behind her, Lionblaze stopped with a jolt.

"What is it?" Cinderheart asked, turning.

Lionblaze stared around the cramped space, hedged by thorns. He had been here once before. Then the sloping ground had been flat and grassy, dipping down in the center to a hole. Now the hole was gone, and instead of smooth grass, rocks and mud had set like a scab on the forest floor.

Lionblaze felt sick. Somewhere below that wounded earth lay his sister Hollyleaf's body. This was where she had fled into the tunnels after finding out that Leafpool was their real mother. The entrance had collapsed and disappeared behind a mudslide, trapping her forever.

"What is it?" Cinderheart's whiskers brushed his.

Lionblaze shook his head. Only he and Jayfeather knew the truth of Hollyleaf's disappearance, the reason she had vanished underground: not just because of Leafpool, but because she had killed Ashfur, the only cat apart from them and Squirrelflight who knew, in order to keep the secret. When Ashfur's death changed nothing in the storm inside Hollyleaf's head, she had announced the truth at a Gathering, then returned to confront Leafpool one final time before fleeing to the tunnel. As far as her Clanmates were concerned, she had died in a tragic accident, and Ashfur's murderer was still unknown, presumed to be a passing rogue.

Lionblaze had been so excited when he'd first seen the tunnels. The wonder of them! A secret place to meet and have fun. Now he stared at the fractured earth and wished Heathertail had never found them. Guilt pricked his pelt as he remembered playing underground with the pretty WindClan warrior while they were both still apprentices.

A growl rumbled in his throat. If Heathertail hadn't discovered the tunnels, Hollyleaf might still be alive.

"Lionblaze?" Cinderheart's anxious mew brought Lionblaze to his senses. His paws ached, and he realized he had been digging his claws deep into the frozen earth.

"What is it?" Cinderheart was staring at him with her head to one side. "Are you still spooked by the owl?"

"I guess so." Lionblaze unhooked his claws from the earth and smoothed his fur with a few licks. "Let's check the ShadowClan border," he suggested, hoping to distract her. "We're almost there."

"Not still scared they're after our blood?"

Lionblaze glanced at the lightening sky, ignoring her teasing. "It's nearly dawn," he meowed. "We can do an early patrol and report back to Firestar."

Cinderheart looked relieved. "You sound like a warrior again." She brushed past him. "You had me worried."

Lionblaze fell in beside her. "Worried about me?"

"Why not?" She stopped and gazed at him seriously. "You're a good friend."

Maybe more than a friend?

Before he could summon the courage to say it out loud, she darted away.

"I'll race you!" she called.

Lionblaze gave chase, keeping up easily as Cinderheart swerved between the trees. Would he ever have the nerve to tell her he wanted her to be more than a friend? His fur prickled with frustration. He could be the bravest warrior in all four Clans, but the thought of telling Cinderheart how he felt drained every drop of courage from him.

Stars glimmered between the trunks ahead. They were nearing the edge of the forest.

He quickened his pace. "Hurry up!" He pulled ahead of Cinderheart, pretending to tease. Truthfully, he wanted to reach the Twoleg clearing before she did. They had fought for it and won it, but he still didn't trust ShadowClan. There was no way he was going to let Cinderheart run into a trap.

He stopped at the edge of the trees, signaling to Cinderheart with his tail to keep back. She ignored him and crouched at his side as he peered across the frost-whitened grass. "I wish Firestar had never asked for it back!" she muttered.

Lionblaze snapped his head around and stared at her, shocked.

She shifted her paws. "I just mean it's impossible to patrol." There was an apology in her mew, as though she sensed she'd spoken too hastily. "ShadowClan can see us patrolling the moment we set paw out of the forest, and the hunting's so poor, and the Twolegs are here all greenleaf—" She broke off.

Lionblaze saw the sense in her argument and wanted to tell her that he'd had doubts about the battle, too. Had it really been worth the blood that had been spilled? But he held his tongue. The Clan had to remain strong and united, now more than ever.

He stifled a shiver. The sound of battle echoed in his ears. Yet again, he felt Russetfur's life ebb away beneath his claws. Sickness rose in his throat, and he pressed his belly to the earth.

"Someone's watching us!" Cinderheart's hiss jerked him back to the present.

"Where?"

Cinderheart pointed with her muzzle, and Lionblaze spotted a pair of eyes gleaming from among the ShadowClan trees on the other side of the clearing.

In a flash, Lionblaze was tearing across the grass. No cat was going to touch the newly won ThunderClan territory. Pelt bristling with anger, he skidded to a halt a tail-length from the ShadowClan border, ears flattened, tail lashing.

The eyes blinked at him calmly; then a cat stepped out from the trees.

Flametail.

The ShadowClan medicine cat stared at him boldly. "Come to kill me like you killed Russetfur?" he growled.

Cinderheart's paws sounded behind Lionblaze. "This is our territory now," she warned the ShadowClan cat. "You'd be wise to remember that."

Flametail snorted and padded closer, crossing the scent

line as casually as if he were padding into his own camp. "I'm a medicine cat," he reminded them. "I can go where I please."

Lionblaze swallowed against the rage that rose from his belly. *ShadowClan arrogance!* "Shouldn't you be back at your camp, treating your wounded?"

"My Clanmates are well." Flametail fixed his gaze on Lionblaze. "Except for Russetfur, of course."

Lionblaze had to stop himself from leaping at the young cat. Didn't Flametail understand the significance of the battle? Didn't he understand how much it had cost both Clans?

He felt Cinderheart's tail brush his flank. "Enough," she murmured, smoothing his bristling fur. "He wants a reaction. Don't give it to him."

Lionblaze let her soft mew soothe him and pulled in his claws.

"You'd best steer well clear of ThunderClan today," Cinderheart told the ShadowClan cat. "We have to set new markers, and yours is not the only Clan that has suffered from the battle."

Flametail blinked at Lionblaze, ignoring Cinderheart. "Once I thought we were kin," he spat. "Now I'm glad we're not. I would hate to share blood with a *murderer.*"

Lionblaze let out a warning yowl, but Flametail turned and, chin high, stalked back into the trees.

"The fox-hearted coward!" Lionblaze wanted to tear Flametail to shreds and feel his life ebb away as Russetfur's had.

"Let's go." Cinderheart circled him nervously, edging him backward, away from the ShadowClan border. "There's nothing we can do here except make more trouble."

Growling, Lionblaze turned and plunged across the clearing. Reaching the ThunderClan forest, he crashed through a wall of brambles, hardly feeling the thorns that slashed his muzzle and tugged lumps from his pelt. Rage and grief blinded him as he raced through the forest. He headed for the hollow, running blindly, ignoring Graystripe and Hazeltail as they welcomed him back. The thorn barrier swooshed past him as he hurtled into camp.

Berrynose was at the nursery entrance, looking rather startled. "Is everything okay?" he called.

"Fine."

Berrynose narrowed his eyes for a moment, then nodded and disappeared into the brambles. Squeaks of welcome sounded inside as Molekit and Cherrykit greeted their father.

"Lionblaze?" Jayfeather was beside the warriors' den.

"What are you doing awake?" Lionblaze panted. "It's not even dawn."

"Checking on the wounded cats."

"Is everyone okay?"

Jayfeather nodded and headed for the barrier. "Come with me," he instructed. "We need to talk."

Lionblaze was starting to feel bone tired from all his running. "What about?" he grumbled mutinously.

Jayfeather narrowed his eyes. "Ivypaw," he growled.

CHAPTER 4

♣

"Ivypaw?"

Dovepaw sat up, blinking.

Lionblaze's disbelieving mew had woken her, ringing in her ears as clearly as a blackbird's alarm. She jerked her head around, searching the apprentices' den for him, but he wasn't there. Ivypaw was sleeping; Blossomfall and Bumblestripe were still snoring in their nests. They'd move to the new warriors' den once it was finished. Then Ivypaw and Dovepaw would be alone, the only apprentices in the Clan until Molekit and Cherrykit became 'paws.

"Yes, Ivypaw." That was Jayfeather speaking.

Dovepaw shook her head. She must be hearing voices outside the den. She reached past the den walls into the ice-cold camp, casting her senses, searching for the conversation that had disturbed her sleep.

"Are you sure?" Lionblaze sounded breathless with disbelief.

What were they saying about Ivypaw? Why did they sound so worried? Trembling, Dovepaw scrambled out of the den. *I'm one of the Three. They should be talking to me. I'm Ivypaw's sister.* She headed for the barrier, hurrying lightly over the frosted earth.

The entrance was less than a tail-length away when a voice called from outside the nursery. "Dovepaw!"

She halted, frustrated.

Berrynose was watching her. "Where are you going?" The young warrior's creamy coat glowed in the pale light. Molekit and Cherrykit huddled beside him, tiny clouds of air spouting from their noses.

"Dirtplace."

"Then use the dirtplace tunnel."

Lionblaze's voice pricked Dovepaw's ear fur once more. "She *knew* him?"

Knew who?

Dovepaw had to find out. She turned and trotted to the dirtplace tunnel. She could slip out that way and find them.

Paw steps followed her. "Are you going to the dirtplace?" Ivypaw, her fur ruffled from sleep, fell in beside her. "Me too."

Dovepaw curled her claws with frustration. There was no way she could slip away now. Ivypaw would want to come with her. As she pricked her ears, searching out Lionblaze again, she noticed that Ivypaw was limping.

"What's wrong?" Her worries swiftly focused on her sister. Ivypaw was favoring one of her hind paws, treading lightly on one, heavily on the other. "I thought you weren't injured in the battle."

"I must have slept on it funny," Ivypaw muttered. The silver-and-white she-cat stiffened as though trying to disguise her limp. "Wasn't the battle exciting?" Ivypaw changed the subject.

"You enjoyed it?" Dovepaw stared at her sister. "But Fire-star lost a life."

"Well, that bit was bad, and Russetfur dying. But it felt so good to use all the skills we've learned."

Dovepaw ducked through the dirtplace tunnel. "I'd rather stick to using hunting skills and save the fighting skills for defending my Clan."

"But we *were* defending our Clan!" Ivypaw followed her. "ShadowClan was going to steal our territory. Don't you remember my dream?"

Dovepaw didn't answer. She still didn't understand why StarClan had sent a dream to Ivypaw and not to her. She made her dirt and headed back into camp.

The Clan was stirring. Graystripe padded past, yawning, heading toward the warriors' den. He cast a baleful glance at the clear dawn sky. "This chill is here to stay. Prey will be scarce before long."

Hazeltail padded after the gray warrior. "That was a long, cold night," she commented.

Graystripe paused to brush muzzles with Millie, who was nosing her way out of the warriors' den. "You're warm," he purred.

Millie pressed against him. "Get some rest," she told him. "It's warm inside. I'll catch you something nice for when you wake up."

The first rays of sun sliced over the top of the hollow and washed the nursery in orange light. Dovepaw reached again for the conversation that had woken her, but Lionblaze and

Jayfeather were heading away from camp, silent now except for their paw steps, which crunched over frozen leaves.

Why are they being so secretive?

"Hey!" Ivypaw hurried from the dirtplace tunnel. "You didn't wait for me."

Dovepaw forced her mew to sound light. "Are you surprised?" She wrinkled her nose.

"Are you saying I stink?" Ivypaw reared and cuffed her playfully, then winced and dropped back onto all four paws.

"Maybe you should see Jayfeather about that leg," Dovepaw suggested.

"It'll be okay," Ivypaw promised. "Look." She turned toward the halfrock, where Brambleclaw and Firestar were organizing the day's patrols. "There are more important things to worry about."

"I want two patrols along the new ShadowClan border." Firestar lifted his chin as he gave the order, but his green eyes were tired. The fur at his throat was still clumped with blood where Russetfur had bitten him.

Toadstep, Icecloud, Cinderheart, and Rosepetal clustered beside the halfrock. Thornclaw, Sandstorm, and Dustpelt sat farther back, while Leafpool and Squirrelflight paced nearby.

"What's the plan?" Cloudtail joined them, his blue eyes bleary with sleep.

"Two patrols," Squirrelflight told him.

Firestar went on. "Brambleclaw will lead the lake patrol; Dustpelt will take the other. Thornclaw, Whitewing, and

Squirrelflight, go with Brambleclaw."

Thornclaw dipped his head. Whitewing nodded. Squirrelflight flashed an uncertain look at Brambleclaw, dropping her gaze when he returned it through narrowed eyes.

Firestar pressed on. "Cloudtail, Sorreltail, and Spiderleg, you go with Dustpelt."

Cloudtail turned at once, fur bristling, and headed for the camp entrance. Sorreltail followed him, her denmates close on her heels. They filed out of camp, tails bushed as though ready for a fight.

"Cinderheart." Firestar turned his attention to the gray she-cat. "It's leaf-bare. The Clan needs skilled hunters, so practice stalking with Ivypaw today. I don't want to let this battle distract our apprentices from their training one moment longer. Lionblaze, do the same with Dovepaw."

Dovepaw stiffened as Firestar scanned the camp. "Where is Lionblaze?" he said.

Berrynose stepped forward. "He went out with Jayfeather just before dawn."

Firestar's eye caught Dovepaw's. She could tell that he wanted to know if something was wrong. Dovepaw shrugged. She knew no more than he did.

Firestar frowned. "In that case, Dovepaw, join Cinderheart and Ivypaw." He turned to Berrynose. "Go with them. You can take Lionblaze's place today."

Ivypaw leaned closer to Dovepaw. "Great," she muttered. "Hunting practice *and* Berrynose."

Dovepaw understood her sister's frustration. They had

fought alongside warriors yesterday. Today they were back to being apprentices.

"Come on." Berrynose led the way to the entrance. As they passed the nursery, Molekit and Cherrykit broke away from Poppyfrost's side and skipped between his paws, almost tripping him. A loud purr rumbled in Berrynose's throat. "You'll be warriors soon enough," he promised. "And when you are, ShadowClan won't dare threaten our territory."

Ivypaw rolled her eyes and whispered to Dovepaw, "Does he have to show off about everything?"

Dovepaw hardly heard her. She was casting her senses after Jayfeather and Lionblaze. *Where are you?*

A shove from behind surprised her. "Stop staring into the trees," Cinderheart chided gently. "Firestar's right. Hunting is our priority in leaf-bare. I want you to focus."

Dovepaw dipped her head and followed Berrynose and Ivypaw out of the hollow.

"Bring us back a vole!" Cherrykit called after them.

As they trailed through the forest to the training hollow, Dovepaw was still fretting. Why were Lionblaze and Jayfeather talking about *Ivypaw*? She recalled the knowing look her sister had exchanged with Tigerheart during the battle. In that brief glance it had seemed the two young cats weren't enemies at all. She frowned. Had Lionblaze seen it too? Was he suspicious of Ivypaw's loyalty? Surely not!

"Dovepaw." Berrynose jolted her from her thoughts. "Concentrate!"

They'd reached the hollow and had stopped in the middle

of the sandy clearing.

"What did I just say?" Berrynose demanded.

Dovepaw lifted her chin and stared at him blankly, her pelt growing hot.

With a sigh loud enough to scare off any prey in the area, Berrynose began to pace in front of her. "I said that even the most seasoned warrior needs to work on his hunting crouch and keep working on it." He halted and whisked the cold air with his tail. "Show me yours."

Dovepaw dropped into a crouch.

"Tuck your haunches in more, or your spring will be weak." Berrynose nudged her flank with his nose. He straightened her tail with a paw. "Keep it off the ground. And stop twitching. The noise of fur on leaves will alert your prey."

Dovepaw lowered her chin, holding it stiff and straight.

"Don't stick your neck so far out," Berrynose corrected. "You must be coiled like a snake, ready to strike, not stretched flat like a weasel sniffing for birds' nests."

Dovepaw dug her claws into the stone-hard ground.

Cinderheart stepped forward. "She looks fine to me."

"I bet she couldn't reach that conker," Ivypaw dared.

"Bet I could!" Dovepaw slowed her breath, focusing on the prickly shell three tail-lengths ahead. She let energy build in her paws, then leaped.

She landed on it squarely. "Ouch!" Its spines jabbed her pads, and she sprang away, fur bristling.

Ivypaw squealed with amusement. "Sorry, Dovepaw! I didn't really think you'd jump on top of it."

"Okay, okay!" Dovepaw sat back on her haunches and lapped at her stinging paws. "I'm a mouse-brain." She couldn't help purring.

Ivypaw skipped around her. "Even a mouse isn't that dumb."

Dovepaw pretended to look hurt, then sprang at Ivypaw, knocking into her and rolling her over.

"Enough," Cinderheart mewed affectionately. "Back to work." She nudged Ivypaw with her muzzle. "Show us your crouch."

Ivypaw pressed her white belly to the earth.

"You're leaning to one side," Berrynose warned.

Ivypaw was still favoring her injured paw. As Dovepaw watched Berrynose and Cinderheart pad around her sister, she pricked her ears and reached for the sound of Lionblaze's mew. Concentrating hard, she let her senses trace down to the lake, her ear fur pricking as she heard waves shifting pebbles at the shore. Familiar scents hit her nose. Jayfeather and Lionblaze were beside the water, huddled close together on the stones.

"And you're sure Ivypaw wanted to be there?"

Dovepaw stiffened. *Be where?* She closed her eyes. Now she could see Lionblaze and Jayfeather shaped in scent and sound, sitting on the shore with the lake lapping beside them, the icy wind lifting their fur.

"She was acting like she belonged there," Jayfeather muttered.

Lionblaze sucked air through clenched teeth. "This is serious."

"*Serious?*" Jayfeather echoed. "This is the *worst* thing that has ever happened to the Clans! The Dark Forest was *filled* with cats from every Clan! So many that a battle with the Dark Forest could destroy us all!"

Dovepaw's fur bristled as Jayfeather's words sunk in. She'd known that some cats were being targeted by Hawkfrost and Tigerstar, but she couldn't believe ThunderClan cats would ever be seduced by their lies.

Something slammed into her side, sending her rolling across the frozen earth.

"Ha!" Berrynose loomed over her. "I told you she was asleep, Cinderheart!"

Dovepaw scrambled to her paws, spitting out frosty soil.

"It's leaf-bare," Berrynose meowed sharply. "How much prey do you think you'll catch in your sleep?"

Dovepaw blinked at him. *Ivypaw's being trained by the Dark Forest warriors!*

On the other side of the clearing, her sister was getting to her paws, her pelt ruffled from rolling on the sandy earth. She suddenly looked small and tired, her eyes dull, her shoulders drooping.

It can't be true! Why would they choose her? She doesn't have any special powers!

Stop! Her thoughts were rushing like a hurricane. She took a gulping breath and steadied her mind. *Jayfeather might be wrong. Perhaps Tigerstar was leading him astray, not Ivypaw.*

"Dovepaw!" Berrynose's harsh mew broke into her thoughts again. "Are you this featherbrained when you train with Lionblaze?"

Dovepaw shook her head. "Sorry." She dropped her gaze. "I'm still a bit distracted after the battle. . . ." She let her voice trail away, relieved to hear Berrynose's tone soften.

"You're young," he mewed gently. "No doubt the battle was hard for you." He brushed his tail along her flank. "Let's concentrate on feeding your Clan. It's every bit as important as fighting. I want to teach you something that will help with leaf-bare hunting." He trotted to the center of the clearing. "You watch too, Ivypaw."

Dovepaw glared at her sister as she crossed the clearing.

Ivypaw met her gaze. "Are you okay?"

"Watch this, you two." Berrynose had dropped into a crouch. He was staring at a small mound of frozen leaves a few tail-lengths ahead. "When the ground is frozen like this, prey can hear every paw step as though it were a woodpecker tapping on a hollow log." He moved forward slowly, sliding his paws over the frosted leaves.

"You look like a snake," Ivypaw mewed.

Cinderheart circled her. "And he'll *sound* like a snake to any prey," she pointed out. "They'll be so busy sniffing for a snake, they won't think *cat* until it's too late."

As she finished, Berrynose sprang forward, darting fast as a hawk, and landed on the mound of leaves. He sat up and turned.

"You try it, Dovepaw."

Dovepaw slithered forward a few paces, her frozen paws slipping easy as ice over ice. Then she jumped.

"Perfect!" Berrynose called as she landed on the leaf mound.

Dovepaw whisked her tail. The sooner they got this training over with, the sooner she could question her sister.

"Your turn," Berrynose told Ivypaw.

Dovepaw sat up straight and blinked at Berrynose. "Why don't I go off with Ivypaw and put it into practice?" she mewed. "It's going to be such a short day." She glanced up through the trees. The sun had hardly cleared the topmost branches. It would begin to sink before long. "Your demonstration was so good that I'm sure Ivypaw will be able to manage this move."

Berrynose puffed out his chest. "Sounds fair."

Cinderheart cocked her head. "Are you sure you've got it?"

"Absolutely," Dovepaw promised. "And if Ivypaw needs any help, we'll come back and find you."

Cinderheart narrowed her eyes. "Ivypaw?"

Ivypaw nodded.

"Stay away from the ShadowClan border," Cinderheart warned them.

"Of course!" Dovepaw was already bounding out of the training hollow. She followed a narrow trail between two gorse bushes and headed up the slope to the top of the hollow.

Ivypaw was close on her tail. Dovepaw could feel her sister's warm breath.

"Good thinking!" Ivypaw puffed. "I couldn't stand another moment of Berrynose showing off."

Dovepaw didn't reply. She was rehearsing questions in her head. *Why are you doing this? How could you be so stupid?*

They reached the edge of the cliffs. Dovepaw pushed on, following the curve of the sheer stone walls, ignoring the sounds of camp life far below.

"Hey, Rosepetal!" Toadstep was calling to his littermate. "Do you want to come hunting with Mousewhisker and me?"

"Leafpool's patrol just brought back a thrush."

"Who knows how long this frost will last? It's best to keep the fresh-kill pile full."

Dovepaw felt a tug on her tail.

"Weren't *we* going to hunt?" Ivypaw meowed crossly.

Dovepaw ignored her, and headed through the beech trees toward the WindClan border. She could hear a squirrel pattering along the ground nearby, but she kept going. She had no intention of stopping to hunt. She had to get Ivypaw somewhere far from the Clan and ask her if Jayfeather was right.

She was suddenly aware that Ivypaw had stopped following. Skidding to a halt on the slippery leaves, she turned back. Ivypaw had dropped into a hunting crouch and was stalking a mouse as it sat nibbling a beechnut between the roots of a tree. Ivypaw pulled herself forward, eyes locked on her prey.

How can you hunt like everything's normal? Rage rose in Dovepaw's throat until she couldn't swallow it back anymore.

"Stop!" she yowled.

The mouse froze, then dropped its nut and darted away beneath the roots of the beech.

"Is it true?" Dovepaw marched toward her sister, pelt bristling, half with fear, half with anger.

Ivypaw blinked at her.

Dovepaw took a deep breath. "Have you been to the Dark Forest?"

"What?" Ivypaw stepped back.

"You heard me!" Dovepaw halted and glared at her sister. "Have you been to the Dark Forest?"

"Of course not!" Ivypaw was bristling now, her green eyes wide. "Why would you say something like that?"

"Jayfeather followed you in your dreams." Dovepaw saw Ivypaw swallow.

"I—I . . ."

"So it's true?" Dovepaw's heart pounded.

Ivypaw's blue eyes hardened. "So what if I did? It's the only way I'm going to learn how to be a great warrior. Everyone's trying so hard to make *you* the best warrior in Thunder-Clan; they hardly bother with me. I'm just Dovepaw's dumb sister—"

Dovepaw couldn't bear to listen. "How could you be so *stupid*? The Dark Forest cats are evil!"

"How would you know?" Ivypaw spat back. "You've never met one!"

Dovepaw stared at her. "Of *course* they're evil. Why else would they be in the Dark Forest? Do you think StarClan sent Tigerstar there because he was *good*?"

"Have you ever met Tigerstar?"

"No! But I've heard nursery tales about him. So have you! He tried to destroy Firestar; he set BloodClan on him—"

"He's different now!" Ivypaw thrust her muzzle in Dovepaw's face. "His time in the Dark Forest has taught him the importance of *loyalty*." Was that a challenge in her mew?

Dovepaw didn't flinch. "You're wrong," she hissed. "He wants to destroy Firestar as much as he ever did. The only thing that matters to Tigerstar is power."

Ivypaw curled her lip. "You haven't spoken to him. *I* have! He told me everything. How he only became ShadowClan's leader after Bluestar forced him out of ThunderClan. How he's always stayed loyal to his birth Clan. Despite everything they've done to him!"

"Everything *they've* done to *him*?" Dovepaw couldn't believe her ears.

"Who won the battle yesterday?"

"What's the battle got to do with it?"

"It was Tigerstar's idea! He's the one who told me to persuade Firestar to fight ShadowClan. He warned me that ShadowClan was planning to steal our territory. And because of Tigerstar, we stole *their* territory instead. What's that, if it's not loyalty?"

"But Tigerstar is part of the Dark Forest! You can't trust him! Don't you see that the battle caused nothing but trouble?" Dovepaw spat. "Winning a worthless piece of land cost Firestar a life and killed Russetfur!"

Ivypaw narrowed her eyes. "Tigerstar is still loyal to ThunderClan. You're just jealous. You're jealous that it's *me* he's visiting and not you! You're scared I might become a better warrior than you! That *I* might be the special one, and that Firestar might start taking notice of me instead of *you*!"

"Don't be a mouse-brain! You're my sister." But Dovepaw found herself yowling at empty air. Ivypaw had turned and bounded into the bracken. Suddenly alone in the frozen forest, Dovepaw started shivering.

Her sister was training in the Dark Forest! How could StarClan have let this happen?

CHAPTER 5

❧

"I think we should just wait and watch." Jayfeather turned up the slope, flinching from the cutting wind. "I'm going home." The watery sun had not softened the frost, and the grass crunched beneath his paws.

Lionblaze remained beside the lake. Jayfeather paused, sensing his brother's struggle to break free from the anxiety that had fixed him at the water's edge. "Hunt for your Clanmates!" he called over his shoulder. "They'll be hungry after the battle."

The pebbles swished as Lionblaze bounded away, and Jayfeather darted over the crest of the slope into the shelter of the trees. As the musty scents of dying foliage touched his nose, memories of the Dark Forest flooded his mind. He couldn't believe that Tigerstar had found a recruit in ThunderClan. Strange that it should be Ivypaw. Perhaps Dovepaw wasn't the only one of the sisters with a destiny.

Jayfeather tried to focus on the familiar scents of ThunderClan territory—prey scuttling over frosty bark, birds calling in the branches above—but only sensed fear beating in every tiny heart as leaf-bare tightened its grip on the forest. It was the season of death, and by newleaf cold and

47

hunger would have slain the weakest.

Shivering, he pushed the thought away and hurried down the brambly trail that led toward the hollow. Cold air pooled outside the thorn barrier, but as he pushed through and broke from the tunnel, he felt warmth wash his pelt. His Clanmates were busy.

"We can lift this branch and prop it up with a beech branch," Leafpool called from the warriors' den. "If we weave new walls around it, there'll be room for at least three more nests."

Jayfeather picked his way through the clutter of twigs piled anew for the warriors' den.

"Watch out," Millie warned as he neared the fresh-kill pile. "Birchfall's digging a hole to preserve prey." When the earth froze, prey could be kept fresh for days by burying it.

Jayfeather lingered at the edge of the prey-hole. "Do you think this weather's going to last?" he asked Millie.

"I'm not sure, but it's best to be safe," she replied. "We need to preserve as much as we can."

"Jayfeather!" Bumblestripe yowled from the medicine den.

Jayfeather jerked his head up and felt anxiety flash from Millie. Was Briarlight worse? He raced for the cave, forcing his way through the trailing brambles that veiled the entrance.

Bumblestripe was standing in the middle of the den, his fur scented with bark and damp green leaves. "Look what we've brought you," he announced cheerfully.

Beneath the forest smells, Jayfeather picked up the dusty scent of cobwebs. "I thought something was wrong!"

Millie ran into the den. "Is Briarlight okay?"

"Everything's fine." Brightheart padded forward. "Bumblestripe found great clumps of web behind the ivy on the Great Oak." The one-eyed warrior sounded proud. "He had to climb a long way up to reach it."

Briarlight fidgeted in her nest. "Isn't he brave?"

Jayfeather sniffed Brightheart's pelt, alert for the sour scent of infection. "How are your wounds?"

"A bit sore," she admitted. "But they were hardly more than scratches. They'll heal."

"Make sure you don't reopen any of the cuts," Jayfeather warned. "Is your torn ear hurting?" he asked Bumblestripe.

"Stings a bit, but in this weather, everyone's ear tips are stinging."

Jayfeather stopped beside Briarlight's nest and bent to listen to the young cat's breathing. The roughness had eased. "Make sure you do some exercise today," he ordered.

"She's already been to the fresh-kill pile," Bumblestripe announced.

"Do you want to check these cobwebs?" Brightheart asked Jayfeather. "They're good and thick."

"I'm sure they're fine." Jayfeather wished his Clanmates' enthusiasm could brighten his mood. "Brightheart," he mewed, "would you take moss to the nursery, please? The kits will need fresh bedding." He felt her stiffen with surprise. "I know it's an apprentice duty," he went on apologetically, "but our two apprentices are out training."

"Of course." Brightheart headed for the entrance. "I'll take

Bumblestripe with me. After finding cobwebs, he'll have no trouble sniffing out some moss."

As they left, Jayfeather turned to Millie. "Birchfall will probably need help with the prey-hole."

"Are you sure Briarlight's okay?" Millie pressed.

"She's better every day."

"You don't think it's too soon to make her do her exercises?" Millie's tail swished over Briarlight's flank. "She looks so tired."

Jayfeather let out a breath slowly. "I'm not making her do more than she can manage."

"It stops me from getting bored," Briarlight put in.

Jayfeather sensed uncertainty lingering around Millie. "Go back to work," he murmured. "Worrying won't help."

As the warrior pushed her way out of the den, Briarlight's nest rustled. "You could have thanked Brightheart and Bumblestripe for the cobwebs," she scolded him. "They found enough to keep you going till greenleaf."

The brambles rustled at the den entrance before Jayfeather could reply.

"Jayfeather!" Dovepaw's fraught mew jangled the air.

Briarlight twitched in her nest. "What's wrong?"

"I'm sure it's nothing," Jayfeather told his patient quickly, knowing exactly what was troubling the young apprentice. "Follow me." He nudged her out of the den. "I need to check on Firestar. His wounds may need re-dressing."

"I know about Ivypaw," Dovepaw hissed as soon as they were clear of the brambles. "She's training with the Dark Forest warriors."

"Keep your voice down!" Jayfeather spat.

"But we have to do something!"

Jayfeather winced as a stray beech twig jabbed his foreleg. "Like what? Order her not to go? Do you think she'll listen?"

"Why wouldn't she?" Fear edged Dovepaw's mew.

Jayfeather steered her to the side of the clearing. "Look," he breathed. "She's made her choice. Perhaps we should just keep an eye on her and see what she does. We might be able to learn something about our enemy."

"Ivypaw's not our enemy!" Dovepaw sounded desperate. "She's my littermate. I can't let this happen to her. StarClan knows what Tigerstar will do to her!"

"I'm not going to stand here and discuss this with you," Jayfeather growled, then turned as the thorn barrier rustled. Mousewhisker, Toadstep, and Rosepetal were pushing their way through, warming the air with the scent of fresh prey. "Not here. Not now." He began to pad toward the warriors' den. "Go help your Clanmates. There's plenty to do."

He left Dovepaw standing in a haze of bewildered fear and headed for Highledge. *I'll talk to her later,* he told himself. *When we have a chance to go into the forest, away from pricked ears and curious eyes.*

From the scents drifting from the fresh-kill pile, Mousewhisker's patrol had brought back thrush, vole, and pigeon.

"We're going to have to dig this prey-hole deeper," Millie meowed.

"Not till I've had something to eat." Soil crumbled as Birchfall hopped out of the hole.

"Mousewhisker!" Cherrykit's mew sounded from the entrance. "You left this behind!"

Jayfeather heard fur brush the earth by the barrier of thorns. Cherrykit and Molekit were dragging something heavy into the hollow.

"A squirrel!" Birchfall licked his lips and bounded toward the pair of kits. "Did you catch it yourselves?" he teased.

"We found it outside," Molekit explained. "Mousewhisker's patrol must have dropped it."

"We didn't catch a squirrel." Mousewhisker's puzzled mew rang from the fresh-kill pile.

Poppyfrost came hurrying from the dirtplace tunnel. "What were you two doing outside camp?" she scolded. "And in weather like this!"

"We're going to need two prey-holes at this rate," Millie commented as Birchfall carried the squirrel across the clearing.

As Jayfeather climbed the rocks to Highledge, Sandstorm poked her head out of Firestar's den.

"How is he?" Jayfeather asked, reaching the top.

"Tired, and complaining about staying in his nest."

Jayfeather squeezed past her into the small cave. The ThunderClan leader yawned and sat up. The wound at his throat smelled clean and dry.

"Does it hurt?" Jayfeather touched the gash gently with his nose tip, feeling for warmth and swelling. The fur was stiff with dried blood, but the flesh beneath felt healthy and soft.

Firestar pulled away. "I'll let you know if it does." He shook out his sleep-flattened fur. "Is Brambleclaw back?"

Sandstorm answered. "Not yet."

"I hope the border marking went well," Firestar growled. "I want ShadowClan to know for sure what is now ours."

Jayfeather's tail twitched. *He thinks we were just two Clans fighting over a piece of territory.*

"Jayfeather?" Firestar sounded tense. "Is there something you want to say?"

Should I tell him about Ivypaw? That the cat who persuaded him to fight for the Twoleg clearing is being trained by Dark Forest warriors? Surely the ThunderClan leader should be warned that dreams and signs no longer came only from StarClan?

No. We can manage this alone.

"They're back!" Sandstorm turned quickly and slipped out of the cave. "Brambleclaw and Dustpelt!"

The rocks clattered as she bounded down to the clearing. Squeezing past Jayfeather, Firestar followed. Jayfeather listened from Highledge as Brambleclaw, Dustpelt, and their patrols halted below him. He could smell the scents of frost and forest rising from their pelts, and the faint tang of ShadowClan lingering on their paws.

"Are the markers set?" Firestar asked his deputy.

"Ours are," Brambleclaw answered.

Dustpelt stepped forward. "ShadowClan hasn't set *their* scent line yet."

Millie trotted over from the prey-hole. "They're refusing to acknowledge the new border!" she declared indignantly.

"They *have* to acknowledge it!" Leafpool had left her work on the warriors' den to listen in.

"They don't *have* to do anything," Birchfall pointed out.

Millie's pelt sparked with anger. "But they lost the battle."

Jayfeather recognized the slow, solid step of Purdy as the loner padded from the elders' den. "Are you sure they *know* they lost?"

"Well, of course they do!" Mousefur jostled past her denmate. "Lionblaze killed their deputy."

No cat spoke, but paws shifted and tails brushed the earth until Firestar stepped forward. "We regret the loss of Russetfur," he meowed heavily.

Where's Lionblaze? Jayfeather's paws pricked. *He should be here to defend himself.*

"Lionblaze should have been more careful," Brambleclaw muttered.

Jayfeather swallowed back his rage. Lionblaze must face the charge himself. If Jayfeather answered for him, it would look as though Lionblaze were hiding from what he'd done. He heard fur snagging on thorns as the barrier moved.

Ivypaw.

She slipped into camp and wove among her Clanmates. "What's going on?"

Jayfeather's pelt grew cold. Light pierced his blind blue eyes, and he could suddenly see Ivypaw, clear as in a dream, her silver pelt bright against the frost-whitened clearing. Foreboding gripped his heart as the vision unfolded. Shadows slid over the top of the hollow, engulfing the dens, swallowing ThunderClan's warriors. Dark Forest cats swarmed down the cliffs, slithering like lizards over the stone. Their eyes shone red, and their teeth and claws glinted like crystal, flashing in the shadows as they crowded the hollow.

With a roar of fury, ThunderClan rose to meet them. Graystripe slashed at a brown-pelted tom, who lunged for his throat and flung the gray warrior flailing to his death. Millie screeched and fell on her mate's murderer, but two warriors ripped the fur from her back and dragged her wailing into the darkness.

ThunderClan was outnumbered and overwhelmed.

Birchfall, shrieking in agony and rage, was slaughtered by merciless claws. Dustpelt sank, his throat ripped by savage fangs. One by one, ThunderClan's warriors fell until the clearing was heaped with bodies. Blood spilled from their mouths, pooled on the ground, and spread a grim shadow over the earth. It oozed from the dens, flooded from the walls of the hollow, and dripped from the thorns of the nursery until the whole camp shone crimson.

Only Ivypaw remained unstained.

Dark Forest warriors swirled around her, triumph lighting their eyes. Ivypaw stood as still as stone, pooled in moonlight, unhurt, unafraid. Jayfeather's heart seemed to stop as she raised her muzzle and stared directly at him, her eyes black as night, her gaze blank.

A hiss of horror sounded beside Jayfeather, and he turned, fur on end.

Spottedleaf crouched beside him, her expression dark with despair. "I'm sorry," she whispered. "I couldn't change anything."

CHAPTER 6
❧

Flametail's paws slid over the frozen pine needles as he raced for camp. He unsheathed his claws to get a better grip and thought again of Lionblaze. *Puffing out his chest as though StarClan likes him best. Typical ThunderClan.*

A blackbird shrilled from high in the pines as Toadfoot sprang into Flametail's path.

Flametail skidded to a halt. "Watch out!"

"Just checking your reflexes," Toadfoot teased, hopping out of the way.

"Check *this*!" Flametail lunged and rolled his Clanmate to the ground.

Toadfoot struggled free and leaped to his paws, purring. "I bet none of the other Clans have a medicine cat who fights like a warrior." He shook out his dark brown fur. "Where've you been?"

"At the new border."

Toadfoot snorted. "Have they marked it yet?"

"Brambleclaw was setting a scent line when I left."

"ThunderClan cats have smaller brains than I thought if they believe we're going to let them keep that land."

Flametail snorted in agreement. "They must know the battle isn't over yet."

Fur brushed the ground nearby. Flametail jerked his head around, wrinkling his nose as he smelled death.

Toadfoot followed his gaze. "They're burying Russetfur."

"Let's join them."

Flametail led the way to where Rowanclaw and Ratscar were dragging the old ShadowClan deputy's stiff body through the sun-striped pines. Rowanclaw was Flametail's father, made deputy only last night.

Pelts flashed among the pines as the Clan filed from the camp to gather around the grave.

"We will miss her wisdom." Tallpoppy's eyes glistened as she took her place alongside the other elders. Cedarheart and Whitewater shuffled to make room for her.

Snaketail held his gray-flecked chin high as Russetfur was dragged toward her resting place. "Many hard-won skills and memories have died with our Clanmate," he rasped.

Ratscar and Rowanclaw halted at the grave's edge and laid Russetfur beside it. Flametail could smell the pine sap he'd rubbed over her pelt as he'd helped Littlecloud prepare the old ShadowClan deputy for vigil.

"A hard farewell," Owlclaw murmured.

Shrewfoot leaned against her denmate. "Was there ever an easy one?"

Blackstar padded to Russetfur's side. "She died fighting. She died bravely." He addressed his Clanmates. "We ask no more than that of our warriors."

Cedarheart's eyes shone. "She was my mentor and taught me well."

Rowanclaw dipped his head. "She came to ShadowClan a rogue and died a warrior."

Blackstar gazed at the sun as it struggled above the pine-tops. "StarClan will welcome her. What we have lost, they will gain. May her memories become our memories, and her skills become our skills." He nodded to Rowanclaw, and the orange warrior gripped Russetfur's scruff in his teeth. Silently, he hauled her body over the grave's edge and let it fall.

Blackstar turned, eyes glittering darkly, and led his Clan-mates away. Flametail caught up to his father at the camp entrance. "Where's Littlecloud?"

"He's exhausted after a night treating battle wounds. Black-star ordered him to rest. He'll share tongues with Russetfur at the Moonpool. He can say his good-byes then." Rowanclaw glanced at his son. "You must be tired, too. You were at his side till dawn."

Flametail was weary to his paws but not ready to admit it. "I can rest later," he insisted. "I just wanted to see the battle-field."

"Good." Rowanclaw nodded. "The land we lost should burn in your mind until it is regained." He touched his muzzle to Flametail's head before squeezing through the entrance tun-nel. Flametail emerged from the bramble thicket in time to see his father disappear with Blackstar into the leader's den.

"Sorry to bother you." Shrewfoot was blinking at him. The gray she-cat thrust a black paw under his muzzle. "Will you check this?" she mewed. "Littlecloud's sleeping."

Flametail inspected the paw. It was swollen at the lowest joint, and her fur was warm to the touch, but she only winced when he touched it with his nose.

"Just a sprain," he assured her. "I'll give you a poppy seed for the pain." He led her through the prickly entrance to the medicine den. It opened into a space deep within the bush. Inside, the sandy floor had been hollowed to make the den roomier, and dried-out pine needles scattered to make it soft.

At the back of the den, Littlecloud stretched and sat up in his nest. The neat tabby tom looked smaller than usual, his eyes wide and his pelt ruffled with sleep.

Flametail frowned. "Are you okay?" He crossed the den and sniffed his mentor's pelt. There was more heat in Littlecloud's fur than he'd expected.

"I'm fine," Littlecloud insisted. "Just tired."

"Stay in your nest," Flametail told him.

Littlecloud didn't argue, but instead glanced at Shrewfoot waiting by the entrance. "Is she all right?"

"A sprained paw," Flametail reported. "I'm going to give her poppy."

Littlecloud shook his head. "Just wrap it with comfrey and nettle." He nodded toward a pile of shredded leaves. "Shrewfoot has always slept a little too heavily on poppy."

"Can you manage the pain if I just ease the swelling?" Flametail asked the she-cat.

She nodded, lifting her paw. Flametail chewed the shredded leaves into a poultice and wrapped up the paw, tying a dock leaf around it to hold the balm in place.

Shrewfoot sighed as he finished. "It feels better already."

"Rest it for a day, then exercise it gently," Flametail advised.

Shrewfoot nodded and slid out through the bramble tunnel. Flametail turned to tell Littlecloud he was leaving, but the ShadowClan medicine cat was already asleep. Flametail's paws felt heavy, and he fought back an urge to curl up in his nest. There were wounds to check.

Nosing his way out of the den, he squinted at the light that bounced around the wide, flat clearing in the forest of pines. Several of his Clanmates were sprawled at the edge, soaking up the meager warmth from the leaf-bare sun. Snowbird rolled and stretched. Her white belly was laced with crimson wounds that made Flametail wince, even though he knew they were all clean now and soaked with marigold juice. Beside her, Scorchfur rested his nose on his paws, ignoring the half-eaten thrush lying by his muzzle. Redwillow lay at the entrance to the warriors' den, clumps of mottled brown fur sticking out on his pelt. He twisted to give his flank a lick, but flinched and lay back again, panting. Olivenose and Owlclaw stretched side by side, pelts ruffled, muzzles scratched.

The bramble wall shuddered as Tigerheart bounded through the entrance. A squirrel dangled from his jaws, and he tossed it toward the fresh-kill pile. Dawnpelt raced in after him, a pigeon in her jaws.

Flametail hurried toward his littermates, sniffing for blood. "I hope you haven't opened any wounds."

"We've been careful." Dawnpelt ducked down to show him

that the gash between her shoulder blades was still sealed with sticky cobwebs, no sign of fresh blood.

Tawnypelt squeezed out of the warriors' den. The tortoise-shell's green eyes lit up as she saw her three kits together, and she greeted each with a lick on the cheek.

Dawnpelt shook her off. "Yuck! We're too old for that!"

Tawnypelt purred and gazed around the clearing. "Where's your father?"

"With Blackstar." Flametail wove around his littermates. "I guess he'll be there a lot now that he's deputy."

Tigerheart flexed his claws. "I can't wait till he's leader."

"Hush!" Dawnpelt nudged him.

Tigerheart shrugged. "Well, it's true. Blackstar can't live forever."

Tawnypelt brushed her tail across her son's mouth. "Don't say such things!"

"At least we always know what Tigerheart is thinking." Flametail flicked his tail at his brother's shoulder.

Tigerheart stuck his nose in the air. "I bet you don't know what I'm thinking now."

Dawnpelt's whiskers twitched. "No, but I bet it won't be long before you blurt it out."

Tigerheart dropped into an attack crouch, eyes twinkling.

Dawnpelt pretended to look scared. "Help!" she squeaked, darting behind her mother.

"Stop it, you two," Tawnypelt chided. "The Clan is still mourning Russetfur."

On the far side of the clearing, Flametail saw that

Rowanclaw had emerged from Blackstar's den and was heading toward his family. Tigerheart and Dawnpelt were too busy chasing each other around Tawnypelt to notice his approach.

Tigerheart rolled Dawnpelt to the ground. "One day *I'll* be deputy, and then you won't be allowed to tease me."

"No, you won't!" Dawnpelt struggled from his grip. "*I'll* be deputy!"

Rowanclaw halted beside his wrestling kits. "Do I have rivals already?" he inquired.

Tigerheart and Dawnpelt leaped to their paws.

"We were just playing," Dawnpelt mewed quickly.

"I'm glad to have such ambitious kits," Rowanclaw purred. "But I'd like to be deputy for a moon or two before you take over." He glanced at Flametail. "Do you want to be deputy, too?"

"I'm happy to be a medicine cat," Flametail replied.

Rowanclaw's eyes glowed. "That's a relief. I don't think I could take on all three of you."

Tawnypelt rubbed her muzzle along Rowanclaw's cheek. "I'm very proud of you all." Her gaze wandered to Blackstar's den.

The ShadowClan leader had appeared in the entrance. His eyes were shining; his pelt was sleek and freshly groomed. "Warriors and apprentices!" Blackstar called as he stepped into the clearing. "You have had time enough to recover your strength! Gather around! There are lessons to be learned from yesterday's defeat.

"You fought hard," Blackstar continued. "But we lost

territory. If we are ever to regain it, we must learn from our mistakes. This defeat is a chance for us to grow stronger."

Give me a chance to heal everyone before you start planning the next battle. Flametail tasted the air. He could smell sourness. The wounds he and Littlecloud had dressed last night were going to need new poultices before infection set in. He glimpsed Ivytail wriggling out of the nursery. Her belly was beginning to swell with her first litter. It would be a while before she was fighting battles again. Perhaps she could help him.

"Ivytail!" He approached the long-furred queen and whispered to her while Blackstar continued his speech. "Will you help me re-dress some wounds?"

Ivytail blinked. "Of course."

In the medicine den, Littlecloud slept as Ivytail and Flametail gathered herbs and slipped back out into the clearing.

Ratscar was pacing back and forth, his brown pelt gleaming in flashes of sunlight falling through the trees. "How in the name of StarClan can we fight cats who swoop from trees like owls?" he demanded.

Flametail dropped a bundle of herbs beside Olivenose. "Your wounds need fresh herbs." Flametail sniffed at the scratches on her flank. "Listen to Ratscar while I fix them." He beckoned Ivytail closer. "Watch what I do." He began to lick the dried ointment from the scratches on Olivenose's flank. Olivenose dug her claws into the ground and concentrated on the debate.

Smokefoot had stepped forward. "Perhaps we can turn what they think is a strength into a weakness?"

Blackstar nodded, eyes like slits. "How?"

"They land heavily," Smokefoot ventured. "It takes a moment for them to regain their balance. We can use that hesitation to make the first move."

Applefur tipped her mottled brown head to one side. "Next time we'll be prepared for their owl tactics. All we have to do is look up. It should be easy to get out of the way while they jump."

Crowfrost's eyes grew round with excitement. "It takes time to climb trees and jump. ThunderClan warriors seem to have forgotten that they're cats, not birds."

Snowbird nodded. "While they're wasting time and energy climbing, we can be preparing to pounce on them when they land."

Dawnpelt joined in. "It'll be easy to defeat them now that we know what they're doing!" She glanced up at a hazel branch stretching over the camp. "Let's practice!"

Tigerheart was already running toward the trunk of the hazel, which was lodged among dense brambles at the edge of the clearing. He scrambled up it and picked his way carefully along the branch. Dawnpelt watched him, shifting her weight from paw to paw, her tail snaking over the ground.

Tigerheart dropped.

Dawnpelt leaped on him as he hit the ground. She rolled him over easily and flattened him against the cold earth.

Blackstar's eyes brightened. "ThunderClan cats think they're clever, but they're pigeon-brained," he growled.

Owlclaw padded forward. "We weren't just weak in the

forest fighting," he reminded his leader. "In the clearing, they split our line in two."

"Perhaps we should arrange our line differently?" Rowanclaw suggested. "Older, more experienced warriors must fight beside younger, less skillful cats. Then, even if they break our line into pieces, each part will be strong."

"Good thinking, Rowanclaw," Blackstar praised his new deputy. "Before our next battle, we will pair our warriors: Skilled and less-skilled will fight side by side."

Flametail felt a rush of pride for his Clanmates. To ShadowClan, defeat meant a chance to come back better, stronger, swifter in the next battle. There was no self-pity, no blame, just the certainty that next time things would be different.

Crowfrost had gotten to his paws. "We could keep a reserve of our strongest warriors," he suggested. "Then when our enemy thinks they're winning, we can send a new wave to crush them."

"Good thinking." Rowanclaw nodded slowly. "Strategy is all very well, but we mustn't forget that fighting skills are what win the battle in the end." He turned to Pinepaw. "You were knocked aside by Hazeltail," he reminded the young cat.

"She's bigger than me, and she took me by surprise," Pinepaw mewed indignantly. "Besides, I was fighting Thornclaw, not Hazeltail."

"True," Rowanclaw admitted. "But I think you could have parried her attack more effectively."

"How?" Pinepaw cocked her head, eyes sparking with interest.

"Come here." Rowanclaw signaled to Oakfur and Ferret-paw to join them in the center of the clearing.

Flametail watched his Clanmates with one eye as he turned to Scorchfur and began smearing fresh ointment on his scratches. Oakfur was still limping, but his pelt was ruf-fled with excitement.

"Ferretpaw." Rowanclaw nudged the cream-and-gray tom into position. "You be Thornclaw."

Ferretpaw fluffed out his fur.

"Oakfur, you be Hazeltail."

Oakfur nodded and crouched, ready to attack.

Rowanclaw nodded to Pinepaw. "Attack Ferretpaw, just like you attacked Thornclaw yesterday. But when Oakfur lunges for you, let yourself roll with him, so the weight of his leap becomes a weight *he* must carry, not you."

Pinepaw frowned for a moment, then turned and leaped at Ferretpaw. As Ferretpaw wrestled beneath his denmate, Oak-fur lunged, hooking his paws around Pinepaw and plucking her off Ferretpaw. Pinepaw went limp, and Oakfur stumbled at the sudden dead weight in his grip. As Oakfur staggered, Pinepaw twisted around, nipped Oakfur's neck, and escaped from his grip. Oakfur quickly found his paws, but the appren-tice was already on his back, churning her hind legs and sinking her teeth into the warrior's scruff.

"Excellent!" Blackstar stepped forward. "We have learned a valuable skill here."

"Great move, Pinepaw!" Ratscar called.

Pinepaw nodded to her mentor, her black fur ruffled with

pride, as murmurs of approval rippled through her Clan.

Flametail licked the last of the ointment into Scorchfur's wound. "How does that feel?"

"Better," answered the gray tom.

Blackstar cast a glance at the fresh-kill pile. "Rowanclaw," he called to his deputy. "Organize hunting patrols, please."

Rowanclaw flexed his claws. "What about marking the new border?"

Blackstar bristled. "Not while there is a trace of warmth in Russetfur's body." His eyes clouded. "Firestar chose a dark path when he asked for that land back. Would a true warrior give a gift, then kill to take it back?"

"Snake-tongue!"

"Fox-heart!"

Insults were spat into the chilly air from all around the camp.

Blackstar signaled for silence with a flick of his tail. "Flametail!"

Flametail jerked his head up in surprise.

"Come to my den and bring Littlecloud. I wish to speak with my medicine cats." The ShadowClan leader turned to Rowanclaw. "Organize the hunting patrols," he repeated. "But stay away from the Twoleg clearing. I don't want any fighting until our warriors are fully healed."

Flametail hurried to the medicine den and nudged Littlecloud awake. The medicine cat still felt unnaturally warm.

He woke groggily. "What is it?" he mumbled

"Blackstar wants to talk to us in his den."

Littlecloud was out of his nest in a moment and hurrying to

the entrance. Flametail was relieved to see that the old cat was steady on his paws. He caught up with him outside Blackstar's den, pausing to let Littlecloud in first. Ducking under the low bramble arch, he followed.

Blackstar's eyes glinted in the gloom. "Did StarClan give you any warning about the battle?"

Flametail shook his head and glanced at Littlecloud.

"Nothing." There was a rasp in the medicine cat's mew, and Flametail was suddenly aware that his mentor was wheezing.

Blackstar was frowning. "No warning at all?"

Both cats shook their heads.

"I would have thought StarClan valued Russetfur more," the leader muttered.

"Perhaps they didn't know," Flametail suggested. "Or it may be that her death was unavoidable."

Blackstar flattened his ears. "*Nothing* is unavoidable!" he growled. He turned to Littlecloud. "Share tongues with StarClan. Find out why this has happened. I want to know if ThunderClan is planning something else. They might be planning to reach farther into the heart of ShadowClan territory. This battle may only be the start. They are at our tree line already, and that is too close to our camp."

Littlecloud blinked at him. "ThunderClan hasn't stolen territory since before the Great Journey."

Flametail shifted his paws, uncomfortable hearing his mentor defend another Clan. This wasn't the first time Littlecloud had treated ThunderClan as friends rather than rivals.

The old medicine cat went on. "I thought Firestar's

leadership had put an end to their greed."

"But not to their arrogance," Blackstar growled. "They have always tried to tell the other Clans what to do. Perhaps they feel as if they've been wasting their words and now is the time for action." He flexed his long claws. "Go to the Moonpool. Speak with StarClan. Find out what you can."

Littlecloud's flanks shuddered as he dipped his head.

"*I'll* go," Flametail blurted out. Littlecloud was in no condition to spend a night in the open, and in such bitter weather.

Blackstar glanced at Littlecloud. The medicine cat's eyes were growing milky, and there was a tremor in his tail. If the ShadowClan leader was shocked that his senior medicine cat was sick, he hid it. "Very well."

Flametail followed Littlecloud from the den. Outside, Littlecloud's tail trembled harder. "Will you be okay on your own?"

"I'll be happy to know you are warm and resting. You've got to take it easy, Littlecloud. Ivytail can help with the simple stuff."

Littlecloud opened his mouth as if he was about to protest, but it turned into a cough. "Thanks," he spluttered.

Flametail dipped his head, uneasy that Littlecloud had given in so easily. The old medicine cat must be feeling really ill.

"Take care." Littlecloud headed back to his den.

"What did Blackstar want?" Ivytail trotted toward Flametail, her belly swaying.

"I'm going to consult with StarClan at the Moonpool," Flametail told her as his mentor disappeared into the brambles. "Will you keep an eye on Littlecloud? He's not well. He needs to rest."

"I'll make sure he does." Ivytail dipped her head. "And I'll keep an eye on everyone's wounds till you get back."

"You remember what to do?"

"If they smell sour, lick out the old ointment and chew up some fresh herbs."

Flametail nodded. "Littlecloud will be able to tell you which leaves to use from the store. I'll be back by sunhigh tomorrow."

"Take care," Ivytail mewed.

Flametail ducked through the entrance tunnel, blinking against the shock of cold air outside the camp. He broke into a run, heading along an old badger path that ran down to the lake. His paws sent up showers of needles; his breath billowed at his muzzle.

As he raced down the slope, the lake glinted through the silver-gray trunks. He emerged from the forest at a sprint, squinting against the sun flashing on the waves. Stones clattered as he leaped onto the shore, and he swerved to run along the water's edge. His muscles felt lean and strong beneath his pelt. Blood pulsed in his ears as his heart quickened.

ShadowClan wasn't going to be bullied by ThunderClan. ShadowClan wasn't a Clan that could be pushed around. Their arrogant neighbors needed to be taught a lesson, and ShadowClan would make sure they learned it.

CHAPTER 7

❧

"What's going on?"

Ivypaw had limped back to the hollow, her foot sore from her training with Hawkfrost the night before. She was still ruffled by her argument with Dovepaw.

How dare she judge me!

As she'd padded through the tunnel, she'd tensed, trying to disguise her sprained paw. But no one had noticed her slip into the clearing. Her Clanmates were gathered around Firestar, their pelts ruffled.

"What's going on?" she repeated.

Then she noticed Jayfeather staring down at her from Highledge as though she'd grown wings. A shiver iced her spine as his gaze locked with hers. Could he *see* her? *He knows I'm training in the Dark Forest.* She pushed away the worry. *Once he sees me becoming a better warrior for my Clan, he'll understand why!*

Blossomfall's mew stirred her ear fur. "ShadowClan hasn't marked the new border."

Ivypaw turned, sagging with relief. "Is that all? I thought there'd been another omen from StarClan." She glanced back up at Jayfeather, but his thorn-sharp stare had relaxed into its usual blind blue gaze.

"Is that *all*?" Blossomfall was blinking at her. "It means ShadowClan hasn't recognized that the territory now belongs to us. That's pretty serious."

Ivypaw shifted her paw, wincing as pain shot up her leg. "Well, yes. But as long as they don't cross our markings . . ."

"They'd better not," Blossomfall muttered as she headed toward the warriors' den, which was misshapen by a half-woven bulge at one side. "Are you coming to help finish the den?"

Dovepaw was already there, working with Leafpool to bend one branch beneath another.

"Later," Ivypaw called.

"Where have you been?" Cinderheart's mew made her jump, and Ivypaw spun around. Was that suspicion in her mentor's eyes? "Dovepaw's been back for ages."

"I wanted to practice my stalking till I got it right." Ivypaw wasn't going to admit she'd been sitting by the lake silently fuming. *I'm as loyal as any ThunderClan warrior. More loyal! I'm the only one who trains to fight for my Clan even in my dreams.*

"You must be hungry," Cinderheart meowed. "Get something to eat. Then you can help Dovepaw and Leafpool with the warriors' den."

Ivypaw looked at her paws. "Isn't there something else I can do?"

Cinderheart leaned forward. "Have you been quarreling with your sister again?" Her whiskers brushed Ivypaw's cheek. "You shouldn't be jealous of her, you know. You're just as good at hunting and fighting as she is."

Of course I am! I've been trained by the best!

"I was proud of you yesterday," Cinderheart went on. "You fought like a warrior."

"Thanks," Ivypaw grunted. Hawkfrost hadn't wasted time with flattery. He'd watched her fight in the battle, and when they'd met in the Dark Forest afterward, he'd shown her how she could fight better next time. So what if she'd sprained her paw; she'd learned so much!

"Get some fresh-kill." Cinderheart nudged her toward the pile of prey. It smelled fragrant, and Ivypaw's belly growled.

"Take what you want." Birchfall was flinging the kill from the top of the pile into a shallow hole beside it. "What you don't eat will get buried for later."

Ivypaw plucked out a fat shrew and gulped it down. As she licked her lips, she noticed Leafpool heading toward her with Foxleap.

"Cinderheart said you'd help finish the new section of the den," Leafpool meowed.

Foxleap could hardly keep his paws still. "It's going to be great once we've finished," he mewed. "There'll be room for Blossomfall and Bumblestripe."

"Okay, I'll help," Ivypaw sighed. She couldn't avoid her sister forever. Twigs were heaped beside the fresh-kill pile, and she grabbed a bunch in her jaws.

"I'll help too!" Rosepetal bounded across the clearing.

"I'm just fixing that patch." Foxleap nodded toward a gap in the den wall where long stems of beech had already been bent and planted into the earth. "You can hardly tell it's a fallen tree anymore."

Rosepetal nodded. "It's become part of the camp now."

"Mind you, there's hardly any hollow left," Foxleap muttered, squeezing past a branch that was sticking out.

"There's enough," Rosepetal mewed. "And it's much less drafty in camp now."

Ivypaw dropped her mouthful of twigs beside Dovepaw. "Here you go." Before Dovepaw could thank her, Ivypaw trotted around the bulging wall and began weaving twigs between the gaps.

"You've got nimble paws." Blossomfall settled beside her and began to help. "Here." She poked a long whip of willow through a hole in the branches. "You guide it, and I'll pull."

Ivypaw poked another twig into a gap in the wall. "Why isn't any cat talking about the battle? It's like they don't remember it happened."

"Why should they?" Blossomfall used her paws to squeeze the woven sticks tighter. "We won. What else should we be doing?"

"We should be learning how we could have fought better."

Blossomfall stared at her. "But we *won!*"

"That doesn't mean we'll win next time," Ivypaw pointed out. "And you can bet that ShadowClan warriors are training harder than ever to make sure that next time they win."

"How do *you* know?"

Ivypaw looked away. "They're ShadowClan."

Blossomfall snorted. "Well, we're *ThunderClan*, and leaf-bare is here, and there's more to worry about than just fighting."

Ivypaw sniffed. *No wonder Hawkfrost doesn't visit your dreams.*

Ivypaw huffed wearily as she circled in her nest. She'd eaten fresh-kill with Blossomfall and had crept into her nest instead of washing, hoping she'd be asleep before Dovepaw followed her in. Now that Bumblestripe and Blossomfall had moved to the warriors' den, it would be hard to ignore her only denmate.

Ivypaw shoved her nose under her paw and closed her eyes.

"Ivypaw?" Dovepaw nosed her way through the ferns and settled in her nest. "Ivypaw?"

Ivypaw slowed her breathing, pretending to be asleep. It had been a long day, and not even the niggling ache in her heart could keep her awake. Soon sleep dragged her deeper into her nest and wrapped her in its warmth.

She opened her eyes into a dream. Mist swirled around her paws, and yowls rang in the cold, dead air. For the first time, her heart sank when she found herself in the Dark Forest. She wanted to sleep all night for once. Her scratches from the battle were stinging, and her paw hurt. Training day and night was exhausting. She closed her eyes, hoping the dream would fade, but the cold mist nipped harder at her paws.

With a sigh, she opened her eyes. A stretch of short, bare grass sloped ahead of her, and the sky above loomed black and starless. Ivypaw stretched, preparing herself for the training session. At least her Dark Forest Clanmates never compared her to Dovepaw.

Paws brushed the grass behind her, and she turned. A brown tom with a black ear—small, lithe, clearly from Wind-Clan—approached. He halted and nodded a curt greeting. Ivypaw frowned, trying to remember who he was. She'd seen him at Gatherings. As she groped for the name, a voice beyond the crest of the slope called to him.

"Antpelt!"

Antpelt. That was it.

As the brown warrior raced toward the voice, Ivypaw reared up on her hind legs, trying to glimpse who had greeted him. Pain shot through her sprained paw. Before she could spot another cat in the shadows, she dropped, landing heavily, back onto all fours.

A mew behind her made her jump. "You look tired."

"Hi, Tigerheart." She was pleased to see a cat she instantly recognized. His thick tabby pelt rippled over his powerful frame, but his eyes looked weary. "You look tired too," she sympathized.

"I wouldn't mind one night's rest." He yawned.

"I guess they want to toughen us up."

Tigerheart didn't seem to hear her. "I don't suppose Dove-paw came with you tonight, did she?"

Ivypaw bristled. "They chose *me*, not *her*!" Not waiting for a response, she charged up the slope toward the trees, following the trail of crushed grass Antpelt had left. Breaking through the tree line, she hurtled into the shadows, rage pulsing in her ears. So much for being free from her sister here!

Why did Tigerheart want to see Dovepaw anyway? Did he have a crush on her?

She snorted. *He's wasting his time.* There was no way Dovepaw would have anything to do with a cat from another Clan. She liked hearing Lionblaze tell her how amazing she was too much to risk breaking the warrior code.

Growling, Ivypaw swerved among the trunks. She saw the matted orange-and-white pelt too late, and slammed into the side of a thick-furred she-cat. Recovering her balance, she turned on the warrior who'd blocked her way. "That was a dumb place to sit!" Ivypaw snarled, still seething.

Before Ivypaw could draw breath, the orange-and-white she-cat leaped on her. Ivypaw felt claws at her neck, and her breath shot from her chest as the warrior thumped her to the ground and pinned her there. Terror flooded Ivypaw as she struggled for air. She froze as the warrior leaned slowly closer.

With stinking breath and lips drawn back, the orange-and-white she-cat snarled, "Show some respect, apprentice." She curled her claws until the thorn-sharp tips sank into Ivypaw's skin. "You don't want to die in a place like this. There's nowhere beyond here, you know. Only darkness."

A tabby pelt flashed at the edge of Ivypaw's vision. "All right, Mapleshade."

Ivypaw fell limp with relief as she recognized Hawkfrost's meow.

"Let her go." There was a menacing growl in his voice, and Mapleshade released her grip.

Ivypaw drew a long gulp of air and began to cough.

Hacking, she scrambled to her paws, her belly brushing the earth as she crouched and tried to catch her breath. She was shaking from nose to tail.

"Pull yourself together," Hawkfrost snapped.

Mapleshade flicked her tail. "Try to keep your visitors under control." She turned and stalked away, muttering, "I preferred it here when it wasn't overrun with wide-eyed idiots."

Ivypaw blinked up at Hawkfrost. "Sorry."

"Never mind Mapleshade," he answered briskly. "She's been here a long time. But not for much longer."

Ivypaw glanced nervously at the departing warrior. The shadows seemed to be swallowing her, and Ivypaw realized with a start that the she-cat's outline hung in the air like mist. She could clearly see the trees on the other side of Mapleshade, where she should only have been able to see the warrior's sturdy body. Ivypaw shivered. "Do all cats fade away?"

"Eventually," Hawkfrost growled. "If they survive long enough."

He headed away through the trees. Ivypaw hesitated for a moment, her belly tight. She never wanted to fade away. She shook out her fur and bounded after Hawkfrost.

"Are you okay?" Hawkfrost was frowning at her hind paw as she caught up.

Ivypaw remembered the sprain. "Fine, thanks."

Hawkfrost leaped a narrow gully in the forest floor. "If you're not up to training, go home."

Ivypaw jumped after him, gritting her teeth as her paw

jarred on landing. "You should be glad I'm here. Jayfeather *knows*." The words tumbled out of her mouth. She hadn't planned to tell, but she couldn't keep it to herself any longer.

Hawkfrost turned his head. "Knows what?"

"That I come here," Ivypaw confessed. "Dovepaw told me."

"So she knows, too." Hawkfrost paused and stared at Ivypaw. "And?"

What does he want me to say? Ivypaw shrugged. "And . . . nothing."

Hawkfrost nodded and set off again.

"After all, I'm not doing anything wrong, am I?" Ivypaw hurried to catch up. "They should be grateful I'm doing extra training. ThunderClan warriors don't seem to care about fighting. I spent all day building dens."

Hawkfrost's pelt brushed the smooth bark of a tree. "You're not doing anything wrong at all," he told her. "Don't you think I'd warn you if you were?"

He led her into a clearing, where a gray-and-black rock jutted from the earth like the hunched back of an ancient badger. Cats circled the stone, and Ivypaw recognized Antpelt and Tigerheart. Tigerheart nodded a greeting, but Ivypaw ignored him. She was too busy looking for other cats she knew. She had never seen so many Clan cats in the Dark Forest before. She spotted the sleek, dark gray pelt of the RiverClan she-cat Minnowtail, and farther along, Breezepelt paced beneath a lightning-blasted pine tree.

Ivypaw halted beside a small white tom. She shivered when she saw the long scar that parted his belly fur and curled over his shoulder to the tip of his ear like a bulging pink snake.

Hawkfrost introduced them. "This is Snowtuft."

Ivypaw nodded shyly, trying not to stare at his scar.

"That's Shredtail, and that's Sparrowfeather." Hawkfrost flicked his tail toward two more Dark Forest warriors. Shredtail's dark tabby pelt was crisscrossed with old wounds, and Sparrowfeather, a small mottled she-cat, had a muzzle that looked as though it had been savaged by a dog. Ivypaw curled her claws and lifted her chin. She wasn't going to let her new Clanmates know how nervous she was feeling.

"Thistleclaw!"

Hawkfrost's greeting made Ivypaw jump. She'd heard nursery tales about Thistleclaw. He'd been Tigerstar's mentor, and some cats said it was Thistleclaw who'd first taught Firestar's old enemy the meaning of cruelty. She jerked around to see a large tom pad slowly into the clearing. Uneven patches of gray mottled his white face. His white shoulders rippled with strength, and he lashed his long gray tail.

"Good evening, Hawkfrost." His sharp green eyes flashed at his Dark Forest ally. "Not many with us tonight."

"Only the best," Hawkfrost replied.

Thistleclaw slowly circled the rock. Ivypaw held her breath. What kind of training session would this be? She lifted the weight from her aching paw, hoping it would hold out.

"You." Thistleclaw nodded to Shredtail. "Get on the rock."

Shredtail scrambled up quickly and stood on the broad, smooth stone.

Thistleclaw's green gaze glittered. "I want you to work

together," he ordered. "You've got to knock him from the rock without letting him strike a blow to your heads." He stared at Shredtail. "Do you understand?"

Shredtail nodded.

Thistleclaw stepped back. "Begin."

Sparrowfeather leaped first. She was small, but she was strong, and she unbalanced Shredtail momentarily with a savage blow to his face. Ivypaw bristled. Blood was welling on the warrior's cheek. Were they supposed to train with unsheathed claws? She crouched down and launched herself at Shredtail, but she was knocked aside by Antpelt, who was making his own attack.

"I said work together!" Thistleclaw yowled. He clouted Antpelt's ear. Ivypaw felt something hot spatter against her neck, and smelled the salty tang of blood. She deliberately didn't look at Antpelt, didn't want to see how he had been punished for getting in her way. Instead she darted around the rock to where Tigerheart was standing on hind paws, batting at Shredtail and ducking to keep his head from being battered in return. Ivypaw reared up beside him and joined in.

Shredtail was becoming frantic as cats swiped at him from every side. Whipping one way and then another, he tried to reach them with carefully aimed blows. Ivypaw ducked as he hooked a paw toward her, then reared as he turned to defend his back. She sprang forward and knocked him with both paws, delight rushing through her as she felt him stagger.

Got you!

But Shredtail spun and faced her, a snarl twitching on his

lips. Ivypaw jerked backward as Shredtail slashed at her eyes with outstretched claws. He missed, but he was close enough for Ivypaw to feel her eyelashes shiver.

Shock pulsed through her. *He could have blinded me!* As she dropped, trembling, onto four paws, Shredtail's eyes suddenly widened in surprise, and he collapsed onto his belly as his hind legs were yanked out from under him. Ivypaw looked up to see Sparrowfeather hauling the young warrior from the rock, her teeth sunk deep into his flesh. Shredtail wailed in agony, his claws scraping over rock as he fought to cling on.

"No!" Thistleclaw roared, and swung a paw that knocked Sparrowfeather off her feet. With a yowl she crashed, sprawling onto the grass.

Ivypaw gasped. *She's not moving!*

The gray-and-white warrior swung his head around, his gaze swooping over the trembling cats. "I told you to *knock* him off." His voice was terrifyingly soft. "Not drag him." He glanced at Sparrowfeather. The small brown cat twitched and lifted her head. "You cheated," Thistleclaw hissed.

"Sorry." Sparrowfeather's mew was little more than a croak.

Thistleclaw circled her slowly, then jabbed her with a paw. "Get up," he growled. "It's your turn." He watched as she dragged herself to her paws and began to haul herself up onto the rock.

"And this time, don't cheat."

CHAPTER 8

Flametail was bone tired.

Clumsily he hauled himself over the lip of the hollow and followed the dimpled rock path that curved down to the Moonpool. He hadn't slept in two days, and he flopped like a defeated warrior beside the water, his paws frozen and raw.

The stone walls of the hollow glittered with ice. A sharp wind made the star-flecked pool shiver. Closing his eyes, Flametail rested his chin on his paws and let the tip of his nose touch the water. At once flames burst around him. The ice on the rock walls hissed and spat as the fire hit it.

Flametail shot to his paws, spinning in panic. A sheet of dazzling orange flames blocked the path that led up from the pool. He cringed away, heart pounding, ears flattened. *StarClan, help me!* Blindly, he raced for the pool.

"No, you fool!" A yowl made him halt.

He turned, squinting as he spotted a feline shape, dark against the wall of fire. "Who are you?" As the cat approached, Flametail could make out the gray tabby pelt of a tom. It wasn't any cat that he knew, though his fur smelled faintly of ShadowClan pines.

"Stay away from the water," the gray cat growled.

"Don't be afraid. Palefoot only wants to help." Now a she-cat shimmered into view. The flames threw flickering shadows over her snowy pelt. Flametail recognized Sagewhisker, the ancient ShadowClan medicine cat.

The StarClan warriors gazed at him calmly.

"Can't you see the flames?" Flametail wailed.

"Look around you," Sagewhisker murmured.

Flametail stared around the fiery hollow. And gasped.

Star-pelted cats lined the ledges and stone shelves of the hollow walls. Fire encircled them, making their fur shimmer, but not a flame touched them. Flametail tasted the air. Frost nipped his tongue. The air was cold. His pelt felt nothing but the icy night breeze. The fire was nothing more than a vision. It flamed silently around him, no more than cold light, illuminating the hollow.

Fear drained from him. Breathing deeply with relief, Flametail scanned the ranks of his ancestors and recognized Runningnose, Nightpelt, and Fernshade. With a rush of joy he saw Russetfur. She looked young and strong, as she must have before he'd been born, her dark red fur sleek, her tail curled neatly over her paws. The light of the flames reflected in her dark, steady gaze.

"Who do you see?" Sagewhisker prompted gently.

"Runningnose, Fernshade . . ." he began. *Why is she asking? She can see for herself.* "Russetfur, Crowtail . . ." He began to recognize more pelts. "Stonetooth, Foxheart . . ." All long-dead ShadowClan warriors he'd met beside the Moonpool. "Just our ancestors." Why was Sagewhisker staring at him so intently?

"Anyone else?"

Flametail scanned the ranks again. "Hollyflower, Flint-fang . . ." He frowned. "All our ancestors," he repeated. His pelt pricked. There were only ShadowClan cats here. "Is Shadow-Clan going to die in a fire?" His heart leaped in his throat. "Is this your warning?"

Sagewhisker shook her head. "Our message isn't that simple, I'm afraid."

"Where is the rest of StarClan?" Flametail shifted his paws.

"They are with their own Clans."

"But in death you are all one Clan." Flametail tipped his head to one side, puzzled. "The borders between the Clans disappear."

A dark pelt flashed through the flames as a large tabby tom jumped down onto the flattened stone. It was Raggedstar, the noble leader of ShadowClan many moons ago.

"There used to be no borders in StarClan." His deep, rich mew rang around the hollow. "But times have changed."

Flametail's claws twitched within their sheaths. "What change? Why?"

"The battle with ThunderClan was unjust and unpro-voked. But ThunderClan's ancestors did nothing to stop it, and Russetfur died." He nodded respectfully to the Shadow-Clan deputy.

"Something terrible is coming." Sagewhisker snatched Flametail's gaze from Raggedstar. Her eyes glittered. "No Clan can be trusted. Each must stand alone if it is to survive."

Flametail's fur bristled. "*What's* coming?"

Sagewhisker leaned closer. "We cannot be dragged down by another Clan's treachery."

Fear tightened Flametail's belly. "Can't you tell me what's going to happen?"

As Sagewhisker shook her head, Flametail turned to Raggedstar. "What is it?" he begged.

Raggedstar glanced desperately at Sagewhisker. "Why don't we just tell him?"

Sagewhisker growled. "If he knew, who would he trust? Suspicion could paralyze the whole Clan."

Raggedstar dropped his gaze to his huge front paws. "This is something far beyond our control," he murmured.

"What can be beyond your control?" Flametail stepped forward. "You're StarClan!"

"We guide you," Sagewhisker meowed. "We advise you. But we cannot stop events that are bound to happen."

"So what *can* you tell me?"

Raggedstar nodded toward the wall of flame. "You must burn as brightly as this fire to protect your Clan. Survival is more important than the code of the medicine cats. You must forget your allegiance to them and pledge yourself only to our Clan. From now on, ShadowClan has no allies. Remember this: A time of war is coming, and your warrior ancestors will stand alongside you. No one else."

A time of war is coming. The fire began to fade, and with it the starry ancestors. *You must burn as brightly as this fire to protect your Clan.*

Flametail blinked open his eyes, shivering. He was lying beside the Moonpool, the hollow dark and silent except for the breeze whispering over the water. The scent of StarClan still wreathed around him.

I'll remember, he promised silently. *I'll protect my Clan, whatever it takes.*

CHAPTER 9

♣

Dovepaw sprang awake, shivering. The fern walls rustled around her, and she tensed against the icy draft. Without Bumblestripe and Blossomfall the den was colder than ever. She pricked her ears. Ivypaw was whimpering in her sleep.

What's wrong?

"Wake up!" Dovepaw jabbed Ivypaw with her paw. What if the Dark Forest warriors were hurting her?

Whitewing poked her head through the ferns. "Is everything okay in here?"

Dovepaw turned quickly, shielding Ivypaw from their mother's view. "Ivypaw's having a bad dream," she mewed. "I was just trying to wake her up."

Whitewing opened the fern wider with a snowy paw, letting dawn light seep through. "I thought I heard her whimper—"

"Really, she's okay." Dovepaw cut her off.

Whitewing shrugged. "If it's just a dream, wake her up and come out. Brambleclaw's organizing the hunting patrols." She ducked out of the den, and the ferns swished closed.

Dovepaw rocked Ivypaw fiercely with two paws. "Wake up!"

"W-what?" Ivypaw blinked open her eyes.

Dovepaw saw that one of Ivypaw's eyes was bruised and swollen around the socket. "You're hurt!"

Ivypaw turned away, hiding her injury in shadow. "It's nothing."

"Did that happen in your dream?" Frustration clawed Dovepaw. "You were fighting in the Place of No Stars again, weren't you?"

Ivypaw thrust her muzzle into Dovepaw's face. "Shut up!"

"You mustn't go there!" Dovepaw felt heat pulsing from Ivypaw's swollen eye.

Ivypaw pushed past her. "Keep your whiskers out of my business."

"Why can't you see how dangerous it is?"

But Ivypaw had barged away through the ferns.

Help her, StarClan! Help her to see that she's wrong. And protect her. Dovepaw closed her eyes. *Please, StarClan.* She steadied herself with a deep breath and nosed her way out of the den.

Hazeltail, Brackenfur, and Toadstep were crowded around Brambleclaw. Bumblestripe and Blossomfall jostled at their heels, and Cloudtail and Brightheart paced while Dustpelt, Sandstorm, and Thornclaw waited quietly.

The ThunderClan deputy's ear tips were just visible. "Dustpelt!" he called. "Take Sandstorm and see if Shadow-Clan has marked the new border." He turned to Cloudtail. "Take Blossomfall and Bumblestripe hunting." He nodded to Brackenfur. "Go out with Hazeltail and Toadstep and see what you can catch. I want another prey-hole filled by sun-down."

Where's Ivypaw? Dovepaw scanned the camp. There was no sign of her sister's silver-and-white pelt, but she spotted Lionblaze at the far end of the clearing. The golden warrior was deep in conversation with Squirrelflight and Spiderleg, their heads almost touching as they murmured to one another. Curious, Dovepaw focused her hearing and listened.

"How big were the paw prints?" Lionblaze sounded worried.

"Big enough," Spiderleg reported. "A vixen, by the smell of it."

"She's used the track more than once," Squirrelflight added.

Lionblaze frowned. "So she's not just passing through."

Squirrelflight unsheathed her claws. "We're going to have to track her down and chase her out."

"It might be better to wait," Lionblaze reasoned. "The forest is harsh in leaf-bare. She may go elsewhere. Foxes prefer crow-food to fresh-kill when the hunting gets hard." He suddenly looked up and stared straight at Dovepaw. "Join Brackenfur's patrol," he called across the clearing.

Dovepaw shifted her paws, aware that he'd guessed she'd been eavesdropping. "What about training?"

"Training can wait." Lionblaze turned back to Spiderleg.

Toadstep and Hazeltail were already filing through the thorn tunnel after Brackenfur. Dovepaw raced to catch up to them. "Lionblaze told me to join you," she mewed to Brackenfur.

"Good." Brackenfur tasted the air. "The more claws the better. Hunting will be hard today. It's too cold to smell a thing."

"And your pelt's going to stand out like a fox in a snowdrift."

Hazeltail circled him, frosty leaves crackling beneath her gray-and-white paws.

Brackenfur snorted. "You'd better go in front then."

Hazeltail led the way up the slope, her pale fur no more than a smudge in the frost-whitened undergrowth. Dovepaw tagged on at the end. She pricked her ears, listening for Ivypaw.

"Wait!" Hazeltail halted at the crest of the slope. She dropped into a hunting crouch, her gaze fixed on the ground ahead. A blackbird was hopping over the frozen leaves. Dovepaw held her breath, while Brackenfur and Toadstep stood like stone. Hazeltail began to waggle her haunches.

Crack!

A twig snapped underneath Dovepaw's foot. The blackbird fluttered away in panic.

"Sorry!" Dovepaw shrank into her pelt.

Brackenfur shrugged. "Twigs are more brittle in the frost."

"Perhaps it'd be better if we split up," Hazeltail suggested.

Brackenfur tipped his head. "What do you think?" he asked Toadstep.

"Sounds good," the black-and-white tom agreed. "At least if we come back with nothing, we'll have no one to blame but ourselves."

Brackenfur nodded. "Okay, let's separate." He glanced around the patrol. "Anyone mind if I take the shore?"

Dovepaw shook her head. She was quite happy to stay in the shelter of the trees. "I'll head toward the stream," she mewed.

Hazeltail was already following the crest of the slope. "See you back in camp, then," she called over her shoulder.

"I'll try the edge of the moor," Toadstep meowed. "There might be a stray rabbit."

Brackenfur brushed against Dovepaw as he passed. "Will you be all right on your own?"

Dovepaw nodded. "I can practice my stalking."

The russet warrior disappeared over the crest of the slope. Dovepaw headed deeper into the forest. She listened, reaching far through the trees, searching out Ivypaw. Then she stopped. Ivypaw had already told her to keep her whiskers out of her business. And why spy on her when she was awake? It was when Ivypaw slept that she needed looking out for.

Dovepaw wove between the trees until she heard the ripple of water ahead. Dovepaw padded to the edge of the stream and leaned down to drink. Ice cracked beneath her paws. She hopped backward in surprise. The still, shallow water had begun to freeze at the shore. There was a narrow strip of sand on the far side where she could reach unfrozen water more easily. Dovepaw leaped the channel and took a long drink. Water dripping from her chin, she tasted the air. There was no warm scent of prey, only the soft promise of snow. Snow was coming. Dovepaw pricked her ears, unnerved by the silence.

The loud cackle of a starling echoed in the stillness.

Prey!

Excited, Dovepaw headed toward the sound, picking her way between the trees as silently as she could. The starling called again, closer now. Dovepaw unsheathed her claws and scanned the branches above. She would climb if she had to.

A rustle in the bracken behind her made her turn. A starling in bracken? *Unusual.* She plunged in, tail lashing excitedly. "Hey!"

A yowl of surprise set her pelt on end. Dovepaw felt fur beneath her feet. This was no starling. Bristling, she wriggled backward out of the bracken. "Who is it?" she mewed, her voice croaking with fear. She tasted the air.

ShadowClan!

The sour stench shocked her, and she tensed, ready to fight. What was ShadowClan doing on ThunderClan territory? The bracken rustled again, and Tigerheart popped out.

Dovepaw stared at him in astonishment. He was on ThunderClan territory! "How dare you come here?" she challenged, ignoring the excitement fizzing beneath her pelt.

"How dare *I*?" Tigerheart's eyes were round. "What are you doing on ShadowClan territory?"

"*ShadowClan* territory?" She frowned. "But this is ThunderClan." She glanced quickly around. Pines mingled with oak and beech. She tasted the air. ThunderClan scents mixed with ShadowClan. Where was the border? She sniffed again.

There! The border was behind Tigerheart.

He spun around and stared at the line of scent-marked trees, as though he was just as surprised to find the border behind him. He turned back. "Sorry!" His amber gaze was wide with apology. "The cold seems to have killed every scent. All I can smell today is frost."

Dovepaw purred. "I know what you mean! I haven't had a whiff of prey all morning."

Tigerheart looked relieved. "I'm glad I'm not the only one." He glanced back at the border. "You're not going to chase me off, are you?" A purr caught in his mew.

"Oh, no!" Dovepaw shook her head. "It was bad enough having to fight you in the battle." His amber gaze swung back toward her, and she felt herself growing hot. "I mean, I know we were having a battle, and we're supposed to fight . . ." The words got tangled on her tongue, and she found herself simply staring at him.

"Borders are more trouble than they're worth," Tigerheart muttered.

"What?" She could hardly believe she'd heard him right. But it was true. Without borders, they could meet whenever they wanted. The thought made her heart prick.

Tigerheart cleared his throat. "Of course, borders are borders." He stopped, his expression growing soft.

"Even when you can't smell them," Dovepaw joked. Why did he have to look at her like that?

Paws thrummed on the ground behind her. "Patrol!" she warned.

Tigerheart's ears were already pricked. "Get back to your side," she told him. "I'll steer them away." Tigerheart hesitated. "Go on!" she urged.

The paw steps were getting closer. Tigerheart bounded toward the scent line. Then he halted. "I want to see you again!"

Dovepaw blinked. "What? When?"

"Here! Tonight. Okay?"

"O-okay." Dovepaw could hardly believe she was agreeing. She turned on her hind paws and darted away.

Lionblaze, Spiderleg, and Squirrelflight were pounding toward her. Their bright pelts flashed between the trees. Dovepaw raced toward them, blocking their path.

"What are you doing?" Lionblaze slowed to a clumsy halt.

"Hunting," she mewed innocently.

Squirrelflight and Spiderleg drew up beside her. Spiderleg sniffed at her. "What have you caught?"

"Nothing yet," Dovepaw confessed.

"Where's Brackenfur?" Lionblaze asked.

"Down by the shore," Dovepaw told him. "We split up."

Lionblaze kneaded the frostbitten leaves under his feet. "Well, with the prey gone to ground to escape this weather, I can't see you'll be much use wandering around here by yourself." He sat back on his haunches and shook tiny specks of ice from his forepaws. "You might as well go back to camp and help patch up the warriors' den."

"Won't Brackenfur be worried if I just disappear?" Dovepaw didn't want to go back to the hollow. She wanted to stay out in the forest and remember Tigerheart's amber gaze.

"We'll find him and let him know." Lionblaze's mew cut into her thoughts. "After we've tracked this fox."

"Was it here?" Dovepaw peered around, suddenly nervous.

Squirrelflight looked puzzled. "Can't you smell it?"

Dovepaw sniffed and felt her fur stand on end. How had she missed it? The forest here was rank with fox stench. "I—I was looking for prey, not fox," she stammered.

Lionblaze narrowed his eyes. "Get back to camp."

Dovepaw nodded, relieved that she didn't have to make any more excuses. As she hurried away, Squirrelflight called after her, "Keep your eyes open!"

"I will," she yowled back.

She figured that she must have given Tigerheart enough time to get clear. And she was going to see him later. She pictured his thick pelt and his long sleek tail, and she hardly felt her paws as she raced down the slope to the hollow. Her heart was pounding when she burst in through the thorn tunnel.

She skidded to a halt. Outside the nursery, Daisy and Poppyfrost were leaning forward, ears pricked. Mousefur peered from the elders' den. Berrynose, at the fresh-kill pile with a sparrow in his jaws, seemed to be frozen to the spot. Leaves fluttered from Leafpool's paws beside the warriors' den.

All eyes were fixed on Millie and Jayfeather. The two cats faced each other, bristling, in the center of the clearing.

"You're pushing her too hard!" Millie's blue eyes blazed.

Jayfeather lashed his tail. "She needs to be pushed!"

"But she's exhausted."

"That's better than lying in her nest slowly suffocating."

"Are you sure about that?" Millie was trembling.

Jayfeather's eyes widened. "You want her to die?"

"I want her to be healthy!" Millie hissed. "I want her to run through the forest. I want her to hunt and fight. I want her to know the joys of being a warrior!"

"That's never going to happen," Jayfeather mewed gently.

"Then what's the point?" Millie raged.

"Isn't there joy in simply being alive?" Jayfeather leaned closer to the distraught warrior.

"Joy?" Millie's mew was thick with disbelief.

Jayfeather lifted his chin. "I won't give up on Briarlight."

A growl rumbled in Millie's throat. "All you're doing is dragging out her suffering."

Leafpool hurried from the warriors' den. "She's not in any pain," she meowed. "Jayfeather makes sure of that."

"But she's not getting any better," Millie pointed out.

"Being a medicine cat is as much about faith as about herbs." Leafpool swept her tail along Jayfeather's flank.

Jayfeather jerked away. "I can deal with this by myself, Leafpool!"

But Millie was muzzle to muzzle with ThunderClan's old medicine cat. "Faith?" she hissed. "If your warrior ancestors are so powerful, why don't they cure her? If this had happened in my old home, my housefolk would have fixed her."

"Millie?" Graystripe's shocked whisper sounded from the entrance as he padded into the clearing. "Is that what you really think?"

Millie backed away. "I don't know what to think," she rasped. "I only see my kit, broken and helpless, struggling through each day, with death stalking her like a fox. . . ." Her mew trailed into silence.

"But she's alive." Graystripe blinked. "She's here with us."

Millie drew a deep breath. "She has to watch her littermates living the lives of warriors, while she just yowls and coughs and drags herself to and from the fresh-kill pile!"

The brambles at the entrance to the medicine den shifted. Briarlight's paws jabbed through the prickly stems as she began to haul herself out. The hollow was silent except for the sound of Briarlight's belly fur dragging over the frozen earth. She stared at Millie. "I'm getting better, aren't I?"

Millie rushed to her kit and licked her cheek fiercely. "Yes, yes you are."

"I'll do all my exercises," Briarlight promised.

"I know you will," Millie soothed. "And I'll help you."

"They make me tired, but they don't hurt me."

"Thank StarClan Bumblestripe and Blossomfall weren't around to hear that." Dovepaw jumped as Poppyfrost's mew breathed in her ear. Closing her eyes, Dovepaw reached out with her senses until she could hear Bumblestripe and Blossomfall pounding along the shore, purring as they raced each other to the stream.

They were lucky. Safe in their small world, they couldn't hear every sound.

Dovepaw glanced around the hollow. Leafpool had returned to her work. Berrynose had carried the sparrow from the fresh-kill pile and was busy gulping it down. Graystripe stood alone in the clearing. Snow was beginning to fall, and the tiny flakes caught in his pelt.

Dovepaw felt a pang of guilt. Her heart was light. She was going to meet Tigerheart tonight.

CHAPTER 10
❧

Afternoon sunlight flashed through thinning clouds as Flametail slipped into the ShadowClan camp. He glanced guiltily around the clearing. He'd only planned to close his eyes for a moment beside the Moonpool, but he'd been so tired he'd woken to find the night gone and the bright air shimmering with snowflakes.

Ivytail was washing outside the nursery, and she looked up as Flametail crossed the snow-dusted clearing. He dipped his head and hurried past her in silence. He had to make his first report to his mentor and then to Blackstar.

As Flametail pushed through the prickly wall of the medicine den, he was relieved to see Littlecloud out of his nest and sorting through a pile of dried herbs. They were smoky with dust, and he coughed as he pawed through them.

"We'll need fresh supplies before the frost withers everything," Littlecloud meowed to Flametail without looking up.

"Perhaps you should take a little of the coltsfoot," Flametail suggested. "It might ease that cough."

"It's just the dust."

Flametail halted beside his mentor. "How are you feeling?"

There was less heat flooding from his pelt, but his eyes still looked milky.

"Better," Littlecloud insisted. "A good night's sleep is all I needed. What happened at the Moonpool? You've been gone a long time."

Flametail stared at his paws. "I fell asleep in the hollow."

"It's a hard journey to the Moonpool, and you were already exhausted."

"But I should have come straight back after a vision like that!"

Littlecloud leaned forward. "What?"

"StarClan warned me that trouble is coming."

Littlecloud frowned. "What sort of trouble?"

"They won't say exactly, but it's serious." Flametail shivered. "There was fire in the hollow. It was everywhere. Raggedstar said war was coming."

"War?" Littlecloud pricked his ears. "What else did he say?"

"That we must forget all of our allegiances and look after our Clan alone."

"Forget *all* of our allegiances?" Littlecloud's tail began to twitch.

"Even our allegiances with the other medicine cats."

Littlecloud blinked. "That's never happened before!"

Flametail willed Littlecloud to understand. "Even StarClan is divided now. We can't trust anyone but ourselves and our own ancestors."

Littlecloud hurried to the entrance. "We must tell Blackstar."

Outside, Blackstar had joined Rowanclaw at the head of the clearing. Oakfur was bounding toward the camp entrance with Snowbird and Ratscar at his heels. Crowfrost and Scorchfur were awaiting orders, while Olivenose and Owlclaw paced impatiently around them.

Littlecloud caught Blackstar's eye.

Blackstar nodded to him. "Crowfrost!"

The black-and-white tom straightened up. "Yes?"

"Finish organizing the extra hunting patrols. I want the fresh-kill pile full by sundown. Rowanclaw, come with me."

Eager eyes turned to Crowfrost as Blackstar withdrew to his den. Rowanclaw padded after his leader, and Littlecloud followed. Flametail waited as they disappeared into the shadows, then pushed his way in after them.

Blackstar's gaze burned through the dimness, fixing on Flametail as he entered. "You dreamed at the Moonpool?"

Flametail nodded. "A time of war is coming. StarClan is divided into the four Clans we know here. We must break all allegiances and look after ourselves."

Blackstar looked puzzled. "But we have no allegiances."

Flametail glanced at Littlecloud. "Medicine cats share a code that crosses boundaries," he reminded his leader.

Littlecloud sniffed. "Are you sure that's what your dream meant?"

Flametail felt the fur on his shoulders begin to prick. "Sagewhisker told me *exactly* what it meant."

"We can't simply turn our backs on the other medicine cats," Littlecloud argued. "Not after countless moons of sharing trouble and help."

Flametail curled his claws into the needle-strewn floor but held his tongue. Couldn't Littlecloud hear him?

"I think," Littlecloud went on, "that we should interpret this dream carefully. StarClan has warned us that trouble is coming, and we must be ready for it. But why must we destroy friendships that have seen us through the most difficult times? It is too soon to forget the Great Journey, or the role medicine cats have played in helping all four Clans to settle here."

Blackstar narrowed his eyes. "I trust your judgment, Littlecloud." He dipped his head to Flametail. "Thank you for traveling to the Moonpool and bringing back this warning. We are not so foolish as to sacrifice ourselves for another Clan, but nor are we so stubborn that we'll ignore help if we need it."

A coughing spasm gripped Littlecloud.

"Go and rest," Blackstar ordered.

Littlecloud swallowed hard against his coughing and padded from the den.

"Thank you again, Flametail." Blackstar flicked his tail, and Flametail knew he was being dismissed. Frustration crawled beneath his pelt as he headed out into the slanting sunshine.

"You should rest, too."

Rowanclaw's mew made him jump. Flametail turned to see his father staring at him. "You must be exhausted." Rowanclaw narrowed his eyes. "What's wrong?"

Flametail snorted and looked away.

"You had something else to say, didn't you?" Rowanclaw pressed.

"I know what I saw at the Moonpool," Flametail growled. "I passed on the message I was given." He saw the tip of his mentor's tail disappear into the medicine den. "Littlecloud's too attached to ThunderClan."

"He's been a medicine cat for longer than you," Rowanclaw pointed out. "It's not surprising he has friends in the other Clans."

"It's clouded his reason," Flametail argued. "A time of war is coming. Didn't any of you hear that? Raggedstar was clear about how we should deal with it. Why can't Littlecloud and Blackstar see that no other Clan will help us if it comes to a struggle for survival?"

"Don't underestimate Blackstar." Rowanclaw's eyes darkened. "He's no fool."

"But he wasn't listening to me!" Flametail lashed his tail. "He was listening to Littlecloud, and Littlecloud is too close to his medicine-cat friends."

"Don't worry." Rowanclaw ran his tail along Flametail's spine. "ShadowClan has always stood alone."

"The warriors, maybe." Flametail ducked away from his father's soothing tail. "But never the medicine cats. Something's happening inside StarClan." A surge of determination stiffened his weary muscles. "All the Clans will be affected. This time we cannot risk relying on anyone but ourselves."

CHAPTER 11

❧

Dovepaw shifted her paws. It was too cold to stand still. The ground was lightly dusted with snow. The sky had cleared, and stars sparkled over the forest. Chilled to the bone, Dovepaw paced the scent line again, keeping her ears pricked. Was Tigerheart coming? She reached through the trees, past the beeches, through the pines, stretching her senses to the ShadowClan camp.

"Move over, Pinepaw! You're crushing my nest."

"Have some juniper before you sleep, Littlecloud. Just to ease the wheezing."

Other sounds crowded at the edge of her hearing. Dovepaw let her senses spread wider.

"Swallowtail!"

The wind whisking the moor nearly swept away the voices from the WindClan camp.

"Where's Whitetail?"

"She's sharing Onestar's den tonight."

Water lapped at the edge of the RiverClan camp.

"Willowshine?" Mothwing called to her apprentice. "Did you make sure Pouncetail's bedding was fixed?"

A dog yapped crossly near the horseplace. It reminded

Dovepaw of the fox, and she drew her senses closer, sweeping the forest nearby just in case the freezing air had fooled her nose again.

Paw steps brushed the thin covering of snow only tail-lengths away. There was weight in them, though they were creeping lightly. Dovepaw tensed, jerking her head to scan the shadowy trees. The paw steps quickened. Dovepaw crouched lower as claws scuffed the ground.

"Dovepaw?"

Tigerheart!

"You spooked me!"

"I thought you'd hear me coming." A purr rumbled in his chest. "You have sharper hearing than any cat I know."

Too sharp. She'd been listening so hard, she'd missed the one thing she'd been waiting for. She needed to remember that hearing *everything* was sometimes not as useful as hearing *something*.

"Dovepaw?" Tigerheart's eyes were gleaming in the moonlight.

She blinked. "Sorry." She wasn't going to let her powers distract her from Tigerheart. He wasn't going to think of her as anything but an ordinary forest cat.

The warrior nudged her shoulder softly with his muzzle. "Stop apologizing."

Above them, the waning moon curled like a claw in the sable black sky and bathed the forest with soft light. Tigerheart's pelt shone beneath it, and Dovepaw felt dazzled by the sight of him.

"Come on." He headed away.

"Where are we going?"

"I know a place where no one will find us."

Dovepaw hurried after him. He was heading away from the lake, following the ShadowClan border. The land sloped gently upward, and the trees began to thin. She started to get breathless keeping up.

"You'll love this place," Tigerheart called back. "No one knows about it except me and Flametail."

The scents of ThunderClan and ShadowClan were growing fainter. Dovepaw glanced over her shoulder. The lake looked like a flattened disc glimmering far away through the trees. "Are we leaving Clan territory?" Excitement prickled in her belly. Was that mountain air she could smell? And what was that musky scent? Her fur pricked as a familiar smell hit her tongue.

Jayfeather.

She stopped and sniffed a low thorny bush. Jayfeather's scent lingered on the tips of the stems. Lionblaze's, too. What had *they* been doing here? She touched a stem with her tongue. The scents were stale. Moons had passed, from the taste of it.

"Hurry up." Tigerheart paused above her on the slope. Silhouetted in the moonlight, his forepaws planted squarely, his chin high, he looked like a Clan leader.

Dovepaw pushed the thought away. "Coming!" She scrambled up the slope to a clearing. Ahead, a tumbledown Twoleg nest rose like a gray tree stump, smaller than the abandoned nest in ThunderClan's territory. Half the walls had fallen down, and there was hardly any roof.

"Wow!" Dovepaw raced past Tigerheart and dashed up the pebbly path that led to the den entrance. She stopped where shadows filled the opening and turned back to Tigerheart. "Is it safe?"

Tigerheart nodded.

Dovepaw crossed the smooth rock that spanned the entrance and padded into the den. Moonlight pooled on the stone floor. She looked up and saw the starry sky. Straight wooden beams crisscrossed it. They must have held the roof up when the nest had been whole.

"How did you know about this place?" she called as Tigerheart followed her in.

"Flametail and I found it when we were apprentices." He leaped up onto a rock jutting above a hole in the wall. "We used to play here." With a second leap he was balancing on one of the crisscrossing logs. It was flat on each side, and he padded along as though he'd done it countless times before.

Dovepaw leaped up onto the jutting stone, her heart lurching as her paws slipped. Dust showered down while she shuffled to regain her balance. She eyed the log where Tigerheart had walked, judging the distance carefully, then leaped. It creaked as she landed, but the wood was rough and soft enough to sink her claws into. Chest pounding, she steadied herself and gazed down at the floor below.

"It's not too far down," Tigerheart called from the other end of the log. "Don't be scared." He flicked his tail, then jumped. In a long, arcing leap he seemed to fly from one log to another, landing solidly and turning to blink at Dovepaw.

"Now watch this." Without pausing, he leaped from one log to the next the entire length of the nest, then turned and bounded back as though he were leaping stepping-stones across a stream.

"Be careful!" Dovepaw gasped. With each jump her heart jumped too.

"That's nothing!" he mewed, landing beside her. He glanced up to where two logs sloped upward and met at a point. Without warning, he reared on his hind legs and leaped, swinging by his claws from a sloping log before hauling himself up and scrambling to the peak.

"Stop it!" Dovepaw could hardly breathe. She couldn't imagine another cat being so strong and nimble—or brave.

Tigerheart slithered down a sloping log and began springing back toward her. As he landed on a log next to hers, it creaked. The sound sent Dovepaw's thoughts spinning back to the hollow when the beech—its great trunk groaning and splintering—had toppled into the camp.

"Watch out!" A shriek ripped from her throat. She leaped across the gap, clasping Tigerheart in her paws and sending them both hurtling to the floor. They landed with a thump on a soft pile of moss. Dust clouded around them.

Her eyes streaming and throat burning, Dovepaw wriggled her paws. "Are you okay?"

Tigerheart didn't reply.

Oh, StarClan. Let him be okay!

"Tigerheart!"

"I think I'm okay." A muffled voice sounded from beneath

her. "But you're going to have to get off me so I can find out."

Mortified, Dovepaw wriggled away. "I'm sorry!" she squeaked. "I didn't mean to land on you."

Tigerheart sat up. He lifted one forepaw, then the other. Then he shook his head. "I'll live," he announced. His gaze was warm but puzzled.

Dovepaw fought the urge to stare at her paws.

"What happened?" he asked.

She glanced up at the log. It was still in one piece. "I heard a crack," she mewed apologetically. "I thought it was about to break."

Tigerheart followed her gaze, squinting a little. "Wow," he breathed.

"Wow?"

"Can you see that tiny split?"

Dovepaw looked harder and saw in the moonlight a small, fresh crack in the log.

"You've got even sharper ears than I thought." Tigerheart's whiskers twitched. "You saved my life!" He scrambled to his paws and began to circle her, tail high, a purr in his voice. "Without you, I'd be dead now. You're my hero. How can I possibly thank you?"

Dovepaw lifted her chin, playing along. "You must bring me mice," she mewed haughtily. "And a fresh squirrel every day for a moon. And new moss for my nest. And . . ." She flicked his chin with her tail-tip. "You must follow me around all day and pick the burrs out of my pelt."

The playfulness drained from Tigerheart's warm amber

gaze. Dovepaw tensed, wondering if she'd teased him too much.

"I'd gladly do all that for you." His mew was as steady as his gaze. "You didn't have to save my life first."

Dovepaw stared back. "I didn't really save your life," she whispered. "It was just a tiny crack. That log could still hold your weight."

"Maybe," Tigerheart agreed. "But you were worried about me. That means you care, right?" Dovepaw saw doubt flicker in the young ShadowClan warrior's gaze. "I mean, you care more than if we were just friends?" he pressed.

Dovepaw swallowed. For the first time she actually felt like she had the power of the stars in her paws.

"Yes," she breathed. "Yes, I care." Her heart twisted in her chest, half in pain, half in joy. "I shouldn't, but I do."

A purr rose deep in her chest as Tigerheart leaned forward and touched his muzzle to hers. Their breath billowed into a single cloud. He twisted his tail around hers, and warmth spread beneath her pelt.

Tigerheart sighed. "We'd better get back, before we're missed." He pulled away, but only far enough to let her get to her paws. Together they padded to the nest entrance, fur brushing fur.

They paused on the smooth rock, and Dovepaw stared out at the forest stretching down toward the distant lake. "This is going to work, right?"

"Yes," Tigerheart promised. "No boundaries are ever going to be strong enough to separate us."

Dovepaw blinked at him. "Really?" She wanted to believe it. She *had* to believe it. Nothing had ever felt so important.

"Let's meet again before half-moon," Tigerheart suggested.

"Tomorrow." Dovepaw felt bold.

"Do you think we could leave camp two nights in a row?" Tigerheart's eyes widened. "You'd take that risk?"

"It's worth it." She brushed his cheek with her nose. His scent felt warm on her tongue. He was hers now. He didn't belong to ShadowClan. They belonged to each other.

"What about your denmates?" Tigerheart pulled away. "They'll notice you've gone."

"It's just Ivypaw now." Dovepaw hooked a clump of moss from Tigerheart's pelt. "She won't tell."

She felt him stiffen. "Ivypaw?"

A cold stone dropped in Dovepaw's belly. Suddenly she remembered the look her sister had shared with Tigerheart during the battle. "D-do you know Ivypaw?"

Tigerheart flicked a strand of dried grass awkwardly from her shoulder. "I've seen her at Gatherings."

"But nothing more than that?" Dovepaw demanded.

Tigerheart sat back and looked her straight in the eye. "Do you mean, have I ever asked to meet her in the middle of the night, and brought her here to risk my life on collapsing logs?" He tipped his head. "Let me think. . . ."

Dovepaw fought the urge to shove him.

". . . No. I'm pretty sure I haven't." He touched his nose to her ear. "There's only one sister I'm interested in."

His breath was warm. How could she have doubted him?

He'd risked so much, coming here and confessing his feelings. She must have imagined the look in the battle with Shadow-Clan.

I trust him.

"Come on." She led the way down the slope until they reached the deeper forest, where he fell in beside her and pulled brambles from her path. She felt wistful as the scents of their Clans grew stronger, and when she began to recognize the trees along the border, her heart began to ache. Tomorrow night seemed a lifetime away. As they reached the clump of beech where they'd met, their steps slowed.

"It'll be tomorrow before you know it," Tigerheart murmured gently. He must have been sharing her thoughts.

She touched her muzzle to his. "See you then," she whispered.

"Definitely," he meowed. "Sweet dreams."

CHAPTER 12

❧

The dawn was bright, and Lionblaze watched as Brambleclaw and Firestar stood below Highledge, their Clanmates pacing eagerly around them.

"Dustpelt, Toadstep, and Foxleap," Firestar called. "Hunt by the Ancient Oak. Sandstorm, Whitewing, and Birchfall, flush anything out of the moorland you can without crossing the WindClan border."

Dovepaw yawned. "Are we hunting or training today?"

"Both." Lionblaze wondered why she looked so sleepy. "I'm taking you out with Cinderheart and Ivypaw." He'd planned the training session with Cinderheart last night as they'd wandered along the moonlit lakeshore. "We want to see how you manage hunting in snow." His thoughts drifted back to the previous night. Cinderheart's pelt had shone in the moonlight, and the stars had glittered as though the sky were as frosted as the hills. "Then we *are* more than friends?" he had whispered into Cinderheart's ear.

She'd pressed her cheek to his. "Hadn't you guessed?"

"I'd *hoped.*"

She'd purred and wrapped her tail around his. "Mousebrain."

"Graystripe." Firestar's mew broke into his remembering. "Take Millie, Brightheart, and Blossomfall and hunt by the lake."

Across the clearing, Ivypaw was circling Cinderheart excitedly. The apprentice had grown and filled out in the last moon. Lionblaze narrowed his eyes. Today's training wasn't just about seeing Dovepaw hunt. He wanted to observe Ivypaw. Jayfeather had persuaded him to wait and see how her visits to the Dark Forest changed her. He'd agreed and had promised not to challenge the young cat yet. But he wasn't completely convinced that they shouldn't intervene. Cinderheart had been fretting over the injuries that appeared fresh each day on her apprentice. Ivypaw had told her mentor that she had fallen out of her nest, or run into brambles while practicing her hunting moves outside the hollow. Clearly the Dark Forest warriors were training the young cat hard.

Firestar issued more instructions. "Squirrelflight, Brackenfur, and Mousewhisker, you can hunt along the banks of the stream. There may be voles."

As the warriors headed for the entrance, Daisy came hurrying across the clearing. Molekit and Cherrykit scampered at her heels. "There'll be no warriors left in camp at this rate," she called to the ThunderClan leader. "The hollow will be empty except for elders and kits. What if ShadowClan decides to take its revenge?"

Cherrykit reared onto her hind legs and boxed at the air. "I'll shred them."

Molekit pressed against Daisy's long cream fur. "I'll tear off their tails."

"Thank you, little ones." Daisy's eyes darkened with worry as she stared at Firestar. "Well?"

Firestar shook his head. "ShadowClan's warriors won't attack undefended kits and elders."

"Are we ready?"

Lionblaze looked up, surprised at the sound of Ivypaw's mew. She was a whisker-length from his muzzle. *She's faster and lighter on her paws than she used to be.*

Cinderheart joined them, yawning. "Let's go before we freeze."

Outside, Rosepetal, Sorreltail, and Brackenfur were tasting the air. "We'd be wasting our time at the shore," Brackenfur meowed to his mate.

Sorreltail nodded. "The deeper into the forest, the better," she agreed.

Rosepetal glanced at them expectantly. "Which way?"

"Up there." Sorreltail flicked her tail toward a thickly brambled slope.

As Rosepetal charged away, shaking snow from the bushes, Sorreltail shook her head. "She'd better slow down, or she'll scare more prey than she catches."

Brackenfur purred and headed up the slope with Sorreltail. They seemed to move as one, their pelts brushing.

Lionblaze stared after them. He wanted to walk with Cinderheart like that someday. His whiskers twitched as he imagined kits bounding around their paws, tripping them at every step. A soft muzzle brushed his, and he realized

Cinderheart had been watching him.

"I'd like that too," she whispered.

His heart quickened as he fell into her gentle gaze. He could still smell the night breeze in her pelt. "How did you know what I was thinking?"

"Hey!" Dovepaw's surprised mew made Lionblaze turn.

The apprentice was shaking snow from her smoky fur. Ivypaw was perched on a snow-laden branch above her sister's head. With a flick of her striped silver tail she sent another avalanche cascading over Dovepaw.

Dovepaw darted toward the tree trunk and began to climb. "I'll get you!"

"Get down, both of you!" Lionblaze fluffed out his fur. "We can have fun *after* the hunt."

Ivypaw leaped to the ground, landing easily. "Which way?" Her eyes shone.

Lionblaze's paws pricked. *She's more confident.*

"The pines," Cinderheart suggested. "They'll give us more shelter."

Ivypaw scampered away. "I'll race you, Dovepaw!" she called over her shoulder.

Dovepaw scrambled down from the trunk and sent up a flurry of snow as she chased after her sister. Lionblaze frowned.

"What's wrong?" Cinderheart tipped her head toward him. "Did you want to hunt somewhere else?"

"That fox has been hanging around the pines," he reminded her.

"Then we'd better keep up with them." Cinderheart darted off, following the apprentices' tracks.

Lionblaze pelted after her. They caught up to their apprentices as beech gave way to pine. The ShadowClan border was close enough to taste.

"Look!" Ivypaw was circling beneath a pine tree, her nose skimming the ground. "Fox prints?" She looked excitedly up at Lionblaze.

She's observant. He hurried to inspect them. The snow framed perfect prints. "Fox," he confirmed.

Dovepaw's ears pricked. "I don't hear anything."

"Let's follow them," Ivypaw suggested.

Cinderheart was already padding along the trail. Lionblaze slid ahead of her, ignoring her growl. He wasn't going to risk her getting hurt just to save her pride. If they bumped into a fox, he was going to be the one to deal with it.

The fat paw prints trailed under a low, spreading elderberry bush. "Wait there," he hissed over his shoulder. Slowly, nose twitching for fresh scents, he slithered below the branches. Under the bush the ground opened into a hole. The stench of fox seeped from the earth, thankfully stale.

"Should we fill it in?"

Cinderheart's mew made Lionblaze jump.

"I thought I told you to stay back."

She flashed him a look that challenged him to argue. He decided not to. "If we fill in this hole," he reasoned, "the fox might just dig a new one closer to the camp." He wriggled backward from under the bush and shook the snow from his pelt.

Cinderheart popped out after him.

Ivypaw was hopping from paw to paw. "Should we report back to Firestar?"

She's still loyal. "When we've finished training," Lionblaze decided. "The fox hasn't bothered us yet; there's no reason it'll start now."

"But keep your eyes open," Cinderheart warned.

"And your ears." Lionblaze looked pointedly at Dovepaw, frustrated to find her staring through the trees. What had happened to her concentration? "Go and hunt!"

She jerked around. "Now?"

"Why do you think we came here?"

Ivypaw was scratching at the snow, clearly keen to start. "Are we hunting together or alone?"

"Alone," Cinderheart told her. "We'll be able to assess you better."

"Okay." Ivypaw bounded past the elderberry, her silver-and-white pelt soon lost among the trees. Cinderheart hurried after her.

Lionblaze watched them go, frowning. Perhaps he should have suggested they hunt together so he could keep studying Ivypaw.

"Which way should I go?" Dovepaw asked.

"You're the hunter," Lionblaze meowed. "You decide."

Dovepaw scanned the forest, ears stretched, nose twitching, then headed up a rise that ran along the ShadowClan border. Lionblaze hung back until she was out of sight before trailing her.

He paused near the crest and peered over. The snow was falling more heavily now, and he could hardly see Dovepaw through the flakes. But he could hear her paws crunching, and every time she sniffed for prey, she snuffled as though fighting back a sneeze. This was impossible hunting weather.

Dovepaw's trail led around a wide swath of bramble, then straightened through a stand of slender maple. Her tracks were already covered with fresh snow. The tinier tracks of prey would be impossible to see or scent. Lionblaze caught sight of her through the trees, no more than a gray blur. But he saw her drop into a crouch. She must be stalking something. As silently as he could, praying the falling snow would deaden his paw steps, he crept closer.

His nose picked up the scent of squirrel. Dovepaw was tracking it over roots that were little more than bumps in the snow. Lionblaze glimpsed a bobbing tail as Dovepaw dived. Then she yowled in frustration as she tripped and tumbled forward. Snow clumps showered her from above as the squirrel fled into the safety of a tree.

"Bad luck." Lionblaze caught up to her.

"Stupid bramble tripped me," she grumbled. "I couldn't see it under the snow."

"These are hard conditions even for experienced warriors," he comforted her. "And this is your first snow hunt."

Dovepaw glanced up at the branches, narrowing her eyes. "Why don't we hunt up there? That's where the prey seems to be hiding."

Lionblaze flexed his claws. He hated climbing, but she was right. "Okay."

He waited while his apprentice scrambled up the trunk of a maple, and then he heaved himself after, relieved to reach the first branch. Dovepaw was already clambering onto the second, and by the time he'd followed, she was scampering along the bough and preparing to launch herself into the branches of the next tree.

Shaking snow from his whiskers, Lionblaze felt like a badger trailing a squirrel. Stretching every claw, he struggled to grip the slippery bark.

"I can see a blackbird!" Dovepaw hissed over her shoulder.

"I'll wait here." Lionblaze could see the bird's black feathers through the snow. It was sheltering in a pine, just a small leap from the branch they were on. Dovepaw drew herself forward, flattening her belly against the bark. She waggled her haunches, then jumped.

The pine shook as she landed. The blackbird squawked, and the branch bent under Dovepaw's weight. With a yelp of surprise, she fell into the snow underneath.

Lionblaze scrambled down the trunk. "Are you okay?"

Dovepaw was staggering on her hind legs while the blackbird struggled and flapped in her grip. She slammed it to the ground and bent to give it the killing bite.

Suddenly, shrieks of terror echoed through the forest. Dovepaw let go of the blackbird. "The fox is in the camp!" She pelted away through the trees as the blackbird fluttered, shouting indignantly, up into the pine tree once more.

Lionblaze launched himself after Dovepaw. Blinded by the snow, he didn't see Cinderheart till she swerved along beside him.

"What's going on?" She matched his pace. "What's all the noise?"

Ivypaw slowed in front of them and hared after Dovepaw.

"The fox is in the hollow!" Lionblaze growled. He pushed harder against the snow, unsheathing his claws.

As they neared camp, Millie came skidding down a slope, showering snow before her. Blossomfall was at her heels. Graystripe and Brightheart were a few steps behind, pelts bristling.

The shrieks from the hollow grew fiercer.

Lionblaze tore through the ragged barrier, shock pulsing through him as he saw the fox. It was circling wildly, huge against the snowy dens, its red pelt like fire next to the icy walls. Poppyfrost and Ferncloud spat, arch-backed, from the nursery entrance, swiping out with unsheathed claws every time the fox whirled near. Jaws snapping, ears flattened, it lashed its tail against the newly built dens. Daisy pressed herself against the medicine den entrance, her fur bushed up, hissing like a cornered snake.

Brambleclaw's patrol had arrived just ahead of Dovepaw and Lionblaze. The ThunderClan deputy darted between the fox's front legs, ducking to avoid its teeth. Dustpelt reared up and swiped at its snout, spattering blood over the white clearing. The fox yelped and snapped harder.

As Dustpelt jumped clear, Toadstep raked his claws down the fox's flank, ripping out hunks of red fur. Blood roared in

Lionblaze's ears. Time seemed to slow down as he crouched with his haunches beneath him, rage welling inside him until he had to force himself to hold back the power pulsing through his muscles. He locked his gaze on the fox until he was blind to everything but its red pelt.

Then he leaped.

He landed square on the creature's shoulders and sank his teeth deep into its flesh. The fox shrieked and plunged away from him. Lionblaze lost his grip and thudded onto the snowy clearing. With a snarl, Brightheart grabbed hold of its tail. The fox whirled around, smacking the one-eyed warrior against a beech branch. But Brightheart clung on, her lips drawn back and her ears flat.

Dovepaw darted under the fox and nipped at its back legs, while Ivypaw clawed at its front. Cinderheart reared and slashed its snout. Foxleap flung himself with flailing claws at its flank. Eyes white-rimmed with terror and confusion, the fox scrambled for the entrance. Bucking and twisting, it threw Brightheart clear as it tore through the barrier. With a final wail, it pelted away into the forest.

Brambleclaw climbed onto the halfrock and surveyed the hollow. "Who's hurt?" he demanded.

Lionblaze scanned his Clanmates. They were checking their pelts and shaking their heads, but Jayfeather was already out of his den and hurrying from warrior to warrior, sniffing for wounds.

"Is Briarlight okay?" Brambleclaw called.

"She's fine." Jayfeather moved on to Dustpelt.

Brambleclaw nodded. "Berrynose, Birchfall, and Foxleap, start repairing the barrier. Graystripe, go and find Firestar's patrol and tell him what's happened." He nodded to Ferncloud at the nursery entrance. "Are the kits all right?"

"It didn't get near them," Ferncloud reported.

Lionblaze stepped forward. "I've seen its den."

Dustpelt arched his back, snarling. "Let's go and teach it a lesson."

Brambleclaw waved his tail. "I think we already have."

Lionblaze felt a warm cheek pressing against his. "Are you sure you're okay?" It was Cinderheart.

"I'm fine." He saw her ruffled pelt. Clumps of fur stuck out around her neck. "What about you?"

"Shaken, but okay."

Ivypaw bounced toward them. "We showed it, didn't we?"

Dovepaw trailed after. "I should have heard it sooner." The words caught in her throat.

"You were hunting," Lionblaze told her. "You're good, but you can't be expected to hear everything." But he wasn't sure that was the truth. Perhaps Dovepaw shouldn't hunt. Perhaps she should concentrate on using her powers to look out for danger.

Ivypaw faced her sister, scowling. "Why should *you* have heard it?" she demanded. "We were the farthest from the hollow! Why do you have to act like you're special all the time?"

Cinderheart flinched.

Lionblaze lashed his tail, angry with himself. Why had he praised Dovepaw in front of Ivypaw? "Don't quarrel," he pleaded.

The thorns rattled, snapped stems dropping, as Firestar raced into camp. Thornclaw and Sandstorm followed with Graystripe. The ThunderClan leader held a starling in his jaws. He dropped it and looked around the hollow. "Is everyone okay? Are the dens damaged?"

"The thorn barrier got the worst of it," Brambleclaw reported.

Sandstorm was already at the nursery entrance comforting Ferncloud. "The kits are safe. You did well."

Jayfeather was wrapping one of Foxleap's paws in a comfrey leaf.

"Are you hurt?" Firestar asked the young warrior.

Jayfeather answered for him. "Lost a claw, I'm afraid. But it'll heal."

Rosepetal gasped and raced across the clearing. "Does it hurt?" she gasped.

Foxleap lifted his chin. "A bit."

Jayfeather gently let go of Foxleap's paw. "We were lucky there weren't more injuries." He carefully folded a comfrey leaf. "My stores are running low, and if this snow keeps up, I'm not going to be able to restock them."

Ferncloud whisked her tail anxiously. "What if the kits get coughs?"

"I've taken all the new growth I can from my herb patch by the Twoleg nest," Jayfeather went on. "I can't risk taking any more, or the plants won't keep growing. We need to search the forest for fresh supplies."

Lionblaze tensed. "Will there be any left in this snow?"

"Not if we delay," Jayfeather warned. "Any leaves that are left will be black and useless before long. We need to gather them now."

Brightheart bounded forward. "I'll go," she offered. "I know what to look for."

"I'll help." Leafpool stepped forward. "I know where to find them."

"Thank you." Firestar nodded to Thornclaw and Dustpelt. "Escort them," he ordered. "Just in case the fox is still around." He turned to Brambleclaw. "Organize more hunting patrols." He kicked the starling he'd dropped. "This won't be enough to feed the Clan." He padded across the clearing and climbed the rock tumble while Brambleclaw assembled the warriors.

Lionblaze hurried after the ThunderClan leader, ignoring the curious stares of Cinderheart and Dovepaw as he scrambled up to Highledge. "Let me fight the fox," he begged.

Firestar turned, eyes wide.

"I'll drive it from our territory once and for all." Lionblaze returned Firestar's green gaze unblinkingly. "You know I won't get hurt."

Firestar sat down.

"It would mean we can hunt safely," Lionblaze pressed.

Firestar frowned. "Are you sure you won't get hurt?" His eyes darkened. "Just because you haven't been wounded yet doesn't prove you can't be. Why risk your life over a fox when we know there are more dangerous enemies waiting in the shadows?"

"It's going to be a hard leaf-bare," Lionblaze reasoned.

"Why make it harder by sharing what little prey we have with a fox?"

"And how will you explain to your Clanmates that you drove away a fox single-pawed?" Firestar queried. "I thought you wanted to keep your powers secret."

"They won't know," Lionblaze argued. "I can tell them that I took the fox by surprise. That winning the fight was just lucky. I'll say that it was already injured after attacking the camp."

Firestar wrapped his tail over his paws. "Okay," he agreed. "But take Dovepaw with you."

"Dovepaw?" Lionblaze's ears twitched. "She might get hurt."

"Keep her at a distance," Firestar ordered. "She can run for help if you need it."

"I won't need—" Lionblaze bit back his objection. *I won't need help; I know it.* He had gotten what he wanted. There was no need to say anything else.

CHAPTER 13

❧

Lionblaze stretched in his nest. His back brushed Cinderheart's. She murmured but didn't wake. Dawn hardly showed through the woven stems of the den. Lionblaze lay still, breathing gently, while shadows stirred around him. Dustpelt yawned and slid out of the den, ready for the first patrol.

Whitewing sat up and reached a paw into Brackenfur's nest. "It's time," she whispered.

The russet warrior grunted and hauled himself to his paws. "Has it snowed again?"

"I haven't looked yet." Whitewing picked her way between the nests and ducked out of the den. Snow crunched as she headed across the clearing.

Lionblaze waited for Brackenfur to leave before he sat up. He wished he'd fought the fox last night while its wounds were still fresh and before it had rested. But Firestar had ordered him to wait.

"If you hunt it now," the ThunderClan leader had reasoned, "the other warriors will feel cheated of a chance to protect their Clan. If you wait, they're more likely to believe you came across it by accident."

Cinderheart rolled onto her back, ears twitching as though she was dreaming. The gray fur of her belly looked downy and warm. Lionblaze felt a sudden pang of guilt. She had no idea about his special powers. He hadn't told her about the prophecy. Now that they'd grown so close, it seemed like lying to keep it from her. But how could he tell her? Their love felt strong, but could it survive the truth?

Lionblaze pushed away the worry and breathed in her warm, sleepy scent. *I'll drive this fox out for you, Cinderheart, so that you can hunt safely all leaf-bare.* He brushed his tail gently over her as he crept to the den entrance. A fresh layer of snow had fallen, and the clearing had the smoothness of water, ruffled only by the tracks of the dawn patrol. The sky showed pink above the hollow, and soft light filtered down into camp.

Lionblaze slid out of the den. Firestar was standing on Highledge, gazing over the empty clearing. He narrowed his eyes when he saw Lionblaze, then nodded. Lionblaze flicked his tail and hurried to the apprentices' den. "Dovepaw!"

His call was barely a whisper, but a moment later the ferns rustled and the gray apprentice pushed her way out.

"Training already?" She stretched with her front paws until her belly dented the snow.

"We have a special mission."

Dovepaw straightened. "Is Jayfeather coming with us?"

"We don't need his powers for this." *I don't need yours, either.*

He headed out of camp, Dovepaw scampering after him.

"Where are we going?"

"You'll find out when we get there."

"Do you need me to listen for something?"

"No." He wasn't in the mood for questions. He should have done this last night and done it alone. He marched along a well-worn trail, his thoughts on the fox. Dovepaw spoke again, but he didn't listen. Lionblaze was picturing the fox whirling wildly in the camp, snapping at Ferncloud, lashing Daisy with its tail. Rage boiled in his blood. How dare it threaten his Clanmates?

A gray pelt blocked his path. "Where are we going?" Dovepaw's frustrated mew made him stop.

"I'm going to chase away the fox." He pushed past her and pressed on.

She bounded along beside him. "Just us?"

"Just *me*. Firestar said I had to bring you to fetch help if I got hurt."

"Firestar knows about this?" Dovepaw sounded surprised.

"Why shouldn't he?" Lionblaze bristled. "He's Clan leader. And he knows about my powers. He knows I won't get hurt."

"But this isn't what we were given our powers for!"

Lionblaze halted and stared at Dovepaw. "You think we should stand by and let a fox terrorize our Clanmates?"

"I didn't mean that." Dovepaw stood her ground. "I mean other Clans deal with foxes without special powers. Why do something alone that a patrol of ordinary warriors could do?" There was something wistful in the way she mewed *ordinary*.

"It'll be easier this way," Lionblaze promised. "And no one will get hurt."

Dovepaw turned away. "It just seems wrong, that's all. Like

cheating." She followed the trail around a sprawling patch of ivy.

"Cheating?" Lionblaze hurried after her. "How can it be cheating to use the powers we've been given to protect our Clan?"

Dovepaw carried on walking. "In a Clan, everyone looks after one another. It's what binds us together. If you can do the duties of every other warrior, what's the point?"

"The point is I won't get hurt and they might."

"I'm sure Thornclaw and Dustpelt would be happy to know that they can move straight into the elders' den. Clearly they're not needed now that the Clan has you."

"For StarClan's sake!" Lionblaze growled. "Why are you making this so difficult?"

"I'm just saying what I think. Or isn't that allowed any-more? Does only your opinion count?"

"You know I don't think that." Lionblaze was surprised to hear Dovepaw sound so fierce. "I'm just being practical. This way, the fox will be gone, and no one will get hurt."

Dovepaw flicked her tail. "I just wish you felt the same way about Ivypaw."

"What do you mean?"

"Have you told her to stop visiting the Dark Forest yet?"

"Jayfeather thinks we should wait."

"For what? Until she wakes up with an injury so bad every-one in the Clan will notice it?"

Lionblaze halted. "Look," he began. "Jayfeather thinks that if we watch her, we might learn how the Dark Forest warriors are training their recruits."

Dovepaw tipped her head to one side and stared at him. "Why don't you just ask her?"

"Would she tell us?"

"Of course she would!" Dovepaw snapped. "She doesn't know they're using her. She thinks she's being trained to be a great warrior."

"In that case, what's the harm in watching her for a little while longer?" Even as he spoke, doubt pricked his pelt. Ivypaw was only an apprentice. Whatever was going on in the Place of No Stars, she was out of her depth.

"What if she gets badly hurt?" Dovepaw snapped. "How would you feel, knowing you could have stopped her and didn't?" She turned and kicked through the snow.

There was no time to reason with her. They were nearing the elderberry bush where the fox hole was hidden. Lionblaze padded ahead and signaled with his tail. "Hide under that holly bush and listen out in case there's trouble."

Fur bristled along Dovepaw's spine. "Be careful," she whispered.

"I'll be okay, but just in case anything goes wrong, get back to camp and get help."

She nodded.

Lionblaze turned away and opened his mouth, letting fox scent bathe his tongue. Dovepaw's arguing had distracted him, interfered with his focus. *The fox invaded our territory,* he reminded himself. It had attacked the camp. Kits could have been killed. Anger started to bubble beneath his pelt, and he ducked under the elderberry bush and crept toward the fox hole.

There were no fresh paw prints leading from the hole. *It must be inside.* He peered into the darkness, wrinkling his nose at the stench. His paws itched with foreboding. The hole disappeared into blackness. Every hair in his pelt stiffened.

I'll draw the fox out.

He crouched at the entrance and gave a sharp, angry yowl.

Silence.

Coward!

Then he remembered with a flash of fury that this fox preferred attacking defenseless kits. He crouched lower, stretching forward. Swallowing against the rank odor, he gave a weak, whimpering yowl.

He pricked his ears. Nothing.

Tentatively, he climbed over the lip of the hole and crept into the darkness. The snow turned to earth beneath his belly as he slithered in. The fox stench was suffocating. He held his breath and crawled farther into the pitch-black lair.

Pain seared his tail as sharp teeth clamped it and dragged him backward. He scrabbled at the earth, struggling to turn, but the fox had caught him, and with a growl it hauled him from the hole and flung him out into the snow. Lionblaze sprang to his paws and faced the fox as it slunk out from under the elderberry bush. It stared back at him, its black eyes bright with hatred. Its snout was still scarred from yesterday's battle.

Lionblaze stood his ground, hissing. The fox showed its teeth. Then it rushed at him. Lionblaze reared up, meeting it with a flurry of swipes. But the weight of the fox hurled him backward. Lionblaze landed with a thump that knocked his breath away. He twisted, tail thrashing as he tried to stand, but heavy paws slammed him harder against the ground. Jaws snapped at his ear, and saliva sprayed his face.

Struggling for breath, Lionblaze dug his claws into the snowy ground and hauled himself forward, leaping to his paws as soon as he was clear. The power of the fox had startled him. He'd never fought an animal as big as this. He'd have to move faster. With any luck, the fox couldn't match his speed. Lionblaze spun around, claws slashing.

Too late!

Pain scoured his flesh, and Lionblaze felt his paws lift from the ground. He churned at the air, panic rising. The fox's teeth were pressing deep into his shoulder. For the first time ever, he feared his flesh would rip.

Dovepaw was standing only tail-lengths away, her mouth wide. "I'll get help!" she screeched.

"No!" Lionblaze twisted and lashed out, blocking agony as the fox's teeth stretched his pelt. Triumph flickered in his belly as he felt fur and flesh rip beneath his claws, and the fox let go with a howl.

Time slowed down.

The snowy ground met Lionblaze's paws. He spun on his haunches and reached out with one paw. Claws stretched wide, he met the fox's snarling face with a ferocious blow. Saliva drenched his pad as a flick of the fox's snout sent Lionblaze staggering backward. It dived again. Lionblaze met it with another vicious swipe. Blood sprayed his muzzle, and he heard the fox wail.

As red fur blurred in front of him, Lionblaze pressed his hind legs into the ground and leaped. He sprang high and clear of the fox's jaws and landed on its shoulders. The fox felt solid beneath him, like warm earth; it bucked and reared, turning this way and that, snapping at Lionblaze over its shoulder and yelping with frustration. But Lionblaze gripped on, keeping just out of reach.

Digging every claw deeper, he sank his teeth into the fox's fur, feeling flesh tear and tugging harder. Blood throbbed from the wound, filling Lionblaze's mouth. The fox sank beneath him with a howl. Lionblaze froze, his teeth still embedded in flesh. He waited for a moment.

The fox lay still, its flanks heaving, a soft whine in its throat. Lionblaze let go and backed off. Crouching, he stared at the fox through a haze of blood. The creature stirred and hauled itself to its paws. Gasping and whining, it headed for the hole. Lionblaze darted forward, snarling and blocking its way. The fox stared at him with wide, terrified eyes and veered past the elderberry bush. With a flick of its scarlet, blood-flecked tail, it headed into the bracken.

Dovepaw slid out from the holly bush, her pelt standing on end. Without speaking, she began to herd the fox onward. Slashing at it from either side, they drove it along the Shadow-Clan border, making sure it didn't cross into ShadowClan territory, growling threateningly if it tried to break away into the heart of ThunderClan's forest. Together they drove it away from the lake and up out of Clan land.

As the slope steepened and oak turned to ash around them, the fox scrambled ahead and vanished under a lump of brambles.

"That's far enough." Panting, Lionblaze sat down.

Dovepaw halted beside him and watched the leaves quiver where the fox had disappeared.

"It won't come back." Lionblaze's legs started to shake. "Let's get back to camp."

Dovepaw eyed him warily. "Are you hurt?"

"Just tired." The fight had crushed all the energy from him, and he found himself leaning on Dovepaw as they headed back. He hardly saw where they walked, letting Dovepaw lead. When the scent of the hollow began to touch his muzzle, he paused. The snow felt wonderfully cold against his stinging claws.

"Just let me get my breath back," he meowed to Dovepaw.

Her eyes were dark. "Are you sure you're not wounded? You're covered in blood."

As Lionblaze gazed down at his pelt, a shriek ripped the air. He stiffened and looked up to see Cinderheart staring at him. Her face was frozen, her eyes wild with horror. "Lionblaze?"

She dashed toward him, sniffing frantically. "What happened? Where are you hurt?" Then she turned and ran. "I'll get help!" she screeched over her shoulder.

Lionblaze wanted to chase after her and reassure her that it wasn't his blood, but his paws were still heavy and his mind thick with exhaustion. Blood dripped from his pelt, turning the snow below him crimson. Cinderheart was going to send panic through the Clan.

"We'd better hurry," he grunted.

"Clean yourself up first," Dovepaw advised.

Lionblaze lapped at his pelt, gagging at the slimy nettle tang of the fox's blood.

"Roll yourself in the snow," Dovepaw suggested.

Lionblaze lay down and wriggled as hard as he could in the cold wet snow. When he clambered to his paws, a wide patch of red stained the white forest floor.

Dovepaw plucked at the ground. "Let's hope we get back before a rescue patrol arrives."

Lionblaze felt his energy returning. The snow had refreshed him, and now his heart quickened as he imagined Cinderheart yowling through the camp that he'd been horribly injured.

They met the rescue patrol on the slope outside the hollow.

"Are you all right?" Firestar headed the patrol. Brambleclaw, Graystripe, and Birchfall paced around them, ears and tails twitching.

"What in the name of StarClan happened to you?" Graystripe sniffed warily at Lionblaze.

"We met the fox," Lionblaze growled.

Birchfall flattened his ears. "Where?" He scanned the trees.

"We've chased it out of our territory," Lionblaze reassured them. "It won't come back."

Graystripe guided Lionblaze toward the thorn barrier with his tail. "We'd better get you to the medicine den.

Cinderheart's already helping Jayfeather prepare herbs for you. She made it sound like you were on your last legs."

Lionblaze's whiskers twitched as he imagined Jayfeather muttering under his breath while Cinderheart insisted he unpack all his herbs for wounds that would prove to be non-existent.

Firestar glanced at Dovepaw. "Are you okay?" he asked.

She nodded. "Lionblaze did most of the fighting," she mewed. "I just helped guide it off our land."

"It didn't stray onto ShadowClan's territory?" Firestar's tail twitched.

"No," Lionblaze told him. "We drove it up toward the mountains." Why was Firestar always so concerned about the other Clans? They should deal with their own problems.

Firestar narrowed his eyes. "We'd better check." He turned to Brambleclaw. "Fetch a patrol and go and make sure the fox has definitely gone."

Brambleclaw bounded back to camp.

"Come on." Graystripe nudged Lionblaze gently toward the hollow. "Let's get you home."

As they entered camp, Lionblaze saw his Clanmates gathered around the clearing.

"Well done, Lionblaze!" Ferncloud called.

Mousefur shook her graying head. "They'll be telling this story in the elders' den long after I've left it."

"How did you do it?" Sorreltail stared at Lionblaze in undisguised admiration.

"Are you hurt badly?" Daisy was frowning.

Graystripe prodded Lionblaze toward the medicine den. "Enough questions. Let Jayfeather check him over first."

Pushing through the brambles, Lionblaze was relieved to be in the peace of the medicine den. Cinderheart looked up sharply as he entered, a pile of herbs at her paws.

"Are you really okay?" she rasped. "I thought they might have to carry you back." The words caught in her throat.

Jayfeather padded forward. "I've had Cinderheart mixing herbs ready to treat you." He nodded to the gray she-cat. "Thanks for your help, but you can go now. I'll need quiet to treat him properly."

Cinderheart's ears twitched. "I could help," she offered.

"No," Jayfeather told her firmly. "Thank you." He fixed his sightless blue gaze on her until she dipped her head and padded toward the brambles.

Briarlight was straining in her nest, craning to see Lionblaze. "I thought you were dead by the way she was carrying on."

Jayfeather tossed her a ball of moss. "Do your exercises," he ordered.

Briarlight grunted but dutifully began to toss the moss ball from one paw to the other, stretching farther and farther each time to keep it in the air.

Jayfeather led Lionblaze to the back of the den. "Are you happy now that you're everyone's hero?" he asked sharply.

"It had to be done." Lionblaze felt stung.

"Not by you alone."

Lionblaze bristled. "The fox has gone," he hissed. "No one's hurt."

"Well, you can be the one to explain how that happened."

"Can't you just clean me up and smear a bit of ointment on me to make it look convincing?"

Jayfeather sighed. "Okay." He led Lionblaze toward the pool at the side of the den and began to wash him with moss soaked in the icy water.

Exhausted by the fight, Lionblaze let Jayfeather clean his fur. But the quarrel with Dovepaw lingered in his mind.

"Are you sure we shouldn't stop Ivypaw from going to the Dark Forest?" he whispered, one eye on Briarlight, still busy juggling in her nest. "Dovepaw's worried about her."

"Ivypaw's okay." Jayfeather dipped a fresh wad of moss into the pool. "She hasn't come to me with any of her injuries and she hasn't shown any sign of disloyalty to ThunderClan. We might as well use her to keep an eye on Tigerstar."

"Then we should speak to her," Lionblaze reasoned.

"And tell her what? To start spying?" Jayfeather swabbed Lionblaze's ears roughly. "Remember what happened when you asked Dovepaw to spy for us? Let's wait, *then* talk to her. She'll have more to tell us, and she won't feel like we're using her."

Lionblaze grunted and closed his eyes, resting until Jayfeather had finished.

"These should convince our Clanmates that you at least got a scratch or two." Jayfeather rubbed a final blob of chewed herbs between Lionblaze's shoulder blades.

Briarlight's moss ball came sailing across the den and landed at Lionblaze's paws. He scooped it up and threw it back.

"Are you okay now?" Briarlight asked.

"Fresh as a newborn kit," Lionblaze told her.

Jayfeather snorted and started bundling away the herbs he'd unpacked from his store.

"Thanks, Jay," Lionblaze murmured.

Jayfeather didn't look up. "Would there be any point in telling you to be a bit more careful next time?" he muttered. "We don't know for sure how far your powers stretch."

Lionblaze touched his nose to the top of Jayfeather's head. "Okay." He headed for the entrance. "See you later, Briarlight," he called as he nosed his way through the brambles.

Cinderheart was waiting outside. She hurried toward him and started sniffing at the streaks of ointment. "I wasn't sure you'd be out so soon. . . ." Her mew trailed away, and she sniffed harder. "I can only smell the ointment," she meowed slowly. "I don't smell blood."

Lionblaze edged away from her. "Jayfeather used some strong herbs," he meowed. "They block most of the scent."

Her eyes grew round. "You sound like nothing happened today." Was that irritation in her mew? "You just took on a fox, single-pawed. You were drenched in blood."

Lionblaze shrugged. "I've been trained to fight."

"You looked like you were bleeding to death!" Anguish shone in her eyes. "I thought I was going to lose you."

Lionblaze pressed his muzzle to her cheek. "You'll never lose me," he promised, his heart pricking with guilt.

"No!" Cinderheart flinched away from him. "I can't do this. I can't feel this way every time you go into battle."

"Don't say that!" Lionblaze's heart lurched. "All warriors go into battle. But that doesn't stop them from having mates."

"Most warriors don't hurl themselves right into the middle of every battle, or go out hunting foxes while everyone's asleep!"

"But I'm okay! Look at me!"

"You can't be!" Cinderheart stared at him, her eyes glazing. "All that blood!" Her tail trembled.

Lionblaze checked the clearing. Dustpelt was organizing hunting patrols. Daisy was washing a complaining Cherrykit while Molekit scrambled up her broad cream back. Berrynose and Hazeltail were busy weaving birch stems into the torn barrier.

No one was listening.

"I need to tell you something," he whispered to Cinderheart. Wrapping his tail around her shoulders, he led her into the bramble patch beside the medicine den. Ducking between the tangled branches, he beckoned with his tail for her to follow. She crept in after him, eyes wide with curiosity.

"There's something you need to understand." Lionblaze stared straight at her. "Something that will reassure you that I won't ever be hurt."

She blinked at him.

"I can't be wounded," he blurted out.

She snorted. "You've certainly been lucky so far."

"No!" Lionblaze shook his head. "There was a prophecy, many moons ago. It was given to Firestar. It was about cats who'd have more power than any others in all the Clans."

Cinderheart tipped her head to one side, listening.

"I'm one of them. I'm one of those cats. I can't get hurt. That's my power. Not in battle, not with foxes, not by anything." He stared at her, willing her to understand. To believe what he was saying.

Cinderheart sat back and stared at him. "There's a prophecy?" she murmured. "About you?"

Lionblaze nodded. She understood!

"And you'll never get hurt." Cinderheart glanced at the ointment smears again.

"No."

"So that you can protect the Clan."

"Yes." Lionblaze leaned forward, relieved that she'd taken it all so calmly. "You never need to worry about me again." He ran his cheek along hers, his heart warming at her scent. "It's all going to be okay."

"No!" She jerked away and backed out of the brambles, her eyes glittering with grief. "We can't do this. I can't be your mate. Not if StarClan has given you this power."

Lionblaze's blood froze. "Wh-what do you mean?"

"You have a much greater destiny than me!" Cinderheart whispered. "We can't do this anymore!" With a wail she turned and fled toward the warriors' den.

CHAPTER 14

❧

Jayfeather began to scoop up the herbs littering the den floor. *What a waste.* He'd used the commonest leaves to patch Lionblaze's "wounds," but even nettle stem and tansy would be hard to replace now that the snows had come. Last night, Brightheart and Leafpool had returned with only a few pawfuls of mallow and thyme. It had taken them half a day to find that much.

"Millie!"

Briarlight's mew jerked Jayfeather back into the present. His mouth watered at the sweet scent of mouse.

"I brought you some fresh-kill." Millie dropped it beside Briarlight's nest. "I thought you might be hungry. You ate hardly anything this morning."

"I told you," Briarlight muttered. "I'm not hungry."

Millie began to tear the mouse apart. "Try a morsel."

"That's not going to make me hungry," Briarlight snapped.

"Just eat a little of it," Millie coaxed.

"I'm not hungry!"

Jayfeather padded to Briarlight's nest. He touched his nose to her muzzle. It was damp but not warm. She wasn't running a fever. But her mind was a whirl of worry and guilt.

"Has her chest infection come back?" Millie asked anxiously.

"Leave the fresh-kill with me," Jayfeather suggested. "I'll check her over and see if I can persuade her to eat something."

Millie stayed beside her kit's nest. "I want to know if she's okay."

"Go back to the hollow." Jayfeather suspected that it would be easier to find out what was troubling the young warrior without Millie hovering. "It'll give me more room to examine her."

Millie hesitated.

"I'll tell you as soon as I know anything," he promised. He felt reluctance weighing Millie's paws as she padded out of the den.

"I don't know why she has to fuss over me so much," Briarlight huffed as soon as she was gone.

"Don't you?" Jayfeather didn't wait for a reply. He leaned forward and sniffed her breath. It was clean and fresh. No sign of infection. He laid a paw on her chest. "Breathe in as deeply as you can." Her breath was deep and clear.

"So, no appetite, eh?" He sensed stubbornness stiffening her pelt and felt the fierce ache of hunger in her belly.

"No."

"Liar."

"What?"

Jayfeather felt surprise flash from the young cat. "You might be able to fool Millie, but not me. Do you really think it's fair to make her worry just because you've gotten it into your head that you don't deserve food because you can't hunt?"

"What are you talking about?" Embarrassment glowed hotly from the young warrior.

Jayfeather softened his tone. "I know you think you're being fair." He settled down beside her nest. "But it's not that simple."

Briarlight turned her head away. "I don't hunt. I shouldn't eat."

"Daisy doesn't hunt," Jayfeather pointed out. "Should she starve?"

"She looks after the kits!" Briarlight grunted.

"What about when you keep them amused by playing moss-ball with them while Daisy rests?"

"Any cat could do that."

"What about Purdy and Mousefur, then?" Jayfeather pressed. "They don't hunt."

"They're old; they've hunted enough for the Clan."

"But they can't hunt anymore. Why don't we let them die now?"

Shock pulsed from the young cat. "We couldn't! They're part of the Clan. It's our duty to look after them." Her nest rustled beneath her paws. "Besides, the Clan wouldn't be the same without them."

Jayfeather left a small silence for her to hear her own words. Then he mewed, "Do you think the Clan would be the same without you?"

She didn't answer.

"The Clan brings you fresh-kill because they think you deserve it, and because looking after their Clanmates is what makes them warriors. They are proud to help you."

"I just wish there was something I could do to help them back." Emotion choked Briarlight's mew.

"Okay." Jayfeather sat up. "Come on. Out of that nest."

Fur brushed twigs as Briarlight hauled herself out.

"If helping look after Molekit and Cherrykit isn't enough work for you, there's plenty you can do here." He swept his tail around the medicine den. "I like to keep balls of moss piled beside the pool so that I can soak them if I need water for washing wounds or quenching the thirst of a sick cat. Bright-heart usually brings me fresh moss every few days. From now on it's your job to check it for splinters or thorns, then divide it into balls and stack it by the pool."

"Okay." Jayfeather felt Briarlight's spirits lifting. "What else?"

"Keep the den floor clean," he ordered. "We have just about every cat in the Clan coming and going at the moment. My herbs seem to get everywhere. Sweep out any dirt and paw up all stray leaves and pile them next to my store."

"No problem."

"And I need to go through my supplies and see what's running low," Jayfeather went on. "You can help me." He padded to the crack in the rock at the back of the den. Sliding into the chilly cleft, he called over his shoulder, "I'll pass them out; you stack them by the wall. We can go through them together."

He began to shove out bundle after bundle of herbs. Many were dry and crumbled in his paws. Reaching to the back, he felt something downy beneath his paw. Hooking it with his claw, he pulled out a scrap of fur. He sniffed it, his heart quickening. *Hollyleaf!* How had her fur gotten here? Had she returned from the dead?

Don't be mouse-brained!

She'd been Leafpool's apprentice once. It must have lodged in a corner then and been there ever since. The warm familiar scent of his sister flooded his heart. For a moment he was back in the nursery, squirming and fighting with Lionkit and Hollykit while Ferncloud sniffed disapprovingly.

Catch this, Jaykit!

Hollykit's a slow slug!

"Jayfeather?" A voice summoned him from his thoughts.

"That's all there is, Briarlight." Jayfeather tucked Hollyleaf's fur into a crack in the rock.

"Jayfeather!" the voice called again.

"Start piling the matching leaves together, Briarlight. I'll be out in a moment."

"Jayfeather." This time warm breath stirred his ear fur.

He jumped around, his pelt scraping the rock. No one was there. Yet the scent of another cat hung heavy in the air.

Yellowfang!

He squeezed out of the cleft. Briarlight was beside the far wall, sifting through the herbs. "I'm matching the leaves," she called.

"Good, good." Jayfeather circled warily, tasting the air. The frosty chill was thick with her scent. Why had Yellowfang come here? It was half-moon. He'd be sharing dreams with her at the Moonpool tonight. Why come now?

"Come with me." Her rasping mew sounded behind him. "Don't worry; no one can hear me except you."

"What are you doing here?" he hissed.

"Visiting you."

Briarlight paused. "What did you say?"

"Nothing," Jayfeather meowed hurriedly. "I—I've got to go out for a while. Keep matching the leaves. I'll be back soon." He followed Yellowfang's scent out of the den and across the clearing.

"Couldn't you have waited till tonight?" he snapped once they were clear of the hollow.

"Do you think I wanted to leave StarClan and come to this freezing place?"

A faint outline shimmered in front of Jayfeather's eyes. He could see Yellowfang's ragged pelt now, and the fuzzy outlines of trees behind her.

"Then why did you come?" Jayfeather's paws ached from the snow.

"You needed to know this before you met with the others at the Moonpool!"

"Okay, okay," Jayfeather muttered. "Just tell me, and we can both go home."

"I saw Lionblaze fight the fox," Yellowfang rasped.

"And?"

"It was a sign."

"A sign of what? That he's a mouse-brain?"

"He fought it alone."

"Yeah. I know. He's a mouse-brain," Jayfeather repeated.

His teeth were starting to chatter. "Can you get to the point?"

Yellowfang's stinking breath billowed around his muzzle as she leaned close. "Stop complaining and start listening," she hissed. "Like Lionblaze, ThunderClan must fight alone."

"When?"

"When the Dark Forest rises, ThunderClan must face its greatest enemy alone."

Jayfeather blinked. "But the Dark Forest threatens every Clan."

"Only one Clan will survive," Yellowfang growled. "Yesterday four patrols could not drive the fox from your territory. Today Lionblaze sent it fleeing for its life. In the great battle that is coming, ThunderClan must fight alone."

"But the Dark Forest warriors are training cats from every Clan," Jayfeather reminded her.

"So every Clan might betray you!"

"But we're *all* in danger. Surely we have to fight together?"

"Why do the Three belong to ThunderClan and no other Clan?" Yellowfang's amber eyes burned. "It must be ThunderClan's destiny to survive while others perish."

What? There have to be four Clans! Around them, the cold wind whipped the snow into drifts. "Yellowfang!"

The old cat was fading, and with her his dream-vision. Jayfeather was plunged once more into blackness.

As the dusk patrol returned and settled down to share tongues, Jayfeather slipped out of the medicine den.

"Good luck!" Millie called as he padded softly around the clearing.

"Take care," Briarlight added.

The young warrior was sharing a scrawny robin with her littermates, and Jayfeather could sense the relief washing over Millie's pelt. He hadn't told her why Briarlight had refused to eat, but Millie hadn't asked. When the gray warrior had come to the medicine den to check on her kit and found her gulping down the mouse, paws stained with herbs, she'd been delighted.

"Keep her busy," Jayfeather had advised. "She still has two paws, and they'll get restless if they're given nothing to do."

Lionblaze and Dovepaw were yet again describing the miraculous defeat of the fox to their Clanmates. No one seemed to notice that the story changed a tiny bit in every telling. Rosepetal and Foxleap were begging for every detail.

"What was your winning move?"

"How did you avoid its teeth?"

Jayfeather hadn't told them about his vision. He wanted to visit the Moonpool first. He wanted to see if the rest of StarClan agreed with Yellowfang. He slipped through the barrier of thorns, leaving the voices of his Clanmates behind.

As he broke from the trees, the moorland wind pierced his fur. Flattening his ears against it, he bounded along the slope to the dip where the medicine cats met before traveling together to the Moonpool. His paws sank deep into snow. It reached his belly where it had drifted, and he was breathless by the time he scented Kestrelflight and Willowshine.

"Not good traveling weather," he called to them.

"At least it's stopped snowing," Kestrelflight responded.

Willowshine shook out her fish-scented fur. "Can we go now? It's freezing."

"Where are Littlecloud and Flametail?" Jayfeather tasted the air but there was no scent of the ShadowClan medicine cats.

"They'll have to catch up." Willowshine was already heading away. "It's too cold to sit still."

Snow crunched as Kestrelflight fell into step beside the RiverClan medicine cat. "Hopefully our tracks will make their path easier."

Their tracks certainly helped Jayfeather. He followed the furrow the others carved in the snow, but even so, keeping his balance on the rocky shores of the stream took all his concentration. He had no chance to focus on the thoughts of his companions. By the time he'd scrambled up the cliff and hauled himself into the hollow, he was panting.

Willowshine was standing on the lip of the hollow. "No sign of Littlecloud or Flametail," she declared. "I hope there's no trouble in ShadowClan."

"We'll find out soon enough if there is," Kestrelflight answered.

"Should we wait?" Willowshine wondered.

Jayfeather was already following the path that spiraled down to the Moonpool. "If you can't see them on the trail by now, they're not coming." Snow covered the dimples in the rock where countless paw steps had passed before him.

"Is the Moonpool frozen?" Kestrelflight hurried after him.

Jayfeather touched it with a paw, relieved to feel it ripple softly against his fur. "No." The hollow must have sheltered the water from the coldest winds. He sank down in the snow and waited for Kestrelflight and Willowshine to settle beside the pool.

"I hope Littlecloud and Flametail are all right," Willowshine fretted. Her fur brushed against the snow as she rested her chin on her paws and touched her nose to the water. Kestrelflight's breathing had already slowed. They would both be in trances before long.

Jayfeather waited. There was no need for him to walk in his own dreams tonight. Yellowfang had already spoken to him. Focusing on Kestrelflight, he let his mind flow into the young WindClan cat's dreams.

Wind tugged his fur, warm and playful. Jayfeather looked around, blinking at the sweep of sky and land before him. He was standing on the arching spine of a rocky hilltop. Forested slopes fell away in front of his paws. Far away the trees darkened toward a shadowy horizon. *Is that the Dark Forest?*

Voices sounded below the crest of the slope, and Jayfeather quickly scooted behind a boulder. As the voices grew nearer, Jayfeather peered around the side. Kestrelflight was walking beside Barkface. The raddled old WindClan medicine cat hung his head and dragged his tail as though the sky weighed heavily on his back. Another WindClan cat walked beside them. Jayfeather squinted. He didn't recognize the light brown she-cat with ginger patches and eyes bluer than the lake in greenleaf.

"Explain it to him, Daisytail," Barkface meowed gruffly. "I knew he wouldn't believe me alone."

"It's not that I don't believe you," Kestrelflight objected. "It's just hard to take in."

The she-cat spoke, her voice as spirited as the wind lifting Jayfeather's pelt. "I stood up for my Clanmates once so that I could protect their future. I led the queens against a leader who believed kits should be trained before they were six moons." Her eyes clouded, and Jayfeather felt pride and grief battling in her heart. "There comes a time when we must stand and fight."

"But I'm a medicine cat," Kestrelflight reminded her. "I follow a different code than a warrior."

"Everything is changing," Barkface growled. "WindClan's greatest battle is coming. We cannot let the treachery of other Clans sap our strengths."

"We must stand alone," Daisytail insisted.

Why? Jayfeather frowned. *Four patrols could not drive the fox from our territory. Today Lionblaze sent it fleeing for its life.* Was Yellowfang's prophecy true?

"You must trust in your ancestors, not in other Clans," Barkface warned. "The past will be your strength, not the present."

Kestrelflight looked ruffled. "But who will this battle be against? Why must we fight alone? Tallstar never saw any weakness in allying the Clan with others to make it stronger."

Daisytail narrowed her eyes. "Tallstar was blinded by

friendships," she mewed pointedly. Jayfeather wondered if she was referring to the long friendship between Firestar and the WindClan leader.

Kestrelflight searched Barkface's gaze. "Is that who we'll be fighting? Another Clan?"

"You don't know your enemy yet," he rasped. "But you'll know them when the time comes."

Jayfeather felt the fur on his neck prickle. Why not tell him? Shouldn't he know that his Clan was going to face an army of the most dark-hearted warriors ever to have walked forest, moor, or stream?

Daisytail padded into Kestrelflight's path, blocking his way. "Don't tell any of the other medicine cats about this," she warned.

Kestrelflight blinked. "Won't they already know?"

"Betrayal could come from anywhere," Barkface growled. "You must stand alone, knowing your ancestors walk with you, and you alone."

Daisytail jerked her head around and tasted the air. Jayfeather ducked back behind the rock. Had she smelled him? Taking no risks, he backed away down a short, steep slope, flinching as pebbles clattered down beside him. He slid into a narrow gully and followed it quickly away from the hilltop. The rocky channel wound down, cutting ever deeper into the hillside. Jayfeather quickened his step until the slopes of the gully began to smooth into grassy banks. Soon he was following a stony path that opened onto a pebbly shore beside a stream.

Willows drooped over its banks. Ferns clustered at the water's edge. Instinctively, Jayfeather headed for cover. This was not his dream. Keeping to the ferns, he headed downstream until he caught sight of a rock. Wide and flat, it broke from the water and split the current around it. He recognized Willowshine's gray tabby pelt silhouetted on the rock, and beside her, Mudfur, the ancient RiverClan medicine cat. Graypool sat with them, paws rooted to the stone even when water splashed and lapped at them.

"You must stand alone," Mudfur ordered.

Jayfeather pricked his ears harder. The rushing of the stream drowned their words.

". . . ancestors will walk with you . . ." Graypool was staring intently at Willowshine.

Willowshine bristled. ". . . cats have always helped each . . ."

Graypool shook her head. ". . . have changed. We must change too. . . ."

"Can I tell Mothwing?"

Graypool flashed a glance at Mudfur. "She won't believe you, but you can tell her."

Mudfur dipped his head. "She's a good medicine cat. She will protect her Clanmates through this terrible battle."

"Please," Willowshine begged. "What is this battle? Who will we be fighting?"

Jayfeather saw the older cats shake their heads. The stream washed around them.

". . . more terrible than your worst nightmares . . ."

". . . darker than you can dream of . . ."

". . . a river of blood . . ."

Willowshine leaned away from them, her whiskers quivering with fear.

Angry now, Jayfeather slid through the ferns, away from the water's edge. It seemed like every cat in StarClan was in a state of panic! Did they really think that dividing the Clans and crippling them with fear would help? He must share what he knew with the other medicine cats. They faced a real enemy.

"Do you believe me now?"

Jayfeather jerked to a halt as Yellowfang blocked his path.

"All four Clans must stand alone," she hissed. "The Dark Forest moves among them. You can't trust anyone. Why do you think the ShadowClan cats stayed away from the Moonpool tonight? They have abandoned you already. And WindClan and RiverClan will abandon you now."

"Not if I tell them what's really going on."

Yellowfang sprang at him, bowling him over. "No!" She pressed him hard to the ground. "Can't you read the signs? Lionblaze beat the fox single-pawed!" she hissed. "If you don't keep quiet, all four Clans will be lost to the darkness."

Struggling, Jayfeather blinked open his eyes and found himself beside the Moonpool, his vision black once more. Fur brushed snow. Kestrelflight was heading away up the path. Willowshine was already at the top, walking quickly as if she didn't want to speak to her companions. Was the bond between medicine cats so easily broken?

Jayfeather scrambled to his paws. He had to warn them. "The Dark Forest—"

Crackling silenced him. Ice splintered behind him, echoing around the walls of the hollow. Jayfeather turned, and his vision was flooded with starlight. The Moonpool was freezing over, ice spreading like fire through grass, reaching over the water until the whole pool was white.

Jayfeather stared around the hollow. Hope flared in his chest. Cats of StarClan lined the glittering walls. The ranks of star-pelted warriors sat silent and still. Jayfeather looked more closely. Was that *Rock* among them? Jayfeather recognized the ancient, hairless cat with a surge of joy. Had he come to help StarClan? Perhaps he'd changed their minds? Perhaps the cats of StarClan were going to face the Dark Forest together after all?

As he watched, pleading silently for some kind of sign, he saw the hollow start to whiten. One after another, the StarClan warriors turned to ice, their fur glistening, their whiskers stiffening, before shattering into cruel, prickling shards in the cold, dead moonlight.

Only Rock remained. He stared blankly at Jayfeather, his bulging blind eyes as frosted as the Moonpool.

CHAPTER 15

♣

Ivypaw opened her eyes. Mouse dung! It was night, and she was still in the apprentices' den. She wanted to be in the Dark Forest. She wanted to perfect the complicated move that Hawkfrost had shown her last night. She pricked her ears.

Silence. Dovepaw wasn't in her nest.

Ivypaw sighed and rolled over. Did Dovepaw think no one was going to notice her disappearing night after night, returning just before the dawn patrol and pretending to wake in her nest as though she'd never been gone?

I know what you're up to. Ivypaw tucked her nose under her tail. *You're sneaking off to practice by yourself in the woods. You've realized that I'm better than you, and you don't like it.*

It was Dovepaw's turn to play catch-up, for a change.

Ivypaw closed her eyes and pictured Mapleshade's move. *If I put a hind paw there and a forepaw there . . .* Her thoughts drifted into a dream.

"Get back, Thornclaw! You might get hurt." She growled at her Clanmate and turned to face the ShadowClan patrol alone. With a single paw, she sent Oakfur flying over her shoulder, then lunged at Smokefoot, kicking out with her hind legs to scratch Crowfrost's snapping muzzle.

Pain tore through her dream as two spiked paws gripped her shoulders. The ShadowClan warriors vanished from her thoughts. This enemy wasn't imagined. The sting of claws in her flesh was real. Ivypaw swallowed a wail of pain as they hooked her pelt and flung her to the ground.

"That'll teach you to pay attention!"

Thistleclaw's rancid breath hit her nose. The Dark Forest swam into focus. With her muzzle pressed into the dank earth, she could just make out the shadowy trunks through the hanging mist.

"Get off me!" she screeched.

"I don't know if begging works on the battlefield." Thistleclaw dug his claws deeper into her neck.

Panicking, Ivypaw flapped her hind legs. Her paws hit something solid. It must be a root. She pushed against it, thrusting herself forward. Thistleclaw flinched, gasping. In a moment she was on her paws and rearing up at the tabby warrior, claws unsheathed, a snarl curling her lip.

"Very good." Hawkfrost's approving growl echoed nearby.

Ivypaw glanced sideways as he stalked from the trees. Suddenly she didn't care about the stinging of her neck or the welling of blood on her fur. Hawkfrost had praised her.

Thistleclaw hissed at her, his back arched and his teeth bared. "You'll be watching for me next time," he snarled.

Ivypaw met his stare. "You might want to start watching for *me*," she spat. "I won't be an apprentice forever." Her gaze darted back to Hawkfrost. "He's always picking on the apprentices," she hissed. "Why don't you give him one of his own so he might leave the rest of us alone?"

Hawkfrost's eyes glinted. "Do you want me to give him *you*?"

Ivypaw lashed her tail. At that moment, she felt ready to take on anything. "If you want. But then you'd have to find a new apprentice and start from scratch."

Amusement lit the tabby warrior's eyes. "I guess I would," he conceded.

"I used to have my own apprentice," Thistleclaw muttered. "She didn't pass the final assessment."

In spite of her burst of confidence, Ivypaw shivered. Something in his tone suggested that failing to pass the assessment meant something more final than trying again after more training.

"Come on, 'paw." Hawkfrost dismissed Thistleclaw with a curt nod and turned his attention to Ivypaw. "We're practicing water fighting tonight."

"Why?" Ivypaw asked as she followed him between the trees. "I'm not a RiverClan cat."

"But you may fight one someday." Hawkfrost flicked his tail. "Hurry up. They're waiting on the shore."

Ivypaw caught sight of pelts through the trees. Antpelt sat with his tail curled over his paws. Beside him was Shredtail. Hollowpaw, a RiverClan apprentice she recognized from Gatherings, paced beside Snowtuft. Ivypaw looked for the river but saw nothing beyond the warriors except shadow. She pricked her ears but only heard the wind whining softly through bare branches. "Where's the river?"

Hawkfrost halted as he reached the other cats. "There."

Ivypaw stared at the flood of dark liquid sliding silently past them. "That's a river?"

A strange sickly stench rose from it. Hollowpaw wrinkled his nose. "It's the best they've got."

"This should be funny." Antpelt scowled at Ivypaw. "I've never seen a ThunderClan cat get wet."

"And I suppose WindClan is always splashing around in the lake," she shot back. She glanced through the trees. "Is Tigerheart here?" She kept her tone casual. She didn't want anyone to guess how much she wanted to see the Shadow-Clan warrior. The thought of getting her pelt wet, especially in that sludgy river, woke butterflies in her belly. She felt safer around Tigerheart. Like the time when they'd trained on the tree trunk and Thistleclaw had knocked Sparrowfeather to the ground.

She frowned, suddenly realizing that she hadn't seen Sparrowfeather since.

Hawkfrost strode to the riverbank. "Are you ready?"

Ivypaw stiffened.

"Before we try it in the water, I'll show you what we're going to practice." Hawkfrost beckoned Antpelt to step forward.

The WindClan warrior lifted his chin and stood stiffly in front of the dark-furred tom. With a quick, low lunge, Hawk-frost knocked Antpelt's hind legs out from under him. Antpelt stumbled and scrabbled back onto all four paws.

A shadow slid from the trees. "Easy to recover on dry land." It was Darkstripe. "But in running water, it's not so easy to regain your balance."

Ivypaw's fur pricked. She didn't like Darkstripe. There was something sly about the skinny black-and-silver warrior that made her nervous. He'd once bitten Tigerheart after they had finished a training match, and then denied it.

Hawkfrost greeted Darkstripe with a brisk nod and went on. "When you're in the water, it's best to keep your claws tucked in. It may feel more natural to try and grip the river-bed, but loose stones rolled by the current may catch a claw and rip it out."

Ivypaw shuddered.

Hawkfrost flicked his tail. "Antpelt, try the move out on Shredtail in the water."

Antpelt padded tentatively into the thick, slow-flowing river. He waded up to his belly, then farther, until the water reached his shoulders. It slapped against him, making a sound unlike any water Ivypaw had heard before.

"Snowtuft, you work with Hollowpaw," Hawkfrost ordered.

Snowtuft nodded, eyes glinting in the half-light.

Hollowpaw waded in. "This isn't water!" he grumbled. "It's too slimy."

Snowtuft shoved the RiverClan apprentice with his muzzle. Hollowpaw stumbled, losing his footing. His shoulders dipped blow the surface as he struggled to find his paws, but he kept his nose high and clear of the dark water.

Ivypaw scanned the forest, wishing Tigerheart would come. She hadn't seen the young ShadowClan warrior for several nights. Had he been training in a different part of the forest?

Darkstripe blocked her view. "I'll partner with Ivypaw if

you like, Hawkfrost." He shrugged. "Since you're supervising."

Ivypaw straightened and lifted her chin. "Okay." She waded into the shallows, hoping the cold water would soothe the stinging scratches on her neck. She was dismayed to find it flowing warm and thick around her legs, tugging at her fur like invisible weeds. She grimaced as she headed deeper, trying to glimpse the riverbed through the murky water.

Darkstripe slid through the water beside her. "Come on, slow slug."

Ivypaw pushed on, shuddering as the slimy water seeped through her pelt and touched her flesh. It rose up past her belly and swallowed her shoulders. She was straining every muscle now, fighting the current to stay standing. She wished she were taller. Darkstripe's spine was hardly covered, while she struggled to keep her head above water.

Suddenly a stone rocked beneath her paws, and she slipped. The water sucked her under before she could take a breath. Paws churning, Ivypaw panicked.

It's not that deep, she told herself sharply, and struck out, finding the riverbed with her paws. Her head broke the surface, whiskers dripping, eyes streaming. She spat out the water she'd nearly swallowed. It tasted rank, like crow-food but worse.

Darkstripe watched her, amusement glinting in his eyes. "I can see you're no RiverClan cat," he meowed smoothly.

"And I wouldn't want to be!" Ivypaw's defiant reply was ruined as she lost her footing again and slipped under the water once more. She struggled, reaching for the bottom, but a lithe shape slid beneath her and knocked her hind legs from under her just as Hawkfrost had demonstrated.

Darkstripe! He'd started the training before she'd had a chance to take a breath.

Ivypaw rolled in the current and floundered with her paws flailing. She fought the urge to breathe in, but her lungs ached for air. Then a paw pressed down on her spine, and she was trapped on the bottom of the river. The water flowed over her. Panic swelled in her chest. She had to breathe. She tried to struggle, but Darkstripe pressed harder, pushing the last gasp of breath from her.

StarClan, help me!

A shadow moved beside her, just recognizable through the muddy water. It was the pale, sleek-furred belly of a River-Clan cat.

Hollowpaw!

The apprentice grabbed Ivypaw's scruff and heaved her clear of Darkstripe's paws. Through the murk, Ivypaw could make out the shadowy outline of the Dark Forest warrior fishing around the riverbed with swiping paws. Close beside her, Hollowpaw signaled toward Darkstripe's hind legs with his muzzle, bubbles spilling from his nose. Ivypaw understood. Though her lungs screamed for air, her panic had faded. She could last a little longer. Together they turned and pulled themselves along the riverbed like a pair of otters and knocked Darkstripe's hind paws out from beneath him.

As he collapsed into the water, Ivypaw shot skyward and broke the surface, gasping. Hollowpaw bobbed up next to her, and they shared a yowl of triumph. Downstream, the water splashed and frothed as Darkstripe struggled to find his footing.

As Darkstripe fought his way clumsily upstream to join them, Hollowpaw whispered to Ivypaw, "Stay clear of his paws." Then the RiverClan apprentice swam back toward Snowtuft.

Ivypaw called innocently to Darkstripe, "Do you want to try the move out on me?"

The tabby warrior narrowed his eyes. Water dribbled from his chin. "Okay." Was that wariness in his gaze?

Ivypaw leaned into the current, bracing her paws against a rock on the riverbed. She wasn't going to cheat. She waited for Darkstripe to take a breath and prepared to feel his paws knock out her hind legs. As he pulled them out from under her, she darted forward like a fish, escaping his reach. She didn't even go under.

Amazed that she felt so at ease in the warm, greasy water, she turned, ready to try the move again on Darkstripe. Utterly focused now, she swiped his paws from under him and swam clear in one clean, quick move. She felt a surge of pride. No other ThunderClan warrior was trained to fight in water.

Breaking the surface, she saw Hawkfrost beckoning the trainees from the bank with his thick, mackerel-striped tail. "Not bad," he called as they padded, drenched, from the river.

Ivypaw shook out her pelt, not caring that she sprayed Darkstripe.

"Though I expected better of *you*, Darkstripe," Hawkfrost sneered at the skinny warrior. "I would have thought you could hold your own against an untrained apprentice."

Darkstripe snorted and slunk away into the trees.

"Ivypaw?" Tigerstar's mew made her jump. She jerked around to see the dark warrior slide from the water and pad up the bank.

"All ThunderClan cats should learn to get their paws wet." He shook out his pelt. "You had some nice moves there."

Ivypaw dipped her head. "Thanks."

"Have you seen Tigerheart?"

The question took her by surprise. "Me?" Did Tigerstar know that she always kept her eyes open for the young tom when she was in the forest? "No."

"He's late again," he growled. "He's been coming later and later every night. Is he sick?"

"I can ask at the next Gathering," Ivypaw offered. Her ear twitched.

"I'll track him down." Tigerstar's tone made Ivypaw shiver. Was Tigerheart in trouble for staying away?

Hawkfrost cleared his throat. "Time to leave." Far away through the trees, beyond the edge of the Dark Forest, the sky was lightening. Ivypaw stifled a yawn as she turned and headed away from the river.

"See you tomorrow," Hollowpaw whispered before vanishing into shadow.

The trees around Ivypaw melted into ferns, and she found herself curled in her nest. She could hear Dovepaw breathing.

She's back.

But only in the last few moments. Her breathing was fast,

as though she'd just settled down, and the scent of snow was fresh on her pelt. Ivypaw's nose twitched. There was another scent in Dovepaw's fur, too. A familiar one. Ivypaw tried to remember what it reminded her of, but her eyes were growing heavy. Exhausted, she slid into sleep.

"What's this?" Whitewing's shocked mew woke Ivypaw.

She jerked up her head. "What?"

"Blood!" Her mother's eyes were round. "Blood in your nest." The white warrior ducked down to sniff at the moss sticking out among the twigs and gasped. "It's on you, too! Are you hurt?"

Ivypaw flinched away. "What are you doing in here?"

"The dawn patrol left ages ago, and neither of you was up, so I came in to wake you."

Dovepaw climbed blearily out of her nest. "I guess we've been training hard."

"Is that why there's blood in your nest?" Whitewing was staring at Ivypaw, her eyes dark with worry.

The ferns rustled, and Bumblestripe poked his head in. "What's all the noise?" he demanded.

"Get Jayfeather," Whitewing ordered. "Ivypaw's hurt."

"No!" Ivypaw protested, "I'm fine." But Bumblestripe had already gone.

Ivypaw felt hot under her fur. No one needed to know about the scratches Thistleclaw had left on her neck. She thought the river had washed them clean, but clearly they'd still been oozing when she'd returned from the Dark Forest. She glanced down at the moss. It was dark where blood had soaked it. Her gaze caught Dovepaw's.

"It must be a thorn in the moss," Ivypaw mewed quickly.

Come on, Dovepaw! Back me up.

Dovepaw shrugged. "Yeah, a thorn," she mewed before pushing her way out of the den.

Thanks a lot! Ivypaw was fuming that Dovepaw had left her to calm down their mother by herself. "Maybe there's a sharp stone in my nest."

"Let me look." Whitewing bundled Ivypaw out of the way and began sifting through the moss with her paws. "I can't feel anything."

Jayfeather nosed his way into the den, carrying a folded leaf. Bumblestripe and Cinderheart barged in after. Ivypaw backed away from her nest.

Jayfeather dropped the leaf at her paws and opened it. It was smeared with thick green ointment. "Let me check you over," he ordered.

Ivypaw shuffled away. "It's just a scratch." *He knows I visit the Dark Forest. He'll guess this isn't a thorn scratch.*

Cinderheart was sniffing in Ivypaw's nest. "All that blood from a thorn?"

"This might hurt a bit." Jayfeather began smearing thick pulp onto Ivypaw's scruff.

Please don't tell. Fear throbbed harder than pain.

Jayfeather sighed. "It's nothing too serious, but I can smell some infection." He wiped another pawful of pulp from the leaf wrap. "You should be more careful."

Ivypaw shrank under her pelt. There was an edge in his

mew. He knew exactly where she'd gotten the wound.

"Will she be okay?" Cinderheart fretted.

Whitewing pushed closer. "Has the bleeding stopped?"

Go away! Ivypaw's ears pounded. The cuts were stinging where Jayfeather was rubbing in ointment. *Just leave me alone!*

"She'll live." Jayfeather sat back on his haunches and refolded the leaf. "Come for fresh ointment tonight." He picked up the leaf in his teeth and headed out of the den.

As he left, Dovepaw slid back in.

"Have you come to watch, too?" Ivypaw snapped.

Dovepaw leaned past Cinderheart into Ivypaw's nest, rummaged for a moment, and then sat up. "Is this what you were looking for?" She spat a long thorn onto the ground.

Whitewing pawed it gingerly. "No wonder there was so much blood!"

Cinderheart frowned. "How did that get in there without you noticing?"

Ivypaw felt a flood of warmth for her sister. As Dovepaw stretched forward and sniffed at her wounds, Ivypaw whispered in her ear, "Thank you."

Dovepaw grunted. "This isn't over." She pulled away.

"Come on." Whitewing flicked Bumblestripe gently with her tail. "Let's leave Ivypaw to rest." She guided the young warrior out of the den. Dovepaw followed, her tail flicking as she disappeared through the ferns.

Cinderheart was staring anxiously at Ivypaw.

"What?" Ivypaw snapped.

Cinderheart sighed. "If those scratches are infected already, they must be deep."

Ivypaw climbed into her nest. All she wanted to do now was sleep.

Cinderheart's tail twitched. "You must be tired." She touched Ivypaw's head with a gentle paw. Ivypaw felt it tremble.

"Is anything wrong?" Cinderheart whispered, leaning closer. "You can tell me anything, I promise. Those wounds couldn't have been caused by a thorn. You'd have been awake and out of your nest at the first prick." She sat back and gazed at Ivypaw. "And a thorn wouldn't have caused infection so quickly, no matter how deeply it scratched. Besides . . ." She peered at Ivypaw's wounds. "Thorn scratches don't rip at the flesh like that."

Ivypaw had grown stiff as dead prey. What could she say? Her mind whirled while her body froze.

"Tell me the truth," Cinderheart pressed quietly. "I won't be angry. I just need to know how I can help you."

Ivypaw took a deep breath. "I've been practicing at night."

"Practicing?"

"I want to be the best ThunderClan warrior ever." *And I'm going to be!*

"Oh." The word escaped Cinderheart as a sigh. "I understand." She sounded relieved. "Of course you want to be the best. And you've been out in the forest training by yourself."

"Yes." Ivypaw cringed. She hated lying to her mentor, who had done nothing but treat her fairly. *It's close to the truth,* she told herself. "Dovepaw's so good at everything. Everybody treats her like a warrior already. Firestar asks her for advice, and Lionblaze never does anything without her . . ."

Cinderheart stiffened. "You're every bit as good as Dovepaw!" she hissed. "I couldn't be prouder of you! If you want to do more training, we'll fit it in during the day. You're a growing cat; you need your rest."

Ivypaw nodded dutifully.

"Will you promise me that you won't go out again at night?" Cinderheart prompted. "There's no one to look out for you when the Clan's sleeping. Who knows what might happen? What if that fox came back?" Worry edged her mew. "You're as good as any warrior. You don't need to sneak around training in secret." Cinderheart's eyes burned into Ivypaw's. "Promise me you won't leave the camp at night again!"

Ivypaw stared at her paws, guilt pricking her belly. "I promise," she muttered.

CHAPTER 16

Dovepaw barged out of the apprentices' den after Whitewing and Bumblestripe. *Let Cinderheart fuss over her! I found her a thorn. She can explain the rest.*

But her rage quickly ebbed. She wasn't angry. She was scared. Every night she went to sleep wondering what wounds Ivypaw would wake with. And what if Ivypaw started *thinking* like a Dark Forest warrior? She needed to talk to Jayfeather. He *had* to help. She headed for his den.

She stalked past the fresh-kill pile, where Purdy was turning over a muddy-looking mouse. "Do you think this will appeal to Mousefur?" he rasped.

Dovepaw paused. "What?"

"It doesn't look like much." Purdy dangled the scrawny mouse from a claw. "But it might tempt her."

"Isn't she hungry?" Dovepaw was surprised. Surely every cat in the Clan must be hungry?

Squirrelflight hurried over. "Does she have a fever?"

Purdy shook his head. "She just seems tired and sad." His shoulders drooped. "I was hoping there would be something on the fresh-kill pile to cheer her up."

"One of the hunting patrols should be back soon," Squirrelflight meowed. "They might bring something." She glanced at Dovepaw. "Isn't Lionblaze taking you out?"

Dovepaw shrugged. "When he's ready." *Besides, I have something else to do first.* She glanced toward the medicine den, hoping Bumblestripe wouldn't be hanging around there long.

Purdy let the mouse fall with a soft thud into the snow. "If I were a few seasons younger, I'd go out myself." He stared dreamily up to the top of the hollow. "I was quite a hunter in my youth. I could catch rabbits." He puffed out his chest. "And pheasants, although . . ." His whiskers twitched. "Pheasants aren't that hard to catch. They prefer eating to flying."

Dovepaw blinked, her attention snatched from Jayfeather. "You caught *pheasants*?" Purdy wasn't small, but even he must have been outweighed by a pheasant.

"When I was younger, nothing was too big for me." Sighing, the old cat headed away toward the elders' den.

Dovepaw dipped her head to Squirrelflight and hurried to the medicine den.

Bumblestripe was pacing beside Briarlight's nest. "You should have seen it! So much blood. All from one thorn. And she'd been sleeping on it all night and hadn't noticed."

Jayfeather was soaking his pulp-stained paws in the pool. "Don't exaggerate, Bumblestripe." He snatched them out and began licking them. "It was nothing more than a couple of scratches."

"I'm going to be checking moss for Jayfeather now," Briarlight announced proudly. "I'm the thorn patrol." She looked across at the medicine cat. "Perhaps I should check the moss for the nursery before it goes in the nests."

Dovepaw was about to call to Jayfeather, but he was already crossing the den toward her. "I'm sure Daisy and Poppyfrost would appreciate you checking the kits' moss," he told Briarlight as he passed her nest. "I've got to go out for a while. Bumblestripe, keep Briarlight company. But no more wild stories, please."

Jayfeather swished past Dovepaw. "Come on," he whispered, pushing through the brambles. "We need to talk."

Finally! Was Jayfeather going to start taking Ivypaw's visits to the Dark Forest seriously? She hurried after him. Without breaking his stride, Jayfeather nodded to Lionblaze. The golden warrior broke away from Firestar and Brambleclaw and bounded after them. Firestar watched, eyes narrowed, as the three padded out of camp.

"Right." Jayfeather halted in a clearing on the bracken-covered slope outside the hollow. He fixed his blind stare on Dovepaw. "You've got to stop Ivypaw coming back from the Dark Forest in such a state. She's going to give everything away."

Dovepaw stared at him, openmouthed. Rage roared up from her belly. "*I've* got to stop her?" she spat. "What do you think I've been trying to do? And not just because all her scratches and swellings and sprains might give away our secret." She thrust her muzzle into Jayfeather's face. "Because I'm scared she's going to get *killed*!"

"Calm down." Lionblaze wove between them. "You're

right, Dovepaw. Ivypaw is getting hurt too often, and it's our duty to protect her."

Dovepaw let out a slow breath. "That's what I've been trying to tell you all along!"

"But," Lionblaze added, "we can't follow her into her dreams."

"Jayfeather can!" Dovepaw pointed out.

Lionblaze shook his head. "Tigerstar's already warned him away from the Dark Forest once. We can't risk him going there again."

"But you can risk Ivypaw going there night after night," Dovepaw fumed.

"She's one of them," Jayfeather reminded her. "They won't hurt her on purpose, as long as they think she's on their side."

"Can't you just talk to her?" Dovepaw looked pleadingly from Jayfeather to Lionblaze. "Tell her she can't go. She might listen to you."

Lionblaze ran his tail along Dovepaw's spine. "Do you really think she'd listen?"

Dovepaw's heart sank. *No.* Ivypaw seemed convinced that Tigerstar was making her a great warrior. She'd never give that up.

"Besides," Jayfeather sat down and tucked his tail over his paws, "we need her in the Dark Forest more than ever."

Lionblaze's attention flashed toward his brother. "Why?"

"Yellowfang visited me and warned me that we must fight the Dark Forest alone."

Lionblaze cocked his head. "Alone?"

"All the medicine cats are being told the same thing. We must cut all ties to other Clans and face the danger alone."

"Do the other Clans know about the Dark Forest warriors?" Lionblaze flattened his ears.

"No." Jayfeather shifted his paws. "StarClan seems to know, but they're keeping it from the medicine cats."

"Why?" Dovepaw demanded.

"They might not want to scare them." Jayfeather shrugged. "They might simply not know who to trust anymore."

"Why don't *you* tell the medicine cats?" Dovepaw asked.

"Yellowfang ordered me to keep my mouth shut." Jayfeather shifted his paws. "And when I tried to warn Kestrelflight and Willowshine, I had a vision."

"What was it?" Lionblaze leaned closer.

"StarClan froze in front of me and shattered like ice until there was nothing left. StarClan was *destroyed*."

Dovepaw stared at him. "So we're on our own?"

Jayfeather shrugged. "ThunderClan has the Three, so ThunderClan must be the one to survive."

Lionblaze began to pace. "So *I'm* supposed to fight this battle for everyone?" The tip of his tail flicked angrily. "Great StarClan, why can't I just have a normal life like any other cat?"

Dovepaw frowned. She thought Lionblaze liked being part of the prophecy. Why was he suddenly acting like he didn't want to be so powerful? He had always encouraged her to embrace her own powers, and at last she was beginning to enjoy them. Thanks to her super senses she could hear

Tigerheart wherever he was. She could hear him hunting with his Clanmates; she could listen to his breathing as he fell asleep in his nest. . . . She jerked her thoughts back. This wasn't the time to think about Tigerheart. "But why does Ivypaw have to keep visiting the Dark Forest?" she demanded.

"We need to know what they're up to," Jayfeather told her.

"We *know* what they're up to," Dovepaw retorted.

"But we don't know when they plan to strike, or if they're behind this plan to divide the Clans." Jayfeather leaned closer to Dovepaw. "Ivypaw could find out for us."

Dovepaw flinched away. "You want her to *spy*? Don't you think she's in enough danger already? If Tigerstar found out she was spying, StarClan knows what he'd do to her." Sickness welled in her throat. "No! There's no way you're going to put Ivypaw through that. Not even if the whole Clan depends on it!"

She spun around, spraying snow, and stormed through the bracken. Lionblaze and Jayfeather didn't care about Ivypaw at all! She was just a way of getting what they wanted. *First they wanted to use me, and now they want to use Ivypaw.*

Pulsing with rage, Dovepaw raced to the top of the slope. The trees thinned at the crest, and she saw the lake below, glittering under a clear blue sky. She might as well use her anger to help her Clan. Plunging down the snowy slope, she headed for the lake. She would hunt.

Where the shore stretched toward the forest stream, Dovepaw picked up the scent of prey. She stopped, her paws aching with cold, and tasted the air.

Water vole.

She padded forward, dipping her nose to sniff the ground. She soon picked up the scent in the snow and saw tracks. Treading lightly, she followed the tiny paw prints along the shore to where the trees lined the stream as it flowed into the lake. After hopping onto the bank, she snuffled her way upstream, weaving through the trees until she spotted the vole—a small, dark shape crouched beside the water. It was focused on the morsel grasped between its front paws.

Dovepaw dropped into a hunting crouch and pulled herself across the snow, keeping her tail and belly high to stop her fur from brushing loudly against the powdery whiteness. She crept closer. The vole kept nibbling, oblivious to the danger. Dovepaw stopped above it. She waggled her hindquarters, then plunged down the bank.

The vole felt warm and fat between her paws, and she finished it off with a sharp, killing bite. Fragrant and limp, it hung in her claws. Her mouth watered from the scent. It was the best piece of fresh-kill she'd seen in days.

"Well done!" Ivypaw called from the opposite bank. Her silver-and-white fur was camouflaged against the snow. She splashed through the shallow, freezing water and scrambled onto the shore beside Dovepaw. "Nice catch."

Dovepaw wrinkled her nose. Ivypaw's fur was still matted with herb pulp. Then she noticed that Ivypaw's eyes were feverishly bright. "You should be resting in camp," she mewed. "Didn't Jayfeather say those scratches were infected?"

Ivypaw bristled. "So?" She lifted her muzzle. "They've got ointment on."

"I wasn't criticizing," Dovepaw mewed quickly. "I'm just worried about you." She dropped her catch in front of Ivypaw. "Here, have a bite." She didn't want to argue with her sister.

Ivypaw shook her head. "That would be against the warrior code," she pointed out.

"Just take a small bite," Dovepaw urged. "You look starving. I'll say it got damaged in the hunt."

Ivypaw narrowed her eyes. "No, thank you," she growled. "I'm not the one who likes breaking the warrior code."

"What?" Dovepaw stared at her in surprise.

"I'm not the one who disappears at night to meet a ShadowClan warrior."

Dovepaw's heart seemed to drop in her chest like a stone. *Ivypaw knows about Tigerheart!* "How did you find out?"

"Did you think I wouldn't smell him on you?" Ivypaw's tail lashed. "Not very loyal, is it? Spending every night with a tom from another Clan?"

Dovepaw stiffened. "At least we're not putting anyone in danger."

"What do you mean by that?"

"Every time you go to the Dark Forest, you betray your Clanmates."

"That's not true!" Ivypaw hissed. "I'm learning to be a great warrior so I can help my Clan!"

"Yeah, right!" Dovepaw snapped scornfully. "Just like Tigerstar. He was a *great* warrior!"

"He *was!*"

"He became ShadowClan's leader. He tried to kill Firestar!" How could Ivypaw be so dumb?

Ivypaw glared at her, eyes cold as ice. "Aren't you going to ask how I recognized his smell?"

Dovepaw blinked, confused. "What?"

"Don't you think it's odd how easily I recognized Tigerheart's scent?"

Dovepaw froze, her blood draining into her paws. She remembered the look Ivypaw and Tigerheart had shared in battle.

"H-how did you know?" Dovepaw cringed beneath her pelt. She didn't want to hear the answer. She didn't want to hear that Tigerheart had been seeing Ivypaw, too. That he'd lied to her. That she wasn't the only ThunderClan cat that occupied his thoughts.

"I meet him almost every night," Ivypaw crowed.

"You can't; he's with me!"

"Not *all* night."

Dovepaw backed away. "Don't say that! He likes *me*, not you. Have you been following him? Find your own mate! Leave him alone!"

Ivypaw padded closer. "Oh, I don't like him in *that* way. I'm not a soppy *dove* like you. I'm a warrior, and so is Tigerheart."

Dovepaw wished she were deaf, wished she could see Ivypaw's mouth moving without hearing the words.

"Tigerheart doesn't spend every night cooing in your ears," Ivypaw taunted. "He's one of the best warriors the Dark

Forest has. That's where his loyalty lies. Not with you!"

"That's not true! You're just jealous!" Dovepaw shrieked at her sister. She couldn't believe these lies. "You're jealous that I'm a better warrior than you. I always have been and I always will be, and you can't stand it. And now you're jealous that Tigerheart loves me and not you! You want to destroy everything I've got because you're jealous. That's all!"

Ivypaw's eyes gleamed. "Really? Why not ask Tigerheart?"

"Shut up!" Dovepaw scrambled up the bank. "If you tell anyone that I'm seeing Tigerheart, then I'll tell the whole Clan you've been training in the Dark Forest with Tigerstar, and then you'll have no friends. Everyone will hate you as much as I do!" She pelted through the trees.

"You forgot your catch," Ivypaw called after her.

"You take it!" Dovepaw yowled back. "Then your Clanmates might think you've done something right for a change!"

She raced on, blocking out the thoughts that whirled in her head. The ShadowClan scent line was close. Its smell bathed her tongue. Had Tigerheart really betrayed the Clans by the lake? She skidded to a halt and pricked her ears. Casting out her senses, she searched for Tigerheart.

She'd done it so often that it was easy to find him. She could hear his mew, hear his paws on the forest floor. She knew their sound—strong and certain. He was with Clanmates. She listened harder. *Ratscar, Pinepaw, and Snowbird.* Purrs rumbled in their throats as Pinepaw fell into a snowdrift with a soft thump.

They sounded happy. Dovepaw wished she were with them.

She wished she were playing in the snow with Tigerheart, certain that he loved her. She wanted to be with him all the time.

Maybe she should join ShadowClan? The idea flashed wildly in Dovepaw's mind, making her heart soar.

Don't be stupid! I'm one of the Three. She couldn't leave Jayfeather and Lionblaze to face the Dark Forest warriors alone. And deep down, she knew that she couldn't leave Ivypaw. Pain pierced her heart like a thorn. She shouldn't have said all those things. She'd been cruel. She'd made it sound like the Clan didn't want her sister around.

Suddenly Dovepaw felt sick. What if Ivypaw decided to stay in the Dark Forest forever? She whirled around and raced for home. She'd apologize to Ivypaw. She'd tell her she'd been wrong.

But that wouldn't be enough! Ivypaw would still keep visiting the Dark Forest. She didn't understand she was being used. Dovepaw pushed harder against the frozen snow. Trees blurred beside her. Ice cracked beneath her paws.

What's the use of all this power if I can't keep my own sister safe?

CHAPTER 17

Flametail scraped snow hopefully from the roots of an old tree stump. He sighed as he uncovered leaves blackened by frost. Why wasn't there a single herb that thrived in the season when sickness was most deadly? Littlecloud was already sick. The Clan was weakened by hunger. It was only a matter of time before whitecough threatened every den.

"Ow!" Pinepaw's mew rang through the trees.

Tigerheart answered her. "That's what you get for messing around."

His brother's hunting patrol was near. Flametail kept digging. "Mouse dung." He cursed as he revealed more rotten leaves.

Tigerheart came bounding through the trees. "What's up?"

Flametail shook snow from his paws. "I can't find any fresh herbs," he sighed. "Not even nettles."

The rest of the patrol caught up. "Need help?" Ratscar offered.

"We've got time," Snowbird explained. "The prey's hiding, too."

Pinepaw leaned over Flametail's shoulder. "What are you doing?"

Flametail's nose twitched. He smelled something green on the apprentice's pelt. He twisted and sniffed harder.

"Do you mind?" Pinepaw ducked away. "I washed this morning!"

"Where've you been?" Flametail demanded.

Pinepaw jerked her head toward the trail they had left in the snow. "Near the larch."

Tigerheart purred. "Pinepaw fell into a snow drift."

"There were brambles underneath it," Pinepaw complained. "I've got prickles in my fur."

"Brambles beneath the snow?" Flametail felt his spirits soar. "That's why I can smell fresh borage on your fur!"

Snowbird narrowed her eyes. "I think your littermate's gone pigeon-brained," she murmured to Tigerheart.

"Flametail knows what he's doing." Tigerheart flicked his tail at his brother. "Don't you?"

"The brambles will have kept the snow off the borage leaves," Flametail explained. "They won't be frost-scorched."

Ratscar padded forward. "I'll show you where we were."

But Flametail was already hurrying back along his Clanmates' trail. "Don't worry," he called. "I can follow your paw prints."

"You won't have trouble finding where Pinepaw fell!" Tigerheart called after him. "The hole's big enough to hide a hare."

Flametail trotted along the tracks left by his Clanmates, his fur pricking with excitement when he saw a drift rise in front of him, the snow dented where Pinepaw had fallen into it. He burrowed through, ignoring the cold that stung his paws, until he felt the first stab of bramble. Wincing, he drew back the stems and saw, safely sheltered, the dark green leaf of unscorched borage.

Thank StarClan! He nipped off as many leaves as he could reach, then shuffled backward out of the snowy burrow. But worry still pricked his pelt. If only it had been catmint or even tansy. Borage was only good for easing fever. It didn't drive out infection, and Littlecloud's lungs were thick with it. What if his sickness turned to greencough? With no catmint, Flametail would be helpless.

He pushed the thought away. *Enjoy StarClan's blessings,* he reminded himself.

Flametail headed for the camp. He liked the cold, crisp weather, and though it made his paws ache, he enjoyed the crunch of snow.

"Flametail!"

As he ducked through the camp entrance, Tawnypelt hurried to meet him. "You've found herbs!" She licked him roughly on the cheek. "Well done!"

Flametail screwed up his face, reminding himself that he was lucky to have such affectionate kin. Sometimes at Gatherings he glimpsed Breezepelt eyeing Crowfeather and Nightcloud with undisguised rage. Crowfeather and Nightcloud never noticed; they were usually too busy exchanging harsh words between themselves.

"You're looking thin," Tawnypelt fretted.

Flametail shrugged. His jaws were too crammed with

borage to speak. Of course he looked thin. It was leaf-bare.

Tawnypelt glanced toward the medicine den. "You'd better go to him. He's been coughing again."

Flametail brushed his mother's cheek with his tail as he hurried away. The medicine den smelled of infection. Flametail dropped the borage beside the store. "You should be in your nest."

Littlecloud was slowly sorting leaves at the back of the den. The fresh herbs were piled on one side; the dry were pushed to the other. "There's no feverfew at all," he sighed.

"Let me help," Flametail offered.

"I can manage." Littlecloud burst into a fit of coughing, which sent the dried leaves fluttering over the den floor.

Flametail gently steered the medicine cat to his nest. "I'll find the comfrey and take it to the elders' den," he promised.

"Stupid cough," Littlecloud grumbled as he climbed into the moss. He looked relieved as he sank into its softness. "It'll clear up in a day or two."

"Of course." Flametail padded to the herbs. Littlecloud had been saying the same thing for days. He'd been too sick to travel to the Moonpool again, and he was no better now.

Flametail had been secretly relieved that Littlecloud hadn't gone to the Moonpool, because he hadn't gone, either. Raggedstar had told them to stay away from the other medicine cats. With Littlecloud too sick to travel, Flametail could obey Raggedstar without arguing with his mentor. When half-moon had come, Flametail had gone alone into the forest and waited out the night in the shelter of a hollow log.

He started tidying the leaves that Littlecloud's cough had scattered.

"Have you had any dreams?" Littlecloud asked suddenly.

Flametail began to roll a wad of comfrey ready for Tallpoppy. "No."

"What about when you went to the Moonpool at halfmoon?"

Flametail stiffened. "It was the same as before. We must stand alone."

A growl sounded in Littlecloud's throat. "Why are you lying?"

Flametail stopped rolling the comfrey. "Lying?" he echoed, trying to keep his voice calm.

"About going to the Moonpool." Littlecloud's nest rustled. "I've been waiting for a quarter moon for you to tell me the truth." He coughed hard. "When you got back, there was no scent of water or stone or the other medicine cats on you. Only damp wood and fear."

Flametail turned to face his mentor. "I'm sorry." He meant it. He searched for the right words to explain what was going on. "Raggedstar told me to stay away from the other medicine cats, remember? I'll go to the Moonpool alone if you like."

"Why are you so sure you interpreted your vision correctly?" Littlecloud challenged.

"There was nothing to interpret!" Flametail swallowed against the frustration rising in his throat. "Raggedstar was clear. War is coming. We must rely on our ancestors to guide us through it. No one else!"

"But Blackstar agrees with me. We must be cautious."

Flametail flexed his claws. "I'm a medicine cat. I answer first to StarClan!"

"If war is coming, alliances may be our only hope!" Littlecloud's mew was growing hoarse. "Joining forces with the other Clans kept us alive on the Great Journey, and before that it helped us to defeat Scourge and BloodClan."

Flametail stared at his mentor. "That was then. This is now. Times have changed."

"The warrior code never changes."

"We're not warriors!" Flametail snapped. "We're medicine cats."

Littlecloud stared back with wide, milky eyes. A cough seized him and shook his body. Flametail rushed to Littlecloud's nest and began to massage his scrawny chest with both paws, trying to ease the tightness he could hear in the cough. He hated arguing with his mentor. Especially when he was sick. Littlecloud had taught him everything he knew, and he trusted him with his life. But Littlecloud hadn't shared the vision of flame. It had been given to Flametail alone.

Flametail jerked away. Why had StarClan shared the warning only with him? He watched Littlecloud being racked with coughs. Was the old medicine cat going to *die*? Grief hollowed Flametail's belly. He began rubbing Littlecloud's back more urgently.

Gradually the coughing eased. Littlecloud lay back in his nest, fighting for breath. "You must always be honest with me," he rasped.

"I'm sorry I didn't tell you about not going to the Moonpool." Flametail smoothed Littlecloud's clumped fur with a paw. "I didn't want to upset you." He met his mentor's anxious gaze. "But I couldn't disobey StarClan."

Littlecloud nodded. "I understand," he croaked. "I only ask for the truth."

"Now you have it." Flametail straightened. "We must stand alone. Raggedstar has made that clear, and I'm going to honor his wish."

"Must *I*?" Littlecloud asked. "I've had no dreams. No visions. I've no reason to abandon old friends." His voice was hardly a whisper.

"Are you thinking of Cinderpelt?" Flametail knew of the close bond between the two medicine cats.

Littlecloud's eyes glistened.

Flametail leaned closer. "She's dead," he murmured. "Jayfeather is ThunderClan's medicine cat now. He's not Cinderpelt. He'll want to fight alone if StarClan wishes it."

"Jayfeather can do what he likes!" Littlecloud propped himself up with a groan. "Cinderpelt saved my life once. That act bonded us closer than friends. I will not abandon the Clan she loved until that debt is repaid."

The stems around the entrance rustled, and Rowanclaw poked his head in. "Flametail?" he called. "Blackstar wants to see you."

Littlecloud tried to clamber out of his nest.

"Just Flametail," Rowanclaw told the medicine cat. "Blackstar heard you coughing. He wants you to rest."

Littlecloud growled with frustration but sank back into the soft moss.

"I'll tell you what he says," Flametail promised, and hurried after Rowanclaw. As he crossed the clearing, he felt pelts brush either side of him. He slowed, puzzled. Rowanclaw was leading. No other cat was near.

Warm scents wreathed his pelt. *Russetfur and Sagewhisker!* He heard their voices, a soft wind in his ears.

"Stay strong!"

"We are with you!"

He nodded and padded into Blackstar's den, leaving the ghostly warriors to the breeze.

"Have you had any more signs?" Blackstar was pacing the cramped den. His tail whipped behind him.

Flametail leaned out of the way. "Nothing," he reported.

"Then why am I having such bad dreams?" Blackstar fixed him with a troubled gaze. "Every night I toss and turn, my dreams filled with blood and violence and death."

Flametail blinked. The old leader looked haunted, darkness rimming his eyes.

"What dangers do we face?" Blackstar demanded. "Will ShadowClan be destroyed?" He peered through the entrance, anguish sharpening his mew. "When you visited the Moonpool after the battle with ThunderClan, you spoke of a war coming. Who threatens us? ThunderClan? WindClan? RiverClan? All of them? How should we face them? What do our ancestors say?"

Flametail dipped his head. "I told you what they said. We

must face the danger alone. Allies will weaken us. So long as we stand alone, we'll be safe."

Hope lightened Blackstar's eyes. "Really?"

"Yes." Flametail looked down at his paws. "We'll be fine." The words sounded hollow, but he had to calm Blackstar. How could they face any battle if their leader lost his nerve?

Blackstar turned away. "We can fight this. We'll be fine." The ShadowClan leader had disappeared into his own thoughts. Flametail backed out of the den.

"I hear you found herbs."

Rowanclaw's mew made him jump. "Herbs?" he echoed.

"This morning," Rowanclaw pressed. "Tawnypelt said you brought borage back. Do you want help to collect more?"

Flametail shook out his pelt, clearing his mind. "Yes," he meowed. "That's a good idea."

Rowanclaw scanned the snowy clearing. "Toadfoot! Dawn-pelt!" The two warriors were patching the nursery wall with leaves. Rowanclaw signaled to them with his tail. "I have a task for you."

"What is it?" Dawnpelt reached her father first.

Rowanclaw purred. "Flametail's found a supply of borage. We should collect it while the leaves are still green."

"There may be other herbs that have been protected from the snow," Flametail added. "We must hunt under every bramble."

Toadfoot shuddered. "We'll be sleeping with scratched pelts tonight."

"Not if we're careful." Dawnpelt was staring into space. "In fact, I have an idea."

"Lift it higher!" Dawnpelt called from beneath a clump of brambles.

Toadfoot groaned as he heaved the stick up with his front paws, balancing on his rear legs and levering the prickly stems from the ground until they were high enough for Flametail and Dawnpelt to squeeze underneath.

"Don't let it drop!" Dawnpelt warned as she wriggled farther under the brambles.

"I won't," Toadfoot puffed.

Flametail followed his sister, his belly scraping the frozen earth. The top brambles were weighted with snow, but here at ground level the stems were bare, and he could see green shoots sprouting among them. "Can you reach?" he mewed to Dawnpelt.

"I think so." She stretched out her forepaws and began plucking the leaves. "Here." She passed a pawful back to Flametail. It was coltsfoot. Even if he couldn't cure Littlecloud, he'd have some way to ease his breathing.

He gathered the leaves Dawnpelt passed him until he was holding a satisfying, green-scented wad between his paws. "Any more?" he called.

"That's it," Dawnpelt answered.

Flametail squirmed backward, out from under the brambles, and shook the prickles from his pelt. Toadfoot was panting with the effort of levering the bush up. Flametail dropped the coltsfoot and put his paws under the stick, next to his Clanmate. Together they held the brambles high until Dawnpelt wriggled out.

Flametail gazed happily at the pile of coltsfoot. "That supply should keep us going for a moon, so long as there aren't too many coughs."

"Let's try another bush!" Dawnpelt circled excitedly, scanning the trees. "What about that one over there?" She hared toward another snow-covered thicket.

Toadfoot rolled his eyes. "I guess I'm carrying the stick." He picked up the sturdy pine branch in his teeth and began to drag it after Dawnpelt.

Suddenly, Flametail heard a sharp crack. Dawnpelt stumbled as ice split underneath her paws. As she started to fall, Flametail felt a rush of dread.

Plunged into a vision, he found himself floundering in freezing black water. It sucked him down, clutching at his fur, filling his ears and mouth. He gasped for breath, and water flooded his chest. Gagging and coughing, he fought his way up, flailing for the surface. His claws hit ice. It blocked the air, trapping him underwater, forcing him back into the sucking depths. Terror roared in his ears as he scrabbled to break it. He felt his claws rip against the smooth surface, and his lungs screamed.

"*No!*" Flametail hurled himself at Dawnpelt before she could sink through the ice. He knocked her into the snow at the side of the trail.

"What in the name of StarClan are you doing?" she yelped,

and pushed him off, scrabbling to find her paws. "Have you gone crazy?"

In the center of the path, a small circle of ice had cracked to reveal a muddy puddle, barely more than a leaf's thickness deep.

"Were you afraid I was going to get my paws wet?" Dawnpelt demanded.

Flametail stared at the puddle, his flanks heaving. "I . . . I . . ." The vision crowded his thoughts, and he could think of nothing but being trapped under that ice in freezing, choking water.

Flametail backed away. Why had a puddle triggered such a vivid vision? He shivered. First fire, now water. He was seeing danger everywhere.

"I know," he whispered to StarClan. "You don't have to keep reminding me."

He must concentrate on what was important right now. Littlecloud was sick. He had to find herbs to keep his Clanmates strong and healthy. Visions could wait.

CHAPTER 18

♣

Sandstorm was coughing. Lionblaze broke off from his work patching the elders' den and glanced at her as she crouched with her shoulders hunched beneath Highledge. She'd been coughing last night, too.

Firestar leaped down the rocks and touched his mate's head with his muzzle. "Are you okay?"

"Just swallowed a snowflake," Sandstorm rasped.

Lionblaze pushed another pawful of leaves into a gap in the branches. Though it was sunhigh, the hollow was gray under a gray sky. More snow had fallen in the past days, weighing down the beech tree so that the freshly built walls creaked and buckled, sprouting holes and cracks. Lionblaze had been working all morning to fill them in and stop the icy drafts that sliced through the new dens. Toadstep and Birchfall had been bringing leaves into camp, their paws muddy where they'd dug through the snow to scrape them from the frozen forest floor.

Birchfall dropped another pile at Lionblaze's paws. Toadstep paced behind him, trying to keep warm. "Do you need more?"

Both warriors were out of breath. Their pelts clung to their bones. Prey had been scarce for nearly half a moon, and the Clan was lucky to eat a few mouthfuls a day.

Lionblaze scooped up a pawful of frostbitten foliage. "If you can find more, I'll be able to patch the back of the den, too."

Birchfall nodded and led Toadstep back out of camp.

"Make sure you patch it up well!" Mousefur's reedy mew sounded through the den wall. "I hardly slept last night, the den was so windy."

Lionblaze purred. The fat water vole Ivypaw had brought back had restored Mousefur's spirits. He scooped up another pawful of leaves and walked gingerly over the branches to the back of the den.

"Is Lionblaze in here?" Brambleclaw had stuck his head through the entrance.

"I'm in back." Lionblaze dropped his leaves, jumped down to the ground, and hurried to meet the ThunderClan deputy. "What is it?"

Brambleclaw was shuffling backward out of the den. "I want you to lead a hunting patrol."

Lionblaze wiped his leaf-clogged claws in the snow. "Great. Where?"

"In the woods near the WindClan border."

Mousefur's head appeared in the den entrance. "What about the drafts?"

Brambleclaw dipped his head. "Birchfall and Toadstep can finish the job."

Lionblaze narrowed his eyes. "Is it wise to hunt near the border?" he ventured. "WindClan has been touchy about it since they started hunting there themselves."

Brambleclaw snorted. "That's precisely why we should make our presence felt. They've chased prey across the scent line before. We don't want them to make a habit of it."

"I guess not." Lionblaze saw the sense in what the deputy was suggesting.

"We're not looking for trouble," Brambleclaw went on. "But WindClan needs to know that ThunderClan is never far from the border line."

Mousefur flexed her claws. "I don't know why they couldn't stick to hunting the moors like they did in the old days." She turned and headed back into the warmth of the den, still grumbling. "WindClan hunting in woodland. What next? ShadowClan fishing in the lake?"

Brambleclaw waited for her to vanish inside. "Don't look for trouble," he told Lionblaze again. "But don't hide from it either."

Lionblaze fluffed out his pelt. "With any luck, we'll catch a rabbit." Rabbits sometimes strayed into the shelter of the forest when the weather hardened.

"A rabbit would be good." Brambleclaw's gaze strayed to the mouse and the scrawny robin that formed the fresh-kill pile. "Take Leafpool, Cinderheart, and Dovepaw," he ordered.

Lionblaze's heart sank. He'd been avoiding Cinderheart. Why had he told her his secret? Why had he believed she'd just accept it? Why *couldn't* she just accept it? His tail twitched.

I haven't changed! I've always had this power. He glanced across the clearing. He knew Cinderheart was there, sharing tongues with Leafpool. He stiffened as she whispered in Leafpool's ear. What if she told someone? Would she give his secret away?

No! Lionblaze pushed away the worry. Cinderheart hadn't changed, either—he still trusted her. "Is Ivypaw coming?"

Brambleclaw shook his head. "Jayfeather says she's still fighting the infection in her scratches. He wants her in camp till she's recovered."

Lionblaze headed toward Cinderheart and Leafpool. He called to Dovepaw as he passed the medicine den. She'd gone to keep Briarlight company. She nosed her way out of the brambles and ran to catch up to him. "What is it?" she asked breathlessly as he reached Cinderheart and Leafpool.

"We're hunting beside the WindClan border."

Leafpool got to her paws. "And checking WindClan hasn't strayed over it, I presume?"

Cinderheart stretched, her pelt ruffled from washing. She twisted to smooth a clump of fur with her tongue.

"We may as well get going." Lionblaze glanced at Leafpool, surprised to find that she met his gaze. She seemed more confident lately. She was quick to offer help to Jayfeather, unflinching whether he accepted or rejected her advice. And she was stronger on patrols, too, often the first to catch prey or to point out where a border scent had grown stale.

Lionblaze scowled. Was she a medicine cat or a warrior now? How should he treat her? He shifted his paws. Was she his mother or his mother's sister? He knew she'd kitted him, but she hadn't raised him. Squirrelflight had done that. At least she had when Clan duties hadn't kept her from the nursery. He shrugged. Daisy and Ferncloud had so often been the queens to warm and wash him; they felt as much like his mother as Squirrelflight, and far more so than Leafpool.

"So?" Leafpool's mew shook him from his thoughts. "Are we going or not?"

"We're going."

Dovepaw was yawning.

"Why are you so tired all the time?" Lionblaze flashed with irritation.

Dovepaw blinked at him. "Sorry." She scampered away and followed Cinderheart out of the camp. As Leafpool headed after them, Lionblaze felt a pang of guilt. He shouldn't have snapped at Dovepaw. She was young. Perhaps her power was too strong for her.

He followed his patrol out of the camp. The smell of the forest pushed away his worries. Fresh snow had smoothed the trails and bushes. The woods looked untouched, and he plunged ahead of his Clanmates, giving in to the kitlike urge to be the first to spoil the soft snow. Cinderheart, Leafpool, and Dovepaw followed him in silence, their paw steps muffled.

As they neared the narrow stream that separated the territories, Lionblaze tasted the air, making sure that no WindClan cat had strayed over the scent line. The stream was hardly more than a frozen ditch filled with snow that left nothing except a dent in the forest floor, but the scent line was fresh, pungent with both WindClan and ThunderClan markers.

"Should I take Cinderheart and hunt up past the brambles?" Leafpool offered.

"We'll cover more ground if we split up," Cinderheart put in.

"Okay." Lionblaze felt relieved. "Take Dovepaw, too." She was yawning again. He'd be better off hunting alone.

As the patrol headed away, bounding past the brambles, Lionblaze sniffed a hawthorn bush on the edge of the ditch, hungry for signs of prey, watchful for WindClan scent.

Frosted snow cracked beyond the ditch, and Lionblaze jerked his head up. Breezepelt was snuffling his way along a trail of small paw prints. Crowfeather followed, ears pricked, fur bristling along his spine.

Lionblaze ducked lower behind the bush. They didn't know he was there. Through the bare stems of the hawthorn, he watched the WindClan cats, skinny and shivering, as they followed the tracks. They weren't even trying to keep low. Did they imagine they were hidden by heather here? *Mouse-brains!*

A shower of snow spattered from the branches overhead. The WindClan cats looked up, their eyes gleaming. Lionblaze could hear the flicker of feathers, and without looking he knew that a thrush was near. He opened his mouth and let the scent bathe his tongue. More snow dropped. Then the thrush fluttered down. It landed beside a larch cone and began to peck for bugs between the bracts. Crowfeather stiffened. Breezepelt tensed. Only their tail-tips twitched. The thrush carried on pecking.

Then Breezepelt leaped. His paws thrust snow out behind him. The thrush exploded into the air, squawking an alarm. Breezepelt shot after it, paws outstretched. He leaped into the air, batting the thrush with a deadly swipe. It bounced from his grasp and shot across the ditch.

Lionblaze sprang out to meet it and swatted at the thrush mid-flight. It fell to the ground, dead.

"Hey!" Breezepelt's outraged mew shrieked across the ditch. "That was mine!"

"It's on my territory." Lionblaze crouched over his catch, his mouth watering. One less piece of fresh-kill for Wind-Clan, one more for ThunderClan. He looked at Crowfeather, the cat who'd made Leafpool betray her Clan. Lionblaze would never admit that this cat was his father. *Your WindClan son couldn't even keep hold of his catch.*

"I killed it." Breezepelt's growl sounded like a challenge.

"Are you sure?" Lionblaze lifted his chin and stared at the WindClan warrior. "Why don't you come and fetch it, then?"

Breezepelt flicked his tail. In one jump, he had crossed the ditch and slammed into Lionblaze.

Lionblaze suddenly felt alive. His fur bushed up as he fell under the WindClan warrior's weight. When Breezepelt's claws tried to hook into his flesh, Lionblaze reared and shook him off like a fly. Then he turned and leaped on top of him, trapping him between his front paws.

"ThunderClan slime!" Breezepelt slithered out of his grip, swiping wildly with all four feet.

Lionblaze's whiskers twitched. This was too easy. Swinging a paw, he thumped Breezepelt heavily across the cheek. The WindClan warrior staggered and fell, then heaved himself up. "That was my thrush," he spat. With a lightning-fast swipe, he knocked Lionblaze's hind paws from under him.

Lionblaze gasped, taken by surprise, and collapsed into the snow. He felt Breezepelt's teeth land in his shoulder. Raging, Lionblaze thrashed like a fish on the slippery snow. Finding a paw hold, he heaved himself to his paws and thrust Breezepelt clear with another hefty blow. Blood spattered onto the snow like crimson rain.

"*Stop it!*"

Leafpool's high-pitched shriek shattered the freezing air as she plunged through the bracken with Cinderheart and Dovepaw behind her. "How can you watch your sons fight?" she screeched at Crowfeather.

Before Crowfeather could reply, his mate, Nightcloud, stalked from the shadows beyond the border. Her black pelt matched Breezepelt's, and her amber eyes glittered with the same venom. "He only has one son." Hatred laced her hiss. "Crowfeather is Breezepelt's father. No one else's!"

Breezepelt crouched down. Lionblaze could see his muscles bunching beneath his pelt, ready for another attack.

"Stop!" Leafpool shot between them.

Breezepelt's lunge hit her square in the side. His claws tore her pelt as he dragged her to the ground. Another jet of blood sprayed the snow. Lionblaze stared in shock. Before he could reach for Breezepelt, Crowfeather had crossed the ditch and hauled his son off Leafpool.

He tossed him aside like prey and leaned over Leafpool. "You chose your Clan, remember?" he hissed.

She stared up at him. "That doesn't mean I didn't love you."

Crowfeather's eyes flashed with pain. "Maybe you did," he growled. "But it wasn't enough, was it?"

"Get away from her!" Nightcloud had crossed the ditch. She sank her claws into Crowfeather's pelt and dragged him away from Leafpool.

Crowfeather turned on his mate, hissing. Breezepelt darted between them with a wail of protest. Lionblaze felt sick. *He's my brother. How can I fight my brother?*

Breezepelt faced his father, tail bushed, lips drawn back. "Leave my mother alone." The thrush had been forgotten. This was about a different kind of blood now, the sort that flowed in a cat's veins, binding him to another.

Lionblaze shook his head, making his ears flap. *These cats aren't my kin.* A few paces away, Leafpool heaved herself to her paws. Lionblaze glared at her. *It's her fault. She made this mess.* Yet her eyes were shot with grief, and he suddenly felt her pain as though it were his own. *She has suffered more than any of us.*

Crowfeather, growling, turned away from Breezepelt and jumped the ditch back onto WindClan territory. "Come on," he snarled. "If ThunderClan is going to starve without that puny bird, let them have it." Breezepelt slunk after him, leaving a thin trail of blood in the snow.

Lionblaze fluffed out his fur. He hadn't felt a scratch. Should he stop fighting Clan cats? *It's cheating.* Dovepaw's words echoed in his mind. Perhaps he should save his powers for the Dark Forest warriors.

Nightcloud leaped the ditch, then paused and turned back. "Next time we'll shred you!" she spat.

Dovepaw darted forward. "Breezepelt started it!"

"Hush." Cinderheart guided her away from the border, murmuring to Lionblaze as she passed, "Perhaps you shouldn't have fought him."

Dovepaw's ears pricked. "Why not?"

Lionblaze narrowed his eyes. "Have you caught anything yet?" he asked his apprentice pointedly.

Dovepaw flicked her tail. "Not yet."

"Then start hunting." Lionblaze watched Dovepaw stamp away, then turned to Leafpool. "You should go back to the camp and get Jayfeather to look at your wounds," he ordered. Leafpool dragged her gaze from the border and nodded.

Lionblaze waited till the two cats had disappeared past the brambles. "Why are you worried about a WindClan cat?" he hissed to Cinderheart.

"You could've really hurt him!"

Do you think I don't know that? "I know what I'm doing!" he growled. "Stop treating me like a two-headed fox!"

Cinderheart stared at her paws. "Well, excuse me for not knowing how to handle this," she muttered. "You're the one who changed everything."

Lionblaze stared at her. Tiredness swamped him like a black wave. "No," he sighed. "This was all decided long before I was born." He turned away. "Let's hunt and go home. The Clan is hungry."

Lionblaze stood back while Graystripe circled the fresh-kill pile, licking his lips. They'd brought back two rabbits, the thrush, and a grouse.

"We should hunt on the WindClan border more often," the gray warrior purred.

Berrynose's mouth fell open. "It looks like a *pile* again!"

Lionblaze stared across the clearing. The good day's hunting hadn't eased the pain in his heart. Cinderheart hadn't even looked at him since they'd talked, and Leafpool had hardly spoken to anyone. He watched Sandstorm coughing. The ginger she-cat was crouched beside the halfrock with Firestar. Brightheart was with them. "She should see Jayfeather," she meowed.

"Really, it's just snowflakes," Sandstorm insisted.

Brightheart circled her. "We're all breathing in snowflakes," she fretted. "You're the only one coughing."

Firestar sniffed her. "Perhaps Jayfeather should check you out."

Brightheart nodded. "It sounds like whitecough." Firestar flashed the one-eyed warrior a sharp look. Brightheart twitched her tail. "If it *is* whitecough, we need to know."

Firestar leaned forward. "Keep your voice down!" Clearly he didn't want the Clan worried.

"I'm going to fetch Jayfeather," Brightheart decided. She hurried away to the medicine den.

"Well done, Lionblaze." Brambleclaw sniffed the fresh-kill pile. "Poppyfrost should eat first, and the kits."

"Briarlight will need some too," Millie added.

Lionblaze rolled a rabbit distractedly with his paw. "There'll be enough for everyone."

Jayfeather was following Brightheart from his den. He stopped beside Sandstorm and leaned over her.

Lionblaze broke away from his Clanmates. "Is it white-cough?" he asked softly as he neared his brother.

"Shhh!" Jayfeather pressed his ear closer to Sandstorm's flank. His tail quivered. "She'll need rest." He straightened. "And keep her warm."

Brightheart shifted her paws. "So it *is* whitecough."

"It may be." Jayfeather touched Sandstorm's ear with a pad. "I'll see if there's any feverfew left."

Lionblaze sat down. It was early in leaf-bare for white-cough. What if it spread? A flash of tabby pelt caught his eye. Leafpool was hurrying toward her mother.

"Sandstorm, what's wrong?" Leafpool bent to sniff Sand-storm's breath and looked up at Jayfeather. "We need tansy. I'll go and find some."

"It's getting late." Firestar rested his tail on Leafpool's spine. "Why not wait till morning?"

"And where are you going to find tansy?" Brightheart shook her head in despair. "We've been scouring the forest for days."

"There's some in your herb patch beside the Twoleg nest," Lionblaze offered.

Jayfeather stiffened.

Leafpool shook off Firestar's tail. "I'll fetch it!"

"It's too delicate," Jayfeather snapped. "If we pick it now, it may kill off the roots, and we'll lose the whole plant."

Leafpool snapped her head around to stare at him. "And if we don't, Sandstorm might get worse!"

"She's strong," Jayfeather countered. "She may not need tansy. I don't want to risk it."

"Risk what?" Leafpool challenged. "The tansy or Sandstorm's life?"

Firestar stepped forward. "It hasn't come to that yet."

Jayfeather kept his blind gaze fixed on Leafpool. "*I'll* decide when to use the tansy," he growled. "*I'm* the medicine cat."

Lionblaze tensed in the chilly silence. Snow creaked beneath his paws.

"Very well," Leafpool meowed at last. "I'll find some in the forest." She turned and stalked away.

"Wait till the morning!" Firestar called.

Leafpool hesitated, then stalked to the warriors' den and disappeared inside.

"Was there any sign of intruders on the border?"

"What?" Lionblaze looked up and saw Firestar staring at him. He'd forgotten to report the skirmish. "We met a Wind-Clan patrol."

Firestar's eyes narrowed. "Did they cross the border?"

Lionblaze felt a rush of confusion. Yes, but only because he'd taunted his half brother. How would he explain that? "There was a small argument about a piece of prey that crossed the border," he meowed at last. "Nothing we couldn't handle."

"Who won the prey?" Firestar asked.

"I did."

Sandstorm started coughing again. Firestar wrapped his tail around his mate. "These disputes are bound to happen," he meowed before turning his attention to Sandstorm.

If only it were that simple! Lionblaze closed his eyes. Today's fight hadn't been about prey, or hunger, or hunting rights. The tangling of relationships between the two Clans had caused the skirmish. It had poisoned feelings, not just between Clans but between Clanmates, weakening the Clan from within as cat turned against cat.

Perhaps Yellowfang was right. Perhaps each Clan should stand alone. When faced with such a treacherous enemy, they couldn't risk letting anything distract them from the final battle.

CHAPTER 19

❧

The roof of the elders' den creaked under the weight of snow. Jay-feather winced. "I hope it holds," he muttered.

"The old den would have been flattened." Beside him, Purdy's fur brushed against bark. "But now, with the honey-suckle woven around the beech branches, this den is strong enough to hold off a hollowful of snow."

Mousefur turned in her nest. "It's the thaw I'm not looking forward to. At least the snow is dry now. When it starts drip-ping through the roof—"

Purdy cut her off. "When the thaw comes, you'll get wet. Like you do every leaf-bare." His tail swished. "Cats that live wild get wet. Not even your StarClan can change that."

Jayfeather touched his muzzle to Mousefur's. "Hold still," he ordered as she pulled away. He smelled her breath. It wasn't sour, and her nose was cool. He listened to her chest, unsure whether the wheezing was infection or just age. Yet it was sunhigh, and the old she-cat was still in her nest. "Are you sure you don't have a sore throat?" he asked again.

"I'm sure," Mousefur grunted.

"Any aching in your joints?"

"Only the usual."

Jayfeather frowned. Why had she refused to play moss-ball with Molekit this morning? He turned to Purdy. "Let me know if she starts coughing."

"I'll fetch you myself," the old loner promised.

Jayfeather nosed his way through the honeysuckle tendrils, shivering as his paws touched snow in the clearing. The big catch Lionblaze's patrol had made had fed the Clan for days, but now the fresh-kill pile was pitifully empty, and Sandstorm's whitecough was beginning to spread. First, Jayfeather had confined Bumblestripe to his nest after coughing and fever gripped the young warrior during the night. Then Poppyfrost had sent Blossomfall to the medicine den.

"She says Cherrykit's got a fever," Blossomfall had told him.

"Tell her I'll come as soon as I've checked on Mousefur."

As Thornclaw led his patrol out of camp, Jayfeather headed for the nursery, praying that Poppyfrost was just being over-anxious. Rasping breath caught his ear. He paused. "Is that you, Mousewhisker?"

"Yes," the warrior croaked from the edge of the clearing.

"Get to your nest and stay there." Jayfeather crossed the clearing, not waiting for the warrior to object. There was no time for argument. The infection was spreading. He'd moved Sandstorm to the medicine den. She couldn't stay with Firestar. ThunderClan needed its leader to be healthy. Jayfeather sent a silent prayer to StarClan. *Please don't let Briarlight catch it.*

"Jayfeather!" Poppyfrost's mew sounded from the entrance

to the nursery. As the warmth of the den surrounded him, tiny claws bit into his back.

"Get off him, Molekit!" Daisy's stern mew sounded from her nest.

Molekit slid down Jayfeather's back. "Just practicing my attack pounce!"

Poppyfrost bustled past Jayfeather. "Go and practice outside," she told the young kit.

"Can Cherrykit come?" he mewed.

Jayfeather cuffed him gently with a soft paw. "Maybe later. I need to check her first."

As Molekit tumbled out of the den, Poppyfrost put her mouth against Jayfeather's ear. "She feels hot," she murmured.

Jayfeather leaned into the nest and touched Cherrykit's small muzzle with his own. "She is a bit warm." He pressed an ear to her chest. "Her breathing is clear, though."

"I feel fine," Cherrykit squeaked. "Can I go and play with Molekit?"

"Does she need herbs?" Poppyfrost's mew was tight with worry.

"Not yet." Jayfeather wanted to preserve his small supply for as long as possible. "Send her out to play in the snow with Molekit."

Poppyfrost gasped. "Outside?"

"The best thing you can do is to keep her cool," Jayfeather advised. "The snow will do that as long as her breathing is clear." He nosed Cherrykit out of the nest. "If you start to feel sick," he told the kit, "come inside and rest." He turned to

Poppyfrost. "Call me if she starts to cough or wheeze."

Jayfeather slid out of the nursery and headed back to his den to check on Sandstorm. "How are you?" he meowed as he leaned into the orange warrior's makeshift nest.

"I've felt better," Sandstorm admitted.

Jayfeather touched a pad to her ears, worried to find them hotter than ever. He turned away from the nest and began pulling herbs from his store. There must be more feverfew somewhere. His chest tightened as he felt the dried leaves and sniffed. Nothing good for coughs.

The brambles rustled, and a fresh tang filled the air. *Yarrow?*

"You forgot to bring these in." Rosepetal's muffled mew sounded at the den entrance. Leaves thumped gently on the floor. *It is yarrow!* Yarrow never survived the first frost.

Jayfeather hurried over to sniff the pile of leaves. "Where did you find these?" There might be other herbs nearby.

"They were lying outside the camp, near the thorns," Rosepetal mewed. "I thought you'd dropped them."

Jayfeather frowned. "Not me."

"Well, someone did." Rosepetal's paw brushed the yarrow, and bitter scent drifted up. "Perhaps it was Leafpool," she suggested.

"Maybe." Leafpool had been scouring the forest for days. She was so tired that it was possible she had dropped some leaves and forgotten about them. "I'll go thank her." Jayfeather brushed past Rosepetal and pushed through the brambles.

Leafpool was tumbling with the kits outside the nursery.

Her pelt smelled of the forest, but there was no scent of yarrow on her.

Jayfeather crossed the clearing. "Thanks!" he called.

Leafpool paused. "Thanks?"

"For the herbs."

"What herbs?"

"The yarrow leaves," Jayfeather explained. "Rosepetal found them outside the camp. We figured you'd picked them and dropped them there."

"It wasn't me." Leafpool's tail-tip brushed the snow as she walked toward him. "Maybe it was one of the other cats?"

Jayfeather twisted and called toward his den. "Rosepetal?"

The young cat came bounding out. "What?"

"Show me where you found the yarrow."

He followed Rosepetal through the thorn barrier. "Here," she announced, stopping in the narrow clearing outside, between the hollow and the trees.

Jayfeather sniffed the ground. No scent of any cat. Just yarrow and snow.

"Perhaps a warrior found leaves and hoped they'd be useful," Rosepetal suggested. "They may have been on patrol and planned to tell you later."

"Maybe." Jayfeather shrugged. "If no one mentions it, I'll ask Firestar to thank whoever found it at the next Clan meeting." Pushing his curiosity aside, he headed back into the hollow.

"Jayfeather!"

Thornclaw's yowl made him stop. "What is it?" Jayfeather

tasted the air. "Mothwing, is that you?" Thornclaw and Spiderleg were accompanying the RiverClan medicine cat down the slope to the hollow.

"We found her by the shore," Thornclaw reported. "She wants to speak with you."

Mothwing snorted and broke away from her escort. "Thanks for your company," she muttered. "I think I could have found my own way here."

Spiderleg's pelt sparked. "We were just trying to help."

Jayfeather flicked his tail. "I'm sure she's grateful." He padded past the warrior, nudging Mothwing along with him. "Let's go to the lake. My den is full."

"Sickness?" Mothwing followed him up the slope.

"Whitecough." Jayfeather wrinkled his nose at the scent of fish on her breath. "Only Sandstorm so far, but possibly three more."

As Mothwing sighed, he wondered if he should warn her that StarClan was trying to divide the Clans. After all, she had no connection with StarClan. They had no power over her. But he couldn't forget Yellowfang's words. Or his vision.

"How's Briarlight?" Mothwing asked.

"She's shaken off the infection."

"Good."

"Her forepaws are as strong as any warrior," Jayfeather went on. "They'll be stronger if she keeps on with her exercises."

"It's going to be a long hard path for her," Mothwing warned.

"Once it becomes the only path she knows, it won't seem so hard." The lake breeze stung Jayfeather's nose as he reached the crest of the slope. He hurried on, breaking from the trees and bounding down the snowy slope. He wanted to stay a few paw steps ahead of Mothwing. It was too easy to fall into the old bond of friendship.

He plunged down the bank, shocked as snow swallowed him up. It had piled along the shore, and he coughed as it shot up his nose. Sneezing, he struggled toward the water's frozen edge until he was free of the drift. "I wish it would thaw," he spluttered to Mothwing.

She lumbered through the snow and settled beside him. "It's just getting colder," she observed. "We're having trouble stopping the kits from playing on the ice. I had to treat three sprained paws yesterday."

Has she just come to gossip about kits? Jayfeather let his thoughts drift into hers.

Her mind seemed empty. He was wasting his time. "What do you want?" he snapped. "I don't have all day."

A purr rolled in her throat. "Blunt as ever." She pawed at the snow, then lowered her voice. "Willowshine told me that StarClan has ordered us to stop talking to the other medicine cats."

"Then why are you talking to me?"

"I want to know if they told you the same thing."

Yellowfang's matted outline suddenly shimmered at the edge of Jayfeather's awareness. His pelt pricked as he sensed the old medicine cat's presence. "I'm not telling you what

StarClan shares with me," he grunted.

"Then they *have* told you the same!"

Jayfeather bit back a reply as Mothwing pressed on. "They told you to stop talking to me, and you have!" Her tail scraped the snow. "If StarClan told you to jump in the lake, would you?"

Jayfeather bristled. "That's not the same."

"Really?" Mothwing leaned closer. "How many times has another Clan helped us save our Clanmates?"

Jayfeather shrugged.

"They're asking us to stop doing something that medicine cats have done since the Clans were born. They're asking us to let cats *die*. Have they gone mad?"

"Remember to hold your tongue." Yellowfang's rasping mew sounded in Jayfeather's ear. "If you don't keep quiet, all four Clans will be lost to the darkness."

"They're StarClan," he muttered. "They have their reasons."

"What reasons?" Mothwing growled. Her fishy breath billowed in his face. "You don't know, do you?"

He pulled away. "I can't explain it to you."

"I know when something feels wrong," she argued. "Our code is different from the warrior code. It reaches across boundaries. To us, every cat is simply that—a cat, with the same right to life as any other. We made a promise to heal and protect, remember?"

"Then protect your Clanmates," Jayfeather snapped back. "But leave mine alone."

"What if Sandstorm's whitecough turns to greencough?"

Mothwing's muzzle was close to his again. "Could you let her die because StarClan told you to?"

"They have their reasons." Jayfeather dug his claws into the snow.

"They're just dead warriors!" Mothwing hissed. "Do you think that when they die, they get clever and brave? Don't you realize that some of them may be as foolish and wrong-headed as they were when they were alive?"

Jayfeather wrinkled his nose against Yellowfang's rancid breath. He felt her matted pelt snag his. She hadn't changed a whisker when she'd joined StarClan. A growl rumbled in his throat. "You've never met a warrior from StarClan," he spat. "You're just guessing."

"So are they!"

Yellowfang growled beside him. "Mothwing was born an idiot. She'll die an idiot."

Jayfeather turned away. "You won't convince me."

Mothwing let out a slow, frustrated breath. "Okay, okay!" She bounded after him, spraying him with snow. "Do you need herbs for whitecough? I've got tansy and catmint—not much, but enough to share if you're desperate."

"No, thank you." Jayfeather forced out the words as he clambered up the bank.

Mothwing halted behind him. "If you do, come find me."

"I won't." Jayfeather trudged up the slope. The snow on the shore crunched as Mothwing headed back toward the Wind-Clan border.

The icy wind tugged at Jayfeather's fur. "Happy now?" he

growled to Yellowfang. But she had vanished.

He broke into a run, bounding up the slope and into the trees. His paws followed the trail home, and his lungs stung harder with each frosty breath, until he skidded, panting, to a halt outside the thorn barrier.

Poppyfrost met him when he wove his way through. "Cherrykit can't breathe!"

Jayfeather pushed past the queen and hurried across the clearing. He could hear the kit's paws scuffing the snow outside the nursery.

Anxiety sparked from Daisy. "We kept her outside like you told us, but now she's wheezing."

Jayfeather stopped Cherrykit with a flick of his tail and pressed his ear to her flank. There was thickness in her chest that rattled every time she breathed in. "Has she been coughing?" he asked Poppyfrost.

"A little," the queen answered.

"Take her inside."

"What about the fresh air?" Daisy demanded.

"She needs rest now." Jayfeather nosed Cherrykit toward her mother. "Wash her. Keep her damp. It'll keep her cool."

Cherrykit yelped with indignation as Poppyfrost scooped her up and squeezed into the nursery.

Daisy trotted after Jayfeather as he headed for his den. "Are you fetching herbs for her?"

"I will, if she gets worse."

"Why not now?"

Jayfeather turned. "I don't have enough," he hissed under his breath.

"What about the leaves Rosepetal brought in?"

"That was yarrow," Jayfeather explained. "Only good for expelling poison."

"But whoever found those leaves might be able to find tansy or catmint."

"When I find out who it was, I'll ask them." Jayfeather wanted to get back to his den and check Sandstorm.

"Is something wrong with Cherrykit?" Sorreltail was hurrying toward them.

"Just a little wheezing," Jayfeather told her.

"Is Cherrykit sick?" Jayfeather prickled with frustration as Dovepaw dropped a sour-smelling squirrel and joined them.

"Just some wheezing!" he repeated.

Daisy's tail swished. "He sent Mousewhisker to his nest earlier because he was coughing."

"And Bumblestripe was coughing half the night," Sorreltail added.

Leafpool's mew sounded close by. "Sandstorm hasn't left the medicine den all morning."

Was the whole Clan going to join in? Jayfeather lashed his tail. "Stop worrying! I can—"

Dovepaw cut Jayfeather off. "There's greencough in ShadowClan," she mewed.

Leafpool's breathing quickened.

"*Green*cough?" Daisy's mew was barely a whisper.

Jayfeather thrust his muzzle toward Dovepaw. "How bad is it?"

Dovepaw's pads brushed the snow as she shifted her paws. "J-just Littlecloud." Her mew was suddenly awkward.

"No one else?" Jayfeather pressed. She must have been listening in to the ShadowClan camp. He knew how uncomfortable she was about spying on other cats.

"No."

"Good." He flicked his tail. He needed to distract the others before they started wondering how Dovepaw knew what was going on in ShadowClan. "Why don't you and Sorreltail fetch Cherrykit a wet moss ball?" he suggested to Daisy. "And Dovepaw, put that stinky old squirrel on the fresh-kill pile before someone trips over it." He headed toward the medicine den.

Leafpool followed him. "What are you going to do?"

"About what?"

She was almost treading on his heels. "About Littlecloud?"

"Pray to StarClan."

"Is that all?"

"What else am I supposed to do?"

"Help him!" Leafpool's mew was sharp.

"Why?"

"You're a medicine cat!"

Jayfeather halted and faced Leafpool. She didn't know that StarClan had ordered him to cut ties with the other medicine cats, and he wasn't about to tell her. When she'd given up being a medicine cat, she'd given up the right to share with StarClan. But he understood her. He'd shared tongues and gossip with Littlecloud at the Moonpool enough times to have formed a bond with the old ShadowClan cat. He lowered his voice. "There's enough sickness here without worrying about other Clans," he murmured. "My supplies are low. I need every scrap to treat our Clanmates."

Leafpool didn't reply. Her silence made his pelt prick. "There is nothing I can do, even if I wanted to," he hissed. He turned and headed for his den.

Could you let a cat die because StarClan told you to? Mothwing's words echoed in his ears.

Leafpool's gaze burned his pelt. Jayfeather could see her thoughts, clear as dreaming. They were focused on the patch of herbs he'd nursed beside the old Twoleg nest. Would she steal them to help Littlecloud?

No!

Yet he couldn't risk it. Her connection with Littlecloud was long and deep. He veered away from the medicine den, tasting the air. Brambleclaw was below Highledge, talking with Spiderleg and Berrynose.

"Brambleclaw?" He padded toward the ThunderClan deputy.

"Yes?"

"I need to ask you something," Jayfeather whispered.

"What?" Brambleclaw lowered his voice.

"There's sickness in the camp," Jayfeather began. "Only whitecough, but that's enough. The herb patches I've grown are more precious than ever. I want you to post a guard around them."

"A guard?" Surprise sharpened Brambleclaw's mew. "You don't think anyone would steal them?"

"There's sickness in ShadowClan, too," Jayfeather explained. "They know about the herbs. They were planning to take our territory to get their paws on them, remember?"

Brambleclaw's tail swished through the air. "That was part of Ivypaw's dream," he growled.

"Exactly," Jayfeather meowed. *Ivypaw's dream may not have come from any cat in StarClan, but maybe it had its uses after all.* "And the forest is full of starving prey who might be grateful for a few juicy stems."

"Berrynose! Spiderleg!" Brambleclaw summoned the two warriors. "Do you know where Jayfeather's herb patches are, beside the Twoleg nest?"

"I do," Spiderleg answered.

"I want them guarded, day and night."

Jayfeather stepped forward. "No cat or prey must get near them," he urged. "They're too precious to lose."

"Don't worry, we'll keep them safe!" Berrynose bounded away.

"I'll send a relief patrol at sundown," Brambleclaw called as the two warriors pounded across the clearing.

Jayfeather closed his eyes. The Dark Forest was growing in strength. The cats in StarClan were frightened. And now he didn't trust his Clanmates. The ground seemed to rock beneath his paws.

"I must stay strong," he murmured to himself. "I must stay strong."

CHAPTER 20

❧

Dovepaw crouched behind a tangle of ivy. She flattened her belly against the snow, keeping low in the gully so that no moon shadow spread out behind her.

Paw steps had nearly reached the top of the gully. Opening her mouth, she tasted the familiar scent. Her belly fluttered. Another tail-length. She held her breath. Almost there.

"Got you!" She shot up the short, steep slope and sent Tigerheart rolling across the forest floor.

"I give up!"

She scrambled off him. "One night you'll get here first."

"I thought I was early tonight." He smoothed his ruffled pelt. "It's as if you know exactly when I leave camp!"

Dovepaw dropped her gaze. "Yeah, right," she mumbled. "Like I can hear you creeping out of your nest." She changed the subject. "I wonder how much longer this snow's going to last."

Tigerheart shrugged. "It's better than rain."

"But it's impossible to go anywhere without leaving a trail."

"A good warrior can follow a trail without snow."

Dovepaw leaned forward and rubbed her nose against his cheek. "I could find your trail on water," she murmured.

A purr rumbled in his throat. "I've missed you."

Border scents filled the air around them, ThunderClan mingling with ShadowClan. "Should we go to the abandoned Twoleg nest?" Dovepaw suggested.

"There's no time tonight." Tigerheart sighed. "Blackstar's sending out extra patrols at moonhigh and dawn."

Dovepaw tipped her head. "Why?"

"We're hunting for herbs as well as prey."

"Is Littlecloud worse?"

"Yes." His belly growled. "And the Clan's getting hungry."

Dovepaw pressed her cheek against Tigerheart's. Thunder-Clan was lucky that whitecough hadn't turned to greencough. "I wish I could help." She pictured Jayfeather's fat clumps of juicy herbs growing by the Twoleg nest, protected from the ice by heaps of bracken. "But Jayfeather's made sure no one can take leaves from his herb patch."

Tigerheart pricked his ears. "Herb patch?"

"The plants he's been nursing since greenleaf."

"He's been growing herbs?"

Dovepaw drew away, surprised. "I thought you knew." She frowned. "Isn't that why ShadowClan wanted our territory?"

Tigerheart stared at her. "We never wanted ThunderClan territory."

"But Ivy—" Dovepaw stopped herself. There was no need for Tigerheart to hear about Ivypaw's dream. "I thought that's why we had the battle."

"It was Firestar who wanted territory," Tigerheart meowed. "He asked for the clearing back."

Dovepaw shifted her paws. *Only because Ivypaw persuaded him to.* She shook out her pelt. She didn't want to argue with Tigerheart. The battle was over. "Never mind."

"But Jayfeather has herbs." Tigerheart leaned closer. "Which herbs?"

"Just some tansy." The words felt sticky on her tongue. She couldn't lie to Tigerheart, but it felt disloyal to tell him about Jayfeather's precious supply. "A bit of catmint."

"Catmint?" Tigerheart's eyes shone. "Would he let us have some?"

Dovepaw felt hot. "Leafpool's asked him to give you some already."

"And?"

"He said no."

"But Littlecloud might die!"

"He said we have to look after our own Clan." Dovepaw wove around Tigerheart, brushing against him. *Come on, Tigerheart, let's have fun!* She flicked his nose with her tail. "Let's see who can climb highest." She glanced up at the pine beside them, wondering if her claws were strong enough yet to make it up the trunk to the lowest branch. It stuck out high above her head.

"Did you hear me?" Tigerheart snapped. "Littlecloud might die."

Dovepaw dropped her gaze, her heart sinking. "I could steal some," she offered. Her belly twisted.

"No." Tigerheart was firm. "You can't steal from your own Clan for me."

Relief swamped her. "I can try and persuade Jayfeather to give you some."

Tigerheart touched his nose to hers. "Thank you," he murmured. Dovepaw felt a rush of affection for him. "I just hope we get some herbs soon," Tigerheart went on. "Otherwise the Clan is going to starve to death while we're scraping the forest floor for leaves."

"Watch this." Dovepaw scuttled backward to the top of the slope. She was going to distract Tigerheart even if it meant falling on her nose. She crouched, pushed up hard with her hind legs, and stretched her forepaws back over her head, trying to reach her tail. Arcing her belly toward the sky, she reached for the ground, praying that she'd manage to complete the backflip.

She landed on her chin with a thump that knocked the wind from her. Thrusting her claws through the snow into the frozen forest floor, she managed to stop herself from rolling down the slope.

Tigerheart was purring with amusement. "Smooth landing."

"Keep watching." She scrabbled to her paws and crouched down, ready to try again, but Tigerheart laid his tail over her shoulders.

"Wait a moment."

"What?" She looked at him.

His front paw flicked up and a clump of snow hit her on the nose.

"Hey!" Dovepaw leaped to her feet, scooped up a pawful,

and flung it at him. Tigerheart ducked as the snow sailed past his ear. Dovepaw lunged at him playfully and tumbled him into the snow.

"Whoa!" Tigerheart pretended to lose his balance and rolled over and over down the short, steep slope, holding Dovepaw in his strong grip. She squeaked as they rolled to a halt. Out of breath, they lay entangled in each other's paws. Dovepaw felt a surge of happiness so strong that she broke into a purr.

Then she stiffened.

"What?" Tigerheart tensed beside her.

"Paw steps." She had forgotten to listen out for danger. Now she could hear fur brushing bracken and pads scraping over the frost-crusted snow. "Someone's coming."

"Who?"

Dovepaw tasted the air. Her tail bushed out. "Ivypaw!"
Too late!

Her sister's white face appeared at the top of the slope. "I knew it!" she hissed.

Dovepaw lifted her chin. "You knew ages ago!"

"But now I've seen it for myself." Ivypaw's eyes glittered.

Tigerheart straightened up beside Dovepaw. "You're on ShadowClan territory," he challenged.

"So's she!" Ivypaw snorted. "At least *I'm* not betraying my Clan."

Dovepaw flashed with rage. "You betray us every night in the Dark Forest!"

Did Tigerheart flinch? Dovepaw glanced at him. His

gaze was fixed on Ivypaw.

Ivypaw lifted her tail. "Are you going to tell her, Tigerheart, or should I?"

Dovepaw leaned forward, her ears flat. "Don't start that again!" *There's no way Tigerheart would train in the Dark Forest!*

Ivypaw's gaze was still locked with Tigerheart's. Dovepaw felt a chill along her spine.

"You see?" Ivypaw snarled at Tigerheart. "My sister doesn't believe me." The tip of her tail began to twitch. "Perhaps she'll believe you."

No! Dovepaw began to back away. *Please don't let Tigerheart be part of the Dark Forest too.*

Bracken rustled behind Ivypaw. Dovepaw gasped as Tigerheart shoved her underneath a pile of dead brambles. "Stay still," he hissed.

Dovepaw flattened herself against the ground and held her breath. The air was thick with ShadowClan scents.

"What's happening here?" She recognized Smokefoot's deep growl.

Tigerheart's paws scrabbled on the snow. "I found her near the border."

Trembling, Dovepaw peered through the tendrils. She could just make out Smokefoot and Applefur at the top of the slope. The ShadowClan warriors were glowering at Ivypaw.

Tigerheart puffed his chest out beside the ThunderClan apprentice. "I was about to bring her back to camp so Blackstar could question her."

"Really?" Applefur narrowed his eyes. "Why were you

wandering about in the middle of the night?"

Smokefoot leaned closer. "You weren't assigned to a moon-high patrol."

Tigerheart met Smokefoot's gaze. "I couldn't sleep."

The ShadowClan warrior turned to Ivypaw. "What are *you* doing on ShadowClan land?"

Dovepaw's heart quickened.

"I was looking for prey."

Please believe her!

"It's a strange time to be hunting," Applefur challenged.

"Food is scarce," Ivypaw answered. "I thought there might be some night prey."

"On ShadowClan land?" Smokefoot challenged.

"I didn't realize I'd crossed the border."

"Can't ThunderClan apprentices smell? Come on," Smokefoot hissed. "Let's take her back to the camp."

Dovepaw fought panic as she listened to the ShadowClan cats lead her sister away. *Tigerheart, protect her!* she pleaded silently.

As soon as they were out of hearing distance, she crawled out from the brambles and dashed for the border. Ivypaw had been captured by ShadowClan! *But I can't tell anyone!*

Dovepaw's heart seemed to stop. How could she explain why Ivypaw had been taken? She might give away her meetings with Tigerheart. How could Lionblaze or Jayfeather trust her again? Would her Clanmates ever forgive her? She pricked her ears, searching for Ivypaw, until she heard voices from the ShadowClan camp.

A kit was squeaking excitedly. "Who's that?"

"Just a ThunderClan 'paw, dear," a queen soothed. "Go back to your nest. It's late."

Dovepaw listened harder.

"Blackstar will see you in the morning." That was Smoke-foot! He must be talking to Ivypaw. "Stay here until you are fetched."

"There's some moss in the corner." She heard Tigerheart's whisper. "You can make a nest out of it. You won't be disturbed. Just keep quiet and don't try to escape."

The tightness in Dovepaw's chest eased. They were treating Ivypaw well. There would be no need for a rescue party, surely? Dovepaw padded home and crept through the dirt-place tunnel. Treading lightly, she slipped past the ferns into her den. As she curled into soft moss, she was painfully aware of Ivypaw's cold, empty nest. Thoughts spinning, heart pounding, she closed her eyes.

The sounds of the camp woke her. Brambleclaw was organizing the hunting patrols below Highledge. Sandstorm was coughing. Poppyfrost was in the medicine den begging Jay-feather for a little tansy for Cherrykit. Ruffled and anxious, Dovepaw climbed out of her nest. She listened hard to locate the ShadowClan camp and finally heard a gruff ShadowClan warrior. "Blackstar will see you later." A small thud made Dovepaw jump. "Eat this." He must have thrown her some prey.

"Thank you." Ivypaw didn't sound frightened.

Dovepaw lifted her chin. She knew what she had to do

now. "Ivypaw?" she called. She waited a few moments, then hopped out of the den.

"Ivypaw?"

Graystripe, Berrynose, Millie, and Whitewing were sitting with Icecloud and Foxleap beneath Highledge. Brambleclaw paced in front of them.

Dovepaw took a deep breath and called to them. "Has Ivypaw already left on patrol?"

Graystripe turned and glanced, puzzled, at Dovepaw. "Do you need her for something?"

Dovepaw shrugged as casually as she could. "She wasn't in her nest when I woke up."

Whitewing got to her paws. "I haven't seen her." Concern edged her mew. "Birchfall?" She called to her mate.

Birchfall paused from digging in the snow. He was unearthing a prey store. "What's up?"

"Have you seen Ivypaw?" Whitewing asked.

Birchfall looked at Dovepaw. "Isn't she in her nest?"

Dovepaw shook her head. "She was gone when I woke up."

Whitewing pushed her way into the apprentices' den, popping out a moment later. "Her nest is cold. She hasn't been in it all night."

Birchfall's fur spiked. "Brambleclaw?"

The Clan deputy looked up. "Is everything okay?"

"Ivypaw hasn't slept in her nest," Birchfall told him.

Brambleclaw glanced around the gathered warriors. "Has anyone seen her?"

"Not since last night," Berrynose answered.

"I shared a mouse with her at sundown," Sorreltail told him.

Cinderheart came hurrying from the dirtplace tunnel. "Did someone say Ivypaw's missing?"

Whitewing paced at the edge of the clearing. "Her nest hasn't been slept in."

"It's too cold to be out of camp for long.," Brambleclaw meowed.

"What if she's hurt?" Whitewing gasped.

Birchfall brushed his tail along her ruffled spine. "We don't know that."

"We'll have to start searching for her," Brambleclaw decided. He nodded to Berrynose and Graystripe. "Take a patrol each and search the forest."

Dovepaw's heart began to race. They mustn't waste hunting patrols! Her thoughts whirled. She couldn't blurt out that Ivypaw was in ShadowClan's camp. They'd wonder how she knew.

Jayfeather! He'd understand.

Glancing furtively at her Clanmates, Dovepaw headed for the medicine den. "Jayfeather!"

"Shhh!" The medicine cat was soaking leaves in the pool. "Sandstorm's sleeping!"

Briarlight propped herself up on the edge of her nest. "What's wrong?"

"Ivypaw's missing," Dovepaw mewed. She stared at Jayfeather, willing him to hear the urgency in her mew. She had to speak to him in private.

Carefully he rolled the soaked leaf into a dripping bundle and laid it beside the pool. "Come with me," he told Dovepaw, and padded past her. Briarlight's eyes were sharp with curiosity as Dovepaw followed Jayfeather out of the den.

Toadstep and Icecloud were clambering over the beech. Toadstep peered down the gap between the branches and the cliff wall. "Ivypaw?"

Rosepetal was checking behind the nursery. "No sign of her here."

"I'm guessing she's not in camp," Jayfeather muttered.

"I know where she is!" Dovepaw could hardly keep the words in. "I can hear her. She's in ShadowClan's camp!"

"What's she doing there?" Jayfeather demanded.

"I . . . I don't know. I can just hear her. I think they're holding her captive. They told her to stay where she was and gave her some food and said that Blackstar would see her later."

"How in the name of StarClan did she end up there?" Jayfeather sounded more annoyed than worried. He headed toward the rock tumble. "Let's tell Firestar before the whole Clan starts to panic."

Dovepaw followed him up the stones. *Say as little as you can,* she reminded herself. *You mustn't give anything away.*

"In the ShadowClan camp?" Firestar blinked with surprise when Jayfeather told him. He turned his sharp gaze on Dovepaw. "How long has she been there?"

Dovepaw stared at him innocently. "She was in camp last night when we went to our nests, but she was gone this morning."

"Do you think she went there herself?"

"She may have gone to the border," Dovepaw ventured. "Perhaps they caught her there?"

"What would she be doing on the ShadowClan border?" Firestar shook his head as though he had a tick in his ear. "I can't think of anywhere more dangerous since the battle."

Dovepaw dropped her gaze, her pelt burning. "I—I don't know."

Jayfeather leaned closer to the ThunderClan leader. "Perhaps you should call off the search."

Firestar ducked out of the den. Dovepaw trailed after him. "We believe that Ivypaw has been taken prisoner by Shadow-Clan," he called down to the clearing.

Dovepaw flinched as her Clanmates stared in shock at the ThunderClan leader.

"How do you know?" Mousefur growled, padding to the center of the clearing.

Firestar shifted his paws. "She was last seen on the Shad-owClan border." He couldn't reveal any more without giving away Dovepaw's powers.

Thornclaw padded past Mousefur. "We should send a patrol to rescue her!"

"I want to go!" Whitewing insisted.

Thornclaw flexed his claws. "I'll lead it."

"We should leave now!" Birchfall yowled.

Firestar flicked his tail. "We must stay calm."

"We can't just leave her there!" Whitewing hissed.

"A small patrol should go and see if it's true," Firestar

reasoned. "If it is, they can ask for her return."

Birchfall bristled. *"Ask?"*

Firestar nodded. "We can't fight them in their own camp," he pointed out. "There are elders and kits there."

Mousefur twitched one ear. "Don't forget, they have Ivypaw. They might harm her if we attack."

Firestar sat down and wrapped his tail over his paws. "Brambleclaw!" he called. "Take Brackenfur, Cloudtail, and Dovepaw."

Dovepaw curled her claws into her pads. She wanted to stay out of this. She wanted to pretend it wasn't happening.

Whitewing darted forward. "I want to go with them!"

Firestar shook his head. "Brambleclaw can handle it," he meowed. "He'll bring Ivypaw back safely." Whitewing turned away, growling. Firestar glanced at Dovepaw. "Off you go."

She scrambled down the rock tumble and joined Brambleclaw, Cloudtail, and Brackenfur as they headed out of camp. "What was she doing on the border at night?" Cloudtail wondered as they headed through the trees toward ShadowClan territory.

"Surely she's not a traitor?" Brackenfur murmured.

Never! Guilt shot through Dovepaw. It was her fault that Brackenfur doubted Ivypaw's loyalty.

"It wouldn't be the first time a cat has met secretly with a warrior from another Clan." Brambleclaw's eyes were dark, fixed on the trail.

It's all because of me! Don't blame her!

At the border, Brambleclaw sat down. Cloudtail stared at him. "Aren't we going to the camp?"

"We'll wait for a patrol," Brambleclaw answered.

Cloudtail snorted.

"We don't know for sure they have her," Brackenfur pointed out.

Cloudtail began to pace the scent line. "It's just the sort of trick ShadowClan would pull."

Dovepaw pricked her ears. Paw steps were crunching through the snow. ShadowClan was awake and patrolling. She waited, listening over the pounding of her heart, until the paw steps came near enough for her to announce without suspicion, "I can hear something!"

Brambleclaw stood up and faced the border, fur smooth, gaze steady. Rowanclaw, Shrewfoot, and Crowfrost wove through the bushes toward them. Dovepaw forced herself to stop trembling. *It's going to be okay.* She spotted Tigerheart as he slid out from behind his Clanmates. She looked down at her paws, frightened to catch his eye in case she gave her feelings away.

"Come to fetch something you've lost?" Crowfrost snarled across the scent line.

Cloudtail bristled. "Then you admit you've taken her!"

Shrewfoot glared at the white warrior. "Tigerheart found her wandering on our territory."

Brambleclaw blinked. "Is she safe?"

Crowfrost hesitated. Dovepaw groped desperately for some sound from her sister in the ShadowClan camp.

"We haven't hurt her," Crowfrost murmured.

Rowanclaw and Shrewfoot exchanged glances.

"May we escort her home?" Brambleclaw addressed the ShadowClan deputy.

"Why's he being so polite?" Cloudtail breathed into Brackenfur's ear.

Brambleclaw flicked his tail. "You don't want an extra mouth to feed," he meowed to Rowanclaw.

Rowanclaw nodded. "True, but we don't want ThunderClan apprentices wandering across our borders either."

Rowanclaw stepped closer to the border. "You can have her back," he growled, "in exchange for catmint."

Dovepaw looked sharply at Tigerheart. His face betrayed nothing. Only yesterday he was worried sick about Littlecloud, and now Ivypaw was being offered in exchange for exactly the herb needed to save the ShadowClan medicine cat? He must have told his Clanmates about the herb patches. How *could* he?

Pain seared Dovepaw's heart. *He doesn't really love me! He was just using me, and now he's using Ivypaw!* Dovepaw froze. Wouldn't she do the same for her Clan? Would her loyalty lie with Tigerheart or ThunderClan?

"Catmint?" Brambleclaw echoed.

"Littlecloud's sick with greencough," Rowanclaw told him. "He needs catmint to survive."

Brambleclaw looked puzzled. "Why ask like this?"

"We don't want to harm Ivypaw," Rowanclaw meowed. The meaning in his words was clear. "We just need catmint."

Brambleclaw tensed, and Dovepaw guessed he was forcing himself not to react to the implied threat. Instead he nodded. "I'll tell Firestar." He signaled to his Clanmates with his tail and headed back toward camp.

"Why didn't Flametail just ask Jayfeather?" Firestar stared in bewilderment at his deputy as Brambleclaw reported Rowanclaw's demand. "We've always helped other Clans in the past."

Beside him, in the clearing, Graystripe curled his lip. "And we've been criticized for helping," he growled.

Jayfeather stood at the entrance to the medicine den. Dovepaw could see his claws digging into the snow.

Leafpool, watching with Squirrelflight from the halfrock, looked grief-stricken. "How sick is Littlecloud?"

Brambleclaw narrowed his eyes. "Sick enough to hold an apprentice hostage."

"I'll go and pick the herbs," Jayfeather muttered.

"Thank you." Firestar nodded. "I know herbs are scarce, but Littlecloud needs them."

Squirrelflight stepped forward. "What about Sandstorm?"

"And Cherrykit!" Daisy trotted across the clearing with her fluffy cream-colored tail held high. "She's no better today."

Firestar dipped his head. "We will try to see to the needs of everyone," he meowed. "But Littlecloud and Ivypaw are in the gravest danger. We must help them first."

Poppyfrost's face appeared in the nursery entrance. Her eyes were round with worry. Firestar's gaze rested on her for a moment before he turned back to Brambleclaw. "Perhaps the cat who found the yarrow can find more herbs," he murmured.

Dovepaw wanted to creep into her nest and hide. What if Sandstorm or Cherrykit got worse? What if they *died*? *This is all my fault!*

CHAPTER 21

A shriveled mouse thudded in front of Ivypaw. "Eat this."

She looked up at the dark tabby ShadowClan warrior who'd thrown it, and sniffed. "Thanks."

The warrior stalked away, around the bramble screen that half hid Ivypaw's corner of the ShadowClan camp.

"I don't know why they're giving you food." Starlingpaw scowled at her. "You were trying to steal ours."

Ivypaw leveled a scornful look at the young ShadowClan tom who'd been ordered to guard her. "I crossed the border *by mistake.*"

"Yeah, right." Starlingpaw turned away and resumed his watch.

Ivypaw rolled her eyes. Anyone would think he was guarding a LionClan warrior. "What exactly do you think I'm going to do? Attack the warriors' den and take over the camp?"

Starlingpaw glanced at her. "Who knows what you're planning? ThunderClan cats are known for being sneaky."

"ThunderClan? *Sneaky?*" Ivypaw couldn't believe her ears. *ShadowClan* cats were the sneakiest cats in the forest. She snorted. *I give up.* She wasn't going to waste time talking to this mouse-brain. She settled onto her belly and began eating the mouse. As she gnawed at the stringy meat, she peered around the edge of the bramble, past Starlingpaw's tail, and watched the ShadowClan camp begin to stir.

Two kits tumbled out of a small hole in the bramble wall. "Come on, Dewkit!" The bigger kit—a tabby tom—crouched down, waggling his tail.

"What?" His littermate—a gray she-kit—stared at him.

The tabby dashed across the clearing. "Race you to the dirtplace!"

"That's cheating, Sparrowkit!" Dewkit pelted after him.

A third kit fell out of the brambles. "Wait for me!" She landed and stared after them, eyes wide.

"Don't worry, Mistkit." A tabby queen slid out behind her. "We'll catch up to them together." She headed after them, Mistkit trotting at her side. The kit's pale gray pelt was as spiky as a pinecone. When they reached the far end of the clearing, they ducked into a tunnel and disappeared from view.

Cedarheart, the graying elder, stretched outside his den. Tallpoppy squeezed out from the brambles behind him and yawned. She looked at the gray sky. "Looks like more snow's coming."

Cedarheart shivered. "We'll be *eating* snow before long."

A pure-white she-cat was crossing the clearing toward a small pile of mangy-looking prey. Was that a dead frog lying on the top? Ivypaw shivered. The white warrior sniffed at it and carried a piece back toward her den. Ivypaw recognized Olivenose squeezing out.

"Do you want to share this?" the white warrior offered.

"Thanks, Snowbird." Olivenose called back over her shoulder, "Do you want to share a vole, Owlclaw?"

Ivypaw chewed on her mouse, a little surprised to see that the ShadowClan camp worked just like ThunderClan's. *What did you expect? Mice and squirrels doing the work for them?*

Rowanclaw ducked into Blackstar's den and emerged a few moments later with the ShadowClan leader. They talked for a few moments before Rowanclaw lifted his chin and called to the Clan, "Let all those ready to hunt gather for patrol."

Pelts swarmed around him. Ivypaw strained to recognize as many warriors as she could. The shapes and colors of these cats were so like ThunderClan, more than stunted WindClan or the fat, sleek RiverClan cats.

"Ratscar, Scorchfur, Snowbird, and Applefur." Rowanclaw nodded to each one. "You will lead the hunting patrols today. Redwillow, you take the border patrol. Tigerheart, Shrewfoot, and Crowfrost"—he flicked his tail—"you'll be coming with me."

Tawnypelt flicked her tail. "The snow has drifted over the training ground," she reported. "We need to find a more sheltered clearing, or else train in camp."

Rowanclaw nodded. "If anyone finds a suitable training area, let me know. Until then, battle training will take place here."

The kits burst out of the dirtplace tunnel.

"Is that strange cat still here?" Sparrowkit squeaked. "The one Tigerheart brought back last night?"

The warriors glanced at one another, surprised. Ivypaw stiffened as, one by one, the cats began to turn and stare at the sheltered corner where she was crouching. She wasn't going to hide like she'd done something wrong to their precious territory. Puffing out her chest, she padded out from behind the brambles and met their gaze.

Rowanclaw took the center of the clearing. "Tigerheart found a ThunderClan apprentice inside our scent line last night," he announced.

Pelts bristled behind him.

"Was she alone?" Ratscar demanded.

"The patrol didn't find any other cats," Rowanclaw answered. "No warrior scent has been found."

"Are you sure?" Olivenose flattened her ears. "They could be trying to take more of our territory!"

"We're *not*!" Ivypaw couldn't stop herself calling out.

Starlingpaw turned on her, bristling. "Be quiet!"

Ivypaw scowled at him as Tawnypelt padded forward and turned to her Clanmates. "She's just an apprentice."

Rowanclaw sat down and wrapped his tail over his paws. "We're holding her for now," he meowed. "No doubt Thunder-Clan will look for her soon. Until then, she's no threat."

"Yeah," grunted Starlingpaw. "No threat."

Ivypaw fought the urge to cuff him around the ear.

Rowanclaw flexed his claws. "The patrols must leave," he ordered. "We can't waste hunting time."

Ratscar, Scorchfur, Snowbird, and Applefur began to weave among their Clanmates, assembling their patrols. Within moments they were thundering through the brambles, out into the pine forest.

A tiny mew made Ivypaw turn. "Hey, Thundercat!"

Sparrowkit had leaped past the bramble screen and was facing her, back arched and fur on end. Ivypaw broke into a purr as Dewkit leaped out after him and Mistkit peeped, trembling, around the prickly stems.

"Can you fly?" Sparrowkit demanded.

Ivypaw blinked. "Fly?"

"The warriors said you flew down from the trees in the battle."

"Oh, yes." Ivypaw nodded. "All ThunderClan cats can fly."

"Liar," growled Starlingpaw.

Ivypaw shrugged. "It's not my fault that ShadowClan kits have poppy seeds for brains."

Sparrowkit raced at her, spitting. "No we don't."

Ivypaw ducked and snarled in his face, baring her teeth. The kit's pelt bushed, and his eyes widened with terror. "Kinkfur! Help!" With a squeal, he turned and hared away. Mistkit and Dewkit went wailing after him.

Starlingpaw turned on her. "What did you do that for?"

"Sorry." Ivypaw winced. "I didn't think I'd scare them that much." Her pelt burned. "I was just joking."

"Those kits have been raised on tales about ThunderClan warriors who eat kits for fun!" Starlingpaw snapped.

Ivypaw stared at him. "Really?"

"They'll have bad dreams for days."

"Let me go and apologize," Ivypaw offered.

The brambles rustled, and Blackstar stalked in. "You *will* apologize," he growled. "But not yet."

Ivypaw straightened up. Blackstar was huge. His one black paw was the size of her head. "I'm really sorry," she mewed.

Blackstar's whiskers twitched. "Don't worry. We're not going to put you on the fresh-kill pile yet." His eyes seemed to glow. Was he amused? He scanned the corner she'd been held in, glancing down at the half-eaten mouse at her paws. "Sorry to keep you like this. Have you had enough to eat?"

"Yes." Hastily, Ivypaw pushed the mouse toward him. "I don't want to use up your food. Prey is scarce."

Blackstar dipped his head. "I expect you want to go home."

Ivypaw felt her eyes glisten. "Yes."

"You'll be back in your camp soon enough." He gazed past her. "First, there's a bargain to be struck. ThunderClan has something we need." He turned and padded away.

Ivypaw watched him go, unease pricking her belly. "A bargain?" she echoed.

Starlingpaw shrugged. "Perhaps we're going to swap you for food."

Tawnypelt padded around the jutting brambles. "Are you all right?" The sympathy in the tortoiseshell's mew made Ivypaw more homesick than ever.

"I'm fine." She swallowed against the lump rising in her throat. "What do you want to swap me for?"

"Herbs," Tawnypelt answered. "Littlecloud's sick. We need catmint and tansy. Tigerheart told us that Jayfeather has been growing some."

"Tigerheart?" Ivypaw was confused. *But Tigerstar told me that ShadowClan knew about the herbs ages ago. That's why they'd wanted to invade ThunderClan territory. Had Tigerstar lied?*

"He overheard some ThunderClan warriors talking about it yesterday," Tawnypelt told her.

No he didn't! Anger throbbed in her ears. *Dovepaw told him!* How could her sister betray her Clan like that? Ivypaw stared around her prison. *How could she betray me?*

Tawnypelt padded closer. "Don't worry, dear." Her eyes were round. "I'm sure Jayfeather will happily give up a few herbs on your behalf. You'll be home in no time."

Ivypaw backed away, bristling.

"Would you like to use the dirtplace?" Tawnypelt offered. "You could stretch your legs. You must be stiff, holed up here." She waved Starlingpaw away with her tail. "I'll keep an eye on her."

Tawnypelt took her across the camp. The clearing was long and wide. All the dens were neatly tucked away inside the camp wall. Ivypaw was impressed. It was perfect for practicing battle moves. Dawnpelt, lying near the edge, looked up from the frog she was chewing and scowled. Sparrowkit was huddling beside Kinkfur. Dewkit and Mistkit were nowhere to be seen. Cedarheart and Tallpoppy had made nests in the snow outside their den and watched her pass.

Ivypaw felt hot under her pelt. She was relieved to duck through the tunnel to the dirtplace while Tawnypelt waited in the clearing. The dirtplace was outside the camp wall, and Ivypaw wondered if she could slip away and make it to the border.

"Are you finished?" Tawnypelt called.

Ivypaw pushed the idea away. The forest was full of patrols that all knew the territory better than she did. She kicked snow over her dirt and headed back through the tunnel. "I want to apologize to the kits," she told Tawnypelt as she emerged.

"What for?"

"I frightened them."

Tawnypelt purred. "I thought Sparrowkit was looking a little quieter than usual." She led Ivypaw across the clearing toward Kinkfur. As they neared, Mistkit squirmed out of the den and hid behind the tabby queen. Dewkit followed and ducked under Kinkfur's tail.

Sparrowkit, trembling, lifted his chin. "You don't scare me!" he growled.

"Good—"

A shriek ripped across the camp, and Flametail came racing through a gap in the brambles, wild-eyed and with his fur bushed up.

Tawnypelt bristled. "What is it?" She raced over to the terrified medicine cat.

"Darkness!" Flametail gasped. "Cold, sucking darkness." The ginger tom's eyes were black with terror.

Blackstar rushed out of his den. "What's the matter?" He barged past Smokefoot and stared at the medicine cat.

Flametail's gaze fixed on his leader. "There is a great darkness coming," he hissed. "I've felt it, all around me. It will engulf ShadowClan like an endless wave and suck us down to our doom."

Blackstar thrust his face closer. "What can we do?"

"We must prepare to fight. StarClan was right. We are alone, and we must fight for our lives!"

Smokefoot leaned forward. "Who? Who must we fight?"

Flametail shook his head. "I couldn't see."

"It must be the other Clans," Blackstar snarled. "If StarClan says we fight alone, it must be them that we fight!"

Kinkfur trembled beside Ivypaw and swept her kits closer with her tail. The brambles shivered. Ivypaw turned to see Tigerheart pad into camp. Rowanclaw, Shrewfoot, and Crowfrost followed.

Flametail straightened up, calmness flooding his mew. "The greatest battle in the history of the Clans is coming, and we must prepare to meet it."

Tigerheart's broad shoulders stiffened. He glanced backward, catching Ivypaw's eye. *We are being prepared already,* he seemed to say.

Ivypaw didn't feel comforted. Flametail's prophecy of doom had scared her; she wanted her Clanmates around her, and Firestar to decide which battles should be fought and which could be left for another day.

If the greatest battle ever was coming, Ivypaw wanted to be home before it arrived.

CHAPTER 22

Dovepaw paced outside the thorn barrier with her ears pricked. She could hear the patrol heading back from the ShadowClan border with Brambleclaw in the lead. Brackenfur and Graystripe padded after, their paws heavy on the snow. Ivypaw was with them, tailed by Squirrelflight.

Dovepaw was unnerved by the patrol's silence. They didn't scold Ivypaw for her carelessness in getting caught. They didn't ask her what had happened in ShadowClan's camp. Her pelt itched with anticipation. Would Ivypaw forgive her for letting ShadowClan take her prisoner?

The patrol appeared at the top of the slope and headed down toward the camp. Dovepaw tried to catch Ivypaw's eye, but her sister's gaze followed her paws, dark with worry.

"Are you okay?" Dovepaw fell in beside Ivypaw. "They didn't hurt you, did they?"

"She's fine," Squirrelflight told her. "Let her rest."

"Won't Firestar want to speak to her?"

Squirrelflight shook her head. "What's done is done." She sighed. "Ivypaw knows she made a stupid mistake. She won't do it again."

Dovepaw paused. Didn't they want to question Ivypaw about what she'd been doing on the border in the middle of the night?

Ivypaw headed straight for her den.

"Please talk to me!" Dovepaw pleaded.

Ivypaw stopped and looked at her with clouded eyes. "I'm fine. Don't worry. I'm just tired."

"Really?" Dovepaw leaned closer.

Ivypaw nodded and turned away.

Stones cracked on the pile of rocks beside the cliff. Firestar's orange pelt glowed in the twilight as he bounded down from Highledge. "Did everything go okay?" he asked Brambleclaw.

"We gave them the herbs; they gave us Ivypaw," the deputy reported.

"Any idea how they caught her?" Firestar prompted.

"She said she was trying night hunting on the border and strayed over the scent line."

Thornclaw was frowning outside the warriors' den. "You shouldn't have sent such senior warriors to fetch her," he grumbled. "It shows too much respect."

Dustpelt paced around him, tail whipping. "If any ThunderClan cat dies because we have no herbs, ShadowClan will have blood on their fur."

Guilt clawed at Dovepaw as she stared after her sister.

"Come on," Squirrelflight murmured in her ear. "Leave Ivypaw to rest. It's time to leave for the Gathering."

Dovepaw spun around. "I'd completely forgotten!" She glanced up at the fat white moon. If she saw Tigerheart tonight, what would she say to him?

Thornclaw and Dustpelt were already waiting by the tunnel. Firestar's tail disappeared through the brambles at the medicine den entrance. Dovepaw guessed he was checking on Sandstorm before he left. Sorreltail padded across the clearing with Blossomfall and Rosepetal, fur fluffed against the cold. Berrynose, Foxleap, and Lionblaze emerged from the shelter of the warriors' den.

Squirrelflight waited beside the nursery until Leafpool slid out of the entrance. "How's Cherrykit?" the orange warrior asked.

"Her breathing's a little rough, but she still has her appetite," Leafpool answered. They headed for the barrier.

Brambleclaw glanced over to the medicine den, breath billowing at his nose, as Firestar and Jayfeather padded out. "Let's go."

They headed for the lakeshore. Jayfeather stuck close to Lionblaze's side as the patrol headed down the bank. The snow had drifted deep in places, but Lionblaze guided his littermate through a gap and dug a channel to where the breeze from the lake had blown the snow thin enough to cross easily.

"Dovepaw?" Lionblaze called to her softly.

She hurried to catch up to him. "What?"

"Do you know what Ivypaw was doing on the border?" Lionblaze hissed. Beside him, Jayfeather's ears were pricked.

"It didn't have anything to do with the Dark Forest," Dovepaw whispered. "She was just . . ." She groped for a reason. "Practicing her night hunting, like she said." Jayfeather's tail twitched, and Dovepaw focused hard on believing that was what Ivypaw had been doing. She didn't want Jayfeather spying on her thoughts and discovering the truth.

"Look!" Squirrelflight was staring up the hillside. They were crossing WindClan's shore, and high on the moorland, the silhouettes of WindClan warriors were lined along the crest.

"What are they waiting for?" Thornclaw growled.

Foxleap shook snow from his tail. "Perhaps they don't want to arrive first."

The moon glinted on the WindClan warriors, sending long shadows spilling down the smooth, white hillside.

"Come on." Firestar quickened the pace. "The sooner we get into the shelter of the island, the better."

Dovepaw waited for Rosepetal and Blossomfall to catch up, then matched their pace. Blossomfall was fretting. "I hope they'll be okay."

"Briarlight will be happy being left in charge of the medicine den," Rosepetal pointed out.

"But Bumblestripe's been coughing all day," Blossomfall sighed. "What if he takes a turn for the worse?"

"Jayfeather put Brightheart in charge," Rosepetal reminded her. "She'll know what to do."

Dovepaw reached out with her senses, up the WindClan slopes where the heather creaked under the layers of snow. The warriors waiting at the top made no sound, only watched. Unease began to prick Dovepaw's belly. She stretched her senses farther, back to ShadowClan territory.

"It could be a trap." Crowfrost's mew was sharp with worry. "Perhaps we shouldn't go."

Blackstar cleared his throat. "We must not show fear," he meowed. "They won't attack under the full-moon truce."

"Can you be sure?" Snowbird demanded.

"It's a Gathering!" Tawnypelt declared. "They wouldn't dare!"

Who are they frightened of? Had StarClan warned them about the Dark Forest warriors? Dovepaw turned her ears toward RiverClan.

"Are you coming?" Mothwing was calling across the camp.

Willowshine's reply was firm. "I'm staying here."

"Will they obey the truce?" Reedwhisker muttered.

Mosspelt's paws pattered over the snow. "Perhaps we should hide the kits and elders until they've left the island."

Fear was darkening every Clan like clouds across the moon. Dovepaw could hear RiverClan warriors pacing the clearing when ThunderClan reached the island. She nosed her way past Blossomfall and Rosepetal and crouched on the shore beside Jayfeather and Lionblaze. "They know!" she whispered.

Lionblaze blinked at her. "Who knows?"

"The other Clans! They know about the Dark Forest."

"You're imagining it." Jayfeather's eyes glinted in the moonlight. "Only *we* know about the Dark Forest."

Dovepaw realized that she hadn't actually heard any cat mention the Dark Forest. "Well, they're scared of *something*," she hissed.

"I know," Jayfeather agreed. "I can sense it in the air.

The medicine cats must have told their Clanmates about StarClan's warning."

"Perhaps we should tell our Clanmates," Dovepaw suggested.

"And scare them to death?" Lionblaze dug his claws into the snow. "We can deal with whatever's coming by ourselves."

"Look!" Foxleap called from the edge of the water. "It's solid all the way to the island!" The young warrior was already slithering across the frozen lake.

Dovepaw padded to the edge and put out a tentative paw. The ice burned, but as her pad grew numb, she tried another paw, and another, until she was standing on the hard white surface.

"Come back!" Sorreltail called. "It might break!"

"Don't worry," Foxleap yowled. "It's shallow here." With unsteady paws he wobbled farther out, picking up speed and falling into a clumsy skid. "Whoa!" He slithered to a halt, purring. "Try it, Blossomfall! It's fun."

Blossomfall hurtled after him, yowling with surprise and pleasure as she glided over the ice. Dovepaw's heart lurched as her paws slid underneath her. Tensing to stay upright, she picked her way across. Every muscle felt stiff with fear, but it was still thrilling to be walking across the lake. She could see the dark shadow of water lapping beneath the moon-white surface. With every paw step, the ice groaned and creaked.

"Come on!" Firestar's sharp order sounded from the island shore. "Get off there."

Dovepaw's claws scraped the ice as she fought to grip it,

and she slithered ungraciously onto the snowy shore, relieved to feel solid earth beneath her.

Brambleclaw and Dustpelt were already pushing through the bracken toward the clearing in the pine trees. Dovepaw slipped through the crackling fronds, lost for a moment as her Clanmates disappeared around her. She followed the sound of their fur brushing stems until she slid out onto the edge of the clearing. The RiverClan warriors froze, as though trapped in ice, while they watched ThunderClan arrive.

"What's up with them?" Rosepetal whispered.

Firestar headed for the Great Oak and climbed onto one of the snow-laden roots. The RiverClan cats drew closer to one another like fish bunching into a shoal. Dovepaw eyed them warily and padded closer to Blossomfall.

"What's spooking them?" Blossomfall hissed.

"Who knows?" Dovepaw stared at her paws.

The bracken behind her crunched, and she turned to see WindClan flooding into the clearing. She bristled, surprised that they were here already. She'd lost track of them while she'd played on the ice. They filed around ThunderClan, hardly making eye contact. Breezepelt's gaze grazed Dovepaw's but quickly jerked away.

Dustpelt was pacing. "I've never heard it so quiet."

"Isn't anyone going to share tongues?" Squirrelflight gazed around, puzzled.

The ShadowClan patrol came last, tense and round-eyed. Dovepaw spotted Tigerheart's dark brown ear tips. He didn't look around for her, but stayed in the knot of his Clanmates.

Dovepaw felt a jab of frustration. How could things change so quickly? Each Clan was acting like it was at war with the others. Was it StarClan who had sown the seeds of mistrust, or the Dark Forest warriors?

"It's so cold; we must be quick!" Mistystar called from the lowest branch of the Great Oak. Firestar sat a little farther along the branch, Onestar and Blackstar stiff as owls beyond him.

RiverClan and WindClan gathered closest to the tree. ShadowClan hurried to take its place beside them. Dovepaw followed her Clanmates as they padded into a pool of moonlight and settled down to listen. She nosed her way past Rosepetal and Blossomfall, seeking the warmth of the crowd and settling between Thornclaw and Lionblaze.

Mistystar, huddled in the moonlight, looked like a small pool of silver. "It's a tough leaf-bare, and with the lake frozen in the shallows, hunting has been hard."

Nightcloud growled. "It makes a change for the fish-eaters to go hungry as well."

Mistystar pressed on. "The bad weather has not kept us from training, and we are thankfully free of sickness."

Onestar stood. "WindClan too is healthy, though rabbits are scarce and the snow is thick around the camp. We have improved our tracking skills and found a way to trace prey to its burrows."

He nodded to Blackstar, who stood and gazed down at the gathered cats for several long heartbeats. "Rowanclaw has become ShadowClan's deputy," he announced at last, appearing to choose his words carefully. "We still mourn the loss of Russetfur. It was not her time to die." He didn't look at Firestar, but went on, "Hunting has been hard, and Littlecloud has been ill. But I'm pleased to report that we have found a remedy, and he will be here with us next full moon."

Murmurs of approval rose from the ShadowClan cats. Dovepaw felt Thornclaw tense beside her and heard Lionblaze's claws scrape the snowy ground.

Firestar stood up. His gaze was fixed on Blackstar. "And how did you find that remedy?" he challenged. Dovepaw heard breaths quicken and paws shift as the Clans tensed around her. Firestar didn't wait for an answer. "You took one of our apprentices hostage, that's how."

There were muffled gasps from RiverClan and WindClan warriors.

"She was on our land!" Blackstar hissed.

"And you would have been within your rights to chase her off," Firestar shot back. "But what true warrior takes a cat, too young to defend herself, and bargains with her like she was prey?"

Blackstar bared his teeth as Firestar pressed on. "A true warrior would have the courage to ask for what he wants." The ThunderClan leader arched his back. "You're lucky we didn't strike back more harshly. We've beaten you once already this moon. Don't think we wouldn't do it again."

Blackstar smoothed his fur. His eyes were slits. "Whatever happens," he breathed, "ShadowClan will be ready."

"We're ready now!" Rowanclaw jumped to his paws, pelt

bristling, at the bottom of the tree. Crowfrost and Smoke-foot stood up beside him and glared into the crowd, their eyes fixed on the ThunderClan warriors.

Lionblaze curled his lip, and a growl rasped in Squir-relflight's throat. Dustpelt flattened his ears. Gulping, Dovepaw unsheathed her claws. Were they going to fight here? She glanced at the bright, clear moon. There was no cloud in the sky to end the truce.

Dovepaw heard whispers spread through the Clans.

"Is this it?"

"Has the darkness come?"

"But the moon is still shining!"

That didn't seem to matter. Every pelt was on end now. Eyes flashed in the moonlight as the warriors glared, half-wary, half-threatening, at the other Clans.

Mistystar got to her paws. "RiverClan! We're going home." She leaped down from the oak and led her Clan through the bristling warriors. Onestar jumped down after her, Blackstar following. They took their Clans out of the clearing in silence.

Dovepaw watched as Firestar scrambled down last from the oak. At the far side of the clearing, the bracken rattled and hissed as the Clans pushed their way through it.

I must speak to Tigerheart!

She raced after the departing cats, finally spotting the tip of his tail. She clawed at it, just scraping the tuft at the end, and he turned and glared at her.

"What?"

"We have to talk!"

His eyes softened. "Come on." He guided her to a quieter spot, where the stiff bracken stems gave way to snow-covered mounds of grass. "Sorry I couldn't talk to you before, but things are tense," he murmured.

Dovepaw scowled at him. "You told Blackstar about Jayfeather's herbs!"

He gazed steadily back at her without saying anything.

"How *could* you?" Dovepaw wailed. "If Sandstorm dies, it'll be your fault!"

"But Littlecloud's sick."

"So is Sandstorm!"

"Not with greencough."

Dovepaw's rage grew. Tigerheart sounded so reasonable. Didn't he understand what he'd done? Tigerheart stroked her flank with his tail, and she flinched.

He frowned. "If Jayfeather were a true medicine cat, he would have given us the herbs."

"He has to put his own Clanmates first!"

Tigerheart tipped his head to one side. "So do I."

Dovepaw felt sick. She wanted this conversation to stop now, but she had to know. "Even above me?"

Tigerheart's tail quivered. "I didn't mean it like that." His amber eyes grew round. "I just—"

Dovepaw cut him off, her mew barely a whisper. "I think you did." She turned and padded away. "I think that's exactly what you meant."

CHAPTER 23

❧

Ivypaw curled into her nest. Snow swished and paws shifted as her Clanmates pounded out of camp and headed for the island. She tucked her nose under her paw.

I'm doing it to be a better warrior! She closed her eyes. *I'm doing it for my Clan!*

As sleep slid around her, she opened her eyes. She was in the Dark Forest. She tasted the air, scenting nothing beyond the sourness of the earth and the reek of mold on the trees. "Hawkfrost?" Her mew echoed through the trees. She needed to see his face. *He wants me to be a great warrior, that's all.*

She padded along a mossy trail. The warmth of soil felt strange against her paws after the sting of snow. The trees parted, and the slimy river rolled in front of her. With a flicker of satisfaction she remembered dunking Darkstripe beneath the water with Hollowpaw.

She followed the dark water for a few paces before spotting light through the trees. She veered onto a path that wound deep into the forest. The light glowed stronger, and she quickened her pace. Thick trunks reared up more tightly around her. Ivypaw kept her gaze fixed on the light. As she neared it, she realized that it glowed from a strange gray fungus, which sprouted from the tree trunks and crowded between their roots. Was the fungus reflecting the moon?

Ivypaw strained to see the round white moon. It must be full here too, right? But the branches grew too thickly overhead. There was no sign of sky or moon. The branches began to clatter, though no wind stirred the forest. A shiver ran along Ivypaw's spine. *Don't be silly.* She pressed on.

With a rush of relief, she heard voices and hurried forward. Beyond the clustering trunks, Tigerheart and Tigerstar were talking.

"You're late." Tigerstar sounded angry.

Ivypaw pricked her ears to hear Tigerheart's reply.

"I had to go to the Gathering."

"Training is more important."

She ducked behind a tree and peered through the shadows. Tigerstar circled Tigerheart. "Don't you know who your real Clanmates are yet?" he growled. "Don't I deserve your loyalty more than those mouse-eaters?"

Ivypaw stiffened. Was Tigerstar trying to turn Tigerheart against *ShadowClan*?

She heard a thump. Tigerheart groaned. Ivypaw slipped forward, ducking behind the next tree before peeking out. Tigerstar had Tigerheart pinned to the ground.

"That's the same mistake you made in the battle with ThunderClan," Tigerstar sneered before letting Tigerheart go.

Tigerheart scrambled up. "What did I do wrong?"

"Don't watch my paws." Tigerstar lunged forward, as if to

knock the ShadowClan warrior's hind legs out from under him. Tigerheart bucked, flicking his back paws high and out of the way, but Tigerstar twisted faster. While Tigerheart avoided the lunge, the dark warrior nipped the young warrior's scruff between his teeth. He dragged him off balance, and Tigerheart landed with a thump on his side.

"Never forget that paws fight, but jaws kill," Tigerstar growled, backing off.

Tigerheart jumped up. "I won't," he panted.

"Lionblaze knows that," Tigerstar snarled. "That's how he killed Russetfur. If you can't match those ThunderClan weaklings, you are nothing."

Ivypaw gasped. *Tigerstar lied to me! He's not loyal to ThunderClan at all!* Tightness gripped her chest, and she struggled to steady her breathing. *He's been telling Tigerheart the same things he's been telling me. He hasn't been training me to help ThunderClan at all.*

"When the final battle comes"—Tigerstar was still talking—"wasting time at Gatherings won't help you. It'll be us against four Clans and their puny ancestors. Then we'll see who the real warriors are."

Ivypaw fled. She raced through the forest, the trees blurring on either side. This must be the battle Flametail had seen in his vision. This was why Hawkfrost had recruited her.

She wasn't special.

She was stupid.

Tigerstar didn't want to help ThunderClan. He wanted to wage war against the Clans. And he was using their own warriors against them!

Gasping, Ivypaw stumbled to a halt. The river blocked her path, sliding silently before her. *How do I get home?* She blinked and blinked again.

Wake up! Wake up!

"Are you okay, little one?"

For a moment Ivypaw imagined she was back in the nursery, Daisy murmuring over her. She snapped open her eyes and saw Mapleshade. The orange-and-white warrior was gazing at her with a mocking gleam in her eyes.

"Leave me alone!" Ivypaw hissed.

"Are you having a bad dream, dear?" Mapleshade sneered.

Ivypaw shrank from Mapleshade's stinking breath. "Why don't you just fade away to nothing?"

Mapleshade flexed her claws. "Oh, I'm not going anywhere until I've settled a few scores."

Ivypaw forced herself not to start shaking. "I . . . I was looking for Hawkfrost."

"He's busy." Mapleshade moved closer. "He wanted me to train you tonight."

Ivypaw swallowed. "Really?"

"Let's try out those river moves you learned last time." Heart sinking, Ivypaw gazed at the river.

"Show me what you learned," Mapleshade ordered before she turned and waded out into the water.

Ivypaw forced herself to follow. The water oozed around her paws and dragged at her pelt.

"Am I deep enough yet?" Mapleshade asked. The water was lapping the warrior's shoulders. Ivypaw had to follow on tiptoes to keep her nose above the water. "Now what happens?" Mapleshade prompted. "Come on, you must remember your lesson."

"I have to knock your legs from under you."

"Go ahead then, dear."

Get it over with quickly. Ivypaw took a breath and ducked under, gagging as the warm, slimy water washed her muzzle. She swam down toward Mapleshade's paws and reached out to grab them. A heavy weight hit her back and pushed her deep into the water, till her chest bumped onto the riverbed. Ivypaw struggled as the blood roared in her ears. Mapleshade had her pinned down. The great she-cat's claws pierced Ivypaw's pelt, pressing her harder against the stones.

Ivypaw writhed on the bottom of the river, bubbles escaping her mouth. Mapleshade was pushing the air from her chest. She fought wildly, kicking out with her legs, hoping to knock Mapleshade away. Ivypaw's lungs screamed. Blackness edged her vision. She fought the urge to suck in water.

Then her flailing hind legs struck a rock. It budged, barely the width of a whisker. Ivypaw flailed again, harder. The stone shifted, then gained speed. Mapleshade's paws shifted as the rock rolled away. With a mighty shove, Ivypaw pushed upward, wrenching herself free as the she-warrior lost her balance.

Desperate for air, Ivypaw forced herself to stay beneath the water. She struck out with her paws and began swimming underwater as far from Mapleshade as she could. As the riverbed sloped up, she followed the curve, emerging from the water on the far bank. She slithered onto the mud, gulping for air.

Glancing over her shoulder, she saw Mapleshade splashing around in the river, searching the riverbed with floundering paws. Low as an otter, Ivypaw crept up the bank and slunk between the trees. When she was sure the shadows hid her, she collapsed, panting, onto the ground and coughed up a lungful of black water. Exhausted, she closed her eyes.

"Ivypaw?"

Dovepaw!

She looked up, relief swamping her as she saw the edges of her nest and her sister's face peering anxiously over its woven stems. Early dawn light was beginning to filter through the ferns.

"Are you okay?"

Ivypaw coughed again, her chest burning. "Yes," she rasped. "I'm okay now." She never wanted to go back to the Dark Forest, not *ever*. "How was the Gathering?"

"I need to ask you something." Dovepaw was looking anxious. The Clan was beginning to stir outside the den.

"What?"

Dovepaw leaned closer as Ivypaw sat up. "Tell me about Tigerheart again." Her ears twitched. "Is he *really* training in the Dark Forest?"

Ivypaw lowered her gaze. "Yes," she murmured. "I'm sorry."

"Don't be." Dovepaw sighed. "I don't think he ever loved me."

Ivypaw jerked up her muzzle. "Don't say that!"

Dovepaw shook her head. "You don't understand."

"I do!" Ivypaw leaped out of her nest and pressed against Dovepaw. "Tigerstar tricked him just like he tricked me!"

Dovepaw stared at her. "What do you mean?"

"It was all a lie—"

"Wait!" Dovepaw cut her off. "Lionblaze and Jayfeather need to hear this, too."

Ivypaw stared at her sister. What was she talking about? What did they have to do with it?

"Just trust me." Dovepaw nosed Ivypaw to her paws and jostled her out of the den.

Jayfeather was padding from the warriors' den with a bundle of withered herbs in his jaws. He seemed to sense Dovepaw, because he turned his blind gaze on them and narrowed his eyes. Then he tucked the herbs under a stone by the den entrance and hurried over.

"Is everything okay?" he asked.

"We're fine," Dovepaw told him. "Where's Lionblaze?"

"I'm here." The golden warrior was bounding down the tumble of rocks from Highledge.

"We need to talk," Dovepaw hissed. She headed for the entrance with Jayfeather and Lionblaze on her tail.

What's going on? There seemed to be as many secrets here as there were in the Dark Forest.

Dovepaw led them up the steep slope outside the entrance, forged her way through the drifted snow, and hopped over a fallen tree. The ground behind was clear where the trunk had held back the drift. Dovepaw crouched against the rotting bark as Jayfeather and Lionblaze settled beside her. Ivypaw balanced on the trunk for a moment before jumping down next to them. They huddled together, cocooned from the bitter wind.

"Go on, Ivypaw," Dovepaw prompted. "Tell them."

Ivypaw looked from Jayfeather to Lionblaze. Their pelts were pricking with expectation. She took a deep breath and began. "I've been visiting the Dark Forest in my dreams."

"Tell us something new," Jayfeather grunted.

Ivypaw blinked. "Tigerstar's been training me," she went on, trying to squash the butterflies leaping in her belly. "And Hawkfrost. They told me they wanted me to be a great warrior so I could protect my Clan."

"And you believed them?" Lionblaze snapped.

Dovepaw turned on him. "Let her *tell* you!" she snarled.

Ivypaw glanced gratefully at her sister. "Tigerstar said that he was loyal to ThunderClan. That he'd been born Thunder-Clan and he'd never stopped feeling like a ThunderClan cat."

Jayfeather was nodding slowly. "Okay."

"I just wanted to be as good as Dovepaw," Ivypaw explained. "I wanted to be so good that everyone would notice me, too."

She was relieved to see Lionblaze's gaze soften. "You're a good apprentice, Ivypaw, and you're going to make a fine warrior. Don't try competing with your sister."

Why not? The old jealousy sparked beneath Ivypaw's pelt. *What's so special about her?* "It's over now. I know the truth. Tigerstar and his warriors are planning to attack all the Clans. They want to destroy us. I'm never going back to the Dark

Forest." She felt bone tired as tension eased from her muscles.

"How will you stop?" Jayfeather's mew took her by surprise.

"Stop what?"

"When you go to sleep, do you *choose* to dream about the Dark Forest?" Jayfeather pressed.

Ivypaw narrowed her eyes. "I . . . I guess not. I just wake up there," she admitted.

Jayfeather sat up. "Good."

What do you mean? What if I wake up there again, without wanting to? Ivypaw felt sick. "W-why is that good?"

"Because you're going to spy for us," Jayfeather declared.

Ivypaw started to tremble. "But I don't want to go there again."

"Too late." Jayfeather shrugged. "You joined the Dark Forest. Do you think Tigerstar's going to let you go after training you so hard?"

"But I don't want to train anymore!"

Jayfeather wasn't listening. His blind blue eyes seemed to be boring into hers. "They don't know you've changed your mind, do they?"

Ivypaw shook her head, unable to speak.

"Then you must keep training with them and tell us everything you find out."

Ivypaw's chest throbbed. "You want me to *spy* on them?"

"Of course." Jayfeather smoothed his whiskers with a paw. "You were ready to betray us. Why not betray them?"

Dovepaw sat up sharply. "She didn't know she was betraying us—"

Jayfeather interrupted her. "She was training with Tiger-star," he snapped. "How was that ever going to be good for ThunderClan?"

Lionblaze tucked his tail over his front paws. "I think it's a good idea."

Ivypaw felt as if she were caught in another terrible dream.

"But only," Lionblaze went on, "if Ivypaw agrees."

Ivypaw felt Mapleshade's paws on her shoulders, pressing her down into the riverbed. "No!" She just wanted to be an ordinary apprentice again, fetching moss for Mousefur and Purdy, learning to hunt in a real forest with real cats. "I'm not going back."

"You may not have the choice," Jayfeather muttered.

Dovepaw's tail was flicking. "Let me talk to her on my own. Please." Lionblaze dipped his head and leaped up onto the trunk.

"Come on," he called to Jayfeather. "Let's leave this to Dove-paw." Jayfeather gave a small sigh and followed his brother.

As their paw steps crunched away through the snow, Ivypaw looked at her sister. "What's going on?"

Dovepaw settled back into a crouch. "There's something that you still don't know."

"What?"

"Climb over the trunk and go do something."

"Like what?"

"Anything." Dovepaw blinked at her. "Throw a snowball; climb a tree. It doesn't matter. Just make sure I can't hear you or see you."

Puzzled, Ivypaw scrambled onto the trunk and bounded away through the snow. She looked back and saw nothing, then headed farther away. Once she knew Dovepaw wouldn't be able to hear her, she slid behind a tree and dug a hole in the snow. Then she filled it in and hurried back to her sister.

"Well?" she panted.

"You dug a hole, and then you filled it in," Dovepaw told her.

Ivypaw felt dizzy. "Did you follow me?"

"Did you see my paw prints?"

Ivypaw shook her head. "Then how did you know?"

Her sister was silent for a moment, gazing at her with wet blue eyes. "I can hear everything," she blurted out. "I can smell everything too, if I set my mind to it."

Ivypaw snorted. "Shut up! You're just showing off again! No cat can smell and hear everything."

Dovepaw lashed her tail. "I'm *not* showing off. Sometimes I wish that I were. I have special powers. I'm part of a prophecy that says three cats will have more power than the stars in their paws. Jayfeather and Lionblaze are the other two cats. That's why they listen to me. That's why Firestar listens to me."

"Firestar listened to me when I told him about my dream!" Ivypaw pointed out.

"But you made it up!" Dovepaw thrust her muzzle in Ivypaw's face. "This is *real*! Right now I can hear Hollowpaw getting lectured for not getting the ticks out of Pouncetail's pelt yesterday. I can hear Dewkit and Mistkit fighting in their nest over who gets first bite of the stinky old sparrow

Crowfrost brought them. I can hear Heathertail showing Harespring a new route through the thickest patch of gorse, and Onestar is washing—".

"Stop!" Ivypaw struggled to keep up. "You can really hear all that?"

Dovepaw nodded. "Everything. I heard the beavers."

"That's how you knew they were stopping the water!" Things that had puzzled Ivypaw for a long time were starting to make a strange kind of sense. "That's why Firestar sent *you* on the mission, even though you were only an apprentice." Her head was spinning. "So Firestar knows, too?"

"Yes, but only Firestar."

Ivypaw's pelt felt hot and prickly. "Why didn't you tell me before?" She didn't give Dovepaw a chance to reply. "Didn't you realize how much it hurt to see you being singled out like some kind of super apprentice?"

Dovepaw shuffled her paws. "I wasn't allowed to tell anyone. No cat knows about Jayfeather and Lionblaze, except Firestar."

"But they knew about each other, right? And I bet Hollyleaf knew!" Ivypaw was starting to seethe. "It's your fault I went to the Dark Forest!!"

Dovepaw stared at her. "Wha-what do you mean?"

"The first time I met Hawkfrost, it wasn't in the Place of No Stars; it was in a field with flowers and sunshine and stuff like that. He . . . he flattered me; he seemed interested in what I could do, not what my sister could do. No cat has ever treated me like that in this Clan. I'm just your shadow here."

"That's not true!" Dovepaw hissed.

"But that's how it *felt*! You can't blame me for listening to Hawkfrost, for wanting to learn all the moves that he taught me."

"No cat is blaming you." Dovepaw sighed.

Ivypaw narrowed her eyes to slits. "Are you sure? Lionblaze and Jayfeather don't trust me. Maybe they want me to go back to the Dark Forest and stay there!"

Dovepaw flattened her ears. "Don't be ridiculous! Can't you see that we *need* you? Without knowing exactly what's going on in the Dark Forest, the prophecy is useless. You got your wish: You're the special one now."

Ivypaw blinked. "I wish I weren't," she whispered. "I'm scared."

Her sister rested her tail on Ivypaw's shoulders. "I know," she mewed softly. "We all are, even the cats in StarClan. I think that we could be all that stands between the Dark Forest and the end of the Clans." Suddenly she looked tiny, huddled into a crouch with the snow banked around her.

"I'll help you if I can," Ivypaw promised in a rush. This wasn't just about her now—in fact, it wasn't about her at all. It was about every cat who lived beside the lake.

"Tell Jayfeather and Lionblaze that I'll go back. I'll pretend I'm still one of them, and I'll find out everything I can about their plans."

CHAPTER 24

Flametail folded the catmint in an ivy leaf and pushed it into his store among the brambles. He began to lay the tansy stems side by side, ready to bundle. They blurred in front of his eyes. A yawn overtook him.

"Flametail."

Far away someone was calling his name.

"Flametail!" Kinkfur nudged him with her nose. "Didn't you hear me?"

"Sorry." Flametail turned, blinking. "Did you want something?" Inwardly he sighed. He didn't know if he had energy left to help any more cats.

"Please, come and check on Mistkit. She's lost her voice."

"I'll be there in a moment," Flametail promised. "I have to put these away first."

As the queen ducked out of the medicine den, Littlecloud's nest rustled. The tabby's brown nose appeared over the edge. "You should get some rest," he advised. His voice was still thick, but there was more life in it than before. "Did you sleep last night?"

Flametail padded heavily over to his mentor's nest. "A bit."

Littlecloud's eyes were brighter, and though his pelt was still clumped, it was freshly groomed. "I thought so." Slowly he sat up. "You were tossing and turning."

"Bad dream," Flametail admitted.

"The same one?" Littlecloud prompted.

"Yes." For the last quarter moon Flametail hadn't had a moment's sleep undisturbed by the same vision of falling far, far down into endless darkness while around him cats shrieked and yowled in terror.

"But no details?"

Flametail turned back to the tansy. "StarClan just sends the darkness," he murmured. "They don't send any clues. I don't know who'll strike first or how we should prepare."

Littlecloud leaned forward. "Our warrior ancestors are with us," he soothed. "Otherwise they wouldn't be warning you. Perhaps they don't know either. They'll share it with you when they do."

"Or with *you*," Flametail countered.

A purr caught in Littlecloud's throat. The first in a while. "Don't worry," he rasped. "I don't plan to be joining our ancestors for a long time." A cough shook him.

Flametail tensed. "Do you want more catmint?"

Littlecloud shook his head. "I'm getting better," he assured Flametail.

"I want to be sure of that." Flametail began to reach into his store.

"My fever has gone, and my chest is loosening. Save the catmint. Leaf-bare always drags on longer than you think."

Flametail turned his gaze toward his denmate. "I'm glad we didn't lose you."

"You and me both." Littlecloud's eyes glowed. "Now go check on Mistkit."

Flametail gathered the tansy stems together, putting one aside, and pushed them into the store with the catmint.

"Check Cedarheart, too," Littlecloud went on. "I heard coughing from the elders' den last night."

"Okay." Flametail picked up the tansy stem and headed for the entrance.

Kinkfur was pacing outside her den. She hurried to greet Flametail. "Mistkit was chattering like a starling this morning, but when she woke after her nap, she couldn't speak."

"Don't worry." Flametail hopped through the den entrance. "Even if she's sick, we have herbs now."

It was warm and dark inside the nursery. Sparrowkit was charging across the sandy floor, a moss ball only whiskers from his grasp. He batted it upward, and Dewkit jumped, snatching the ball in her paws. Sparrowkit lunged, knocking Dewkit into Flametail. Flametail dodged out of the way.

"Careful," Kinkfur warned, pushing into the den.

Mistkit peeked out from a nest woven from hazel stems.

Sparrowkit untangled himself from Dewkit. "Mistkit's really sick!'

"We'll have her better in no time." Flametail dropped the stem beside the nest. He sniffed at the kit. She was warm, but there was no sourness on her. If anything, it was whitecough. He nipped off one end of the tansy and laid it carefully at Kinkfur's paws.

"Chew it up and give her the pulp to swallow after her next feed," Flametail instructed.

Kinkfur nodded and pawed the stem out of the way as Sparrowkit and Dewkit bounced over to investigate.

"Blargh!" Dewkit shuddered.

Sparrowkit made a face. "Does she have to eat herbs?"

Flametail leaned down till his nose was level with theirs. "Don't go too near her, or you'll have to eat herbs, too." He left Sparrowkit squeaking with disgust and nosed his way out of the den.

Cedarheart was lying outside the elders' den, his flanks shuddering as he swallowed back a cough.

"Here." Flametail dropped the rest of the tansy stem in front of the old tom's muzzle. "Chew this," he advised. "Make sure you swallow it all."

Cedarheart pushed it away. "Save it for the young 'uns," he croaked. "I've survived this long. A cough won't harm me."

"Probably not," Flametail agreed. "But swallow it anyway. It'll make my life easier."

"In that case . . ." Cedarheart scooped up the tansy with his tongue, chewed it, grimacing, then swallowed. "I'll be more glad to see this newleaf than I've ever been," he grunted.

Flametail yawned. "I think I'd better stretch my legs," he meowed. "Or I'll be asleep before the dusk patrol leaves."

He headed for the camp entrance. Outside, the air was already brittle with frost.

Shrieks sounded from the lake. Flametail pricked his ears.

Was a cat in trouble? Then he recognized the voices of Redwillow and Pinepaw. They didn't sound in fear for their lives. In fact, they sounded *happy*.

Paws pounded over the frozen snow toward him. A tortoiseshell pelt flashed, and Olivenose skidded to a halt beside him. She was out of breath. "We're playing on the lake! It's completely frozen," she panted. "You could walk right over to RiverClan territory if you wanted."

Dawnpelt caught up to her. "I'm going to fetch Scorchfur and Owlclaw!" She trotted past, heading for camp. "Go and play, Flametail," she called over her shoulder. "You've been looking much too worried lately. Go and have some fun." She disappeared into the brambles.

Flametail's paws pricked. It had been a long time since he'd felt carefree. He'd been turning into an elder, obsessed with aches and pains and worrying about every cough and sneeze.

Olivenose bounded away. "Come on!"

Flametail raced after her, weaving between the bushes down to the shore. The Twoleg halfbridge jutted out into whiteness, clamped by ice. Olivenose trotted along the wooden boards and beckoned from the end with her tail. Flametail caught up to her and stood at the edge of the bridge.

The lake was completely frozen, a broad sheet of ice glowing pink under the sinking sun. Redwillow, several fox-lengths from the shore, raced over the gleaming whiteness, then flung himself down and skidded, spinning, on his belly. Yowls of amusement followed him from where Crowfrost and Ratscar stood watching. Even the senior warriors were enjoying themselves.

Olivenose jumped down from the halfbridge and landed on the ice. "Come on; it's safe," she called.

Nervously, Flametail hopped down, relieved to find the ice firm beneath his paws. He tentatively padded away from the halfbridge, heading for where Starlingpaw and Pinepaw were sliding stones to each other.

"What are you playing?" Flametail called.

Pinepaw jumped up. "Well done, Olivenose!" she meowed. "Now we've got enough players."

Starlingpaw trotted up to Flametail. "We want to play prey-stone. It's this game we just made up." He called to Pinepaw. "Slide the stone over here!" He stopped the smooth fat stone with an expert paw as Pinepaw slid it fast over the ice.

"This is the prey," he explained, pushing the stone toward Flametail. "Over there is the prey-hole." He flicked his tail and Flametail peered across the ice.

"It's not a real hole, but all the ice between that tree and that holly bush"—Starlingpaw flicked his tail toward the shore—"is where the stone's safe. If you get in there, you win. If me and Pinepaw stop you, we win, and we have to swap places."

Flametail narrowed his eyes. "Got it." He put his paw on the stone.

Olivenose padded past him. "I'm on your team," she told him. "Slide the stone to me if they block your path."

Starlingpaw and Pinepaw were already taking up position guarding the "prey-hole."

Flametail quickly realized it would be impossible just to slide the stone past them. Instead he turned and began batting it away from them. "Keep up with me!" he called to Olivenose. She scampered a few tail-lengths away from him and stayed level as he pushed the stone farther out across the lake. The ice was freezing under his paws, lightly dusted with snow, but wonderfully slippery.

Out of the corner of his eye, Flametail spotted a group of ThunderClan cats stepping gingerly onto the ice near their territory. He didn't care. There were no boundaries on the lake. Anyway, he was a medicine cat. He could go wherever he chose. As he picked up speed, he stopped lifting his paws and let them skate over the surface instead. The wind rippled his fur, and he felt as if he were flying. He let himself glide, then shoved the stone toward Olivenose.

She stopped it with a paw and spun around. "Let's attack!" she yowled.

Flametail turned and, matching Olivenose's speed, headed back toward Pinepaw and Starlingpaw. They were crouched on the ice, eyes narrowed and fixed on the stone, ready to lunge and stop it whisking past them.

"Here!" Olivenose sent the stone toward him.

Flametail caught it, not missing a step as he skated forward. He batted it back to Olivenose. She was ready and parried it back toward him. Starlingpaw and Pinepaw looked from side to side, trying to follow the stone as Flametail and Olivenose flicked it between them faster and faster, all the time closing in on the prey-hole.

Flametail fixed his gaze on the gap between the two apprentices and, with an almighty shove, flung the stone across the ice. It whizzed toward the gap, straight as a diving hawk. Flametail slowed to a halt and watched it get closer and closer with excitement rising in his belly.

"I've got it!" Pinepaw yelled to her denmate, and flung herself across the ice. She slid on her belly as fast as a snake and stopped the stone dead with an outstretched paw. Yowling in triumph, she hurled it back out across the ice. It hurtled past Flametail, shooting toward the middle of the lake. Flametail turned, paws skidding, and raced after it.

He skated past Ratscar and Crowfrost, chasing the stone as it whirled onward. With a rush of satisfaction he saw it slow and slide to a halt. Dropping onto his belly, he slid after it.

Crack!

The world split beneath him.

Terror gripped Flametail's chest as he felt the ice heave under his paws and tip him into the water. He slid into the freezing depths with a shriek. The water was instantly black around him. It dragged at his fur, so cold it felt like claws.

Above him, the light faded as the water sucked him down.

This is what I was seeing in my dream!

He began to churn with desperate paws, fighting for the surface.

Why didn't StarClan tell me?

He blinked, focusing on which way the bubbles around him were drifting, then headed upward with a surge of hope. His paws thudded against a solid wall.

No!

He could see light beyond the whiteness, and scrabbled toward it. This time his claws ripped against the jagged underside of the ice. He saw movement above him, shadows over the ice. He heard yowls and mews calling his name as paws thundered above him.

Then the water began to pull him down. He was too tired to fight it. As the noise and chaos faded, Flametail felt numbness spread through his body. He let his paws grow still, allowed the water to cradle him.

Such quiet.

Such calm.

Suddenly the water started to churn. Flecks of ice and bubbles floated around him. He saw silky gray fur wafting near him.

Jayfeather? Had the ThunderClan medicine cat fallen in, too? *It's quiet here.* He wanted to reassure his fellow medicine cat that everything was okay. *Don't fight it.*

Suddenly claws tugged Flametail's fur. Jayfeather had grabbed hold of him. He was trying to pull him up. *Where did you learn to swim underwater?*

Through the darkening depths, Flametail could see Jayfeather's eyes; though blind, they seemed to be pleading with him. He stared back. *It's hopeless. The ice has blocked us in.*

The current was pulling harder now, drawing them down despite Jayfeather's flailing and struggling.

Then Flametail saw another pair of eyes. Bulging and white. There was a third cat in the water. A grotesque creature.

Hairless and scarred. Flametail stared at it as it seemed to float beside them. A tiny part of his mind wondered if this was a StarClan cat he hadn't met yet. But did any warriors, past or present, ever look like that?

The ugly cat reached toward Jayfeather.

Let him go!

Flametail heard the voice in his head. It wasn't speaking to him. It was speaking to Jayfeather.

It is his time to die, not yours. Let him go!

Flametail felt Jayfeather's claws unhook from his pelt. He began to sink, gazing up at the fading light.

Darkness swept over Flametail and the sunlight vanished forever.

CHAPTER 25
🍀

Ivypaw spotted a shrew scampering over the snow. She shot after it, lunging and pinning it by its tail before it realized what was happening. She muttered her thanks to StarClan and bent to give the killing bite.

The shrieking from the lake swelled. Now a shrill edge sharpened the yowls. Ivypaw lifted her head. The prey dangled from her jaws as she strained to hear, and she wished for a moment that she had her sister's abilities. Then she unwished. It must be a real nuisance to have such power. How did Dovepaw ever manage to sleep?

The screeches from the lake echoed strangely in the frosty air. Ivypaw had wanted to go and play on the ice with Blossomfall and Rosepetal. But she'd promised herself she'd hunt for the Clan until she'd caught enough to make up for the herbs she'd cost her Clanmates. She knew she had to take at least half the blame for getting caught on the ShadowClan border. And it sounded like ThunderClan already owed Dovepaw more than they could ever repay.

She padded to a gnarled oak and began to dig between its roots. Beneath the snow lay a mouse and sparrow. She'd hunted since before sunhigh, and now weariness weighed down her paws. Scooping the two bodies out, she picked them up gently between her teeth and headed back to camp.

By the time she reached the barrier of thorns, the sun had dipped behind the treetops, and shadows enfolded the camp. Her Clanmates milled beneath Highledge, their pelts ruffled.

Jayfeather was padding toward his den. Ivypaw saw with surprise that his pelt was drenched. Leafpool fluttered around him and followed him through the brambles.

Ivypaw dropped her catch on the solitary squirrel and skinny starling that made up the fresh-kill pile. Graystripe came to admire her contribution. "Nice catch."

"I've been hunting all day," Ivypaw confessed.

Firestar's mew rang across the clearing. "Let all cats old enough to catch their own prey gather beneath Highledge."

Thornclaw and Dustpelt padded from the warriors' den. Poppyfrost hurried from the nursery while Daisy shooed the kits back inside the bramble den. Foxleap was already pacing, fur standing on end, at the foot of the rocks. Rosepetal watched him, her eyes round and dark, while Berrynose barged past Toadstep and Icecloud to sit at the front. Brambleclaw settled at the bottom of the rock tumble and stared at his paws, while Squirrelflight sat down a few tail-lengths away.

Ivypaw spotted her sister scurrying from the dirtplace tunnel. She joined her beside Whitewing. "What's going on?" she whispered.

Whitewing shook her head and sighed.

"I have bad news," Firestar began. "Flametail was playing

on the lake and fell through the ice," the ThunderClan leader announced.

Poppyfrost gasped. "Is he dead?"

"His body has not been found." Firestar glanced toward the medicine den. "Jayfeather tried to save him, but Flametail was too heavy."

Squirrelflight's pelt bristled. "Is Jayfeather all right?"

Firestar nodded. "He's cold, but Leafpool is with him. She'll know what to do."

Brambleclaw's eyes darkened. Flametail was his littermate's son. Ivypaw knew he'd feel the loss most sharply.

"In the future"—Firestar's mew hardened—"any cat caught on the ice will be severely punished."

Foxleap's whiskers twitched. "Yeah," he whispered. "By *death*."

Squirrelflight hushed him with a flick of her tail.

Ivypaw felt her mother's tail slip around her. "Promise you won't go on the ice," Whitewing murmured.

"Of course not," Dovepaw meowed.

"No way." Ivypaw shuddered, remembering her terrible panic when Mapleshade held her underwater in the black river.

Firestar leaped down from the Highledge and headed for the medicine den.

"Did any other ShadowClan cats fall in?" Dovepaw called to Foxleap as the young tom headed for the fresh-kill pile.

He shook his head. "Just Flametail."

Ivypaw shuffled closer to Dovepaw. "Are you all right?"

Her sister's ears were twitching. "We nearly lost Jayfeather," she murmured.

"But he's alive, right?"

Dovepaw nodded. "What if it had been Tigerheart?" Her eyes clouded.

"But it wasn't." Ivypaw brushed Dovepaw's flank with her tail. "I bet you can hear him now."

Dovepaw lifted her muzzle. Ivypaw could see her ears twitch as she strained to listen. Her sister's faraway gaze softened. "He's sitting vigil with the others." She snapped her attention back to Ivypaw. "It's like I can hear the emptiness where Flametail was." Dovepaw pressed closer. "It must be awful to lose a littermate." She wrapped her tail around Ivypaw. "You don't have to go to the Dark Forest, you know."

Ivypaw's chest tightened. She wasn't sure that she had any choice. It wasn't like in the beginning, when her dreams had carried her to the meadow and she'd chosen to follow Hawkfrost into the woods. Now she opened her eyes straight into darkness whether she wanted to or not. But she had promised she would do this.

She wanted to help her Clan.

She wanted to help Dovepaw.

As she settled into her pile of moss, Ivypaw felt her sister bend over her.

"I'll sleep next to you in your nest if you want," Dovepaw offered. "Then I can wake you up if you seem to be in trouble."

Ivypaw shook her head. "I've been there loads of times before, remember?" she mewed under her breath. "I'll be okay." *I hope.* She closed her eyes.

It was a long time before sleep overtook her. Dovepaw's breathing had slowed by the time Ivypaw's weary limbs relaxed and she slid into darkness. She opened her eyes and tasted the air. For the first time, her paws trembled.

"Hello, Ivypaw."

She turned, flustered. Tigerstar was standing beside a straight, dark pine as if he'd been waiting for her. Fighting back panic, Ivypaw swallowed hard. She forced her muscles to loosen and met the dark warrior's curious gaze. "Hi."

Tigerstar watched her a moment. "Have you seen Tigerheart?"

"He's sitting vigil for Flametail," she mewed. "He may not come tonight."

"Flametail, eh?" Tigerstar shrugged. He clearly knew all about the medicine cat's death. "That's one less, I guess."

You fox-heart!

Tigerstar padded around her, letting his tail sweep her flank. "I'm glad *you* came."

"What are we practicing tonight?" Ivypaw prayed the brightness in her mew was convincing.

"We may train later, but first I thought we should all get to know each other a little better." He padded away between the soaring trunks. Mist puddled around his paws, swirling as he walked. "Are you coming?"

Ivypaw trotted after him. She felt sure her heart was

pounding hard enough for anyone to hear. *I must keep calm. I'm doing this for Dovepaw and my Clan.*

She saw shapes in shadows around her. The dark outlines of warriors. As she followed Tigerstar deeper into the forest, she became aware that cats were everywhere, waiting in the mist, their paws scuffing the earth as they paced.

Were these Clan cats or Dark Forest warriors? She peered through the shadows, trying to recognize pelts. There was Mapleshade, scowling from the darkness. Scarred and ragged warriors circled her, growling and muttering to each other.

"I—I didn't know there were so many cats here," she mewed to Tigerstar.

"There are enough to match StarClan," he answered calmly.

The trees opened into a gloomy clearing. She recognized the boulder they'd trained on almost a moon before. Thistle-claw was sharpening his claws on the smooth rock, admiring their clean tips between each scratch. Hawkfrost nodded a greeting to Ivypaw, while Darkstripe paced behind him. Shredtail and Snowtuft were there too. And, in the boulder's shadow, unmoving and watchful, sat Brokenstar.

Ivypaw was relieved to see Hollowpaw, Antpelt, and Breeze-pelt. She'd begun to fear she was the only Clan cat here. Tigerstar glanced back at her. "You may as well sit with your friends," he murmured. "I've an announcement to make."

They're not my friends! Yet she hurried toward the familiar faces and felt less nervous as she settled among them.

Tigerstar jumped onto the boulder. "Gather all cats old enough to catch their own prey." There was a sneer in his voice, and the cats circling the rock purred in mocking amusement.

"The time is close!" Tigerstar growled.

Shapes moved from among the trees. More warriors began to stream from the shadows. Ivypaw's heart pounded harder, and she huddled closer to Antpelt.

"The day is nearing!" Tigerstar's growl became a hiss. "We are going to invade the world of the Clans and destroy them and their warrior code, once and for all."

Ivypaw felt Antpelt tense beside her. Was he shocked? She searched his face, then Hollowpaw's and Breezepelt's. Their eyes were shining! It was as if they were truly Dark Forest warriors. Struggling to hide her horror, Ivypaw scanned the clearing. Cats filled every tail-length, yowling in fury.

"We'll kill them all!"

"The days of the Clans are over."

Mapleshade reared and slashed at the air. "They'll be sorry we ever kitted them!"

Ivypaw pricked her ears. When were they going to attack? But Tigerstar only bared his teeth and slid, hissing, from the boulder. He slipped into the throng of cats, and Ivypaw lost sight of him. The air crackled with excitement as the cats paced and wove around each other, bristling.

A pair of eyes glinted at Ivypaw, and she found herself unsheathing her claws as Darkstripe padded toward her.

"Are you ready for the battle of your life?" There was a taunt in his mew.

Ivypaw glanced at the forest, wishing she could disappear into its shadows.

"Or do you want to leave?" Darkstripe seemed to guess what she was thinking.

"N-no, of course not."

"Good." He circled her, letting his tail slither over her spine. It felt like a snake, cold and heavy. Ivypaw wished Tigerheart were with her.

"Ivypaw!"

She looked up hopefully, disappointed when she saw Brokenstar heading toward them. The massive, scarred tom dipped his head to her. "Greetings, Ivypaw. I've been watching you train." He shouldered Darkstripe out of the way. "Very impressive."

Ivypaw met his gaze, keeping Darkstripe at the edge of her vision. Why was Brokenstar singling her out? Was he trying to make Darkstripe jealous?

"I have a special mission for you," Brokenstar went on.

Ivypaw blinked. "Really?" Maybe it was a kind of assessment.

"Follow me." Brokenstar headed into the trees.

Ivypaw trotted after him, her breath quickening as the dark tom climbed over a low rise and jumped down into an empty streambed. The gully meandered between twisted trunks and led them under low-slung branches that dripped with dusty gray moss. Ivypaw ducked beneath them, shuddering as the moss left cobwebby smears on her pelt.

She paused. Something was flitting through the brittle ferns on the bank. She peered through the mist, stiffening when she recognized Darkstripe's pelt.

"Go away, Darkstripe!" Brokenstar's yowl made Ivypaw

jump. She wasn't the only one to have spotted the shadow.

The scrawny outline froze, then slid from sight.

"He's no better than a whining kit," Brokenstar muttered. He flicked his tail toward the nearest tree. "Show me your climbing skills."

"Okay." Ivypaw leaped onto the lowest branch and clawed her way up the thick, knotted trunk. When her paws started to ache, she stopped to catch her breath and looked up. There was still no sign of sky. *How tall is this tree?* Far below, she could see Brokenstar watching from the streambed.

"Not bad!" Brokenstar called. "See if you can get down faster, though."

Concentrating hard, Ivypaw let herself drop a tail-length at a time, clutching at the bark to control her fall. As the ground grew near, she pushed away from the tree and landed nimbly on a patch of slimy grass at the edge of the gully.

Brokenstar bounded up the bank and joined her. "Now show me an attack lunge."

Ivypaw crouched down, unsheathed her claws, and focused on a clump of moss a few tail-lengths ahead. She sprang and hit the moss squarely, then flipped over, lashing out with her hind legs before jumping back onto all fours.

"You're fast." Brokenstar faced her. "How are your defensive moves?" The words still hung in the air as he pounced.

Just in time, Ivypaw saw his claws flash and ducked. With a jerk of her spine, she rolled out of his way. She guessed he'd anticipate her and shot forward as soon as her paws hit the ground.

She was right. Brokenstar's claws pierced the spot where she'd been a half moment earlier. She spun around and confronted him, hackles up, teeth bared, prepared for another attack.

Brokenstar sat down. "Nice."

Ivypaw's heart was thudding so loud she was convinced Brokenstar would be able to hear it. Where was her mission? Was he just testing her skills?

"I have one final task for you before you can fight alongside your new Clanmates."

Ivypaw pricked her ears. This *was* an assessment! "What is it?"

Something moved in the shadows at the edge of the clearing. *Darkstripe?*

"Come out!" Brokenstar called.

Ivypaw gripped the earth as an orange-colored cat padded out of the ferns.

"Flametail?"

The ShadowClan medicine cat's eyes were stretched wide. "Did you fall through the ice, too?"

Ivypaw shook her head. "I—I . . ." Words choked in her throat. How could she explain why she was here? "H-how did *you* get here?"

"I was in StarClan." He squinted, puzzled, up through the branches. "I heard a noise in the bushes and followed it. It kept moving ahead of me, whispering my name, so I followed it until I got here. But . . . but this doesn't feel like StarClan anymore." He shifted his paws. "Do you know the way back?"

Ivypaw stared at him, not knowing what to say.

"Kill him." Brokenstar's order cut through the silence.

A bolt of panic shot through Ivypaw. "What?"

He can't mean it!

Then she understood. It was a trap—one that she wasn't going to fall into like a dandelion-brained rabbit. "I can't." She looked triumphantly at Brokenstar. "He's already dead."

He's not catching me out with stupid questions.

Brokenstar's whiskers quivered. "So young, so innocent," he growled. "No cat stays in StarClan forever. They all fade in the end." His gaze ran over Flametail as if the medicine cat were a juicy piece of prey. "Unless someone kills them first."

Ivypaw narrowed her eyes. "That's not true! This is where cats come for the rest of all the moons!"

"Oh, it's true," Brokenstar assured her. "It's also unimaginably painful to give up the last dying echo of one's life."

Ivypaw started to back away. "I'm not killing him."

Brokenstar's muzzle was suddenly a whisker from hers. His hot, rancid breath stung her eyes. "Why?" he hissed. "Are you a Dark Forest warrior or not?"

Ivypaw blinked. "I—I . . ."

Brokenstar's gaze scorched her. "I don't know why Hawkfrost chose you," he snarled. "I think your loyalties will always be with your Clanmates beside the lake." He stepped closer. "Which makes you dangerous."

"I thought you wanted dangerous cats," Ivypaw spat back. If she could defend herself convincingly, surely Brokenstar would let Flametail go?

Brokenstar's gaze didn't waver. "I know what your sister is."

"So?"

"You're her littermate."

"If you know so much," Ivypaw hissed, "then you must know that I'm not part of the prophecy."

"But you share her blood. Would you really betray that? Or should I kill her instead, to be sure that your loyalties are not divided?"

Leave Dovepaw out of it! Without Dovepaw, the Clans would be lost. Ivypaw lifted her chin. She was ready to die.

And yet . . .

If she died here, who would warn the Clans? She'd heard Tigerstar say that the battle was near. She had to go back. Which meant she had to persuade Brokenstar to let her live. There was only one thing to do.

"I'm loyal to the Dark Forest." She rounded on Flametail and crouched down, lashing her tail. *I'm sorry, Flametail, but I have to do this for the sake of our Clans!* She unsheathed her claws. *Forgive me, StarClan!*

As she sprang, there was a blur of dark brown fur, and something hard slammed into her. The force knocked her sprawling across the clearing. Blinking, she staggered to her paws.

Tigerheart!

"What are you doing?" he screeched, standing in front of Flametail. Horror and bewilderment flared in his eyes. "I won't let you destroy what's left of my brother!"

Tigerstar stalked from the shadows. "Oh, very brave. I see

my blood flowing in yours."

I'm sorry! Ivypaw tried to catch Tigerheart's eye. But the young warrior's gaze was darting between Tigerstar and Brokenstar. Spitting, he pressed against Flametail. "Leave him alone."

"Brokenstar." Tigerstar's mew was soothing. "There's no need to kill Flametail. He's no threat. He can only mix herbs."

Brokenstar swung his head around. "He means nothing to me, alive or dead. But what about *her*?" He flicked his tail toward Ivypaw.

Ivypaw hung her head, trying to catch her breath. Had she done enough to convince the Dark Forest cats that she was loyal to them, and not the Clans by the lake? She didn't dare think about what Tigerheart would do to her when they got back to the lake.

"We need all the warriors we can get," Tigerstar answered smoothly. Ivypaw jerked her head up.

"I believe that Ivypaw is loyal to the Place of No Stars. When the final battle comes, she will stand with us."

WARRIORS
ADVENTURE GAME

*Visit www.warriorcats.com
to download game rules, character sheets,
a practice mission, and more!*

Written by Stan! • Art by James L. Barry

UNINVITED GUESTS

Whichever previous adventure you played, consider that two moons have passed since then. Determine what age that makes all the cat characters (including the cat belonging to the person who will take the first turn as Narrator) and use the information found in the "Improving Your Cat" section of Chapter Four in the game rules to make the necessary changes.

Unless you are the first Narrator in this adventure, stop reading here. The information beginning in the next paragraph is for the Narrator only.

The Adventure Begins

Hello, Narrator! It's time to begin playing "Uninvited Guests." Make sure all the players have their character sheets, the correct number of chips, a piece of paper, and a pencil. Remember that the point of the game is to have fun. Don't be afraid to go slow, and refer to the rules if you aren't sure exactly what should happen next.

When you're ready, begin with **1** below.

1. Fox Hunt

Special Note: "Uninvited Guests" begins with the cats already in the middle of the action, hunting for a fox, but the players will not immediately know how their cats got there or why they're chasing the fox. The scene is set up so that you can have a flashback that gives the players that information. This can be a little tricky at first, and your players may be anxious about it, but by the time the scene is finished everything should be fine. If you are particularly nervous about this style of storytelling, simply use the material below to improvise an opening scene that begins in the Clan camp.

Read Aloud: "Your target is fast and clever, running through the woods at top speed, making sudden turns, and diving into deep brush. Following the trail is difficult, but that's your mission. The question is: Are you up to the job?"

Narrator Tips: Have all the players make Smell Checks (the Track Knack will be useful here, if any of the cats have it). The players may want to know what's happening, but tell them that everything will be explained *after* they make the Smell Check. If a cat's result on the Check is 5 or lower, that cat smells nothing. If the Check is between 6 and 10, the cat can smell the distinct scent of a fox, but it seems to be coming from several different places at once. Any cats who have totals of 11 or higher on the Check can pick up a clear scent leading away from the Lake.

Now explain to the players that their cats are on an important mission to track down a fox that has been stalking the Clan territories for a couple of days. Once they find the fox, they are supposed to chase it out of the area permanently. The Clans are all working together on this mission and every able-bodied warrior who isn't needed to protect the queens and kits is out doing the same thing the players' cats are.

Let the players act out the scene where they received their orders from a Clan leader (their leader, if they are all from the same Clan, or whatever leader you, as the Narrator, prefer if the cats in the group come from different Clans). This is a flashback scene, but it is also a chance for the players to ask questions and gather background information.

There isn't a lot that the leader can tell them. The fox's scent was first discovered a couple of days ago, but it seemed to be staying on the edges of the Clans' territories, avoiding the places that warriors and other Clan members went most frequently. Then, about a day or so ago the fox was scented and even seen near all the Clan camps—particularly close to each Clan's nursery. The Clan leaders thought the fox might be trying to steal kits, so they called for this massive hunt.

When the players are finished asking questions, the flashback is over and it's time to go back to the fox hunt. Tell the players that their cats started searching at dawn, finding nothing but stale scents of cats, mice, voles, and other creatures. But then they came across a reasonably fresh trail, and that's what they're following now. The scent is getting fresher, and the fox seems to be trying lots of tricks to throw off anyone that tries to follow her. That means there's a good chance she knows the cats are after her—she might even be nearby.

What Happens Next: The next phase of the adventure depends on the Smell Checks the players made at the very beginning of the scene.

If none of the cats' Check totals was higher than 5, continue with **17**.

If the best of the cats' Check totals was between 6 and 10, continue with **6**.

If some, but not all, of the cats' Check totals were 11 or higher, continue with **4**.

If all of the cats' Check totals were 11 or higher, continue with **5**.

2. Wrong Scent

Read Aloud: "The scent grows stronger as you come to a small meadow—where the trail ends. This is the spot."

Narrator Tips: Let the cats look around briefly, perhaps making See Checks to try to spot the fox. After a few moments it will become clear to them that there is nowhere in this meadow for a fox to hide. However, there are a few rabbits here, munching contentedly on the grass. As yet, they have not noticed the cats' presence.

What's happened is that the clever fox ran along a path used regularly by the rabbits, hoping that the appetizing smell of a potential meal would distract the cats from noticing that the fox scent is not particularly fresh. Unfortunately, the cats seem to have taken the bait and fallen off the fox's current trail. Now they are in a meadow full of rabbits, and they're starting to feel a little hungry.

Although the cats know that their duty is to rush back onto the fox's trail, their stomachs are beginning to grumble. Would anyone notice if they took a very brief break to catch a quick meal?

As the Narrator, your job here is a little complicated. You should make the players aware that their cats are tempted to take a break and hunt the rabbits, but also that they all know the proper thing to do is to get back to the fox hunt. It is up to the players to decide what the cats actually do.

What Happens Next: If the cats want to stay here and try to catch a quick meal, continue with **7**.

If the cats want to get back on the fox's trail, this is the end of the chapter. Hand the adventure to the next Narrator and tell him or her to continue with **3**.

3. An Important Message

Read Aloud: "Suddenly, you realize why the trail has been so difficult to follow. Not only did the same fox run over these paths multiple times, there is *also* the scent of a second fox along the trail! Between the pair of fox scents and the scent you cats are leaving on the trail, it's a big mess. But now you've got the scents straight!"

Narrator Tips: The insight the cats have made is going to make tracking down the fox much easier. However, things are about to get more complicated for the cats. After the players have finished processing this new information, tell them that their cats hear another warrior calling out their names.

A moment later, Ashfoot, the WindClan deputy, comes bounding up to the group. She has important news—two kits are missing.

A pair of WindClan kits—a brother and sister—have gone missing. They were last seen in the WindClan camp very early this

morning. They're a rambunctious pair who often find trouble in unlikely places. This time, though, it seems like trouble found them. When the queens went to the far corner of the WindClan camp, where the two usually go to hide, there was a hole in the camp's thorny wall and the kits were gone. What's worse, on the outside of the wall, they found fox scent everywhere. The Clans are now worried that there may be a pack of foxes moving into the territory.

Depending on how well the players' cats did on the earlier Smell Checks, the cats may already have some information about this. They may know that the fox has three cubs, and they may know that there is a WindClan kit out there somewhere. Let them share their knowledge with Ashfoot and talk about the best way to proceed.

When the discussions have ended, Ashfoot will tell the players' cats that they are doing well. She will go off to deliver her message to the groups of cats who are searching elsewhere. If the players' cats have given her any information, she will bring it back to the Clan leaders.

The cats now have a clear choice, based on the scents they've identified: They can either follow the adult fox or follow the new fox. (If they know about the fox cubs, or previously identified the scent of the WindClan kit, that will also help inform their decision.)

What Happens Next: If the cats follow the scent of the original fox they've been stalking, continue with **12**.

If the cats follow the new scent (of the fox cub), continue with **14**.

4. Mixed Scents

Read Aloud: "This is definitely the right scent trail! You're clearly getting closer to the fox. But wait . . . there's more than one scent in this trail!"

Narrator Tips: It becomes clear to the cats that there's more going on here than just a single fox running around in the Clan territories. The scent trail indicates that there are several foxes, but one scent is clearly dominant over the others. And there's another scent mixed in there but the cats can't immediately tell what it is.

Have each cat make either a Ponder or Smell Check (player's choice). These Checks may be boosted by the Animal Lore or Track Knacks, if the players like. Rather than working alone, a cat may decide to help one of the other cats with his or her Skill Check. To do this, the helping cat makes a Focus Check. The cat being helped then gets a bonus to his or her Check equal to half the total of the Focus Check. In this way, the cats can work together to get the best possible result.

If the highest Check total (including help) is 10 or higher, the cats figure out that there are five scents mixed into the scent trail. If the total is 14 or higher, they realize that four of the scents are fox cubs and the strongest scent is the mother fox. If the total is 17 or higher, they realize that there really are only three fox cubs—the fourth scent is a kit from WindClan.

What Happens Next: If the best of the cats' Check totals was 9 or lower, continue with **6**.

If the best of the cats' Check totals was 13 or lower, continue with **2**.

If the best of the cats' Check totals was 14 or higher, continue with **5**.

5. There She Is!

Read Aloud: "The scent trail is absolutely plain now—the overlapping tracks are easy to sniff through to find the freshest, most recent path. It is clear that the fox came this way only a short while ago. You've nearly got her!"

Narrator Tips: Improvise a final dash through the underbrush or over an obstacle, something that gives the players a sense of completion for their chase. At the end of that action, they find themselves on one side of a glade while the fox sits at the other side. It feels almost as if she has been waiting for the cats to arrive—and that in itself is more than a little suspicious.

Allow the cats to make Ponder Checks (or other Skill Checks that may seem appropriate) to figure out what's going on. Any cat that has the Animal Lore may use it without having to spend the Intelligence chip that is usually required to access a Knack. If the Check total is 8 or lower, the cat is sure that the fox is just toying with the group—making it *seem* as if she's running away, then doubling back to a section of the woods they've already searched. If a cat's Check total is 11 or lower, he or she notices that despite the fox's apparent relaxed posture, she seems poised to flee—and she's already leaning in the direction she will run. If the Check total is 12 or higher, the cat notices that while the fox is leaning and getting ready to run in one direction, she is glancing back in the opposite direction—almost as if she wants to go that way but is afraid to lead the cats there. If the Check total is 17 or higher, the cat realizes that the fox's backward glance is just another attempt to confuse the cats—perhaps it's a ploy to help her escape, or perhaps there really is something over there that she wants the cats to see. The fox is being so sly that it's almost impossible to tell what her *real* intentions are.

The big question is: What will the cats do with all this information? Because no sooner do they get it than the fox dashes away in the direction she was leaning.

Of course, the cats may not want to even think about such things. If they just want to charge ahead and chase after the fox, by all means allow them to do so.

What Happens Next: If the cats think the fox is going to double back to a place they've already searched and want to beat her to the location, continue with **6**.

If the cats want to follow the fox in the direction she is running or investigate the section of woods she was staring at, this is the end of the chapter. Hand the adventure to the next Narrator and tell him or her to continue with **3**. Tell the new Narrator to make note of which direction the cats were heading.

6. Running in Circles

Read Aloud: "Over the rotten log, through a bush, around that tree, back through the bush, back over the log . . . wait a minute! You've lost the trail."

Narrator Tips: The fox is very sly. She knows that there are many cats in the area, so wherever she went she carefully used as few paths through the woods as possible. The result is that her new scent trails are difficult to separate from her older ones, and that makes it hard to follow her. The cats have gotten caught in a loop, following the scent around in a circle that leads them back where they started, but at least they figured out the problem quickly. They still have time to get back on the right track.

Have each of the cats make another Smell Check, making sure they understand that they must find a way to do better than before—spending chips or using Knacks—otherwise they will not be able to find the fox.

What Happens Next: If none of the cats' Check totals was higher than 5, continue with **17**.

If the best of the cats' Check totals was between 6 and 10, continue with **2**.

If some, but not all, of the cats' Check totals were 11 or higher, continue with **4**.

If all of the cats' Check totals were 11 or higher, continue with **5**.

7. Stalking

Read Aloud: "So far, the wind is in your favor, and none of the rabbits are aware of your presence. There are three or four small and lean rabbits near you, and a much meatier one on the far side of the meadow."

Narrator Tips: The players need to decide which rabbit (or rabbits) they want to try to catch. They can easily leap onto one of the small ones nearby, but it won't make much of a meal. The larger rabbit is farther away and would have to be stalked, which would be difficult. In either case, going after one rabbit will certainly scare away all the others.

If the cats want to catch one of the small rabbits, they have to Pounce on it. The rabbit's Jump score is 5, and it can be taken down by just 1 chip's worth of damage. There are three small rabbits nearby, but the cats must time their Pounces so they happen at the same time. Otherwise, when the first cat Pounces, the remaining rabbits will flee.

If the cats want to catch the larger rabbit, they must first stalk it. What's more, they must do so without any of the rabbits in the field becoming aware of their presence. To do this, all the cats who are participating in the hunt must make Sneak Checks. The only result you, as Narrator, are concerned with, though, is the lowest total in the bunch—if one cat is clumsy, it will ruin the hunt for everyone.

If the lowest Sneak Check total is 7 or lower, the large rabbit senses the cats' approach and flees before they can Pounce.

If the lowest total is between 8 and 12, the large rabbit is unaware of the cats, but the smaller rabbits catch wind of them and flee. This warns the larger rabbit, who starts to flee before most of the cats are in position, but the group may select one of the cats to try to Pounce on it before it escapes.

If the lowest total is 13 or higher, all the cats get in position around the larger rabbit, and they can Pounce on it together.

The large rabbit has a Jump score of 8. In order to take it down, the cats must do 3 chips worth of damage to it; otherwise, it will escape before the cats can Pounce again.

If the cats succeed in catching a rabbit, they get to have a quick meal before going back on the fox's trail. If the cats caught the large rabbit, they can Refresh all of their spent chips. If they caught one or more of the smaller rabbits, each cat can Refresh one chip (and only one) from those that have been spent so far.

What Happens Next: If the cats decide that this was a bad idea after all and want to get back on the fox's trail, this is the end of the chapter. Hand the adventure to the next Narrator and tell him or her to continue with **3**.

If they tried to catch a rabbit, whether or not they were successful, continue with **9**.

8. Fox Fight

Read Aloud: "The fox looks at you, her eyes cold and vicious. If you want to fight, she is more than ready to oblige."

Narrator Tips: This scene focuses entirely on the fight between the players' cats and the fox. It uses the rules for fighting found in Chapter Five of the game rules.

Once the cats make it clear that they are going to attack, the fox will stand up and leave its den, nudging the cubs so that they stay put and glaring at the kit so that she does, too. But now the kit is free to call out to the cats. She asks them *not* to fight but to listen to what she has to say.

If the fight begins, it follows all the usual rules for fighting. The fox has a Jump score of 10, a Pounce score of 7, a Swat score of 10, and a Bite score of 8. The fox has Ability chips just like the players' cats do, and spends them in the same way. She has 5 Strength chips, 8 Intelligence chips, and 7 Spirit chips. For the purposes of this fight, the fox is treated just the same as a player's cat except that the Narrator controls all its movements.

The fox will fight until she is knocked out because she is fighting to protect her cubs. However, if the cats want to stop the fight at any time, she will also stop. Fighting is not what she wants to do, but if forced to she will fight to the best of her ability.

What Happens Next: If the cats decide to delay the fight and listen to what the kit has to say, continue with **16**.

If two or more of the cats are knocked out during the fight, continue with **13**.

If the cats win the fight and they've already found and

rescued the missing fox cub and WindClan kit, continue with **22**.

If the cats win the fight but they haven't yet found the missing fox cub and WindClan kit, continue with **16**.

9. Picking Up the Scent

Read Aloud: "The fox's scent is still around, but the trail is far from fresh. It has clearly been back and forth over this ground many times in the past few days, and finding the newest trail is even more difficult than before."

Narrator Tips: Taking a break to hunt has made the cats' work even harder. They are going to have to work together to find the right trail. Ask the players if they can think of anything the cats can do to improve their chances of finding the right scent. This is an opportunity for the players to get creative. If any of the ideas sound like they really would be helpful, give each player's cat a +1 bonus on the Check below.

Have each of the cats make a Smell Check (allowing the use of any Knacks that seem appropriate). Then have them add their Skill Check totals together to get a group total.

What Happens Next: If the group total is 20 or lower, continue with **17**.

If the group total is 21 or higher, this is the end of the chapter. Hand the adventure to the next Narrator and tell him or her to continue with **3**.

10. Up a Tree

Read Aloud: "The scent is getting stronger. The missing cub and kit must be close, but their scents are not on the ground.

They're drifting through the air. That's very strange, but surely it will all make sense once you find—wait . . . what's that new scent?"

Narrator Tips: The scent trail leads up to a copse of trees. The players' cats can smell the WindClan kit and fox cub's scents on the wind but not on the ground. This is very unusual—it's generally the way an owl's scent or a sparrow's scent comes through. The players may want to puzzle over that, but they have a more pressing issue—there's a new scent, too. This one is on the ground and coming from very nearby.

Have each of the cats make a Ponder Check (the Animal Lore Knack will be helpful) to see if they recognize the scent. Anyone who gets a Skill Check total of 7 or higher realizes that the new scent is a raccoon.

If the cats follow either scent trail, they enter into the copse of trees and find a strange sight. The kit and fox cub are in one of the trees, clinging to a narrow, low-hanging branch. Below them, a round-bellied raccoon is hissing and barking and swiping the air with its claws, furiously trying to get to them.

The kit sees the players' cats and calls out, telling them what happened.

He and the cub were just running around, having fun, when they accidentally tumbled into a raccoon. This made the raccoon angry, and it chased after them. At first this seemed

17

fun, too. The raccoon was heavy and slow, and the kit and cub were small and fast—they expected it would give up the chase soon enough. But it didn't. It kept coming, and it kept getting closer as the kit and cub grew tired. Soon it was almost on top of them, and they noticed just how sharp its teeth and claws were. In order to get away, he and the cub climbed this tree. This turned out not to be a great plan because the raccoon just climbed after them, so they went out on a branch that seemed too thin to bear the raccoon's weight. The plan worked—the raccoon couldn't come out on the branch after them—but they still underestimated its anger. Rather than going away, the raccoon simply climbed back down to the ground and has been there ever since.

The kit and cub both look terrified, exhausted, and desperate for the players' cats to do something to help. The question is: What will the group do?

What Happens Next: If the players' cats want to attack the raccoon, continue with **15**.

If the players' cats want to try something other than fighting, continue with **11**.

11. A Test of Wills

Read Aloud: "The raccoon hisses and growls at you. Even after all this time, it's still seething with anger at the kit and cub, but it's aware of your presence and seems to realize that you have it outnumbered."

Narrator Tips: The raccoon has no intention of leaving, so it is up to the players' cats to convince it otherwise. How they try to do that is up to them and, in great measure, the results depend on you, the Narrator. The players' cats can try any tactic they can imagine—using the Hiss or Arch Skills, charging at the raccoon as if they plan to attack and then backing away, finding some fresh-kill to offer in order to distract it, etc. It is up to you to decide how to use the game to resolve their actions.

The raccoon has a Strength score of 10, an Intelligence of 4, and a Spirit of 6, and it has Ability chips to spend just the way the players' cats do. It doesn't have as many advantages as the cats, but it does have a few Skills and Knacks. The raccoon has 4 levels of Hiss, 3 levels of See, and 2 levels of Smell. It also has the Leap Knack.

As an example, if the cats decide to try to scare the raccoon away by making noise, you'll probably want to have them make Hiss Checks. You may want to set a target number for a cat to try to beat on a single Skill Check, or set a higher number and have all the cats generate a group total, or let the raccoon make its own Hiss Check. Do whatever you think best fits the situation.

As the Narrator, your best guess is automatically right.

This scene continues until the cats succeed in chasing the raccoon away or they decide to switch tactics and fight it.

What Happens Next: If the cats decide that this isn't working and that it would be better to fight the raccoon, continue with **15**.

If the cats succeed in scaring away the raccoon, this is the end of the chapter. Hand the adventure to the next Narrator and tell him or her to continue with **20**.

12. Home and Family

Read Aloud: "The scent trail is finally clear. Before long, you come to a small clearing with a fallen log at the far end. Sitting in the hollow of the log is the fox. She glares at you, then looks down between her paws where you see she has one of the WindClan kits pinned. The kit is struggling to call out to you, but its words are muffled by fox fur."

Narrator Tips: Allow the players to ask any questions they want about the situation—don't rush them into making a decision about what to do next. Exactly what they find out will depend on what they ask, but below is a detailed summary so that you know how to answer clearly.

The fox, noticing how close the players' cats were to catching her, headed back to her den in the hollow of the log. When she went searching for her missing cub, she left the other two cubs and one of the WindClan kits, the she-cat, here sleeping. Knowing that the cats would arrive momentarily, she put the kit up front under her paw—a warning that she will hurt it if the cats come too close. Really, she has no plan to hurt the kit at all. She simply wants to get her missing cub back, and she blames the Clan cats for the fact that it is missing at all. (The kit can explain this reasoning, if the cats can get the fox to let her up so she can speak.) The other two fox cubs are now awake but hiding behind her, deeper in the den.

The fox is a clever animal, capable of communicating basic feelings by emotions—angry looks and sad whines—and pointing. She is not able to speak to the cats or make complex plans. The fox wants the cats to know that she is holding the kit until such time as her missing cub returns. She's also hinting that if she finds out that the cats hurt her cub, she will retaliate by hurting the kit. This may be too complicated a message to get across without words, but it's what the fox is thinking.

At first, it may seem that the fox is intentionally keeping the kit silent by covering its mouth with her paw. In fact, she is just trying to keep the kit from wriggling away and running back home. Unfortunately, at the moment, she is preventing the kit from calling out to the cats, which would help to clear up the situation.

What happens next depends entirely on how the players' cats react to this situation. The fox is not going to make the first move.

What Happens Next: If the cats decide to attack the fox, continue with **8**.

If the cats decide to leave and follow the other scent trail, continue with **14**.

If the cats do anything that involves staying near the fox's den but not starting a fight, continue with **16**.

13. Knocked Out!

Read Aloud: "When your eyes flutter open, you can see the friendly face of your Clan's medicine cat peering down at you."

Narrator Tips: A significant portion (or perhaps all) of the cats have been knocked out in a fight. While it might have been possible for the other cats to finish the adventure alone, they succeed or fail as a team.

Improvise an appropriate conclusion for the cats based on their actions. As long as they acted nobly and fought courageously, their Clan leader will be proud of them and say so. There is no shame in failing as long as you try your best. If they acted rashly or, worse, failed to uphold the warrior code, the leader will give them a more stern talking-to.

Some other warriors succeeded in finishing the mission and finding the kits. As Narrator, you can decide how that happened and tell the players that tale.

What Happens Next: The adventure is over. The players' cats do not get any Experience rewards for this adventure. The group *can*, however, play the adventure again, hopefully either being more careful about when to pick a fight or merely being better fighters.

14. The Other Trail

Read Aloud: "Knowing that there is a second scent on the trail makes everything clear. In fact, you're certain that this scent belongs to a fox cub, and the fox you've been chasing is its mother. But the cub hasn't been moving around nearly as frequently, so the trail is difficult to follow because it is hidden under the mother fox's scent."

Narrator Tips: The cats are hot on the trail of the second fox. This scene will require the cats to make one final Smell Check as a group. It also provides a chance to be sure that they have put together all the various snippets of information about the cub into an accurate understanding of the situation. As Narrator, you may ask the players to have their cats make Ponder Checks to see which ones understand things most clearly, but whatever the results are, the group as a whole should get all the following information.

The two main scent trails are the cub running around and exploring the woods and the mother fox looking for him. Sometime early today, the cub's scent was joined by the scent of a WindClan kit, and the two youngsters seem to be exploring and playing together. But then suddenly their scents stopped—they were no longer moving around—and their trail was buried under the scent of the mother fox as her search became more frantic.

In order to figure out the last place the cub and kit went, have each player make a Smell Check for his or her cat, and then add the Check totals together to get a group total.

What Happens Next: If the group total is 13 or lower, continue with **17**.

If the group total is 14 or higher, this is the end of the chapter. Hand the adventure to the next Narrator and tell him or her to continue with **10**.

15. Raccoon Ruckus

Read Aloud: "After the better part of a day, the raccoon is still snapping at the kit and cub. Clearly it's ready for a fight."

Narrator Tips: This scene focuses entirely on the fight between the players' cats and the raccoon. It uses the rules for fighting found in Chapter Five of the game rules.

From where it stands, the raccoon will hiss at the players' cats, but it remains focused on the kit and cub perched on the branch above. The cats will need to force it away.

If the players' cats decide to fight the raccoon, the fight will follow all the usual rules for fighting. The raccoon has a Jump score of 7, a Pounce score of 10, a Swat score of 12, and a Bite score of 10. The raccoon has Ability chips just like the players' cats do and spends them in the same way. It has 10 Strength chips, 4 Intelligence chips, and 6 Spirit chips. For the purposes of this fight, the raccoon is treated just the same as a player's cat except that the Narrator controls all its movements.

The raccoon will fight until it only has 7 chips remaining, and then it will try to run away. If this happens and the cats decide to chase the raccoon, they can easily catch up with it and continue the fight. However, if they let it go, the raccoon will leave Clan territory entirely and never be heard from again.

What Happens Next: If the cats decide to delay the fight and instead try to scare the raccoon away, continue with **11**.

If two or more of the cats are knocked out during the fight, continue with **13**.

If the cats knock out or chase off the raccoon, they win the fight and this is the end of the chapter. Hand the adventure to the next Narrator and tell him or her to continue with **20**.

16. The Truth of the Matter

Read Aloud: "With a tiny grunt of exertion, the kit lifts up her head and calls out, 'Wait! I can explain everything!'"

Narrator Tips: The kit gets her head free from the fox's paw and attempts to explain what happened. The details are below. Use them to improvise a scene where she is trying to make things clear quickly in order to prevent a fight, but also is struggling with the fact that she is just a frightened kit and doesn't really understand all the details of what's going on.

The brother and sister had snuck away from the queens and the other kits, as they often did, and were poking around in one of the furthest corners of the WindClan camp. They smelled a strange scent and heard something scratching on the other side of the camp's wall. It didn't smell dangerous, and the scratching sounded like it was coming from something no bigger than they were.

Their curiosity got the better of them, and they started scratching on their side of the wall, curious to see what was out there. Soon they'd poked a hole through the wall, and on the other side they saw a fox cub. They started sniffing and pawing at one another. Before long, they were rolling around and play fighting, just like old friends. This quickly turned into a running and tumbling game of tag and soon they were far away.

They spent some time running and playing together—this was the first time the kits had been out of the camp. After a while, though, she got separated from her brother and the fox cub. She thought she saw the fox cub's tail, so she pounced on it, but it wasn't the cub—it was his mother!

The mother fox was frantic, searching for her cub. The kit could tell because her face had the same look the queens got whenever one of the kits went missing. Then there was the sound of other cats in the area—Clan warriors who were out looking for the fox—so she grabbed the kit by the scruff and carried her off to this den.

"She's been very kind to me but won't let me leave," the kit tells them. "I think she's waiting until her missing cub comes home. But I have no idea where the cub or my brother is, and I just want to go home!"

The kit begs the players' cats not to hurt the fox. She bets that if they find and return the cub, the fox will probably take her whole litter and get out of Clan territory as fast as they can.

What Happens Next: If the cats decide to go look for the missing kit and fox cub, continue with **14**.

If the cats decide they want to fight the fox first, continue with **8**.

17. Outfoxed

Read Aloud: "The scent trail heads up the hill, away from the Lake. As it leads you deeper into the woods, the other trails fade away until only this one remains. But then you realize that this scent trail is older than all the others. You've accidentally followed the path the fox first used when she entered the Clan territories."

Narrator Tips: There are several scenes that can lead to this bad ending, so you will have to improvise the specific details of this scene. All of the possible lead-ins, though, are similar in that after following tracks around in circles for the better part of the day, the cats ended up focusing on the wrong one. They've now gone far enough away that it will take the rest of the day to get home, and by the time they do, other warriors will have resolved the situation.

What Happens Next: Not every adventure can end in success, and this one hasn't. Although they tried hard, the cats failed to solve the problems being caused by the fox in Clan territories. They do *not* get any Experience rewards for this adventure. The group *can*, however, play the adventure again, hopefully finding a way to get a better result next time.

18. Making the Trade

Read Aloud: "As you enter the small clearing, you can see the fox perched in her den within a hollow log. She's looking right at you, as though she has been expecting you."

Narrator Tips: The fox has the she-cat kit beneath her paws, but luckily the kit is free to call out to you. She says that she is all right, and she is happy to see her brother. Although she struggles to get free and come over to you, the fox maintains her hold.

The fox cub will immediately run to its mother unless the players' cats stop it, which they can do easily. It will whine and keep trying to go, but there is nothing it can do to overpower the cats.

The fox will not let the kit go until the players' cats let her cub come back to her. She does not like or trust the cats, and so will not release the kit until it is absolutely clear that they are not trying to trick her. The cats may want to talk to her or try to negotiate a situation where both the cub and kit are released at the same time. However, while the fox is clever, she at best only understands the very basics of what the cats are saying.

This might be a tricky scene for you, as Narrator, to improvise, but try to make the fox's meaning and intention as plain as possible without actually putting words in her mouth. It is up to the players to figure out how to solve this situation, but if they are having too difficult a time of it, allow their cats to make Ponder Checks (using the Animal Lore Knack, if they wish). If the Skill Check total is higher than 8 (the fox's Intelligence score), they understand the situation and know what the fox is demanding.

If the cats are not willing to release the cub, nothing will change. The only other option is to start a fight with the fox, though it's doubtful anyone really wants that to happen.

Once the cub is free and very close to the hollow log, the fox will let the she-cat kit go and move to nuzzle her pup. At that point, the kit will run directly over to her brother.

What Happens Next: If the cub and kit are both back with their families, continue with **19**.

If the cats won't let the cub go, choosing instead to start a fight, continue with **8**.

19. The Stare Down

Read Aloud: "The kit dashes across to her brother and they roll about with wild enthusiasm. Meanwhile, the fox nudges her cub into the den with its siblings, then steps out and glares at you angrily."

Narrator Tips: The fox has gotten just what she wanted, but she's still not very happy about the situation. The cats know where her den and, more important, her cubs are. Now she will have to take her cubs and go find a new den, preferably far away from the Clan territories. The angry glare is her way of saying "Leave my family alone . . . or else!"

As with the previous scene, there really isn't any way to have direct communication between the fox and the players' cats. Through an improvised scene and a few well-placed Ponder Checks, though, you should be able to get the players to understand what's going on.

The big question is how the players' cats will respond to such an aggressive stance. The fox doesn't want to fight; she just wants the cats to know that she *will* if it's necessary. If the cats are feeling aggressive, though, that might be enough to get combat started. If they simply acknowledge the fox's anger and concern, though, she will gladly let the tension ease.

What Happens Next: If the cats accept the fox's message

without escalating to violence, continue with **21**.

If the cats decide to take the tension up to the next level and start a fight, continue with **8**.

20. Climbing Down

Read Aloud: "The kit is so relieved that the situation with the raccoon is over that he almost leaps off the branch. It's then that he realizes just how high up he and the cub are. 'H-how do we get down from here?' the kit asks."

Narrator Tips: This scene is all about getting the tom kit and the fox cub out of the tree. They're both much better at climbing up than they are at coming down. Plus, after such a prolonged and frightening experience, they're both more than a little tired.

It is up to the players' cats to figure out how to get the two out of the tree, and it is your job, as the Narrator, to use the game rules and your imagination to improvise a scene that lets the group find a workable solution. If the idea they have seems impractical or unlikely to work, tell them so—or hint at it strongly. If possible, think of an Ability or Skill Check that goes along with the actions they suggest, and an unpleasant result that will happen if they fail at those Checks.

Don't make it anything too harmful—just inconvenient. After all, they beat the raccoon. This is merely a small inconvenience when compared to the sharp claws and teeth they just avoided. But a few added bruises or embarrassments can certainly be gained if the cats use bad judgment.

In the end, if necessary, help the group find a way to

succeed in getting the kit and the cub out of the tree. This scene should be a memorable diversion, not one where the adventure grounds to a halt.

If the cats have already interacted with the mother fox near her den, they will know just where to go next. If not, have the cub dash off, following its own sense of smell and memory of where the den is, and have the group follow.

What Happens Next: If the players' cats have fought and knocked out the mother fox, continue with **22**.

If the mother fox is still in her den waiting for the return of her missing cub, continue with **18**.

21. Farewell Fox

Read Aloud: "The fox seems satisfied that the cats mean her family no harm—at least for the moment. She walks over to the hollow log and climbs in with her cubs. They nuzzle and rub against one another so happily, you almost expect them to purr."

Narrator Tips: The fox and her cubs are reunited. So are the WindClan kits, who the players' cats now have to guide back to the Clan's camp. The brother and sister spend the whole trip apologizing for the trouble they've caused and promising they'll never do it again.

The leaders of all the Clans will be pleased with what a good job the cats did, and everyone will be fascinated with the tale of the fox and her cubs. The cats who know the most about Animal Lore will say that the Clan warriors should probably stay away from the fox's den for a few days, just so she feels safe. As soon as she doesn't feel threatened anymore, chances are good that the mother fox will take her cubs and find a new den—they like to keep the location of their homes secret, especially from potential enemies. In fact, it's most likely that the fox will take her cubs and leave the Clan territories entirely.

If the players' cats go against this advice and go back to the hollow log within the next day, they will get there just in time to see the fox and her cubs walking up the hill away from the Lake and out of Clan territory. The fox will look back with a warning glare, as if to say "Don't follow us!"

If the players' cats wait a few days and then go back, they will find the fox's den abandoned, and a fading scent trail leading up the hill away from Clan territory. Either way, the foxes are gone and they will not return to this part of the woods.

What Happens Next: The players' cats should be proud of their accomplishments. Dealing with a fox is never easy, but dealing with an anxious mother fox is even more dangerous. They handled the situation wonderfully, and the leaders and other warriors will tell them so. All the Clans will tell stories of these deeds for many, many moons to come, and the two WindClan kits will grow up thinking of the players' cats not just as warriors but as *heroes*!

22. Tending the Cubs

Read Aloud: "The fox lies limp on the ground, out cold. You feel a great rush of success momentarily—then you hear the whines and sniffs of fox cubs as they rush out to see what's wrong with their mother."

Narrator Tips: While beating the fox in battle may give the players' cats a momentary sense of accomplishment, the truth is that it is a bad ending to the adventure. With their mother injured, the cubs' lives are in jeopardy. While she is hurt, no one will be around to feed them or protect them from other forest animals.

Improvise a scene where other Clan cats arrive, including one or more of the Clan leaders. Have them point out that the warrior code says that all kits must be protected—and it seems reasonable to say that applies to these three fox cubs.

It should be clear that the players' cats did well by rescuing the kits. But their actions also make them responsible for the fox cubs while the mother fox recovers. They will have to spend a day or two shepherding the cubs around, the way a Clan's queens do for its kits, and even bringing food to the mother fox (who is too weak to hunt).

What Happens Next: When all is said and done, the fox and her cubs will leave the Clan territories, and the kits will be returned to WindClan. The adventure is a success and the players' cats should be proud of their accomplishments. A fox is always a wily opponent, but a mother fox who is protecting her cubs is even more dangerous. Beating her in combat shows just how strong the cats have become, and the leaders and other warriors will tell them so. All the Clans will tell stories of these deeds for many, many moons to come, and the two WindClan kits will grow up thinking of the players' cats not just as warriors but as *heroes*!

33

AFTER THE ADVENTURE

A fter the last scene of the adventure has been played, the game itself is not necessarily over. There still are a few things you can do if the players want to keep at it.

Play It Again

Maybe you just want to try the whole thing a second time, starting back at the beginning or perhaps picking up somewhere in the middle where it feels like things went wrong. In either case, your cat would be right back where he or she was and have another chance to try to find a more favorable outcome.

One of the great things about storytelling games is that you can always tell the story again. And, since the actions of the fox are very much dependent on not only what the players' cats do, but what order they do it in, this adventure could easily have several distinct twists in how the story unfolds.

Plus, however they handled the interaction with the fox the first time through, the cats may want to see what happens if they try a more aggressive tactic—or a less aggressive one. Playing again will let everyone see all the parts of the story and give other players the chance to try their hands at being the Narrator.

Experience

If the cats completed the adventure successfully, then they all get Experience rewards. It is important to note, though, that each cat can only get experience from this adventure once. If you play through and successfully finish the adventure several times, your cat only gains the rewards listed below after the *first* time he or she completes the adventure.

If you use different cats each time, though, each one can get the Experience rewards. The rule is *not* that a player can only get experience once, it's that a *cat* can.

There is more than one way to successfully conclude this adventure. The players' cats could have solved the situation by being diplomatic or by defeating the mother fox in a fight. As long as the fox and all her cubs were able to find a new den and carry on with their lives, it counted as a victory for the cats. However, the two resolutions have slightly different Experience rewards, as described in the Knack section below.

Age: Although the action in this adventure clearly happens over the course of a handful of days, the presumption is that this is the most interesting and exciting thing that happens to your cat during the whole of that moon. Increase your cat's age by 1 moon and make any appropriate improvements described in Chapter Four of the game rules.

Skill: On top of the improvements your cat gets from aging, he or she also gains 1 level in the Smell Skill and 1 level in the Ponder Skill.

Knack: Dealing with a mother fox and her cubs certainly gave the players' cats some lessons they would never have learned any other way. As a result, they each get a Knack based on what approach they used to resolve the situation.

If the players' cats finished the adventure without having

to fight and knock out the mother fox, they each gain 1 level of the Animal Lore Knack from interacting so closely with the mother fox and correctly interpreting her moods and intentions.

If the players' cats finished the adventure by fighting the mother fox and knocking her out, they improved their fighting skills by facing down a very fast and dangerous foe. Each cat learned a few new sneaky combat moves and gains 1 level in the Feint Knack. If a cat already has 3 levels in Feint, then there wasn't anything new for him or her to learn from this encounter.

More adventures can be found at the back
of each novel in the Omen of the Stars
series, and you can find extra information at
www.warriorcats.com.

KEEP WATCH FOR

OMEN OF THE STARS #4

SIGN OF THE MOON

Dovepaw slid out through the thorn tunnel and stood waiting in the forest for her sister, Ivypaw, and their mentors to join her. A hard frost had turned every blade of grass into a sharp spike under her paws, and from the bare branches of the trees, icicles glimmered in the gray dawn light. Dovepaw shivered as claws of cold probed deeply into her fur. Newleaf was still a long way off.

Dovepaw's belly was churning with anxiety, and her tail drooped.

This is your warrior assessment, she told herself. *It's the best thing that can happen to an apprentice. So why don't you feel excited?*

She knew the answer to her question. Too much had happened during the moons of her apprenticeship: important events beside which even the thrill of becoming a warrior paled into insignificance. Taking a deep breath, Dovepaw lifted her tail as she heard the paw steps of cats coming through the tunnel. She couldn't let the cats who were assessing her see how uneasy she was. She needed to do her best to show them that she was ready to be a warrior.

Dovepaw's mentor, Lionblaze, was the first cat to emerge,

fluffing his golden tabby pelt against the early morning chill. Spiderleg followed him closely; Dovepaw gave the skinny black warrior a dubious glance, wondering what it would be like to have him assessing her as well as Lionblaze. Spiderleg looked very stern.

I wish it were just Lionblaze, Dovepaw thought. *Too bad Firestar decided that we should have two judges.*

Cinderheart appeared next, followed closely by her apprentice, Ivypaw, and last of all Millie, who was to be Ivypaw's second assessor. Dovepaw's whiskers quivered as she looked at her sister. Ivypaw looked small and scared, and her dark blue eyes were shadowed with exhaustion.

Padding closer, Dovepaw gave Ivypaw's ear an affectionate lick. "Hey, you'll be fine," she murmured.

Ivypaw turned her head away.

She doesn't even talk to me anymore, Dovepaw thought wretchedly. *She's always busy somewhere else when I try to get close to her. And she cries out in her dreams.* Dovepaw pictured how her sister twitched and batted her paws when they were sleeping side by side in the apprentices' den. She knew that Ivypaw was visiting the Dark Forest, spying on behalf of ThunderClan because Jayfeather and Lionblaze had asked her to, but when she tried to ask her sister what happened there, Ivypaw replied only that there was nothing new to report.

"I suggest we head for the abandoned Twoleg nest," Spiderleg announced. "It's sheltered, so there's a good chance of prey."

Lionblaze blinked as if he was surprised that Spiderleg was trying to take over the assessment, but then nodded and led the way through the trees in the direction of the old Twoleg path. Dovepaw quickened her pace to pad beside him, and the other cats followed.

"Are you ready?" Lionblaze asked.

Dovepaw jumped, startled out of her worries about her sister. "Sorry," she mewed. "I was thinking about Ivypaw. She looks so tired."

Lionblaze glanced back at the silver-and-white she-cat, then at Dovepaw, shock and anxiety mingling in his amber eyes. "I guess the Dark Forest training is taking its toll," he muttered.

"And whose fault is that?" Dovepaw flashed back at him. However urgent it was to find out what the cats of the Dark Forest were plotting, it wasn't fair of Lionblaze and Jayfeather to put the whole burden on her sister's shoulders.

Ivypaw isn't even a warrior yet!

Lionblaze let out a sigh that told Dovepaw he agreed with her privately, but wasn't prepared to say so. "I'm not going to talk about that now," he meowed. "It's time for you to concentrate on your assessment."

Dovepaw gave an irritable shrug.

Lionblaze halted as the old Twoleg nest came into sight. Dovepaw picked up traces of herb scent from Jayfeather's garden, though most of the stems and leaves were blackened by frost. She could hear the faint scutterings of prey in the grass and in the debris under the trees. Spiderleg was right: This would be a good spot to hunt.

"Okay," Lionblaze began. "First we want to assess your

tracking skills. Cinderheart, what do you want Ivypaw to catch?"

"We'll go for mice. Okay, Ivypaw?"

The silver tabby gave a tense nod.

"But not inside the old Twoleg nest," Millie added. "That would be too easy."

"I know." Dovepaw thought her sister sounded too weary to put one paw in front of another, let alone catch mice. But she headed off into the trees without hesitating; Cinderheart and Millie followed at a distance.

Dovepaw watched until the frostbitten bracken hid Ivypaw from her sight, then sent out her extended senses to track her as she padded behind the abandoned nest toward the group of pine trees. Mice were squeaking and scuffling among the fallen needles; Dovepaw hoped that her sister would scent them and make a good catch.

She was concentrating so hard on following Ivypaw that she forgot about her own assessment until Spiderleg flicked his tail-tip over her ear.

"Hey!" she meowed, spinning around to face the black warrior.

"Lionblaze *said* he'd like you to try for a squirrel," Spiderleg meowed. "If you're sure you want to become a warrior, that is."

"I'm sure," Dovepaw growled. "Sorry, Lionblaze."

Lionblaze was standing just behind Spiderleg, looking annoyed. Dovepaw was angry with herself for missing his order, but even more with Spiderleg for being so obnoxious about it.

It's mouse-brained to have two judges, she grumbled to herself. *Mentors have been assessing their own apprentices for more seasons than there are leaves on the trees!*

Raising her head, she tasted the air and brightened when she picked up a nearby scent of squirrel. It was coming from the other side of a clump of bramble; setting her paws down lightly, Dovepaw skirted the thorns until she came out into a small clearing and spotted the squirrel nibbling a nut at the foot of an ivy-covered oak tree.

A wind was rising, rattling the bare branches. Dovepaw slid around the edge of the clearing, using the bracken for cover, until she was downwind of her prey. Its scent flooded strongly over her, making her jaws water.

Dropping into her best hunter's crouch, Dovepaw began to creep up on the squirrel. But she couldn't resist sending out her senses just once more to check on Ivypaw, and she jumped as she picked up the tiny shriek, quickly cut off, of a mouse under her sister's claws.

Her uncontrolled movement rustled a dead leaf, and instantly the squirrel fled up the tree, its bushy tail flowing out behind it. Dovepaw bounded across the grass and hurled herself up the trunk, but the squirrel had vanished into the branches. She clung to an ivy stem, trying to listen for movement beyond the wind and the creaking of the tree, but it was no use.

"Mouse dung!" she spat, letting herself drop to the ground again.

Spiderleg stalked up to her. "For StarClan's sake, what do

you think you're doing?" he demanded. "A kit just out of the nursery could have caught that squirrel! It's a good thing none of the other Clans saw you, or they'd think ThunderClan doesn't know how to train its apprentices."

Dovepaw's neck fur bristled. "Have you never missed a catch?" she muttered under her breath.

"Well?" the black warrior demanded. "Let's hear what you did wrong."

"It wasn't all bad," Lionblaze put in before Dovepaw could answer. "That was good stalking work, when you moved downwind of the squirrel."

Dovepaw flashed him a grateful look. "I guess I got distracted for a heartbeat," she admitted. "I moved a leaf, and the squirrel heard me."

"And you could have been faster chasing it," Spiderleg told her. "You might have caught it if you'd put on a bit more speed."

Dovepaw nodded glumly. *We haven't all got legs as long as yours!* "Does this mean I've failed my assessment?"

Spiderleg flicked his ears but didn't answer. "I'm going to see how Millie is getting on with Ivypaw," he announced, darting off toward the abandoned nest.

Dovepaw gazed at her mentor. "Sorry," she meowed.

"I guess you must be nervous," Lionblaze responded. "You're much better than that on an ordinary hunting patrol."

Now that she was facing failure, Dovepaw realized just how much she wanted to pass her assessment. *Being a warrior is way better than being part of the prophecy with my so-called special powers.*

She tensed as another thought struck her. *What if Ivypaw is made a warrior and I'm not?*

Her sister deserved it, Dovepaw knew. She didn't have any special powers of her own, but every night she put herself in danger to spy for Lionblaze and Jayfeather in the Dark Forest.

Ivypaw's better than me. I can't even catch a stupid squirrel!

"Cheer up," Lionblaze meowed. "Your assessment isn't over yet. But for StarClan's sake, *concentrate!*"

DON'T MISS

RETURN TO THE WILD #1

SEEKERS

ISLAND OF SHADOWS

Lusa

Excitement tingled through Lusa's paws as she padded down the snow-covered beach. Ice stretched ahead of her, flat, sparkly white, unchanging as far as the horizon. She didn't belong here—no black bears did—yet here she was, walking confidently onto the frozen ocean beside a brown bear and two white bears. Ujurak had gone, but Yakone, a white bear from Star Island, had joined Lusa, Kallik, and Toklo. They were still four. And a new journey lay ahead: a journey that would take them back home.

Glancing over her shoulder, Lusa saw the low hills of Star Island looming dark beneath the mauve clouds. The outlines of the white bears who lived there were growing smaller with each pawstep. *Good-bye,* she thought, with a twinge of regret that she would never see them again. Her home lay among trees, green leaves, and sun-warmed grass, a long, long way from this place of ice and wind as sharp as claws.

Lusa wondered if Yakone was feeling regret, too. The bears

of Star Island were his family, yet he had chosen to leave them so that he could be with Kallik. But he was striding along resolutely beside Kallik, his unusual red-shaded pelt glowing in the sunrise, and he didn't look back.

Toklo plodded along at the front of the little group, his head down. He looked exhausted, but Lusa knew that exhaustion was not what made his steps drag and kept his eyes on his paws and his shoulders hunched.

He's grieving for Ujurak.

Their friend had died saving them from an avalanche. Lusa grieved for him, too, but she clung to the certainty that it hadn't been the end of Ujurak's life, not really. The achingly familiar shape of the bear who had led them all the way to Star Island had returned with stars in his fur, skimming over the snow and soaring up into the sky with his mother, Silaluk. Two starry bears making patterns in the sky forever, following the endless circle of Arcturus, the constant star. Lusa knew that Ujurak would be with them always. But she wasn't sure if Toklo felt the same. A cold claw of pain seemed to close around her heart, and she wished that she could do something to help him.

Maybe if I distracted him. . . .

"Hey, Toklo!" Lusa called, bounding forward past Kallik and Yakone until she reached the grizzly's side. "Do you think we should hunt now?"

Toklo started, as if Lusa's voice had dragged him back from somewhere far away. "What?"

"I said, should we hunt now?" This close to shore, they

might pick up a seal above the ice, or even a young walrus.

Toklo gave her a brief glance before trudging on. "No. It'll be dark soon. We need to travel while we can."

Then it'll be too dark to hunt. Lusa bit the words back. It wasn't the time to start arguing. But she wanted to help Toklo wrench his thoughts away from the friend he was convinced he had lost.

"Do you think geese ever come down to rest on the ice?" she asked.

This time Toklo didn't even look at her. "Don't be bee-brained," he said scathingly. "Why would they do that? Geese find their food on *land*." He quickened his pace to leave her behind.

Lusa gazed sadly after him. Most times when Toklo was in a grouchy mood, she would give as good as she got, or tease him out of his bad temper. But this time his pain was too deep to deal with lightly.

Best to leave him alone, she decided. *For now, anyway.*

As Star Island dwindled behind the bears, the short snow-sky day faded into shadows that seemed to grow up from the ice and reach down from the sky until the whole white world was swallowed in shades of gray and black. When Lusa looked back, the last traces of the hills that had become so familiar had vanished into the twilight. Star spirits began to appear overhead, and the silver moon hung close to the horizon like a shining claw. The bears trekked between snowbanks that glimmered in the pale light, reaching above their backs in strange shapes formed by the scouring wind.

"It's time we stopped for the night," Kallik announced, halting at the foot of a deep drift. "This looks like a good place to make a den."

"I'll help you dig," Yakone offered. He began to scrape at the bottom of the snowbank.

Lusa watched the two white bears as they burrowed vigorously into the snow. This would be Yakone's first night away from his family, away from the permanent den where he had been raised. Yet he seemed unfazed—enthusiastic, even, as he helped Kallik carve a shallow niche that would keep off the worst of the wind. The white bears' heads were close together now as they scraped at the harder, gritty snow underneath the fluffy top layer. Yakone said something that made Kallik huff with amusement, and she flicked a pawful of snow at him in response.

Lusa turned away, not wanting to eavesdrop. A pang of sorrow clawed once more at her heart when she spotted Toklo standing a little way off, watching the white bears without saying anything. After a moment he turned his back on Kallik and Yakone and raised his head to fix his gaze on the stars.

Looking up, Lusa made out the shining shape of Silaluk, the Great Bear, and close to her side the Little Bear, Ujurak. Seeing him there made her feel safe, because she knew that their friend was watching over them. It helped to comfort her grief.

But there was no comfort for Toklo. All he knew was that his friend, the other brown bear on this strange and endless journey, had left them. His bleak gaze announced his loneliness to Lusa as clearly as if he had put it into words.

"We're here, Toklo," she murmured, too faintly for the brown bear to hear. "You're *not* alone."

She knew that Toklo had been closer to Ujurak than any of them; he had taken on the responsibility of protecting the smaller brown bear. *Toklo felt like he failed when Ujurak died,* Lusa thought. *He's wrong, but how can any bear make him understand that?*

Kallik's cheerful voice sounded behind her. "The den's nearly ready."

Lusa turned to see the white she-bear backing out of the cave that she and Yakone had dug into the snow. Kallik shook herself, scattering clots of snow from her fur. "Are you okay, Lusa?" she asked. "You look worried."

Lusa glanced toward Toklo, still staring up at the stars. "He's missing Ujurak. I wish I knew what to say to him."

Kallik gazed at Toklo for a moment, then shook her head with a trace of exasperation in her eyes. "We're all missing Ujurak," she responded. "But we know that he's not really dead."

"Toklo doesn't see it like that," Lusa pointed out.

"I know." Kallik's voice softened for a moment. "It's hard out here without Ujurak. But think what we've achieved together! We destroyed the oil rig and brought the spirits back so the wild will be safe. Toklo should remember that."

"Toklo just remembers that Ujurak gave his life for us."

While Lusa was speaking, Yakone emerged from the den, thrusting heaps of newly dug snow aside with strong paws. Kallik padded toward him, then glanced back over her shoulder at Lusa.

"Ujurak has gone home," she said. "He's happy now, with his star mother. There's nothing for Toklo or any other bear to worry about."

Lusa shook her head. *It's not as simple as Kallik thinks,* she told herself. *And not as simple as* Toklo *thinks, either. He might not be here on the ground with us, but I think we've still got a lot to learn about Ujurak.*